FRANCO

D1021572

EYE OF THE STORM

Staring at each other, neither of them able to break away, he knew they were standing in the center of a storm. 'Twas quiet, motionless, with scarcely a breath being drawn that could be heard. Yet the calm was deceptive, for he knew that mere inches—seconds—away, the storm raged out of control. All it needed was a step in the wrong direction and . . . disaster.

They'd made all the gestures to leave. They had exchanged all the pleasantries people exchange. And yet . . .

They moved at the same time, each taking a single step toward the other. She hesitated, then took another one. And another.

With a muttered oath, he closed his eyes and held out his arms to her, and when she stepped into them, he wrapped her close, a long, groaning sigh escaping him. Her head came to rest against his chest, and he knew she must hear the quickened beat of his heart. Then, lowering his head, he fitted his lips to hers. . . .

Starfinder

Patricia Potter

🐿 BANTAM BOOKS

NEW YORK TORONTO LONDON SYDNEY AUCKLAND

STARFINDER

A Bantam Book

PUBLISHING HISTORY
A Bantam Book / November 1998

All rights reserved.
Copyright © 1998 by Patricia Potter.
Cover art copyright © 1998 by Robert Hunt.
Stepback art copyright © 1998 by Franco Accornera.

ISBN 0-553-57880-4

Published simultaneously in the United States and Canada

Bantam Books are published by Bantam Books, a division of Bantam
Doubleday Dell Publishing Group, Inc. Its trademark, consisting of
the words "Bantam Books" and the portrayal of a rooster, is Regis-
tered in U.S. Patent and Trademark Office and in other countries.
Marca Registrada. Bantam Books, 1540 Broadway, New York, New
York 10036.

PRINTED IN THE UNITED STATES OF AMERICA

OPM   10 9 8 7 6 5 4 3 2 1

Acknowledgment

With appreciation to Stephanie Kip,
whose skill has contributed so much to *Starfinder*
and whose enthusiasm and support
has meant so much to me.

Prologue

The gallows had never been so crowded. So many braw Scots dying today.

As so many had died months ago at Culloden Moor.

Ian Sutherland wished he had been one of the latter as he awaited his turn to march up the steps, feel the rough rope fitted around his neck, and end his life in front of a drunken, cheering crowd of turncoat countrymen.

Better to have died quickly at the end of a sword, or even to have bled to death from the jagged wound in his side, which still ached at times. Aye, death in battle would have been far better for both his brother and himself than spending four months shivering together in jail only to be led to this public slaughter. They'd been fed enough to keep starvation at bay but not enough to relieve the spasms of hunger.

Ian's arms were bound behind him, the rope so tight it ate into his flesh. Yet he relished the pain, for, in minutes, he would never feel anything again. Not the cold wind sweeping the Highlands, not the soft touch of a woman, not the strength of a good horse under him as he raced over the hills of the land of his birth.

The sound of the trapdoor mingled with the roar of the crowd, and six more Scots met their death, swinging back and forth from the ropes. At least the hangman seemed competent. A mild comfort.

Two English soldiers came to where he stood with his brother, Derek. They took Derek's arms, and Ian started to follow. But he was pushed back.

"Ah, we have an anxious one," one of the soldiers said. "You can wait yer turn."

His brother turned to him. There was no fear on his nineteen-year-old face. He gave Ian a cocky grin. "I'll see ye soon, brother. In heaven or in hell."

"Be hell for sure," muttered one of the guards as he pushed Derek forward along with five other Scots.

The six who had just died were being cut down, and new ropes were being affixed to the sturdy gallows. Ian tried again to move forward, but one of the king's burly guards pulled him back, and he watched helplessly as his brother mounted the stairs, the irons around his ankles making him awkward. Derek stood quietly as the noose was drawn over his neck. His eyes met Ian's, and he nodded as if to reassure him.

On the eve of Culloden, Ian had listened as Derek admitted his fear and, with some embarrassment, murmured that he had prayed he would not disgrace the Sutherland name. He had not. He had brought honor to their clan at Culloden. He would bring the clan more honor today.

Watching his brother, Ian felt his heart—already broken on Culloden field—die. He'd seen his clansmen decimated. His older brother, the marquis of Brinaire, had died along with thousands of other Scots. Ian himself had been wounded and would surely have died had not Derek stayed with him to bind his wound and see him safely to a crofter's stable. If not for Ian, Derek might have escaped.

Instead, the young Scot was about to hang, as Ian himself would soon hang. Then all that would be left of the Sutherlands of Brinaire was their seven-year-old sister, and God only knew what had happened to her.

With King George wreaking havoc through the Highlands, hunting the last of the rebels and dispossessing what was left of the families who had sided with Bonnie Prince Charlie, Katy's fate was, at best, uncertain.

The breath caught in Ian's throat, nearly suffocating him, as the trapdoor opened again. He turned his face away, unable to bear the sight of the swinging bodies. His brother's body.

"God bless you, Derek," he whispered, feeling the sting of tears behind his eyes. He did not let them spill down his cheeks. He would show no weakness to these English bastards.

Instead, he tried to think of home, of the magnificent keep with its tapestries and long tables, where he and his family and the clansmen had taken their meals. He thought of the sea and the mountains, the rushing waterfalls and the long hours of the gloaming. He thought of his parents, dead these past ten years. For the first time he was glad they weren't alive, glad they weren't here to witness the death of their children and the destruction of their way of life.

Guards were approaching again, selecting the next group of victims from the thirty or so remaining prisoners—young and old men of good family, of good name. To make sure there would never be another uprising, the duke of Cumberland was systematically murdering all who had somehow escaped the killing fields of Culloden: Stewarts, MacPhersons, MacLarens, Grants, Camerons . . . and so many others. Under the scrutiny of King George, anyone with even the slightest connection to Jacobin families was slaughtered. Trials were a sham, the verdicts foreordained.

A passing guard jostled Ian, and he fought to keep his balance. The irons on his ankles limited his movement, though, and he was weak from his wound and from the lack of decent food. He swayed as the guards passed him by again, taking another six men.

Was he to be the last? Was he to watch all the others, friends and kin, die before he could find his own oblivion?

Were it not for his sister—beautiful, loving little Katy—he would have gone gladly. With his brothers dead and Brinaire seized and given to a Royalist, a traitor, he had nothing else left in this world. But thoughts of Katy plagued him. A smuggled message, given to him in prison by a captured MacPherson, had said she'd disappeared.

Where was she? Ian's hands balled into fists. He would never know.

Now more doomed Scots were being led up the steps of the gallows. He wished he could look away from them, yet they deserved his attention, deserved to have faces filled with pride and defiance upon which to rest their eyes as they faced death. But, dear God, he prayed, take me next.

He sensed the tension of the condemned men around him as they waited for the trapdoor to fall again. No one cried out for mercy. No one begged for his life. They had joined Prince Charlie, well aware of the price of failure for themselves. Yet they had not begun to realize how great a price their families would pay.

Ian flinched at the crack of the trapdoor. The bodies were being carried to a wagon, to be taken off and burned. Cumberland wanted no graves.

A few minutes more. Then another selection. Again he was left standing, now with only two others. He met their eyes with shared resignation. They would be next.

Ian heard the clank of chains on the steps, the muttered prayers of the men around him, the ribald shouts of the crowd. The rabble was no longer happy. They had wanted—expected—to see fear, begging, trembling. Instead they were seeing braw, proud men, defiant to the end.

Time seemed to stand still. Mayhap Ian was growing numb with the horror of it, and the loss. The scene blurred, and he felt himself swaying again. No. He must not fall down. He would not.

One of the remaining prisoners moved closer, allowing Ian to lean briefly against him. Damn his weakness. Damn the wound. Damn the English.

The momentary support steadied him, and he nodded thankfully to the man in Cameron plaid. "My thanks," he said.

The man nodded, his eyes unblinking as the trapdoor sprang open once again.

Then the sergeant was back with two guards, come for the last of the victims. The two men alongside Ian were taken, but again, when he tried to move forward, the sergeant shook his head.

"We 'ave other plans fer ye, my lord," he said. "But ye can stay and watch the festivities."

Chapter 1

The Eastern Shore, Maryland, 1747

Fancy Marsh carefully fed the fox through the wire pen, watching as it delicately devoured the hunk of venison. The sleek, bushy-tailed animal was nearly full grown, and his wounds were healed. Soon it would be time to let him go.

Noting the frown on her seven-year-old son's brow as they sat side by side on the ground outside the pen, she realized Noel was thinking about it, too. He and Fortune, her younger sister, had found the fox kit when he was only a few weeks old. He had been huddled next to his mother, who lay dead in a trap. The grieving kit was starving and had badly infected wounds on his front paws and legs. Noel had his aunt's—and her own—protectiveness toward wounded and helpless critters. He and Fortune had brought the hapless kit home, and Noel had presented him to Fancy, tears glinting in his eyes. "Save it," he had begged.

She hadn't hesitated. As long as she could remember, Fancy had loved all living things, as had her father, and she had never been able to resist the impulse to help a wounded animal.

Having finished his meal, the now healthy and beautiful red fox lay down and looked at her, his silvery blue eyes trusting after so many weeks of being in her care. Knowing that John, her husband, would not approve—indeed, would glower at her for the risks she took—she reached through the wire fence and scratched the animal's head. The fox responded by licking her hand, then laid his head on his paws and went to sleep.

"It's almost time to let him go, isn't it?" Noel asked anxiously.

Fancy glanced at her son and smiled. "Yes, it is." Seeing his crestfallen expression, she added, "We'll wait another week or two, until we're sure he can take care of himself."

Her son nodded. In the past, he had begged to keep the critters they seemed to collect, but he'd since learned that the animals were better off in the woods, far away from livestock and the rifles of men protecting their own. Besides, his father would not have allowed it.

John tolerated Fancy's mending ways, but he worried about her being bitten and about Noel and their three-year-old daughter, Amy, becoming too attached to animals that were not meant to be domesticated. And the children *had* become attached, more than once, which was why the household included a fairly large permanent animal population.

John had frequently surrendered to the inevitable, muttering to himself and never seriously chiding Fancy. But a fox? No. He would never agree, and Fancy had to admit that in this case he would be right. She was grateful that he had let her nurse the fox this long; he had even built a pen for it along the back wall of their house.

John Marsh was a good man, and he, too, had protective instincts. She'd known that from the start, when, after their father died, John had saved her and six-year-old Fortune from a terrible fate. She'd been nothing but a fifteen-year-old woodsy, but he hadn't hesitated, even though she had, at first. He was so much older than she, and, at fifteen, she was frankly scared of the whole idea of marriage—especially marriage to a stranger. She had never regretted the decision, though. John was kind, if sometimes impatient, and he had a generous heart, a heart she had recently come to realize was much too soft for the Maryland wilderness.

Between her own mothering tendencies and John's gentle nature, they'd collected quite a brood in their nine years of marriage. In addition to their two children and her sister, Fortune, there was Bandit the raccoon; Posey the squirrel; Unsatisfactory, a motley calico cat who'd been brought to America to hunt rats but who preferred not to; Lucky, a three-legged half dog, half wolf she had rescued from a trap; and Trouble, a crow that Fortune had found as a fledgling with a broken wing.

John was always able to ferret out a newcomer, possibly because of the children's sly, mischievous expressions.

John would shake his head. "What now?" he would ask wearily. "A lion? A tiger? An elephant?"

Noel and Amy would giggle, then slide into his lap, and it wouldn't be until later, when he and Fancy were in bed together, that he would haltingly wonder whether she should try to heal the whole world.

Lately she'd been biting her tongue so that she wouldn't say she'd be happy if she only could heal him. For they both knew that his soft heart was failing.

Sighing, Fancy rose from the ground, shooed Noel off to play, and went inside the house. John had taken one of his prized two-year-old horses to an auction two counties away, and he would be exhausted—and, she guessed, discouraged—when he returned. Before he arrived, she had work to do.

John had been feeling poorly for over a year now, especially so the past few months. And planting would begin as soon as it rained, probably any day now. They had to harvest at least half a hogshead of tobacco and several acres of corn to support themselves and the horses through the winter. There was always so much work to be done on their small farm. John was determined to make a success of his stables, but the work was backbreaking and, along with tending the crops, nearly impossible for one man alone, even a man in fine health.

It seemed they were always one step away from disaster and never more so than now. It galled Fancy to know that John's brother, Robert, was waiting like a vulture to grab their land. He had always frightened her, but these days she cringed at the very thought of him. He had opposed John's marriage to her as unsuitable, but now that he was a widower, he looked at her with what she recognized as the gleam of lust in his eyes.

Brushing away the uncomfortable thought, Fancy took a broom to the floor of the large room that served as both the dining and gathering area. John had added a small room on either side, one for them and one for Fortune and Amy. The house was larger than that of most yeomen, but then, John wasn't exactly a yeoman, just a second son of a small planter. And unlike his brother, Robert, his ambitions had been modest. He'd wanted only a family and a small farm where he could breed and raise horses. He hadn't wanted hundreds of acres, nor had he wanted to own the numerous slaves required to work those acres. He had no stomach for it.

Fancy hoped he had the stomach for the apple pie she was going to bake for him. She had already started a stew bubbling in a huge pot in the fireplace, filling the room with a delicious aroma. Surely the pie and the stew would spike his flagging appetite.

After putting the broom away, Fancy went to a table where she measured out some flour, a small amount of precious butter, some sugar, and dried apples. She would have a feast ready for John when he returned home.

"I'll go to Chestertown tomorrow," John said as he picked at the meal Fancy had worked so hard to provide. "I heard that a ship carrying indentured servants is arriving."

He had arrived home after dusk, long after the children were asleep, and had fallen into a chair with a heavy sigh.

In quick, surreptitious glances, Fancy had noted that his face was gray and his breathing ragged. "I think you should take a couple of days' rest before going off again," she said, worry twisting inside her.

Lines creased his forehead and the skin around his eyes as he replied. "We have to replant the young tobacco, or we won't make it through the winter."

"But a day or two—"

He shook his head. "You know redemptioners are sold fast."

Fancy frowned. John had been talking for a month or more about obtaining a redemptioner—a bond servant—to help him in the fields. To say she had reservations about the idea was a gross understatement. The very word "redemptioner" raised ugly memories.

Fancy herself had tried to help with the farmwork while Fortune looked after Noel and Amy, but that was not a long-term solution. Fortune was without speech and little more than a child herself, a shy sprite who had a tendency to disappear into the woods, preferring solitude or the company of other nonspeaking creatures. Often she slipped off before dawn and did not reappear for hours.

Still, a redemptioner—a man bound by law and not desire . . . ?

"Are you sure?" she asked, her tone reflecting her thoughts.

"It is the only way, Fancy," John explained with a heavy sigh. "And redemptioners are willing to indenture themselves to get to America. 'Tis nothing like slavery. Regardless, if we don't get a tobacco crop, we won't be able to feed the horses this winter, and I can't do the planting myself. You know how I felt about selling Pretender, but I had no choice. Nor do we have one now."

Pretender, at two, had shown the promise of tremendous speed. But keeping their breeding stock was even more important than owning a winning racehorse, so Pretender had been sold so that they could buy an indentured servant with the money. That John had been driven to such a choice told her how poorly he must be feeling.

She went over to him and put a hand on his shoulder. There was a grayish pallor under his skin. He was forty-four but he looked ten years older.

Affection welled inside her. She could never understand how he and Robert could have come from the same parents. Robert was the opposite of John in every way—greedy, cruel, ambitious. As the elder son, Robert bitterly resented the fact that his father had left a small but prime piece of land on the river, along with the best of the family's horses, to John. Robert had inherited the bulk of his father's estate, but the piece that he didn't get stuck in his craw to this day.

And it could go on sticking, Fancy thought with a surge of anger. He could have helped his brother, if he'd been so inclined. Instead, he'd used his considerable influence to prevent any of the other local planters from offering John aid since he'd become ill. And if Robert knew *how* ill his brother was . . . well, he'd probably be gleefully planning the funeral.

Gritting her teeth so as not to let anger get the better of her, Fancy wished she could provide some magic potion for her husband. She had brewed teas and given him healing herbs for his heart, but she knew of nothing more she could do. A doctor had confirmed that his heart was not as strong as it should have been, but even he could offer no medicine that would help. Perhaps a bondsman *was* the best thing. It was certainly a better alternative—and perhaps the *only* alternative—to John working himself to death.

She rubbed his shoulders. "Shouldn't the children and I go with you?"

He shook his head. "You couldn't go to the auction, and I'll be away for several nights. Someone has to take care of the horses, and Fortune . . ."

When he trailed off, she understood that he was reluctant to say anything disparaging about Fortune. He looked on the girl as a little sister, with both fondness and exasperation. But Fancy knew that Fortune could not always be relied upon.

Yet anxiety for John's well-being still clawed at her. She didn't like the idea of him traveling all the way to Chestertown alone, and even less did she relish him returning alone with a bond servant of unknown background and morals. But then, surely John wouldn't be foolish enough to purchase a convict.

"Maybe you can find one who can read and write," she said hesitantly, "who can teach . . . the children."

"I'll do what I can," he said wearily. "But the most important thing is to find someone strong enough to plant and tend the tobacco and corn."

She had to stifle the impulse to beg him, please, to try very hard. John had never learned to read, though he and his brother had been tutored. All the figures that Robert had learned so easily were only gibberish to John. It was a failure that bothered him deeply.

Fancy knew how he felt. She couldn't read, either, and it was her greatest regret, just as her greatest ambition was that her children learn. Although there was no school and no one to teach them, she had sworn they *would* learn. Somehow. And she *would*, too. She already had books sitting on a shelf above the hearth, books she had bought whenever she could, awaiting the day when she would be able to read them. Her dreams, her hopes, lay in those books.

John stopped playing with his food and rose from the table. "I think I'll go to bed."

When Fancy nodded, he started to walk toward their room. Then he turned back to her, catching her hand in his.

"I missed you," he said.

Instead of being pleased by his declaration, Fancy was alarmed. John rarely, if ever, gave her an outward display of affection. Even in the privacy of their bed, he had never said he loved her. He had married her as an act of kindness, and they had not even lain together as husband and wife until a year after their marriage. She was too young, he'd said. And in all the years since they had consummated their marriage, although she knew he cared for her, he had never been demonstrative in his affection or admitted to any tender feelings toward her.

So why now?

The most obvious answer to that question sent shivers up her spine, and her hand tightened around his. She wanted so much to make him well again. He had once been so strong, so sure. She couldn't bear to consider the possibility of losing him.

"I missed you, too," she said, holding his gaze.

He nodded and looked as if he wanted to say something more, but he had never been easy with words. "Good night, wife."

"I'll be to bed soon," she said, trying to keep the worry from her voice.

But she couldn't stop thinking about the as yet unpurchased indentured servant as she took John's nearly full plate outside and set it down for Unsatisfactory, Lucky, and Posey. The pets shoved each other goodnaturedly for the most advantageous position, Posey skittering in and out between the others' feet. Fancy smiled at their antics, looking past them toward the barn. The servant could sleep there, she supposed. She would have to clean out a corner, and prepare some kind of mattress.

Slowly, hope began to surface. Fancy had discovered that most things worked out for the best—like her marriage to John. If the redemptioner could take on some of the labor, perhaps John would get better. And maybe he really would find someone who could teach her and the children to read. She'd heard that there were teachers among those seeking new opportunities in this land.

What a fine present that would be.

How many days had he been chained in the hold of the ship? Ian had lost track. Nor did he know how long he'd been in prison before being put aboard. The days had blurred together into one unending nightmare, and he knew only that it had been a long time—a very long time—since he'd last tasted freedom. He was only surviving now, not living. He was surviving for Katy's sake.

The air in the ship's hold was hot, suffocating, stifling. Although there had been moans earlier during the voyage, the convicts with whom he shared his quarters were now too miserable to make any sound. The crossing had been too rough for them to be taken above deck for air or exercise.

One of the sailors who had brought water and bread earlier in the day had said they were only two days from Baltimore, their destination.

As bad as the voyage had been, Ian had no better expectations of its conclusion. He was to be sold at auction to the highest bidder for a term of fourteen years. He had already been informed of the consequences of trying to escape: an extension of the term, whipping, even death. The British soldiers had branded his thumb, marking him as an indentured convict, to prevent his return to Scotland.

It didn't matter, though. He would escape. Ian Sutherland, who had once been marquis of Brinaire, would be no one's slave.

He shifted, trying to change his position. Any was difficult. Each convict was allotted two and a half feet of space. A long chain, threaded through rings on the men's leg irons and locked to the sides of the hold, held them in place. Most of his fellow prisoners had been sentenced to transportation for poaching or theft. Only Ian and two others were Scots taken at Culloden Moor.

He had not been hanged, he had discovered, because of the intervention of the Macraes. He had fostered with them as a boy—but they had fought for the Hanover, King George. Ian's death sentence had been commuted to transportation for fourteen years. And he could never return to Scotland on pain of death.

He'd damned both the pardon and those Macrae traitors, inviting death, but the officer who presided at the hangings had only laughed. The plantations of the Caribbean would teach him manners, he'd said. But later, while being loaded on this ship with the other human cargo, he had learned that he was being sent to America. It was a distinction of little comfort. Guilt was a festering sore inside him. For Derek. And for

Katy. Now there was no one to look after her, to provide for her. If she lived.

If she lived. Ian might have found a way to meet his own death in that hold were it not for that possibility.

Four prisoners *had* died, and Ian had barely survived the starvation, fever, and filth. His only clothes were the same bloodstained garments he'd worn at Culloden, and a dark beard now covered his cheeks and chin. His thick hair, which he'd always kept unfashionably short, for comfort, was now long and dirty.

Dear God, how he longed for a bath. His brothers used to call him unnatural because he bathed daily; he would most certainly die of ague, Patrick—who, as first born, carried the first name of his famous ancestor—and Derek would say in all seriousness. But nothing, it seemed, could kill him.

He heard the rattle of chains as someone else tried to shift his aching body. It was incessant, that sound of iron against iron, iron against wood. So was the pain from the leg shackles and the manacles circling his wrists. His skin was raw and bloody from chafing.

He rested his shoulders against the bulwark and tried to think of the Highlands, his home, the sweet air from the pastures mixed with the tangy scent of the sea. The mountains, the waterfalls . . .

He thought of Katy, her ringlets of auburn hair. She had always badgered him to tell her stories—one story in particular—about their ancestors. Ian had first told it to her as they'd stood together one night on the parapets of Brinaire. The story was a family legend about his great-great-grandfather, Patrick Sutherland, a man they called the Starcatcher. A man who had united two warring clans and won his lady love. It was Katy's favorite tale, and she had asked to hear it over and over again.

"I want my own starcatcher," she'd said.
"And you will have one," he'd promised.
"Katy," Ian whispered. "Where are you?"
He would find her, or die trying.
But first he had to escape.

Chapter 2

John Marsh looked at the scraggly bunch of men whose indentures were for sale, and his heart sank.

He had hoped against hope he would find a reliable man who was willing to work for his freedom. But there were no redemptioners here, only convicts, some so thin he knew they couldn't survive a summer in a tobacco field.

Still, a large number of potential buyers surrounded the freshly scrubbed and newly clothed newcomers. Labor was far too scarce, and bondsmen were cheaper than slaves.

John looked at the eyes, not the brawn. Strength was important, but he needed someone he could trust with his family.

He almost left. Not only because the men were all convicts but also because he was opposed in principle to slavery, and was this not a form of the evil practice? Yet he knew he couldn't plant the tobacco this year; he just didn't have the strength any longer. He felt it slipping from him day by day.

It was as he had told Fancy: he had no choice. And he would treat the man well, like a member of his family. The man would be far better off with him than with any of the other potential buyers. With this rationalization, John straightened up and looked harder at the lot before him. The bidding would begin shortly. He looked at the other would-be buyers, and distaste filled him. Small planters or farmers, all of them. Men who couldn't afford slaves. But he knew most of them worked their bond servants to death. He could barely stand being among them.

His gaze returned to the twenty or more souls who stood on the wooden platform. The best of the group, he knew, had already been sold in Baltimore, leaving this sorry bunch to the buyers farther inland.

"Do any of them read and write?" he asked the man who seemed to be in charge. If the man was literate, perhaps Fancy wouldn't be so opposed to the purchase.

The man shrugged and turned to the convicts. "Anyone 'ere know 'is letters?"

John saw one man, one of two in irons, look up, something flickering briefly in his eyes. But no one spoke. Then another convict nudged the man who had glanced up.

" 'E's a lord, 'e is," the second man said derisively.

John took several steps closer. The "lord" was so thin he'd probably been passed over in Baltimore. Or it could have been the irons on his wrists and ankles. No one would want to buy a troublemaker. His eyes were a startling shade of green, and John saw no emotion there, only a studied blankness. His thick, dark hair had been recently cropped close to his head, and he was dressed in a rough canvas shirt and trousers.

But his shoulders were straight, though set as if against blows, and ill-fitting clothes couldn't mask his instinctive pride. Then, for the briefest second, John saw something other than emptiness in the man's eyes. He saw intelligence.

"Your name?" he asked.

The man's gaze met his own, contempt blazing in those green eyes. Then he looked away.

One of the overseers aimed a club at the man's stomach, and he doubled over in pain.

"You answer the gentleman," the overseer said. "Give him yer name."

The man straightened but was stubbornly silent.

The guard started to draw back the club again, but John stopped him. "His crime?"

"Treason. He's one of 'em Scots that thought to rebel, then ran from the king's army." Arteries in the Scotsman's neck throbbed, but he remained silent as the overseer continued. "His term's fourteen years of work. And the price is only forty pounds."

John drew back. The man was a far cry from the gentle schoolteacher he'd thought—no, hoped—to find. A Scot. He would be gone from the farm the next day unless John watched over him constantly.

John forced his gaze from the man's face. He had watched a muscle move in the Scot's cheek at the mention of his crime. Rebellion yet lived in that soul.

Moving down the line, John saw only dull, sullen eyes, slack jaws, and bodies ravaged by starvation and God only knew what diseases. His gaze went back to the Scot. The man was terribly thin, but there was strength in those wiry muscles. Two other potential buyers were looking at the Scot, one demanding that he open his mouth. In response, he only clenched his jaw tighter.

He met another blow with stoic silence. But the show of defiance didn't deter one of the two men examining the Scot. John knew him: Caleb Byars, a man known for his cruelty.

Knowing he was a fool—but then, the other bondsmen were clearly worthless, and he had to purchase one of them, didn't he?—John stepped over to the factor who was conducting the sale.

"I'll give ye thirty pounds, no more for him," Byars was saying.

"Thirty-five," John said.

Byars looked at him with dark, malevolent eyes. "Ye'd be buying trouble. He needs taming."

"I expect he knows the penalties for escaping," John said, even as he wondered whether the Scot's knowledge of penalties would keep him in check. Yet for some reason—he chose not think what it might be—he couldn't let the Scot go to Byars. He turned back to the seller. "My offer is thirty-five pounds."

"Forty," the man insisted. "It's twenty-five for a term of seven years, and 'is is fourteen. I'll take 'im farther inland before I sell him for less than that. I'll throw in the irons."

John looked at the bondsman again. The Scot was several inches taller than he was, and he was considered a tall man. Their eyes met, and he felt, more than saw, the burst of fury suddenly revealed in the green gaze. Hate. Contempt. He knew he should withdraw from the bidding.

Yet this might be his last chance to ensure that his family survived the winter.

John nodded. "Forty pounds it is," he conceded.

The bondsman's lips tightened as he was pushed away from the others, and the seller motioned John over to a table, where another man sat with a pile of papers in front of him. John counted out forty pounds, five pounds less than the sum he'd received for Pretender, and took the convict's papers. He wished he could read them but was grateful he could sign his name. Still, he looked over the papers, feigning comprehension; he often faked the ability to read to keep people from cheating him.

He turned to his bondsman. "Your name?"

The man hesitated, then answered in a deep, lyrical voice. "Ian Sutherland."

John nodded. "I'm John Marsh. I have a small farm twenty miles from here."

Sutherland didn't acknowledge the words.

"I'll have those irons removed if you swear you won't try to run."

"I willna promise that."

Byars had approached, two of the other bondsmen behind him. "I warned you he would take taming," he said with a malicious smile.

John felt his face redden. His breathing was more difficult suddenly, just as it was at the end of a day in the fields. For a moment he felt dizzy; then a pain seized his chest. He placed a hand on the table and steadied himself, then turned to the man who had sold the indenture.

"Take the chains off him."

The seller took a key from his pocket. "I told you the chains go wi' him."

"Take them off."

One of the guards unlocked the irons and John watched the Scot rub his wrists, which were raw and bleeding.

"Come with me," John said. He was surprised when Ian Sutherland did so.

Ian clenched and unclenched his hands as he followed the man who had just purchased his body. His stomach still hurt from the blow he'd taken, but he had felt many such blows since his arrival in the colonies. When he was unchained to change clothes several days earlier, he'd vented his frustration on the guard who'd told him to remove his filthy plaid, obviously expecting to be obeyed immediately. When Ian didn't move fast enough, the guard had taken aim at his ribs with a club, not anticipating any opposition from one of the sorry, sick victims of the long voyage.

Ian had stopped the swinging club with one fist; at the same time the other fist plowed into the man's face.

It had been pure pleasure after the beatings and starvation and abuse he'd endured, but his satisfaction hadn't lasted. He was soon surrounded by burly guards with clubs, one of which had struck his head, plunging him into blackness.

When he regained consciousness, he saw that his body had been washed, his hair cropped, and his beard shaved. He was clothed in hot, itchy garments, and his wrists and ankles were chained again. He was lying alone in a small windowless room, an iron collar padlocked around his neck and attached to a ring on the wall. His ribs hurt, as did every part of his body.

He didn't know how long he remained there before a large, squat man unlocked the door.

"Most of the lot with you were sold today," he said. "I'm taking the remainder of you to Chestertown. They ain't so choosy down there about their bondsmen. You give me any more trouble and I'll kill you."

Ian stared up at him, hatred boiling in his gut.

"Mebbe you think I won't," the man continued. "Mebbe you think I want the forty pounds I'm asking for you. But using a Scot traitor as a lesson to the others would suit me jest fine. You attack another of my men or try to escape, I have the right to have you whipped. Law don't say how long. I'm yer master until someone pays good coin fer you."

Ian stiffened, but the collar held him close to the wall.

"We sail tonight. My men will bring you to the ship in a few hours. You just sit there in all that jewelry, milord, and think about whether you want to live or not."

The door closed behind him, and Ian knew what his answer would be: Katy. He would force himself to live for her.

The collar stayed on his neck for the next three days.

It was taken off only when he and some twenty other prisoners were finally unloaded from the ship and escorted to the local jail. The next morning a man came in and shaved him again. He was told to wash and ordered to answer whatever questions were asked of him. If he was asked to open his mouth and show his teeth, he was to do so.

Ian knew the chains that bound him would hurt the chances of a sale, as would the *T* branded on his thumb. *T* for "treason."

Marquis of Brinaire. He'd carried the title for only a few weeks before his lands were confiscated and the title voided. But he'd been called "my lord" all his life.

Ian thought about all of this as he followed Marsh docilely enough, but inside he was anything but docile. He'd been sold like a horse on an auction block. No longer was he Ian Sutherland, scion of a powerful clan. But he wasn't going to make another mistake. He didn't know this country, and his canvas clothes marked him as clearly as the brand. He had listened to Smythe, the seller, much more closely than the man imagined, and he didn't intend to be easy prey.

It might take a week, a month, mayhap longer, but he *would* escape and find a ship back to Scotland. And he would find his sister.

Seething inwardly, he followed John Marsh down the street of a town he had heard called Chestertown. 'Twas little more than a village, new and raw but humming with energy. He marked its streets, the port with its merchantmen and small craft, and stored the information for future use.

The air smelled fresh, and at any other time he might have taken pleasure in the soft, pleasant breeze, particularly after months in the ship's hold. But pleasure was only a distant memory now. Even so, his body did feel lighter, relieved of the heavy chains.

If only he could shed the chains on his soul. That weight, he knew, would never leave him. The sight of one brother falling at Culloden and the other swinging from an English rope would be with him always.

Marsh stopped at a brick building with a small sign on the door and told him to wait outside. For a moment Ian wondered at the man's foolishness, but then he understood that misplaced trust had nothing to do with the order. Marsh knew he had no place to go.

His new "owner" was gone only a few minutes, and when he came back outside, Ian noticed that he no longer carried the indenture papers. Perhaps Marsh was not such a fool after all. He was not going to risk being attacked by his bond servant and having the papers stolen—a thought, along with a thousand others, that had indeed crossed Ian's mind.

"Are you hungry?" Marsh asked, eyeing him worriedly.

"Feeling cheated?" Ian retorted, knowing how thin and weak he must appear.

Marsh shrugged off the hostility. "I need some rest and a bite myself before we start back. I don't imagine they fed you overwell on the voyage."

Ian didn't reply. He had no idea what to make of John Marsh. He was English, and he was willing to buy another human being. Ian had only contempt for both of those traits. He remembered the collar, as well he was meant to remember it; it had been one of Smythe's small lessons. Marsh could put him back in one, could have him whipped, could, Ian supposed, have him killed.

Still, his stomach rumbled at the thought of food. It had not been full since before Culloden.

He followed John Marsh into a dark tavern and sat opposite him, watching as the man seemed to slump into the chair. His face was an unhealthy gray, but his brown eyes were steady. Ian said nothing as Marsh ordered ale, stew, and bread for both of them, and he tried not to show his eagerness when a large dish wafting aromatic flavors was set in front of him.

Ian's eyes seldom left Marsh as he ate carefully, slowly chewing each bite. He knew he couldn't fill his stomach, not yet, or it would rebel at the sudden bounty. The ale was lighter than what he was used to, but he sipped that slowly, too.

Marsh ate very little before leaning against the back of his chair and simply watching him. He waited until Ian had finished, then sighed and leaned forward.

"I will make a bargain with you," Marsh said slowly.

"What do I have to bargain with that you don't already own?" Ian asked, allowing the bitterness to sharpen his voice.

"Your loyalty."

"You canna buy loyalty."

"No," Marsh agreed wearily. Then he added, "But stay with me—with my family—five years, and I'll give you your freedom. Five years instead of fourteen."

Ian hid his surprise behind hostility. "You think you will be safe with me around? A treasonous criminal?"

"Will I?" Marsh asked softly. "And my wife and children?"

Ian only stared at him. He wasn't going to answer the Englishman. Let him wonder.

"One of the men called you a lord. Is it true?"

Resentment and fury swirled inside Ian. This man, this . . . Englishman, had no right to question him, no right to expect a respectful answer. "Do I look like a lord?"

"You hold yourself like one."

"Then I'll ha' to work on changing that, to be a proper slave," Ian said caustically.

"I didn't buy a slave."

"Then wha' did you buy?" Ian snorted. "I saw coin change hands. You ha' papers claiming me as property. Wha' else am I if not your slave?"

"I need . . . help, willing help."

"You hire help. You *purchased* me," Ian said, his burr deepening with the anger he felt. "But donna you think you can buy anything else. I willna ever trust an Englishman. So donna think you can persuade me to stay, with your *kind* offer."

Marsh fell silent. After a moment he rose. "We have a long ride home."

It felt extraordinarily good to be astride a horse again, and it *was* a fine horse. Under other circumstances, Ian thought, he would have enjoyed a ride through this lush green countryside.

But enjoyment, like pleasure, was something he didn't ever expect to experience again. A year ago he'd had a family, a home, a country, a title. He had studied at the University of Edinburgh, and he spoke four languages fluently.

Now he had nothing.

But he had been surprised when he'd followed Marsh to a livery stable and two very fine horses were brought out. He'd seldom seen such horseflesh, even among his own horses in Scotland. They had been bred for endurance more than speed, and they had none of the stark beauty of these animals. One was a stallion, another a mare, small but exquisitely formed, and he couldn't help but admire them both.

"The mare is gentle . . . and tractable," Marsh had said, watching Ian's reaction to the animals, "though I suspect you ride well."

"I can ride," Ian replied curtly.

Marsh gave a tired-sounding sigh. "Taking care of

horses will be among your duties. I breed them for racing."

Ian stiffened at the casual expectation of his services.

John Marsh's face changed, the tentative smile disappearing. "You don't have any reason to trust me, but you don't have to. I don't care what you did to get here or why you did it, but I need your labor, and I sold one of my horses to pay for it. You will be well treated. And I meant that offer: give me good service for five years and you go free."

He paused, then added in a tone stronger than any he had yet used, "But I warn you, I will have you returned if you try to escape. Then I will sell your indenture. Another seven years could be added to your sentence, and I could easily recoup my money." His voice hardened further. "I'm no fool, Ian Sutherland. Those indenture papers are safe with a friend, and should anything happen to me on this journey, or to my family, you will be hunted down and executed."

Ian's hands clenched at his side, but he remained silent.

"Do you understand?" Marsh persisted.

"Aye, I understand."

"I have no wish to lock you up at night," the older man added, "but I will if it is necessary."

"You prefer a willing slave rather than an unwilling one," Ian said bitterly. "You should have bought someone else, then."

Marsh shook his head, then apparently decided to let the matter drop. "You take the mare."

Ian didn't say anything, but swung up into the saddle. Despite the mare's small size, he could feel her sleek muscles beneath him. John Marsh obviously treated his animals well.

That's all he was now. An animal. It was no comfort that he was to be well treated.

Chapter 3

ancy waited anxiously. Every new sound sent her running to the door. John had been gone three days. He should have been home by now.

She had tended the vegetables, fed the horses with Fortune's help, baked three loaves of bread, and started a stew using precious pieces of a ham she had been saving. Then she'd cleaned. And cleaned and cleaned.

Where was John? Had something terrible happened to him? She should never have allowed him to go alone.

After checking on a sleeping Amy, she returned to the porch in time to see two riders approaching. Shading her eyes against the noonday sun, she recognized John, and relief coursed through her. Her happiness at seeing him safely home was marred only slightly by seeing the second rider. Obviously John had been successful in his mission.

With trepidation, she watched the two men approach. The stranger, riding behind John, was lean—gaunt, really—but she gave him only a cursory glance, more interested in seeing how her husband had weathered the journey. When the two men pulled their mounts to a halt in front of the house, she watched John slowly dismount.

She started forward, then held back when Noel barreled past, eager to greet his father, with Lucky barking excitedly behind him. As John patted his son's shoulder, she noted that, although it was only noon, he already looked tired. More than tired. Drained. The knot of worry tightened in her stomach. At least he'd found someone to help them.

But when her gaze went to the stranger, her heart sank. Here was no willing redemptioner. His back was stiff with resentment, and his striking, hawklike features were stamped with bitter hostility.

He stayed in the saddle, watching John, who was answering Noel's incessant questions. Although John was not a demonstrative man, he loved his children fiercely. When his gaze flickered up to hers, she saw worry and even a little fear in his eyes.

Turning, John said something to the man on horseback. The stranger dismounted, and she noted that, despite the proud, stiff way he held himself, he completed the maneuver with the ease and grace of a practiced horseman. As he took several steps toward her, she thought, Dear God, he's tall, even taller than John. His ill-fitting, coarse clothes hung on a rail-thin form, and the wrists revealed by his too short sleeves were raw and bleeding. Raising her gaze, she found him staring at her. His eyes were a dark green—greener than emeralds—and unreadable. They weren't dull or empty; they were . . . like glass, reflecting rather than revealing.

"This is Ian Sutherland," John said belatedly. "My wife, Fancy Marsh."

Nothing flickered in those eyes, and for a moment she thought he wouldn't even acknowledge her. Then he nodded. But that nod had nothing to do with submission, she sensed immediately. Rather it was an inborn courtesy. A gentleman's instinct?

A dangerous gentleman. She felt it in every fiber of her being.

Odd, then, that Lucky, who distrusted strangers and always let them know it, was strangely quiet.

"Mr. Sutherland," she acknowledged.

He looked surprised at the returned courtesy, and she was pleased to have startled some reaction from a face that otherwise resembled granite. His jaw tightened slightly, but he said nothing. She was beginning to wonder whether he had a voice.

"Hello," a small voice said, and she looked down. Noel was staring at the stranger with fascination. "I'm Noel," he said.

Something shifted in the stranger's green eyes, but he didn't move. Or speak.

"Do you talk?" Noel asked, almost as if he'd read her own mind. "Fortune doesn't." To Noel, not talking was not extraordinary at all, and his matter-of-fact tone said as much.

A muscle throbbed in the man's cheek, and his gaze rested on Noel's face for a moment. "Aye," he said finally, obviously reluctant to admit even that much.

"That's my dog, Lucky," Noel said, then added, clearly awed by his dog's acceptance of the bondsman, "He usually growls at strangers. He must like you. I have a cat and a crow and a raccoon, too. Even a squirrel. His name is Posey. You like animals, don't you?"

For a moment, Ian Sutherland looked as if he had taken a blow to the body. Then his lips tightened, and his shoulders became, if possible, even more rigid. Fancy held her breath, waiting to see if he would respond to the eager glow in her son's eyes. He didn't want to. That was apparent.

"Aye," Sutherland said at last. Then he turned to glare at John.

Fancy saw John's shoulders slump, and she knew her own bearing must mirror his disappointment at this most inauspicious beginning. Handing the reins of his horse to the bondsman, her husband said, "Rub them down and give them some feed. Fancy will have a meal ready for us later."

The stranger took the reins of both horses and, without any further acknowledgment of either the Marsh family or the order he'd been given, easily led the mare and John's often temperamental stallion toward the barn.

Fancy watched him. He was obviously far more comfortable with animals than with human beings. Like Noel, she was stunned that Lucky had seemed to accept him right away. Yet she couldn't help but feel uneasy.

Her gaze slid to her husband. "John," she said finally, "what have you done?"

"I don't know," he answered. "I really don't know."

Ian curried the horses, trying not to feel satisfaction at the soft nuzzling the mare gave him. He didn't want to feel anything. And yet . . . he couldn't prevent his hand from stroking the animal's neck. She really was a beauty.

He quickly fed and watered both animals. Two other horses occupied stalls behind him, and he'd seen several others in the two paddocks. All of them were fine-looking animals, as fine as any he'd ever seen, and it was impossible not to appreciate the care that had obviously gone into breeding such superb creatures.

Impossible also to keep himself from enjoying these brief moments of quiet among them. Some of the tension left his body as he worked, and when he'd finished, he took a moment to lean against one of the stalls and simply admire the stallion.

But he paid for letting his guard down. He had dropped it only slightly, but that was enough. Enough to let in the pain. It sliced through him, deep and dark and fierce, and he knew, in that instant, that he'd failed utterly in his attempt to sever himself from painful emotions. He'd succeeded only in masking his loneliness and despair.

Swearing under his breath, Ian moved away from the stall. Noting briefly the makeshift bed and assuming it was to be his, he looked for anything that he might use as a weapon. All the usual farm implements were there: a scythe, several axes, a pitchfork. John Marsh was a trusting man.

Sighing, he sat on the narrow bed. It felt odd after all this time sleeping either on the stone floor of a cell or the bare boards of a ship's hold. Last night he had lain on the ground, but he hadn't slept. He had thought about running off with the two horses, one to ride and one to sell.

Two things had stopped him. He knew almost nothing about this colony called Maryland, not even which direction to run. And his scarred wrists and coarse clothes would betray him in a moment. Better to wait. And yet freedom had been so close he could taste it.

He rubbed his tender wrists now, well aware that yesterday had been the first day he hadn't worn irons in . . . How long had it been? The date on his indenture papers was May 25, 1747. A year and a month since the tragedy at Culloden. He and Derek had hidden for several weeks before being captured. He'd been in irons since then. An entire year.

It seemed like an eternity. An eternity during which he'd become a stranger even to himself. Gone was the studious lad who'd followed the family's second son tradition and studied classics at the University of Edinburgh. Then he had managed the clan's business affairs for his older brother. He had continued to train at arms, as did every Highland male, but he'd discovered his heart was in books, not war. Still, he had not hesitated when his older brother sided with Bonnie Prince

Charlie. And he had seen more death and destruction, more hideous waste, since that day than he had known existed.

Images of his brothers' deaths were seared into his mind, and anxiety about his sister was a permanent knot in his gut. In the days before he and Derek were captured, he'd heard terrible stories: women and children burned alive in barns, young girls raped. Katy was lost out there somewhere, Katy who had always been so loved and protected.

The lad, Noel, reminded him of Katy. Quiet, eager, ingenuous. He'd had a devil of a time not giving the lad, at the least, a smile. "You like animals, don't you?" Noel had asked. The question had shaken him. It could have been Katy speaking. She loved animals; indeed, she'd had her own pair of ferrets—another tradition in the Sutherland family. Were the little beasts with her now? Or had they been taken, along with everything else?

Ian was exhausted, yet his mind would not stop spinning. He couldn't decipher John Marsh—or his wife, who looked to be a good thirty years younger than her husband. She had obviously been shocked by Ian's appearance and had said little, yet he remembered the way she had spoken his name and the soft smile she had given the boy. Her eyes had been wary, though, when she looked upon him. With good reason, he thought. He was certain she realized her husband had brought home no tame servant.

Well, it was no matter to him. He owed Marsh nothing, and his family even less. He would not hurt them, but neither did he plan to stay one hour longer than necessary. He was well disabused about kindness and loyalty. After spending his boyhood fostering with the Macraes, he hadn't believed they would turn against Scotland, against its true prince. Yet he had seen them fighting and killing Sutherlands. And the fact that the Macraes had allowed Derek to die while interceding for Ian himself did nothing to lessen his hatred for all Scotsmen who had sided with the English. It had also taught him an important lesson: even those one trusted were perfectly capable of betrayal.

Ian heaved a deep sigh and lay down upon the narrow but comfortable mattress. A few good meals couldn't erase the effects of a year of near starvation, nor did months of confinement prepare one for two days of sitting in a saddle. He was as tired, and as weak, as if he were recovering from a grave illness. Mayhap he was tired enough to sleep.

Tired enough that his sleep might not be plagued by nightmares.

Fancy watched as John looked in on the napping Amy, touching his hand to her face and watching her sleep for several moments. Then he returned to the main room and slumped into a chair.

Before questioning him about the bondsman, she gave him a glass of ale and watched him anxiously. Was he feeling worse? His face seemed even pastier than usual.

Fancy waited what seemed like hours before his body appeared to relax. Then she could wait no longer. "He looks angry," she said. "He didn't come over here of his own free will, did he? He didn't indenture himself for passage?"

Setting his empty glass on the table, John sighed. "There were only convicts, Fancy."

She bit her lip. She'd known it the moment she saw the scars and open sores on his wrists.

"He was the best of the lot," John said, "and he can read and write."

Even that welcome news paled in the face of the

threat Ian Sutherland posed to her family. "What was his crime?" she asked.

"Treason," John said. "He fought with the Scots against King George."

Fancy's breath caught in her throat, her apprehension increasing. She had heard of the fierceness of Scottish warriors. Yet she also felt a measure of compassion for the bondsman, who apparently was guilty of little but following his conscience. She suddenly understood the rancor on Ian Sutherland's face.

"Caleb Byars was going to buy him," John continued. "I couldn't stand by and allow it."

Pulling out the chair across from her husband, she sat down and met his gaze. "What are you going to bring home next?" she teased gently. "An elephant?"

John did not smile. "The indenture is for fourteen years," he said slowly. "I told Sutherland I would give him his freedom in five if he stayed willingly."

But he would not. Fancy knew that as surely as she knew the sun set each evening.

"I will offer him a small wage, too," John said after a moment's pause. "At least Robert can't scare him off."

Fancy was envisioning the bondsman in her mind. She doubted anyone would intimidate him, including her husband. But she thought—no, prayed—they could persuade him to stay. He wouldn't be able to go back to Scotland. She knew well enough that any man transported as a convict could return only on pain of death.

"His wrists need tending," she said finally.

John nodded. "His ankles too, probably. They had him in irons. And you can see that his stomach is in sore need of food. Dammit, he's nearly starved to death!" He glanced at her. "That's why I was late. He needed food and rest. I half expected him to run last night while I was asleep. But he's smart enough to know he wouldn't get far in a strange country with that brand on his thumb."

She hadn't noticed. The very thought sent ripples of pain through her.

Hesitating, John studied her for a moment, then continued slowly. "Fancy, I don't think he would hurt any of us. I wouldn't have purchased his indenture otherwise. But still . . . be cautious."

Fancy knew that keeping Noel away from the man would be difficult, if not impossible. The boy had a cat's curiosity. Seeing the worry on her husband's face, however, she nodded.

John looked as if he wanted to say more, and she tipped her head in question.

After a short pause he said, "One of the other convicts said Sutherland had been a lord of some kind."

She felt not even a flicker of surprise at this information. Ian Sutherland had a natural grace about him, an arrogance in the way he held himself, that spoke of breeding and position. The kind of breeding and position that poor clothes and obvious exhaustion could not mask. Any tentative spark of hope she might have been nurturing was quashed. How could a man who had been a lord adjust to being little more than a slave?

"Will he eat with us?" Fancy wasn't sure she wanted the glowering Scotsman at her table. Lord, she had no idea what Fortune would make of him—or what he would make of Fortune. Yet he must be terribly lonely, being forced from his own country and family.

John took a long time to answer. Finally he nodded, saying, "I want . . . I hope he will become part of the family."

Fancy strongly doubted it, but she didn't argue. "I'll get you some stew," she said, rising. "Then you should rest."

"I'm not hungry," John said. "But take some out to the Scotsman. And do something for those wounds."

She hesitated. "What should I call him?"

John looked as uncertain as she felt. The man certainly didn't invite familiarity. Her husband finally shrugged helplessly. "I don't know. I've never owned anyone before." With a weary sigh, he rose and headed for the bedroom, hesitating at the doorway to look back at her. "Perhaps I should go with you."

She shook her head. "I don't think he could hurt me even if he wanted to. He looks too weak to frighten a fly." She paused. "I hope he's not too weak to help you."

"I won't put him to work tomorrow or the next day," John said. "But I suspect he'll regain his strength soon. Especially," he added with a slight smile, "eating your good cooking."

Despite the warmth in his voice, she saw the concern in his eyes, and she knew its cause: he didn't want her to go alone to the barn, but he didn't have the strength to go with her.

"Sutherland knows . . . the penalties for escaping," John said, trying to reassure both of them.

Fancy wasn't mollified. Something about the Scotsman deeply disturbed her. "I'll be all right," she said with feigned confidence.

"Where's Fortune?"

"She went to gather herbs," she said.

If he'd been feeling well, she knew he might have pursued that subject, questioning the wisdom of allowing her sister to wander alone in the woods. Instead, he merely dragged his feet into the bedroom and closed the door.

Vowing that she would *make* John spend the following day in the same pursuit he had planned for his bondsman—resting—Fancy went to collect the ingredients she needed for a poultice.

Outside, she slipped down into the cool cellar where she kept fruit and herbs and collected a handful of wild garlic. Taking the strong-smelling plant to the kitchen, she cut it into small pieces and added it to a pot of water. After hanging the pot over the fire to boil, she poured stew into a deep bowl and placed it carefully in a basket, along with a loaf of the bread she'd baked that morning. She added butter, jam, cheese, and a spoon, then, after hesitating for a moment, dropped a blunt knife into the basket.

By then her garlic medicine was ready. She poured it into a jar and placed that, too, in the basket, along with some clean rags for bandaging.

Amy had awakened from her nap, and the children were playing with the animals in front of the house, Noel keeping a protective eye on his younger sister. He often seemed far older than seven, and he was curious about everything. She longed for him to learn to read and write. Of course, she longed for those skills herself, too, but her father—himself an educated man—had seen no purpose in it. He had run from his past and wanted no reminder of it, choosing to live among the Indians with whom he traded. He had decried civilization as the opposite of its definition and taken a Cherokee wife, in part to give Fancy a mother. That had completed his isolation from white society. Fancy had grown up in Indian towns and had fled along with her stepmother's people from white influence. Thus she had never learned to read so much as a single letter.

Perhaps the Scot could change that, and teach the children as well.

The thought made her heart feel lighter.

She opened the barn door, allowing daylight to flood the interior. As her eyes adjusted to the difference in brightness, she saw the lean figure on the bed jerk to a sitting position. Apparently he'd been resting. Slowly, very slowly, he stood as she walked toward him.

"You were asleep?" she asked.

"Nay, not that," he said.

"I brought you some food."

"Did you, now?" Cold amusement made the question condescending.

She tried not to act as awkward as she felt, but the hostile, arrogant look on his face made her feel very much in the wrong. She knew how she and John must seem to him. People who bought other people.

"And those wrists need attention. I brought a poultice."

"I donna need it."

"You do, or they will become infected."

"I see," he said contemptuously. "You'll be wanting to get your money's worth."

Her gaze met his, and a shudder ran through her at the intense anger in his vivid green eyes. Those eyes were not reflective now, nor were they empty or closed. They were filled with a simmering rage.

"We do not have money to waste," she admitted, "and we do need help, as you have surely seen for yourself by now. But John planned only to purchase the indenture of someone who was willing to sell labor in return for passage." She wanted to tell him about Byars, but she knew he wouldn't listen. All he knew was that he had been sold, and bought. And she could well understand that humiliation. She'd come very, very close to it herself.

"How noble," he sneered. "And when he couldn't find such a man, he decided to buy a convict. I imagine I was cheaper."

She decided not to take his bait. "Sit down," she ordered him sternly, and was astonished when he did so

after only a moment's hesitation. Taking one of his
wrists, she gently explored the lacerations with her fingers. He would probably always have scars, but she
knew any sympathy she might have expressed would be
rejected. So she tried not to allow any feelings to show
as she washed the wounds, then soaked fresh cloths in
the still steaming water. Allowing the cloth to cool only
slightly, she wrapped first one wrist, then the other,
tying the poultices securely with narrower strips. He
held himself perfectly still throughout the procedure
and made no sound.

"Your ankles. Do they need tending? John said they
might."

"I donna need anything from you," he said arrogantly. Then his nose twitched. "What is in that potion?"

"Wild garlic," she said. "It is good for healing open
wounds."

He looked doubtful, and it occurred to her that he
would probably make a liar of her through sheer force
of will.

"You'll see," she said, trying to sound confident.
"Now let me look at your ankles."

He didn't move.

She sighed. "All right. I will leave some cloth and
the mixture. Use it or not, as you choose."

He didn't answer.

She tried again. "There is stew and fresh bread in
the basket."

He still didn't answer.

She started for the door. Then, determinedly, she
stopped and turned back. "John said you can read.
Would you . . . teach me and the children?"

He stared across the barn at her, and she could see
him weighing his response. "Do I have a choice?"

"Yes," she said softly. "John needs your help in the fields. Anything else would be . . . a favor."

"Why does your husband not teach you?" Sutherland asked.

She bit her lip for a moment, then nibbled on it; it was a habit she'd developed long ago and hadn't been able to break. She didn't want to admit that John couldn't read or cipher, that something in his head prevented him from seeing things as others saw them. His tutor had called him stupid—he had told her that—but she knew he wasn't. He was a shrewd judge of men, yet he had always felt inferior among them because he wasn't able to read.

John. Tears started to well up in her eyes. She was losing him. Slowly but surely. His face was growing more ashen by the day, his breath was becoming more ragged, and the foxglove didn't seem to help any longer. They needed this hostile stranger so badly, and she knew that he felt no loyalty to them whatsoever. And why should he?

His eyes were still questioning her. She thought about lying to him, but lies always meant more lies. Yet John was ashamed of his lack.

"He doesn't have the strength after working all day," she finally replied. It was a truth, if not *the* truth.

The Scot's gaze seemed to thrust right through her, and she thought he was seeing everything. But his face, that stone-hewn visage, never changed.

"You should eat," she said to him. "Then get some more rest."

"At your order, mistress," he said with mock servility.

She started to leave, then hesitated once more to speak over her shoulder. "I'll fetch you for supper tonight."

"I would rather eat here," came the growled response.

"My husband wants you to join us."

"Ah, he thinks to make me a member of your foine family," the Scot said. "Well, tell your husband it willna work. My body might have been sold, but no' my mind. Or my soul."

Fancy took a slow, deep breath. "I will expect you," she said, then left before he could taunt her any further.

Chapter 4

Ian waited to hear the bar fall into place outside the door, but the sound never came. After several moments he walked to the door and pushed. It opened.

He stood in the late afternoon sunlight and looked across the yard. The lad was there, watching a child Ian had not seen before, a lass of about three. The lad looked up, his tawny hair glinting in the sunshine. He grinned, an open little-boy grin that tugged at Ian's heart.

The dog stood and stretched on its three legs. Yellow and ugly, it barked once, as if finally deciding it had a duty to do so. Then the animal moved toward Ian with surprising speed, halting a foot away and sniffing curiously. Sitting, it gave him a look of such entreaty that Ian could almost imagine the missing leg pawing the air.

He resisted the urge to squat down and pet the sorry beast. He had no intention of allowing himself the slightest feeling toward any member of the Marsh family, including the animals. He had his own family—or what might be left of it—to consider.

He'd be damned if he would let himself become attached—and obligated—to the Marshes.

The bloody dog whined and cocked its head, its ears perked, and that phantom paw might have bobbed again, begging to be clasped in greeting. Much against his will, Ian leaned over and rubbed behind the dog's ears, which caused a display of embarrassingly grateful wriggles.

The dog's fur was warm from the sun, and the heat seemed to transfer itself to his fingers. How long had it been since he'd touched anyone, or anything, with gentleness? Far too long. Until today he hadn't realized how much he'd missed—how much he needed—physical contact with other living beings.

Yet even as he allowed himself a moment's escape, a flood of other emotions almost overwhelmed him, and he realized, as he had done in the barn, that he could not open even a crack in his heart, or he would be overtaken by grief.

He stood straight, glowering at the two children as if they were the king's soldiers come to take his freedom. God knows, they were every bit as dangerous, albeit in a different way.

But while the lass shrank back slightly, the lad only looked puzzled and interested. A braw one, he would be. Ian glared at the dog, but it wasn't intimidated, either. Instead, it rolled over, sticking its three legs in the air, pleading to have its stomach scratched.

He wouldn't succumb this time.

Ian's thoughts went to the horses, in their stalls behind him and in the fenced paddocks beside the barn. Marsh had told him he was breeding them for speed, to compete in the races in Chestertown and Baltimore. Ian could take one now and be miles away in only a few hours.

He had thought about escape many times in the past two days, and now he saw the necessity for doing so. He had realized it even more strongly when the woman entered the barn and gently tended his wrists.

The woman. He told himself to keep thinking of her that way. No name. No thoughts about how very bonny she was, especially given that she was another man's wife. His owner's wife.

Ian cast one more glance at the lad, who still watched him, then walked back inside the darkened barn, trying to erase the memory of sun-streaked tawny hair and wide amber-colored eyes and a smile so guileless it hurt.

Feeling restless, he started to work in the barn, not because he had to but because if he didn't, he would go quite mad.

John rested most of the afternoon, hoping that a fraction of his strength would return. He knew that Sutherland needed rest and food before he could transplant the young tobacco plants from their seedbeds. But the tobacco had to be transplanted in wet weather, so he and Sutherland must be ready when the rains came.

If he rested, John figured he could do some of the work himself. Next winter's survival depended on that crop. Closing his eyes, he reminded himself that if anything did happen to him, his family had the Scotsman now.

He would find a way in the coming days to bind the man to them. It occurred to him that Noel would help, if unwittingly, for John had seen the flicker of warmth in the Scotsman's eyes when they had rested on the boy. It also occurred to him that Ian Sutherland had risked everything to fight for a cause destined for defeat. He was obviously an honorable man—another weapon that might be used to win his loyalty. John knew it was unfair, but he was desperate. The safety of his family was at stake. He just needed time. A little time to overcome the man's resentment.

Trouble was, he wasn't sure he had that time. His strength was ebbing day by day, and each breath was harder to come by. He felt a vise tightening around his heart. Only Fancy's concoctions seemed to help, and even they were losing their effectiveness.

Lying in bed, John knew from the angle of light filtering into the room that it was near suppertime. He wasn't hungry; he never was anymore. Still, he would sit at the table, demanding the Scotsman's reluctant presence. He would watch.

He would pray.

Fortune returned home at dusk, her apron full of mushrooms, wild onions, and garlic, and her basket full of berries.

Fancy helped sort the items, and managed to refrain from scolding her sister for being gone so long. Trying to keep Fortune at home was like trying to anchor a butterfly.

Fortune's black hair was windblown and tangled, and her dress was dirty. Even so, at fifteen, she was strikingly beautiful, with her Cherokee mother's dark coloring and high cheekbones. Men always looked at her twice, but their admiration would turn to contempt when they realized she was part Indian. The contempt often turned even uglier when they discovered she was also mute and communicated only with her hands. Because of such reactions, Fortune avoided going to town and usually disappeared when visitors approached the farm.

She was Fancy's half sister, but Fancy thought of her as her child. They had been with the Cherokees in Virginia when their father died, and another trader had taken them to Baltimore, to their father's partner. Fancy felt a familiar coldness as she thought of Josiah Manning, and, as always, thoughts of that man were followed by waves of gratitude toward John. She would never forget what he'd done for her and Fortune.

She put the onions Fortune had brought home in

the simmering stew, and checked the bread baking in the fireplace. She'd made a berry pie earlier in the day. Supper would be ready shortly, and she went to tell John.

She opened the door to their room and stood quietly, watching her husband for a moment. He was standing next to the window, his shoulders slumped, his face pale in the softly colored rays of a setting sun.

He turned.

She went to him and put her hand in his. "Fortune's home and supper's ready."

He was quiet a moment, then asked, "You talked to the Scotsman?"

"As much as he would allow."

"He's bitter."

"Yes," she agreed softly.

"Did he give you any reason to fear him?"

"No," she said. "You're right. I don't think he would hurt any of us, but I do think he will run away as soon as he feels he can succeed."

John nodded sadly. "I wondered why he didn't take one of the horses on the way home, but of course he knows nothing of the country, nor the constabulary. It's a measure of the man that he *would* wait. The question is how long."

"How much did you pay for him?"

"Forty pounds," he said. "Five less than I got for Pretender." He looked at her steadily. "He was considered a troublemaker. I think that's why I got him cheap. Byars didn't want to pay even that; he knew the man wouldn't last fourteen years on his place."

He turned his gaze back to the window, to the sunset. "Fancy, the indenture papers, as well as the papers for the farm, are with Douglas Turner in Chestertown. So is my will. But you know Robert will try to take this place. I trust Douglas as much as I do any man, but I know my brother. He will try anything. If something happens to me, I want you to get the papers immediately. I want you to put them someplace safe."

His voice was more intense than she had ever heard it before. He didn't want false assurances, and she respected him enough not to give any. Instead, when he looked at her again, she simply nodded.

"And now I am ready for supper," he said with false heartiness. "I'll get the Scotsman."

"He said he preferred to eat in the barn."

"I am sure he does, but I want him to eat with us. If he gets to know us, perhaps . . ." John let his voice trail off, lifting one shoulder in a shrug.

"He will resent being forced," Fancy warned.

"He's still a bond servant," John said with resoluteness. "He will do as I tell him."

Fancy kept her doubts to herself. Going to the front door, she called to Noel and Amy, who came skipping inside, chattering about how Lucky had run to the stranger and the man had petted him.

"Is he going to stay?" Noel asked.

"Yes," Fancy said, hoping she spoke the truth.

"Lucky likes him." It was the greatest compliment Noel could give.

Fortune was looking at her curiously.

"John has brought someone to help," Fancy said cautiously.

Fortune cocked her head in question.

"A Scotsman," Fancy added uncomfortably. "He's a bondsman."

"He hardly ever talks," Noel added helpfully. "He's tall. Taller than Pa. And he can read and write. Pa says so. He'll teach us."

Fortune's gaze went to the row of books Fancy had slowly, sometimes painfully, collected. Those useless books had cost money that could have been put to better purpose, John had often said. But Fancy had never been able to rid herself of her obsession for them. Fortune didn't seem to care if she could read, but Fancy knew her sister understood her own desire to comprehend the words printed on those pages.

Fancy wondered whether she should warn Fortune that the bondsman wasn't entirely happy about being here. But then Fortune, fearing discord, might flee and keep out of the way until late.

"You might wash," she suggested.

Fortune smiled and headed for the pump outside. But Fancy could tell that, in that brief exchange, Fortune's curiosity about the newcomer had been roused.

Please, God, she prayed, don't let the Scotsman say anything to scare her off. She wouldn't allow herself to think that his reaction would be more cruel than that. She only hoped he didn't think Fortune was stupid or mad because she didn't speak.

And why did she care what the Scot thought?

She didn't know why, but she *did* care a great deal what he thought of all of them.

Her hand trembled slightly as she took a pot of boiling water from the fire for tea, then placed dishes on the table along with spoons and knives. It was not an elegant meal, she knew, but it was a hearty one.

Would he come?

Fortune shyly emerged from her room, her hair combed and her face and hands clean, although she still wore her spotted gown, and slid into a seat. Noel and Amy were already seated. The door opened, and all four heads turned toward it expectantly.

John entered, his steps a little slow and his lips in a tight, thin line. Behind him came the Scot.

He was still wearing the ill-fitting clothes. His hair was so short it probably hadn't required combing. His face was clean, but stubble darkened his cheeks and chin, making him look dangerous. A deep frown marred his brow, and anger sparked in his eyes. He was here against his will: that much was plain.

"He cleaned the barn," John said, nodding to the Scotsman to take one of the empty chairs.

Sutherland said nothing, but sat in the chair John had indicated. His gaze slowly moved around the table, lingering for a moment on Fortune. Fancy felt herself stiffen until she realized he had done the same for each of them. His expression showed no lust, as she had feared, but only a searching curiosity. Then the interest vanished from his face, replaced by a hard glare.

Fancy swallowed hard. She wondered how John had managed to get him to come to the house and whether it had been worth the trouble if he was going to glower throughout the meal. He dominated the table. He dominated the room.

She spooned several large ladlefuls of stew onto his plate, giving a smaller helping to John, who didn't eat much, then smaller ones still to Fortune and the children before ladling out a portion for herself.

John said a quick blessing, unlike his usual long-winded prayers, then lifted his spoon to eat. The Scotsman waited a moment, then started to consume the stew, slowly and steadily. He hadn't spoken a single word. It was almost as if he were sitting alone in the room. He was making it clear that, though he was forced to eat with them, he would not be forced to do one thing more.

Fancy's spirits fell.

Noel, though, was not to be discouraged. He stared at the Scotsman's movements with fascination. Instead of gobbling his own food rapidly, as he usually did, his spoon remained empty while he watched the Scot's methodical, efficient movements.

A loud screech, followed by a feline howl, brought

every head at the table up as two small critters streaked through the room.

"That's Unsatisfactory and Bandit," Noel explained to the bondsman, whose spoon had halted halfway to his mouth.

"Unsatisfactory?"

"My cat," Noel said.

"*My* cat," Amy wailed.

"And Bandit," Fancy added.

"The raccoon," John explained, surprising Fancy.

Confusion broke the stark control the Scot had imposed on his features when Lucky came barreling past in hot pursuit of the other two, and suddenly all three animals were weaving in and out among the chair legs. In the midst of this fray, a crow suddenly landed on the table, flapping its wings and knocking over a cup of milk.

"Trouble!" Fancy warned in her sternest tone, and the crow obediently flew across the room to roost on the back of a chair.

"How did Trouble get inside?" John asked sternly, but a smile tugged at his mouth.

"She must have been in the loft," Fancy said, noting that the Scotsman was looking at each of them in turn, his brows knitted in something like bewilderment, as if he thought them all mad.

"The crow," she tried to explain.

Sutherland's brow furrowed deeper.

"Her name is Trouble," Noel added helpfully.

"For obvious reasons," John submitted.

"She's Mama's pet," Noel put in.

"Mine, too," Amy said.

"Bandit's yours," Noel informed his sister. "Unsatisfactory is mine. Trouble is Mama's, and Lucky belongs to all of us. Posey likes Unsatisfactory."

The recital of animal relationships only seemed to

confound the Scotsman further. Fancy could barely hold back a smile at his pained expression.

"Posey," she said helpfully, "is a squirrel that Unsatisfactory raised. Posey lives in the trees now, but he comes back for visits." She paused and added, "Now you know everyone."

"Not the fox," Noel pointed out.

"The *fox*?"

Good Lord, he spoke. The Scotsman had actually *volunteered* two words. Fancy saw that she wasn't the only one surprised at the sound of the deep, accented voice; four additional pairs of eyes all turned upon him.

"Our baby fox," Noel explained. "Except he's not really a baby anymore. Fortune and I found him when he was really little. His mama was dead, and he was hurt. So we brought him home, and Mama fixed his wounds and saved his life."

The crow cawed and took a strutting step on the chair, ready to return to the table. Fancy hurriedly picked the bird up, took her to the door, and thrust her outside. She cawed indignantly as she flew to a fence post.

"Supper isn't always like this," John explained somewhat apologetically.

"Yes, it is," Noel said happily.

Fancy returned to the table and mentally blessed the creatures. Despite himself, the Scotsman was interested. He might think them all mad, but the haunting loneliness and raw anger, at least for the moment, had left his eyes.

He spoke again with apparent reluctance. "A cat named Unsatisfactory?"

"He was brought from England to chase rats and mice," Fancy said, "but he didn't want to do that. One of our neighbors was going to drown him because he was unsatisfactory."

The Scotsman lifted one eyebrow slightly, then let it settle back down in place. He looked disgruntled, as if suspicious that the whole performance had been designed for the express purpose of disconcerting him.

He started eating again.

But Noel couldn't stop talking about the animals, especially the fox.

Fancy looked at her husband and smiled.

He didn't smile back. His gaze was still on the Scotsman, his look speculative. He had put his spoon down, and Fancy wished he would eat more. Perhaps some pie.

She looked over at Fortune, who was also watching the Scotsman with interest. She didn't seem to have any fear of him, nor was she intimidated by his silence. That was odd.

So was Lucky's lack of suspicion.

Fancy had always felt that children and animals were the best judges of character, far better than she who'd always had a tendency to like everyone, even after an early betrayal. Fortune's acceptance of the Scotsman told Fancy a great deal.

She watched the Scotsman's startling green eyes. A flicker of amusement appeared in them at something Noel said, but it disappeared almost instantly, as if he had caught himself doing something wrong, and his lips turned downward once more. Now, however, Fancy knew there was something other than bitterness inside the man.

Somewhere inside her heart a smile began to bloom.

Bloody hell, but she had a smile that would light the heavens.

So did the boy. And the little girl—Amy. He remembered Katy at that age. All curiosity and needs and wants. Bursting with life and love. Running to him and throwing her chubby arms around him and declaring her "lob."

Pain assaulted Ian like a streak of lightning as he gazed around the table, taking in each member of the Marsh family.

Family. The pain burned deeper. He remembered the raucous suppers and gatherings of his clan, the mock battles and songs and glorious tales repeated until he knew each one by heart. He remembered his mother singing to Derek as a baby, and his gruff father, who had understood his love of books, telling him about other Sutherland men who had studied philosophy and law and ideas. He remembered the library, and the fierce fires that raged inside the giant fireplace that ran its length. And the great hall filled with voices, the stone steps that had rung with the sound of boots running up and down them.

He was blinded by the sudden flashes of remembrance, and his throat closed. He could barely breathe. He had to leave. He had to.

Abruptly, with more instinct than conscious thought, he pushed back his chair and fled out the door.

Almost mindlessly, trying to escape the intolerable pain, he made for the woods that bordered a river beyond the house. His steps grew faster, and then he was running. Running to escape the memories, running to escape the past. Running to escape the images of his brothers and Katy. Katy, alone and afraid, when he should have been able to protect her. He ran until he could run no longer, until he came to a wide ribbon of water. The river. There he sank down on the sandy bank amid the tall, prickly grass.

He would not let the Marsh family entrap him. He would *not*. He would not let them keep him from doing what he must do.

He looked up at the night sky with its million stars and wondered if Katy was looking at the same sky. Was she alive? After so many months of imprisonment, the sky looked glorious to him. But he found little hope in it, and no answers.

Ian put his head on his knees. The emptiness inside him was more excruciating than any wound he could imagine. He had never cried, never. Yet now he felt tears flowing down his face. And he did not try to stop them. Instead, he gave in, finally letting the grief he'd kept bottled up inside pour from him.

Chapter 5

The Scotsman didn't return. Fancy waited with John deep into the night for some sign of him, but the house and yard remained ominously quiet.

John finally went to the barn and locked the door. He couldn't afford to lose a horse, and, though he hadn't said it, she knew he worried that the Scotsman might steal one of his precious animals. When he returned to the house, he looked defeated. Defeated and extremely worried.

She tried to comfort him. She fixed him tea with a touch of foxglove in it. Surely, she said, the man would come back. But even she heard the doubt in her voice; the truth was, she didn't know any better than John what Ian Sutherland would do.

They both finally went to bed, but John's restless movements kept her awake until nearly dawn, when she drifted into a fitful sleep.

The first rays of the sun woke her. She tried not to jostle John as she got up and was pleased when he didn't awaken. Thank God he was finally getting some genuine rest. She walked to the window and looked toward the barn. Had Ian Sutherland returned? For John's sake, she prayed that he had.

The morning showed promise. The sun was just appearing on the horizon over the flat, empty expanse of the field where the tobacco would soon be planted. The first golden rays pierced the gray of early morning, but in the growing light she saw no one.

Fancy sighed and turned back to the bed. John still had not moved. Odd, since he usually stirred at first light.

Staring at the form of her husband, lying so still beneath the covers, a sudden thought made her heart skip a beat, then begin to race. In the next instant a river of gooseflesh crept over her.

Slowly she moved to the bed, unaccountable dread putting a lump in her throat. When she reached John's side, she looked down at the face that had become so dear to her. Then slowly, she placed a hand on his cheek.

Shudders ran through her, and her breath caught on a small, choked cry. His skin was cool, his expression peaceful. And still. So very still. Not a whisper of breath passed through him.

Kneeling by his side, she placed her face next to his. "Oh, John," she whispered. "Dear, dear John."

Ian woke, blinking in the early morning sun. It felt good, those rays of sun streaming down upon him. For a moment he imagined he was back in Scotland. The air was fresh, the sky endless. . . .

And then he remembered.

He wondered whether John Marsh was hunting him, whether he'd alerted the constabulary and the neighbors about the runaway bondsman.

Drained from the previous night's emotional outpouring, Ian rose slowly from the ground. When he swayed and had to put his hands on his knees to steady himself, he became aware, fully and for the first time, exactly how much strength he'd lost in the past year. He hadn't thought about it last night; he'd been moving on pure instinct. But in the light of day he had to acknowledge the truth: when he'd collapsed here, on the riverbank, he couldn't have run another step if his life had depended upon it.

Nor could he simply keep running today; he would be caught within hours. After being gone all night, he supposed he could already be considered a runaway and his sentence lengthened. English justice, he thought bitterly. Part of him still wanted to flee, but the reasoning part of him said that only a fool would try to run under these circumstances. He had no resources. No tools, no weapons, no food, no knowledge of the geography or the people.

He had to go back. Return to captivity. In some ways, doing so voluntarily was worse than if he'd been dragged.

Ian looked around, trying to get his bearings. The river stretched before him, the sun glittering off of its choppy surface. It was wide, and a strip of sandy beach, littered with shells and driftwood, stretched along its bank as far as he could see in either direction. No trees grew this close to the water, only a sea of tall, spiky grass, some of it with odd-looking, fuzzy brown pods about a handspan long at the top of the stems. Behind him, though mayhap fifty feet away, a stand of tall, straight pines marked the margin of the woods.

He had no idea where he was, no notion how far he had run. Bloody hell, he didn't even recognize the plants growing around him. The entire landscape, flat and endless as it was, seemed foreign and inhospitable to him. Yet he could see quite well that the river flowed in a southeasterly direction, and he remembered seeing it flow through John Marsh's property.

He would follow the river back to the Marshes' farm. He should be able to see the barn from the riverbank.

With his lips thinned to a grimace, Ian began walking toward the rising sun.

* * *

Fancy dressed John, and when the rest of the household was awake, she broke the news to them.

With Fortune close by her side, she led the children into the bedroom and allowed them to see their father, to kiss him, to say good-bye. Noel understood that his pa was dead, but Fancy could see in his wide but dry-eyed expression that the full impact had not yet hit him. Amy seemed to understand, but long after they left the room, she kept asking when Papa would wake up, which made Fancy realize that her daughter really didn't know what death was.

She told both children that their father had gone to heaven to join the angels. She'd always tried to make heaven a wonderful place for them. When their pets died, she told them the animals had gone to a place where they could play all day and eat their fill.

Amy asked if her pa was playing, and Fancy could only nod, unable to speak past the lump in her throat.

"When will he be back?" Amy asked again.

"He won't be back, sweet pea," Fancy said. "But you will see him again someday. I promise."

Amy digested that information while Noel stood silent, arms at his side. His reaction worried Fancy considerably. Not a tear had fallen, and his expression was stoic. A little boy shouldn't be able to act so grown up.

She remembered losing her own father, the terrible emptiness she'd felt, as well as the insecurity and fear. She never wanted Noel and Amy to know that uncertainty.

But how could she instill confidence in the future in her children when she herself felt at such a loss? How would she manage the farm by herself?

And who was going to tell Robert about his brother's death? For he did have to be told.

Her stomach knotted at the thought. Robert would

try to take everything. She knew it. And she wasn't sure she was up to the battle. Not alone.

And she *would* be alone, Fancy thought, watching Fortune inch toward the door. Her sister's capacity for coping with unpleasantness was low in the best of times; in the face of tragedy, the girl simply had no resources at all.

When her sister reached the door, she looked at Fancy, her eyes pleading.

Fancy nodded. "Go ahead. But please help me with Amy this afternoon."

With a sad but grateful look, Fortune escaped.

Her sister felt things deeply—probably too deeply, Fancy thought—and the only way she seemed able to face them was alone.

Sighing, she looked down at the children. "Come with me," she said, wanting to keep them busy, wanting to keep herself busy. "We'll feed the horses."

Noel usually responded with eager exuberance to being offered such adult responsibilities, but he remained quiet and serious. Very adult. He simply put his arm around his sister, and the three of them went out to the barn together.

The door was locked. Of course. Fancy had forgotten that John had locked it. And why.

"Noel, you know where the key is kept," she said.

His gaze left the barn door and swept around the yard. Then he looked up at her, his expression questioning.

"He disappeared last night," she said wearily.

Noel's shoulders stiffened, as if he sensed the loss meant more responsibility for him. Without a word, he turned and trotted toward the house, leaving Amy clutching Fancy's hand.

Fancy struggled to keep the tears from falling. She didn't want the children to see them; they had grief of their own to handle. They would have to bury their father.

A coffin. A service. A minister. She couldn't imagine how to accomplish any of those things. She had no idea how to build a coffin. And a minister? There was only a circuit rider who wasn't due for another ten days.

Thinking about the details overwhelmed her. Such terrible details. Yet they kept her mind busy so she didn't have time to think about other, more important things. Like how alone they were . . .

Noel came running back with the key. She allowed him to turn it in the large lock and open the barn door. Without further prompting, he straightened his slight shoulders and hurried inside toward the feed sacks.

Amy toddled in behind him, and she actually took the bucket that Noel handed her and held it still, or mostly so, as he shoveled feed into it. Her lips were pursed in concentration, and Fancy realized that her daughter at least understood that something very grave had happened and that her cooperation was needed.

It took them over an hour to feed the horses, far longer than it should have. Noel worked hard, but before they were half finished, Amy was scampering about, climbing the rungs of the stalls, jumping on hay bales, and generally being more hindrance than help. Not surprising given her age, but the difficulty involved in accomplishing that one critical daily chore made Fancy even more aware of how utterly impossible it was going to be for her to run the farm alone.

Back at the house, she sent Noel to play with Amy in the other room so she could sit on the bed beside John. Burying her face in her hands, she fought off a wave of grief. But it was grief laced with guilt. She had loved John, but not with passion. If she had, would his heart have been stronger? Would he have had a greater desire to live? She felt she had cheated him, although he had never uttered a word of complaint.

At that moment, with him lying dead beside her, she was nearly paralyzed with regret for what had not been. John had always seemed content with their marriage. Why hadn't she been content as well? Why had she always felt slightly . . . yes, it was true . . . disappointed? Wasn't friendship enough? Why had she harbored this small, secret belief that there should be more than that?

Oh, but she would miss John sorely. He had been her best friend, her protector, her anchor, and his death would leave a ragged, gaping hole in her life.

She was trying not to think about exactly how big that hole was when a knock at the door brought her head up.

They rarely had visitors, and of all times . . .

She forced herself to stand and go to the door. When she opened it, her eyes widened in shock.

The Scotsman stood before her, his clothes wrinkled and his hair mussed, although he'd apparently made some effort to wash at the pump. His face and hands were still wet.

"You came back," she said stupidly. For a moment she simply stared at him, then in the next instant, anger roiled inside her. While part of her knew that John had been sick for a long time, the part of her that needed someone to blame saw a scapegoat in the errant bondsman. Certainly his abrupt departure had caused John a great deal of anxiety.

"My husband is dead," she said in a clipped tone.

Sutherland frowned, his eyebrows knitting together as if in confusion.

"He died last night," she continued, amazed at the calmness of her voice. She wasn't calm. Not at all. She was reeling. And she was angry.

The confusion left the Scotsman's expression, but otherwise, his features remained impassive. Was he thinking that this was his chance to escape?

She hated him then. She hated the hope he had given John, only to snatch it away. She hated him for being alive when her husband was dead. She hated him for disappearing last night.

But after a long, silent minute of glaring into dark green eyes that were filled with an emotion she couldn't identify, the hate drained away, leaving her empty. Ian Sutherland was a stranger, here by no choice of his own. It was foolish—and unfair—to blame him for anything, much less John's death.

She bit her lip and turned away. In sudden need of support, she leaned against the wall beside the door.

At least the Scotsman didn't say he was sorry. She didn't think she could bear that.

"What do you want me to do?" he asked, his voice harsh, empty of sympathy, empty of feeling.

Yet he stood there, waiting.

What *did* she want him to do?

She had no notion. She knew her chin was trembling, and she hated it. She wanted to be strong, but she had two children, a sister who had disappeared, animals to feed and water, horses to exercise, and a farm she couldn't possibly manage. And her husband was gone.

Dredging up some remnants of the anger she'd felt only moments ago, she asked, "Where were you?" Her voice was more bitter than she'd ever heard it, but she was afraid that if she didn't hold on to her fury at the bondsman, she might somehow move closer to him, to the strength she instinctively felt in him.

"Downriver," he said simply. "I don't know exactly where." Then, after a pause, he asked, "What happened?"

"He died in his sleep. His heart . . . I didn't know until . . ." She waved a hand in a small, helpless gesture, then took a step away from the wall, away from him. But she could barely hold herself upright, and she felt herself swaying.

She jumped as his hand cupped her elbow, steadying her. Warmth from his touch was like fire to the coolness of her skin, the chill of her spirit. She jerked away, backing up against the wall as if he were an enemy.

"You'd not be thinking I would hurt you?" Sutherland said in a curiously soft voice.

Indeed, she had been thinking exactly that. She remembered others, people who had said they would help her after her father's death. Instead, they had stolen her father's furs and sought to sell her and her sister as servants—or something worse. So how could she trust this cold-eyed man who made no secret of his hostility?

But she also knew she couldn't show weakness in front of him, couldn't allow him to think he could take advantage of her.

Ignoring his question, she said, "I want you to go with me to John's brother. I have to tell him that John is dead."

His first instinct was to say no. She could see it in the way he hesitated, the way his gaze moved toward the barn. This was a chance for him to escape. There would be no one to stop him, no one to ride after him.

"John's friend in Chestertown has your papers," she said, forcing the words out reluctantly. "My brother-in-law would see that you were brought back." It was an empty threat. She would do no such thing. She would never give Robert that power over this man— over *any* man. But if she could make the Scotsman stay a few days, a few weeks, maybe he would understand that she meant him no harm, that they could reach an arrangement advantageous to both of them.

She needed him so badly. The farm needed him. Dear God, her children needed him. She could never let them fall under Robert's influence.

His eyes swept her. If there had been a hint of sympathy in them, there was none now. Instead, his presence was almost threatening as he stood in the door of the farmhouse. Despite his thinness, despite the lines in his face, there was something overpowering about him.

Suddenly he bowed mockingly. "Your servant, mistress. I'll hitch the buggy."

"I have to wait until Fortune returns to look after the children."

"Where is she?"

"She went to the woods to be alone. She does that."

He leaned against the doorframe, and for the first time she suspected the depth of a weakness he was trying to hide. There was also something else, a hesitancy she hadn't seen before, perhaps even the slightest hint of regret.

She tore her gaze from him. She needed help from this man, not pity. He was a bond servant. *Her* bond servant.

"Can you find her?" he asked, surprising her.

"Yes, but I can't leave the children."

A long, low sigh came from his mouth. "I'll look after them."

She hesitated.

"*If* you trust me with them." It was a question.

"Should I?"

He shrugged. "Probably not. Didn't your husband ever tell you not to trust the slave?"

Her stomach clenched. *Her husband.* Her husband now lying in the next room. She wondered whether the pain would ever go away. She forced herself to confront his question. "You're not a slave," she said fiercely.

"Splitting hairs, mistress," he said. "A moment ago you mentioned my papers, the papers that say you own me."

"We own your services, not you."

He gave her a dark look. "I canna leave your property without permission. I canna own anything without your permission. I canna write a letter without your permission." His jaw moved even after he stopped talking, as if he was straining to keep from saying something else.

After a moment's silence he seemed to force himself to relax. "I gi' you my word, I will stay until your husband is buried. I will look after your children, and they will be safe wi' me. More than that, I canna promise."

She believed that he would do as he said. Perhaps because he'd drawn the line so clearly.

She swallowed hard. "I'll go find my sister."

Sutherland looked down at her—and it seemed a very long way down. When he was close, the disparity between her height and his seemed much greater. She felt small and inconsequential. And uncertain again. Was she foolish to trust him?

Even more foolish to leave him with her children, the most precious part of her life.

"They will be safe wi' me." How surely he had said those words.

"I ha' a sister," he said suddenly, his burr deepening even further. "About the age of your lad. I would never see harm come to a bairn."

Realizing he had sensed her reluctance, she wondered why it was, the thicker his accent became, the less threatening he seemed. And the more she trusted his words.

* * *

The woman said little during the six-mile trip to her brother-in-law's home. Before they left, she had put on a dark dress and tucked her hair under a plain bonnet. She sat very still.

Ian drove the horses carefully, keeping his eyes averted from the woman and riveted on what was little more than a wide trail. He didn't want to look at her, at the sad, wistful face with the huge brown eyes.

He also wanted to pay attention to every landmark, every trail and path they passed. What he saw mostly was water. It was everywhere. Broad marshes filled with more of that strange-looking grass with the fuzzy brown tops. Narrow creeks and larger streams that branched out into other streams and branched again, like the wrinkles on an old man's face.

And a very flat face it was, at that. Coming as he did from the Highlands, Ian was struck by the fact that, no matter where he looked, there was not a hill, not so much as a five-foot rise, in sight.

The best he could say about what was to him such boring landscape was that it made life easier on the horses. He had felt almost guilty hitching them to the cart. They were far too fine for such work, and it was fast becoming clear to him that John Marsh had spent what money he had on developing a fine strain of racing horses, not on purchasing work animals.

Except Ian himself, of course.

The reminder dimmed the brightness of the day. So did the reason for the trip. He couldn't ignore the feeling of guilt that nagged at him. If he had not disappeared last night, might John Marsh still be alive?

He hadn't admitted it to the woman, but he felt it deep in his bones. God knows, he didn't want to be responsible for another death, nor did he want to see sadness the likes of which he'd seen in the Marsh children's eyes.

The woman had given him a grateful glance when she returned with her sister and saw the children playing quietly in front of the house.

He wondered why she hadn't taken them with her, and why she seemed so tense. But it was none of his business and he wanted no confidences that would bind him any tighter to her. The brother-in-law would take care of them, and Ian could escape, back to Scotland.

He was musing over his options when her quiet voice broke his thoughts.

"Thank you," she said.

"For what?" he replied curtly. "I'm just following your orders like a good servant."

"I don't think you will ever be a *good* servant," she said tartly.

His hands tightened around the reins, but he held back his retort. He didn't want to engage in conversation. He didn't want to know her better. He didn't want to worry about her. Yet he was very aware of her presence beside him. A slight scent of flowers clung to her, and she continued to surprise him with flashes of spirit and independence despite her obvious grief. She had cried; red-rimmed eyes gave proof to it. But she had not cried in front of him.

He'd wanted to reach out and comfort her. All his instincts demanded it. But a single act of kindness would lead to others, and . . . well, he knew a trap when he saw one. And he would never be trapped again. He couldn't afford it.

"A good servant?" he replied after several moments had passed. "No, I won't be one of those."

He saw her glance at his hands, and he knew she could see the calluses from years of weapons training. "Did you farm in Scotland?"

"My clan raised sheep and cattle," he answered abruptly.

She wanted to talk, perhaps needed to talk, but he wouldn't allow himself that familiarity.

She didn't try again, but occasionally his arm would brush hers, the sweet flowery scent of her would drift over him, and his senses would lurch. He disliked that in himself—that he was thinking about her as a woman. She was newly widowed; even if he hadn't been in the position of bondsman, he had no right to have carnal thoughts about her.

It had been so long, though. So long since he'd felt a woman's softness. Her light scent was different from the often heavily perfumed women he had known, and a hundred times more enticing.

At her direction, he turned onto a narrow lane and was startled several minutes later to see a large brick home sitting amid well-tended fields. Behind the house lay more fields, dotted by numerous bent figures, hard at work. Her brother-in-law's farm? Ian had assumed that the man would be a small farmer, much like John Marsh.

He looked at the woman. Her face was set and her body rigid. Her hands were clasped together in a hard, tight knot. As much as he hated to acknowledge it, even to himself, he was plagued by curiosity. He knew the danger involved in asking questions, in learning anything more than absolutely necessary about this woman and her family; knowledge could lead to caring, and he definitely did not want to care.

Yet Fancy Marsh interested him. He wanted to ask why her husband had been so desperate for help that he'd purchased a bondsman when his brother had so many men working his fields. He wanted to know how she'd come to be married to a man so much older than she. He wanted to know why she had a sister who looked nothing at all like her, who didn't speak at all, and who seemed more than a little fey.

Clamping his jaw against the words, Ian urged the horses up the lane. As they approached the house, a lad of about twelve ran up and took the reins from him. He stepped down, helped Mrs. Marsh, then turned at the sound of the front door opening. A tall black man, dressed immaculately in black-and-white livery, stood in the doorway.

Ian noticed that Mrs. Marsh stiffened her shoulders before asking, "Is Mr. Marsh at home?"

The man's glance flickered over Ian, rested a moment on his servant's clothes, then dismissed him, returning his attention to Mrs. Marsh. "Massa Marsh is in the fields," the man said.

But Ian saw a horseman galloping toward the house, and the woman noticed the rider, too, for she turned and watched him approach.

Ian stood to the side, instinctively knowing that this man must be the brother-in-law and that, for some reason, Fancy Marsh did not like him—in fact, might even fear him.

The rider jerked his mount to a swift halt, dismounted, and strode swiftly toward them. Ian saw the man's gaze rake over him, and his poor clothing, with contempt, then focus intently on Mrs. Marsh.

"I saw your wagon from the field," he said to her, taking off his riding gloves, switching a wicked-looking quirt from one hand to the other. "This is an unexpected pleasure."

Ian noticed that, though the words were courteous enough, and certainly proper, the man's leer was not, nor was the way he put a hand on Mrs. Marsh's arm and ran his fingers down it. His demeanor was, in fact, distinctly unbrotherly.

She pulled away from his touch. "John's dead," she said starkly. "He died this morning. I thought you should know."

The man's hand paused in midair, then dropped to his side.

"How?" he asked.

"His heart."

For a moment the man's face remained devoid of emotion, then a look of concern slid across it. "Ah, poor John. You must let me look after everything for you."

Something about the way he said the words rang a warning bell in Ian's head. The man's concern was feigned—he would have sworn to it—and there was an ugly hint of something like satisfaction in his tone as he offered his help.

Taking a step backward to distance himself, Ian took a long look at Robert Marsh. He was of an age with John Marsh, though he looked far healthier. He wasn't as tall as his brother had been, but he was more substantial in body—not fat but well muscled. And he carried himself with an arrogance that had been lacking in his brother. His hair was thinning, and his face was hard, his eyes set close together, blue—a glittering pale blue that held no warmth.

"I don't need your help, Robert," Mrs. Marsh said. "I just wanted you to know. We'll be burying him under the oak tree this afternoon, and we'll hold services when the circuit rider comes next week."

Ian was surprised at the strength in her voice, particularly as he recalled how frightened she had seemed.

"You and your sister and the children, of course, will stay with me," Robert Marsh said.

"No," she replied. "I have my own home."

"Now, you know you can't manage that farm alone," he pressed.

"Not when you scare everyone away from working for us," she said bitterly. "You as much as killed John. But you won't get that farm."

"You misjudge me, Fancy," Robert said. "All I've ever cared about was John's health. He never should have tried to farm that land. It belongs to Marsh's End." A hardness crept into his voice, despite his obvious attempts to be solicitous.

Ian felt distaste roil up inside him.

"No. It belongs to me now," she said with defiance.

He shrugged. "You will be coming to me soon enough." Then he turned and stared hard at Ian. "Who is he?"

Ian waited for her to say the humiliating words, to tell him that he was her bondsman.

"Ian Sutherland," she said. "He is . . . working for us."

Robert Marsh looked him over, just as the buyers had days ago when his indenture was sold. Like a horse or cow.

"He's not from around here."

"No," she said without elaboration.

"Doesn't look like much."

Ian wanted to strike the man. He wanted it so badly his arm ached. He was being discussed as if he weren't present, as if he were livestock waiting for a buyer.

He forced himself to remain perfectly still, but he couldn't force his gaze to drop, couldn't prevent himself from meeting Robert Marsh's glare squarely. A most unservile attitude, but he wouldn't give the man the satisfaction of thinking he'd intimidated him.

"He is stronger than he looks," Mrs. Marsh replied.

Her brother-in-law's lips turned up at the corners, but by no one's most generous thought could the movement have been considered a smile. He turned to Ian. "I pay far better than anyone in this county."

As offers went—an attempt to bribe the only help his brother's widow had into abandoning her—Ian thought it might be the most loathsome proposal he'd ever heard. His fists knotted. He understood now why Mrs. Marsh had appeared so tense about this trip to visit her brother-in-law.

But she hadn't revealed Ian's true status as a bonds-man, and for that he felt he owed it to her to maintain control in front of this contemptible man.

"I'll be remembering that," he said slowly. "But it looks as if ye ha' plenty of help."

Robert shrugged. "Slaves. Convicts. I can always use a good freeman to help my overseer." Then his gaze went down to Ian's hand, looking for the telltale brand. But Ian had already tucked his thumb inside his fist.

Robert studied him for a moment, then turned his attention back to his sister-in-law. "I think we should bury John in the family cemetery."

"No," she said. "He loved that oak tree. He told me . . ." Her voice trailed off.

He ignored her words. "I'll send some of my people to get him."

"No," she said again in a stronger voice.

"Now, Fancy," Robert Marsh began, as if she were a child, "the community would expect it. Just as it would expect me to take you all in. You can't live out there by yourself—a widow and a young girl—with no one but this . . . this stranger," he finished with obvious dis-approval.

It took every ounce of self-control Ian possessed to remain passive. He'd thought the past year had taught him something about self-preservation and looking out for his best interests. He had certainly done his best to bury any protective instinct he might feel toward any-one but Katy, for she was his only real concern. But as he watched the slim woman before him stand up to an obvious bully on the day her husband died, he wanted nothing so much as to jump to her defense. Bloody hell, what he *wanted* was to smash his fist into Robert Marsh's smug face.

Despite the man's solicitous words, an underlying threat was as obvious as the look in his eyes. Ian could almost feel the heat radiating from the other man's body, a lust so strong that the man couldn't keep his hands off his own newly bereaved sister-in-law. His fingers were touching her arm again, but his eyes were on her breasts.

She took several steps away, toward Ian. Instinctively, he moved closer to her and was gratified when Robert Marsh dropped his hand.

"I am going to bury John under the oak tree," she said again, "but there is something you can do."

Ian heard the reluctance in her voice, and could tell she hated asking her brother-in-law for anything.

"A coffin."

Robert shifted his weight to his other foot. "If you bury him here, where he belongs."

"No," she said flatly. "We will manage without a coffin, then."

She turned and started toward the buggy. Silently Ian followed her, helping her up onto the seat, then climbing into the driver's seat. He flicked the reins, and the horses drew the buggy toward the lane.

Ian looked at the woman next to him. Her face was like marble, her back even straighter and stiffer than before.

A glance over his shoulder showed Robert Marsh watching them depart. He had a slight smile on his face, and he was flicking his quirt against his leg.

Chapter 6

ancy's heart was beating so loud she was sure the Scotsman could hear it.

Robert always did that to her. She didn't scare easily, not after growing up the way she had. But Robert had power and influence in Kent County. And he had always made it clear, when John wasn't around, that he wanted her. Suddenly Fancy was only too aware that she didn't have many more weapons now than she'd had nine years ago when her father died.

The Scotsman hadn't said a word since they'd ridden out of Marsh's End. Had he seen how afraid she was? Whether or not the Scotsman had intended it, she had felt supported by his presence, standing behind her as she'd faced Robert. She was grateful to him for that—and for returning to the farm that morning. She wondered why he had, but she wasn't going to ask.

When she could no longer stand the silence between them, she cast him a quick sideways glance. "What did you think of Robert?"

Sutherland shrugged. "It's no' my right to think anything."

She bit her lip at his harsh tone. "I would like to know," she persisted.

"Crabbit," he said.

"Crabbit?"

"Bad-tempered."

"Is that Scottish?"

"Aye."

It seemed a fitting description to her, if not complete.

"We need you," she told him then.

"So do others," he said flatly.

"Who?"

He didn't answer, merely clucked to the horses, asking them for more speed.

Yet his words had sent a chill through her: "So do others." So it wasn't only his resentment against being a bondsman or his anger at the sentence imposed on him that made him want to escape.

"Three years," she bargained, cutting even further the offer John had made. "And at the end of that time, you can have one of the horses." She hated begging. John had spent precious coin to purchase labor. Didn't she have a right to expect the bondsman to work for her?

Maybe. But she knew the notion of earning his keep, of paying back in labor what had been spent on him in coin, mattered not one whit to the hard, determined man beside her. And, truly, how could she expect it to when she herself didn't believe in indenturing human beings against their will?

The answer came swiftly: she could do nearly anything to protect her family.

A muscle moved in Sutherland's cheek. His gaze flitted to her, then focused once more on the road in front of him. "My term is fourteen years."

"I know," she said. "But I will only need you until Noel is old enough to help, and until we've established a reputation for our horses."

He turned to her again, and this time the look he gave her was long and searching. Then, almost reluctantly, he said, "I canna do that."

She turned her face away from his piercing gaze, toward the creek that ran alongside the road, and fought to keep the tears from falling. She couldn't afford to show weakness to this man. "I can't lose the farm," she said, desperate to keep the quaver from her voice.

A minute passed in silence, and then he spoke unexpectedly, into the chasm that had formed between them.

"Your sister," he said. "She doesna look like you."

Fancy cleared her throat. "She's half Indian. Cherokee."

Her estimation of him rose a notch when interest, but no revulsion, flickered across his features.

"I've read about your Indians," he said.

She felt the familiar hunger inside her at the mention of reading. How wonderful to be able to take adventures that way.

"Are there Indian tribes around here?"

"No. They were pushed west long ago."

"Then how . . . ?"

She looked at him. His eyes were straight ahead, but she'd heard the curiosity in his voice. That it was reluctant was as clear as the blue sky above them.

"Our father was a trader. After my mother died, he took a Cherokee wife. We lived with them."

"Your sister is very . . . shy," he said after a moment.

Fancy started to say that Fortune had not talked for nearly ten years, but then she checked the impulse. She feared that she had thrown enough at the Scotsman for one day; no sense in adding yet another thing that he might consider a problem.

Searching his face in surreptitious glances, she said, "Fortune has been called many names. People look down on . . . half-breeds."

"As they do convicts," he said bitterly.

"You aren't a convict," she retorted automatically. "You fought for your country."

" 'Tis the same thing to the Sassenach."

"Sassenach?"

"English," he said contemptuously.

He said the word with so much hatred that she knew the emotion went deeper than his own imprisonment. She wondered whether he considered her a Sassenach—one of the enemy.

She hesitated. She wasn't sure she should stir this particular pot, and yet talking helped divert her thoughts from John. "Your family?"

"Ye donna want to know," he said, his burr deepening. "And 'tis none of your business." With that, his expression hardened, and he retreated once more behind that granite wall.

She wanted to rail at him, tell him that she had lost a mother and a father and now a husband. Yes, she too had faced grief, but she had never shut herself off from the world as he was trying to do. But then, she thought, she'd always had someone who needed her. Her father. Then Fortune, when their father died. And now, with John's passing, the children needed her. At no time in her life could she simply have retreated into her own grief.

So do others. His words came back to her. *What* others? And why did they need him? Could they possibly need him more than she did?

Loneliness deepened inside her. Loneliness and desperation. She'd always been an optimist, always believed that somehow things would work out. But for the first time in her life, she considered the possibility that things might not work out at all and, indeed, that nothing would ever be right again.

* * *

Ian helped Fancy Marsh bury her husband under the old oak tree.

He had looked for materials to build a coffin, but there were no boards, and in any case he had no tools, nor was there time to make one. Instead, together they wrapped John Marsh in a quilt. Then, as the children watched in silence, Ian dug a deep hole in which to place the body.

It took hours. Though the earth was rich and loamy, it was dry and hard from lack of rain. Still, Ian welcomed the work, mindless labor that required naught but his hands. He welcomed the pull on muscles too long inactive. He even welcomed the pain.

Once, he looked up and saw Fancy Marsh watching him. He had seen no tears, but her eyes were red, either from sleeplessness or from tears shed in private, and her face was pale with worry. Her arms were wrapped around the children.

We need you. Her words echoed in his mind, beating into him with the rhythm of the digging. Other words quickly followed: *Trap. Trap. 'Tis a trap. Think of Katy. Katy. Think of Katy.*

His thumb tightened around the handle of the shovel. He couldn't see the brand through the dirt embedded in his skin, but he knew it was there. He knew it was there every waking moment of every day. That brand would be a death sentence if he returned to Scotland. And yet he must. He must find his sister.

The shovel struck the dirt again, plowed into it with the force of pent-up anger and frustration. Noel was watching him with tragic eyes and little Amy with tearful ones. Even the dog was slinking around as if he knew that death had made an unwelcome call at the farm.

But this was not his business. His loyalty was to his family, or what was left of it. He owed these people nothing. Nothing! Damn John Marsh. He would have preferred any other buyer. Anyone at all.

Finally the hole was as deep and as long as his own height, and Ian climbed out of it. He was covered with dirt, his rough clothes layered with it.

The woman let go of the children and came to him. When she took his hands in hers and turned them, palms upward, he saw the raw blisters beneath the grime. Her fingers touched his skin with gentleness. She had been strong at Robert Marsh's home and at other times when facing him, but there was an underlying kindness about her that appealed to him.

Awareness flared again within him, the raw attraction of man to woman that knew neither propriety nor honor. When she dropped his hands suddenly and stepped back, he knew that she too had felt it.

"Wash your hands," she said. "I have something that will make them heal quickly. And you can change into some of my . . . some of John's clothes."

He nodded and strode away from her. He didn't want to feel desire for her any more than she wanted to feel it for him, which, surely, was not at all.

Going to the well, he pulled up a bucket of water, splashed it over his hands and face, then emptied the dirty water onto the ground. When he turned, she was standing there, holding several garments. He took them from her, noting that the shirt was of soft cotton, the trousers well worn but of good material.

A dead man's clothes. Not much better than a convict's. But he had bloody few choices at the moment. Moreover, the garments were clean, and his ingrained sense of decency demanded that he not attend a burial in filthy clothing.

He went to the barn and changed quickly, then caught himself feeling the stubble on his face. Although he had no mirror, he knew he must look like a brigand.

He hadn't been given anything to use for shaving, and he now had a four-day growth of beard. It reminded him again of exactly how little he had. Nothing at all but his pride. Aye, he had that.

Fancy Marsh met him in the yard, and together they returned to the house, where he picked up the shrouded body and carried it outside. With the woman and her children following him, he carried the body to the grave and lowered it gently into the earth beneath the oak. Then, handing the widow the shovel he'd used, he stood back and watched as she and the lad each tossed a shovelful of dirt into the hole. When the wee lass demanded a turn, too, her brother helped her. Then the lad handed the shovel back to Ian, and he finished filling the grave for them.

He was gratified by the look on Fancy Marsh's face when he produced the small cross he'd made with the name John Marsh carved into it. Though she did not say thank you, her gratitude was clear in her expression.

Every man deserved a marker, Ian thought as he stuck the cross into the dry, sandy soil at the top of the grave and piled rocks around its base to hold it upright. It sickened him to know that neither of his brothers had one. His older brother Patrick's body had been left for the wild animals, and Derek's had been burned. The Sassenach wanted no martyrs.

Standing back from the grave, Ian watched as Fancy Marsh ran her fingers over the lettering on the cross. It was not so poor a piece of work, especially given the brief time he'd had to make it. The new widow dropped a flower onto the fresh mound of dirt, and her sister did the same.

Ian eyed Fortune Marsh with her wild, uncombed hair and disheveled dress. She had not shed a tear—at least he hadn't seen one—yet her nearly black eyes were luminous with pain. She seemed so fragile, so easily wounded. When she turned to catch him watching her, she shied away as if in fear.

Her reaction caught him off guard. He had never hurt a woman or child and would never intentionally do so. In truth, though he'd killed men in war, he'd never wanted to hurt anyone. All he'd ever wanted was to be a scholar, a teacher. Nor had he ever wanted to be anywhere except the Highlands, where he could read and think, perhaps wander along the rugged coast or sit beside a pool of clear spring water.

Instead, he was standing under an American oak tree in borrowed clothes, listening to Fancy Marsh say a brief prayer over her husband's grave.

He didn't blame her for his plight. She and her children were innocents, and he'd been cast among them. But he had his own innocent to find, and he greatly feared she needed him far more than even Fancy Marsh and her brood.

When the burial was over, Ian went to the barn, to the horses, which were in dire need of care. They'd been fed and watered, but they needed to be exercised. Ten horses. Fancy Marsh could not possibly take proper care of all of them.

No, but she could sell them. They were fine horses and would bring good prices. The new widow could buy a house with the money, and eventually she would find a husband. She was a fine-looking woman, and so was her sister. The best thing he could do was encourage that solution to her problem. Then he would feel free to leave without guilt. He had no reason to feel guilt, anyway.

Suddenly feeling better, Ian saddled the stallion, then led the animal out so he could talk to the woman. She was still standing next to the grave, holding her children's hands. Her sister had disappeared again.

Ian watched them for a moment. They made a striking portrait. She stood straight in her dark dress, her
fine tawny hair blowing in the wind. The lad mimicked
her pose, his back rigid and his features stoic. The lass,
Amy, was very still, too still for a child her age, her
mouth trembling and her eyes swimming in tears; it
was beginning to dawn on her, he could see, that her
father was not coming back.

Ian felt the depth of their loss, despite his efforts to
remain aloof. He had been a young man when he lost
his parents, but he remembered the pain, the agony of
losing people who were so much a part of oneself that
it was difficult to think of life without them.

The memory made him wonder how Katy was surviving, having lost everything she knew, everything she
loved. Did she know that he was alive? Or did she believe him dead, along with the rest of their family?

When Fancy Marsh turned and saw him, he took the
final few steps toward her.

"The horses need exercising," he said.

She looked at him for a long moment, and he knew
exactly what she was thinking: if he rode out, he might
never come back. But then, he could have left hours
ago, and taken one of her precious horses with him.
She had little power and even less protection. And they
both knew it.

"Can I go, Mama?" Noel gave his mother a beseeching look.

Ian started to shake his head.

"Noel can ride one of the mares," she said.

Ian saw the plea in her eyes, then looked down at
Noel's solemn face. The lad needed a distraction, and
he could not, in good conscience, deny him.

He gave the lad's mother a single nod.

"Thank you," she said. "And thank you for the
cross. You didn't have to do that."

"Yes, I did," he said shortly.

"You're a strange man, Ian Sutherland."

But instead of acknowledging her words, he just turned and headed back toward the barn, Noel trailing his steps.

The Scotsman was quiet at supper, and so were the children. Fortune had returned, but she, as always, was silent. No one except Sutherland ate much, although he made up for the others.

Fancy was again aware of how his presence seemed to dominate the room, and she wondered whether it had been a mistake to invite him to eat with the family, tonight of all nights. Yet Noel seemed to take some comfort in his presence.

She hated to admit it, but so did she. There was a steadiness about Ian Sutherland, despite his bitter demeanor. His inner strength had helped her get through John's burial that afternoon without breaking down. The Scotsman had accomplished the excruciating task for her with grace and sense, doing far more than she'd asked him to do.

But how much longer would he stay? She'd seen the faraway look that haunted his eyes. No, she could not depend upon him remaining with them for long, perhaps not even through tomorrow.

To her it didn't matter who else needed him; Fancy could only see, at that moment, that she needed him desperately. And she was willing to use any means—the children, gratitude, guilt, threats—to secure his agreement to stay, at least until the tobacco was planted. Their very survival depended on it.

Watching him throughout the silent meal as he sat with his head bent over his food, she noticed that his gaze occasionally flicked toward the mantel, to the books she kept there. Perhaps she only imagined it, but his eyes seemed to have a hungry look about them as he eyed the volumes in brief stolen glances.

After finishing his last bite in his usual efficient manner, he shoved back the chair.

"Don't go yet," Fancy said. "Will you read something to the children?"

He looked at her suspiciously, then at Amy and Noel, his gaze softening as he did so. Then he turned his gaze to Fortune.

To Fancy's amazement, Fortune met the Scotsman's look. She didn't lower her gaze as she usually did with a stranger and often even with someone she knew. Fancy understood why her sister behaved as she did, and she had never tried to push her. She only hoped that someday Fortune would, or could, learn to trust someone again. Could that time be now? And with such an unlikely person?

In answer to the Scotsman's unspoken question, Fortune nodded with an eagerness that surprised Fancy even more, until she realized that all of them, even Fortune, would have jumped at any excuse not to go to bed this night.

She herself was dreading it, knowing that the bed she had shared with John for nine years would feel very empty. Although he had not touched her intimately since his illness became severe a year ago, she'd grown used to his presence next to her. Even if she had not genuinely wanted to hear the Scotsman read aloud, she would have found a reason to postpone bedtime.

The Scotsman hesitated, then looked at her and nodded. "Aye, I'll read. For a while."

Fancy rose from the table and showed him her small collection of books. They had come from peddlers who had passed by the farm and all were well worn. Two, she knew, were schoolbooks. One was a Bible. The other three were thick and leather-bound. She watched as the Scotsman looked through them, and she saw a brief smile touch his lips as his fingers lingered on one of the spines.

"Your husband never read to you?" he asked.

"He could not read," she said.

His brow furrowed and she could guess his thoughts. He had seen Robert's fine house. There should have been tutors.

"He said he couldn't learn," she explained, her voice low so that it wouldn't carry to the children. "He had tutors, but the marks on the pages didn't look the same to him as they did to his brother." With bitterness coloring her whisper, she added, "Robert always called John stupid, but he wasn't. He was smart in many ways, and no one was ever better with horses. That's why . . ." She hesitated, then finished, "That's why John's father left the horses to him, even though he was the younger son."

Sutherland looked at the books again, then raised one eyebrow in query. "So you bought these books because . . ."

He thought she was foolish. "I knew I would learn someday," she said defensively.

That muscle throbbed in his cheek again—she was coming to recognize it as a sign that something had affected him—and for a moment she thought she saw a flash of approval in those usually cloaked eyes. But the look disappeared quickly, and he pulled out the book that had made him smile.

"*Robinson Crusoe,*" he said.

She watched as his hands fondled the worn leather binding, and she realized he was a man who found much pleasure in books. She remembered exactly what he had said about his former life: "My clan raised cattle and sheep." But he was far more than a farmer or a sheepherder. She wondered whether she would discover exactly how much more before he disappeared.

Her gaze followed his movements as he sat down at the table again and opened the volume. Something about the way he fingered the pages told her that he was far more at ease with a book in his hands than he'd been with a shovel.

Fancy's musings stopped when the Scotsman started to read, and she lost herself in the words and in the deep accented voice that spoke them with such power that the images they described seemed to take on life.

She wished John were here to share the rare experience with them. But then, perhaps he was. Perhaps he was looking down from heaven, smiling. He had, after all, brought the Scotsman to them.

Chapter 7

Holding a candle steady in one hand, Ian sat on the narrow bed and studied the book he had brought from the house. It was a history of Maryland colony, founded in 1632 under a royal grant. Maps of the land were scattered throughout the text.

Unable to believe he'd been so fortunate to have the very information he needed almost literally handed to him, he found Chestertown, on the Chester River, and figured his approximate location. Then, having satisfied his immediate curiosity, he widened his study of the map to take in the entire peninsula that was the eastern portion of the Maryland colony, a great slice of land that lay between the Atlantic and the Chesapeake Bay. The area was veined with waterways both large and small, the Chester River being one of the largest, located at the upper end of the Chesapeake.

Moving the candle closer to the map, he considered escape routes. Once away from the Eastern Shore, as the peninsula was called, he could find a port and seek passage as a seaman. Of course, Chestertown was the closest port, but it would be the first place the constabulary would look for an escaped bondsman, and, as small as the town was, they surely would find him.

Would Fancy Marsh alert the authorities if he disappeared? She would be a fool not to. Her husband had paid forty pounds for him, and she had made it very clear how much she needed his help. She might not want to set the hounds upon him, so to speak, but he couldn't discount the likelihood that she would.

She had asked for only three years, but he couldn't give them to her. He couldn't give her even three months. Nor could he say anything about his sister to Fancy Marsh. If he did, she would know that he was headed back to Scotland, not simply off to find freedom elsewhere in the colonies. His life would be forfeit if he was found in Scotland. If anyone knew of his return.

With another look at the map, Ian realized that if he could find a boat, he might be able to make it to Baltimore, where there would be less chance of being recognized as an escaped bondsman. A boat would also get him to Annapolis, on the Chesapeake's western shore; it was the capital of the colony, and so more ships would probably dock there than in either Baltimore or Chestertown. He would look for a ship headed for a neutral port, and from there he'd make his way to France. Then, from France, he'd be forced to go by stealth to Scotland.

As for staying alive once he reached Scotland . . . He could burn the brand off his thumb, but what could he do about the scars around his wrists? The bloody English had marked him well and for life.

After closing the book and blowing out the candle, Ian set both aside. Somehow he would hide his scars. Gloves. Long cuffs. He lay in the dark, pondering different plans. Now at least he had something to hold on to. A beginning. Hope.

He refused to let himself think about the family who slept—or mayhap did not sleep—in the house only a short distance away, or of the fresh grave outside, under the old oak tree.

Robert Marsh sat in the Chestertown tavern with an employee of the firm that sold slaves and indentured servants. Robert had come to town with his questions about Ian Sutherland. It hadn't taken long to discover that John had purchased the fourteen-year indenture of a Scot who'd been convicted of treason.

"Mean bastard," his companion said. "Had to beat 'im some. Didn't know 'is place. I told the gentleman who bought 'im to keep 'im in chains, but 'e paid no mind. Gonna 'ave trouble with that one."

"Fourteen years," Robert said thoughtfully.

"Righto. Don't 'ave many of those. Most terms are seven, but treason's different. Heard he was almost hanged."

"How much did my brother offer?"

"Forty pounds, but my bet 'e be a runner. Glad to 'ave 'im off my 'ands."

Robert called for more ale for both of them and sat back. "Know anything else about him?"

The man swallowed the last of his ale, drops of it clinging to his lips. " 'E's arrogant for a bloody convict. One of the other convicts said 'e were a lord or some sech in Scotland. Didn't look like much to me, though."

A lord. Perhaps that explained why the man had so haughtily refused his offer to work for him, Robert thought. But such airs didn't impress him. As far as he was concerned, this Sutherland was no more than a slave who'd belonged to his brother and, now, to Fancy. Robert's eyes narrowed. If the man belonged to him, he would soon whip that arrogance out of him. The thought gave him some pleasure. He still felt the sting of the contempt Sutherland had radiated as he stood there in that ill-fitting clothing.

At the memory, Robert felt his anger rise. What right did a convict, no matter his background, have to judge him?

None, he concluded. None at all. And he'd made certain, in the years since inheriting Marsh's End, that no man had that kind of power over him. He was still living with the result of his father's judgment, and it galled him as much now as it had then, seeing that look in another man's eyes: superior, slightly disgusted, and full of doubt about what it saw.

He'd told his father he would look after John. And he *would* have. Yes, he would have seen to it that his brother was provided for. But his father hadn't trusted him. Hadn't believed him. And so, the old man had given John the choicest piece of land and the best horses from the stable.

Robert had felt then and he felt now that the land and horses should have been his. After all, John had been a dull-headed fool as well as the second son. Yet Robert understood quite clearly that because John had a way with horses, and because their father valued horses more than the tobacco that had produced his wealth, the old man had valued John above his firstborn son.

Robert would never forget that. Nor could he forgive it.

In all the years since the old man had died, Robert's only consolation had been that the bulk of the estate had come to him. For his father had at least understood that John did not have the intelligence to run a large plantation.

Still, Robert thought, John had managed to infuriate him again when he'd married Fancy, a girl of dubious lineage. His own wife having died five years ago, childless, Robert had been looking for another wife these past three years. But there was no one of his own class available, certainly no one of attractive face or figure. And no one as attractive as Fancy. He found it galling as well as secretly embarrassing that, over the years, he'd developed an attraction to that confounded, lowborn woman.

Thou shall not covet thy brother's wife. Robert prided himself on being a God-fearing man, yet he had been lusting after his brother's wife for years, and that had made him furious with himself, with John, and with Fancy.

But now John was dead, buried without benefit of clergy, and in unhallowed ground. And Fancy . . . Fancy was alone with a convict.

He swore at her stubbornness. He wanted her under his roof. He wanted the horses, and he wanted that piece of prime riverfront land. God help him, he wanted it all. And no convict was going to stand in his way.

He knew now what he would do.

Robert rose from the chair. The trader started to rise with him. A man who knew his betters.

"No, no," Robert said effusively. "Have another." He threw several coins on the table and left the tavern.

Ian stretched in the sunlight, letting it soak into him.

He felt good. Too good. Dear God, but it felt fine being free.

Relatively free, he reminded himself.

Nightmares had haunted his sleep the night before. He was back in the hold of the ship, an experience even worse than the prison cell in Edinburgh where he'd waited out the uncommonly bad winter until the ship could make the Atlantic crossing safely. At least in the cell he'd had some space to move, and though he hadn't been well fed, he'd still had more to eat than he was given aboard the ship. He would never forget the hopelessness, the total despair, of those months chained in the ship's hold.

As he stood in the barn doorway, basking in the sunlight, free of chains, anything seemed possible.

His gaze swept over the small farm: the dilapidated

fence, the chicken coop, a pig and four piglets in a pen that hardly seemed solid enough to hold them. The horse pasture. The nearby field with the flats of small tobacco plants and, beyond, the greater acreage, furrowed and ready for planting. And of course the small white single-story house.

The sounds and sights of life, of living.

The three-legged dog bounded toward him, eagerly wagging its tail. The crow was perched on a fence post, the cat sunning himself. The children were nowhere in sight, but he knew someone was up, because he saw smoke curling from the chimney.

Walking to the side of the barn, he looked around the corner toward the grave and saw Fortune kneeling there.

She looked up, obviously startled, and for a moment he thought she would dash off toward the woods that bordered the river. She didn't, though, and indeed tentatively held out a hand as if beckoning to him.

He walked slowly toward her, stopping about ten feet away. "Fortune?" he said.

She pointed to him, then placed the palms of her hands together and put them against the side of her head, miming sleep.

He understood her. "Aye, I had enough sleep," he said. What kept her from talking? he wondered. Fancy Marsh hadn't said why her sister couldn't speak, and he hadn't wanted to ask. He was curious, though. Fortune had an immense vulnerability about her that touched something tender inside him. "Thank you for asking," he said.

She hesitated, then pantomimed holding open a book. Then she spread her hands as if asking a question.

"Aye," he said. "I'll read tonight."

A smile broke over her face like a ray of sunshine breaking over a lake after a storm.

Lucky barked, as if he too felt warmed by her happiness. With her smile still in place, she pointed at Lucky, then at him, then back to Lucky.

He thought she was trying to convey that it surprised her that Lucky approved of him.

"I think he likes everyone," Ian observed wryly.

She shook her head and made a face.

"He *doesn't* like people?"

She held up her thumb and index finger, giving him a clearer message.

"He likes only a few people?"

She nodded, clearly pleased that he understood.

Her hands moved again, telling a story. He watched her. A trap. A dog struggling to get out. Someone—Fortune?—opening the trap. Then she feigned fear and pointed at Lucky.

"He was afraid?"

She nodded. Then with one hand pointing toward the house, she stooped to touch the dog, stroking his leg as if rubbing something on it.

"Fancy healed him," Ian guessed.

Fortune nodded. Then, taking a few steps toward him, she motioned toward his wrists, then rubbed her own.

"Aye," he said, "she tended me, too." And already the pain had faded. Fancy did have a way of taking care of things. If he wasn't careful, she would take care of her problems by giving them to him—and he already had quite enough of his own.

"Fancy said you were part Cherokee," he said.

Fortune's eyes suddenly lost their glow, and she turned her head away.

"I have read that they were a braw people," he said. At her puzzled look, he explained, "Fine."

Her gaze questioned him as if she didn't quite believe his words. Then she nodded.

"You should be very proud."

Her shoulders straightened, and her dark eyes seemed to reach into his soul. She was a pretty thing, even disheveled, as she always tended to be. Her face was striking with high cheekbones and dark, mysterious eyes that seemed to hold a thousand secrets. She was slender and lithe, almost ethereal. He couldn't imagine Fancy Marsh ever having been that fragile; for all her prettiness, the woman had a core of steel in her that Ian didn't think this girl had ever had, or ever would have.

Taking a few more steps, Fortune came closer to him. Reaching out with one hand, she touched him, her fingers just barely skimming his hand before she moved quickly away, her hurried steps taking her behind the barn.

Ian stood watching for a moment, surprised and pleased and disgruntled at once; he was humbled to think she trusted him, yet he didn't want her, or any of the Marshes, forming an attachment to him. Nor did he want to form an attachment to them.

Sighing, Ian turned and headed back inside the barn, but he stopped when he found Fancy Marsh standing between him and the open barn door. He wasn't sure he was ready for this, or for the questions in her eyes.

"Where did Fortune go?"

"She just . . . disappeared. She was telling me about Lucky—"

"*Telling* you?"

"Aye, with those gestures of hers." He hesitated, then asked, "How did she come to lose her speech?"

Fancy was quiet a moment, then said softly, "She used to speak, but then . . ."

She didn't continue, and Ian didn't pry. It was none of his business. And he would keep telling himself that, he vowed, every time he was tempted to ask a question about any of these Marshes.

"I'm afraid I may ha' wounded her. I told her tha' I knew she was part Cherokee, tha' I ha' heard they were a braw people, and tha' she should be proud. Then she ran away. Did I say something wrong?"

Fancy's face relaxed. "A lot of people, including Robert, have called her half-breed. They haven't been kind about it. I think she was surprised that someone was."

"I meant only to be . . ."

"Kind," she finished for him.

"I'm sorry," he said.

"Don't be," Fancy said. "Fortune likes you very much. I don't think she's ever tried to communicate to anyone before. No one, of course, but John and the children and me. She told me yesterday that she thinks God sent you."

Ian closed his eyes. If God had sent him, the means He'd employed to accomplish the deed were bloody cruel.

"I ha' to see after the horses before I eat," he said brusquely, his burr thickening even further in his fear of the sudden emotion swamping him. He didn't want, nor could he afford, more of this conversation.

"Breakfast is almost ready," Fancy said.

He nodded curtly.

"Thank you for being so good to her."

Bloody hell.

He nodded again, then escaped into the barn.

Fancy watched Ian Sutherland disappear, then went back to the house.

The book he'd read last night was still lying on the table, and she picked it up, fingering it reverently as she tried to fathom the mysteries of the Scotsman, the contradictions she kept seeing in him. His accent, for instance. It seemed to come and go, though she wasn't certain what brought about the shifts. A few minutes ago she'd had to listen hard to understand him as he spoke, yet last night he'd read *Robinson Crusoe* with barely a burr to his words.

And his voice had been mesmerizing. She'd watched Noel's eyes light up as he listened to the story. Even Amy, as young as she was, had been transfixed, though Fancy was unsure whether her daughter's fascination came from the story itself or from the deep, magnetic cadence of Ian Sutherland's voice.

Goodness knows, the Scotsman had seemed as consumed by the tale as they all were, although she sensed it was not new to him. He hadn't hesitated over a single word, as their minister sometimes did at services, and his tone had varied as he read. When he'd described the storm that struck young Crusoe's ship, his voice had filled with tension; he'd made the story so vivid, so alive, that she'd seen the lightning and heard the thunder and pounding rain.

Reluctantly, Fancy put the book down and checked the johnnycake baking in the fireplace. It was golden brown, and she placed it on the table along with the cornmeal pudding, then went about preparing the rest of the meal. As she gathered plates to set the table, she caught herself counting out six.

Looking at the sixth plate for a moment, she put it back with a sigh. She missed John's gentle presence, although he had been a quiet man, particularly in the morning. Even the sound of Noel's voice, as he talked to the fox while feeding it, didn't fill the emptiness.

Last night had been so lonely. She hadn't truly realized until then how much she appreciated John, his steadiness, his patience, his tolerance of what he fondly called her peculiarities. Not until the long, dark, empty night had come.

The children came into the kitchen for breakfast without her having to call them, as if a sixth sense told them when food was ready. Amy emerged from her room, carrying her doll, Petunia, and Noel arrived, followed by Unsatisfactory.

Wondering if they should wait for the others, Fancy went to the door. As she looked toward the barn, Sutherland came out of the open doorway, and, to her amazement, both Lucky and Fortune trailed behind him.

She noticed immediately that the Scotsman had used the razor she'd given him the night before. John's razor. His short, dark hair was damp and obviously wanted to curl, though it settled on merely being crinkly. His face, pale from months of confinement, made his green eyes that much more formidable. He appeared to be feeling much better than he had three days before, she thought. His skin was already starting to show some color, and he moved with more confidence. Was it only three days ago that he'd come into their lives?

Yes. And Ian Sutherland, she noted, was a handsome man.

Appalled, Fancy wondered what kind of woman would notice a man's appearance the day after she'd buried her husband. But then, she reasoned, it was merely an objective observation. He *was* a very handsome man. She had not noticed before, what with the ill-fitting clothes and the beard and, of course, all that had happened.

As the Scotsman approached the porch, looking every inch a vital man, her brother-in-law's words came back to haunt her: "You can't live out there by yourself with no one but this . . . stranger."

God help her, was Robert right?

Apprehension wrapped itself around her, making it difficult to draw a deep breath. Fancy knew what others in the county would say—and what Robert could do to make sure they knew all the details of the situation. She knew of his influence. He had already made it impossible for John to hire help. And if he took a notion to use Ian Sutherland's presence against her, that was exactly what he would do.

But she couldn't lose the Scotsman. If she did she would lose the farm. It had been John's dream, and now it was her independence. If she lost it, she and Fortune and the children would be under Robert's thumb—exactly where he wanted them to be.

Whirling away from the doorway before the Scotsman reached it, she went to the fireplace and made herself busy. She heard the clomp of his footsteps as he crossed the small porch and entered the kitchen.

"Can I be doing anything for you?"

She gave him a quick look over her shoulder, surprised by his offer. She shook her head. "Just sit," she said. Then, struck again by how different—how good—he looked, she watched him, marveling at the easy grace with which he moved to the chair and folded his long body into it.

The children were already seated, and extraordinarily quiet. Noel was petting Unsatisfactory, who was curled up contentedly in his lap, while Amy was clutching Petunia to her as if she would never let the doll go. Both children, she thought, seemed to need to hold on to something.

A frown flickered across Fancy's brow as she looked again at the cat in Noel's lap. He knew the rules about animals at the table, but she didn't have the heart to remind him. Not today.

With a sigh, she picked up the teakettle and carried

it to the table. As she poured the steaming liquid into Ian Sutherland's cup, she caught his bemused look.

"How many more?" he asked.

"More?" she repeated.

"Animals," he said with just a trace of humor. He glanced at the cat in Noel's lap, then at the raccoon, curled around the boy's feet on the floor. "So far, I've seen the raccoon, the cat, the dog, the crow, and the fox. Are there others lurking somewhere?"

Before she could answer, Noel piped up with a bright reply. "Papa used to say that Mama would bring an elephant home." But then his lower lip trembled, and he looked down at his empty plate.

Without a word, Fancy quickly ladled food onto plates, then sat down and bowed her head. The children followed her lead. The Scotsman, who'd picked up his spoon, dropped it abruptly but he didn't bow his head.

"Noel," she said.

The boy thought for a moment, then spoke in a clear, bold voice. "Bless this food, and . . . and please look after Papa, your servant."

Fancy bit her lip. John had always given the blessing. It had usually been long, and the children had fidgeted. This was probably an unsatisfactory prayer, but then . . . she couldn't think of anything better at the moment.

A smile crossed the Scotsman's face so quickly that she wondered whether it had been there at all.

"That was short," Amy noted admiringly.

"I know, sweet pea," Fancy said.

"Papa prayed a long time," Amy contributed further.

The Scotsman's lips quivered slightly.

"Do you have an opinion, too?" Fancy asked.

"Nay," he said. "Not me. I thought it was just fine."

She held his gaze for a moment, wondering whether he was laughing at her. It was important that he respect her and that he acknowledge her authority.

"Good," she said, and started eating.

The children only picked at their food, as did Fortune. The Scotsman ate with his usual precision but without any apparent enthusiasm. He kept his eyes on his food and said nothing until he finished. Then he looked up at her.

"What do you want me to be doing today?"

She hesitated. There was so much to be done. The most urgent task was the transplanting of the tobacco plants, but they had to wait for rain to do it.

"Can you work with the horses? Exercise them?"

"Aye."

"Do you know anything about training them?"

"Training?"

"For races?"

"Nay, but I do know horses," he said.

She was aware of how well he rode, having seen him riding out yesterday with Noel. But riding was one thing, and training was quite another. She suspected that he was understating his skills—whether out of modesty or out of a desire to make himself less valuable to her, she wasn't sure.

So how was she ever to know what she could trust to his skills and what she would have to do herself?

Realizing how very little she knew about Ian Sutherland, the man she now owned, she also realized that the fate of the farm—and, consequently, of her family—depended entirely on the two of them working together.

God help her.

Chapter 8

Ian woke to the sound of rain splattering on the roof of the barn. Rising from his bed, he went to the wide doors and opened them.

It was impossible to see more than a few feet into the darkness through the downpour. Still, the cool air, after the hot summer day, felt good. He'd been in the colony only a week, and he'd already come to hate the suffocating humid heat. Mayhap some became used to it, but he didn't think he ever would. He missed the Highlands and the brisk, fresh wind that always blew them clean. He missed . . .

He missed many things.

In any event the storm was a welcome relief.

Wearing only his trousers, Ian stepped outside into the rain, letting it cleanse him, relishing the prickly feeling of the cold water as it struck his face and chest. While the trees swayed, their branches waving like a demented man's arms, the sky boiled with clouds that shrouded any glimmer of dawn's light.

A streak of lightning was followed quickly by a clap of thunder. Behind him, in the barn doorway, Lucky whined. The dog had become his shadow, and as much as he would have liked to discourage the animal, he didn't have the heart. Still, he ignored the dog's current whimpers—doubtless the animal thought a man should have sense enough to come in out of the rain—and continued to let the storm wash over him.

Another bolt of lightning streaked across the sky, and, in the brief light it provided, Ian looked toward the fledgling tobacco plants that awaited planting. He hoped they were weathering the storm.

That he'd even thought about the bloody plants angered him. A week, he thought. He'd been here only a week, and already the Marshes—and their desperate needs—were undermining his intention to escape quickly. There was that tobacco, and it had to be planted. Ian understood quite clearly that the family desperately needed the money the crop would bring. How, in good conscience, could he abandon them at a time like this?

On the other hand, how could he stay even a minute longer, when his sister, assuming she was alive, might be in terrible need?

Plant the tobacco, he thought. Plant the tobacco for them. Then you can leave with a clear conscience. He would feel better about leaving if he knew he'd given Fancy Marsh what she needed to keep body and soul— and her family—together. By the time the tobacco was ready for harvest, this year's foals would be ready for sale, along with the yearlings. She could sell the horses and, along with the tobacco crop, the family would have a nice sum to tide them over until . . . until when?

Until the widow Marsh found herself a new husband. God knows, she was pretty enough to attract one. . . .

Ian stood for a long while in the pouring rain, thinking of Scotland, of his sister, of his plans for escape. Thinking of anything but exactly how pretty Fancy Marsh was and how rapidly the unwelcome desire to help her was growing inside him.

A thunderclap woke Fancy. Rain. She said a brief prayer of thanksgiving. It would be late to transplant the tobacco plants to the large field where they could spread out and grow. But not too late.

Rolling out of the bed that now seemed much too large, she went to the window. Lightning forked through the sky, briefly illuminating the yard. In that moment she saw the Scotsman. Shirtless, he was leaning against the barn, letting the rain pound against him. What on earth was he doing out in the storm?

Holding her breath, she waited for the lightning to flash again. When it did, and the inevitable rumble of thunder followed, her shoulders shrank inside her white cotton nightdress. Ian Sutherland might like the thunder, but she did not. She liked gentle rain, friendly and nourishing, not this violent, pounding torrent.

Another brilliant fork of light illuminated the farm. He was still there, unflinching under the onslaught of the storm. Unflinching and alone.

Was he thinking of Scotland? Of those others who needed him?

Since they'd buried John, the Scotsman had performed every chore she'd asked of him. Yet he'd refused to teach her or the children to read. "I'll no' start something I canna finish," he'd told her coldly. He'd also refused to eat any more breakfasts or the noon meals with them. " 'Tis not my place, nor do I ha' the time."

She'd let him go about his business, carrying a johnnycake with him, Lucky following behind. But she felt as if she'd lost an important battle. Eating meals together made them seem more like a family, and she wanted him to feel like a part of her family. She wanted him to stay.

She waited for another glimpse of him, but the storm was moving. The brief flashes were too far away now to cast any light onto the farmyard.

Sighing, Fancy returned to bed, hoping she'd be able

to sleep a little longer. If the rain gentled tomorrow, she and Noel and the Scotsman would begin to transplant the tobacco. It was backbreaking work, but it had to be done.

And the day after tomorrow the Methodist minister would be here—as would Robert with all his righteous disapproval—for the funeral service. Robert would probably bring the Anglican priest from Chestertown, and then there would be another argument about which clergyman should commend John's soul to his Maker.

John, like the rest of his family, had been a member of an Anglican church until he'd married her and brought Fortune into his household. Even now Fancy remembered the priest publicly condemning her sister because of her Indian blood. John had glared at him, grabbed her hand and Fortune's, and stalked out of the church. After that, they had sought a more tolerant man of God and found him in the unassuming person of Reverend Rufus Winfrey.

Fancy didn't blame the Anglicans for the priest's behavior. She had seen intolerance from all manner of people when they learned that her father had lain with an Indian. None, except the Quakers and Reverend Winfrey, who had brought the new Methodist religion to this part of Maryland, had accepted her marriage to John as blessed.

What a pity it was, she thought, that more people weren't like Reverend Winfrey and Ian Sutherland, who also seemed to have no prejudices.

Lying in the darkness, Fancy wondered what the reverend would think of the Scotsman. Would he, too, be horrified that she and her nearly grown sister were living, for all intents and purposes, alone on the farm with a young, handsome man? She didn't believe he would condemn her, but neither did she think he would entirely approve.

God, help me, she prayed. I can't live with Robert, and Ian Sutherland is my only hope of keeping the farm. I can't lose him. Help me find a way to keep him. Please, help me.

With Fortune and the children in tow, Fancy attended Reverend Winfrey's camp meeting, held in a field near the river. She'd invited the Scotsman to join them, but he'd asked whether it was an order and, when she said no, he'd curtly refused.

Before the service began, Fancy told Reverend Rufus Winfrey about the death of her husband.

"We've buried him, but we would be so grateful if you would come out to our place and pray over him."

"Of course I will," he said with a sad smile on his weathered but kind face. "I'll be there this very afternoon."

Fancy was surprised when, throughout the morning, others came up to her, not only to offer condolences but to ask if they might attend John's service. Most of the small farmers around them had generally kept their distance; Fancy had guessed that their reticence was due either to Robert Marsh's reputation or to her sister being a half-breed. Perhaps both. She knew people were afraid of Robert and the influence he had as a large landowner. Then, too, folks still repeated stories of long-ago Indian atrocities, and they had little sympathy for the tribes that had once occupied the land.

Either way, she had always felt that she and John were very much alone, with no real friends whom they could count on. By the end of the service, though, with all the people who'd expressed their sympathy and said they'd like to attend the service, she was beginning to wonder if she'd been wrong.

"He was a good man."

Fancy looked up to see a familiar face. Tim Wallace. With him was his son, Tim, a youth of seventeen or eighteen years. Fancy had heard them called Big Tim and Little Tim, although the latter was taller than his father.

She knew them, had spoken to the elder man on rare occasions, but like her other neighbors, the Wallaces had maintained a wary distance. She had heard that Big Tim was once an indentured man himself, though he had given his bond willingly in order to reach America. His indenture had been bought by a blacksmith, and he'd learned the trade as well as earned enough coin to start his own small farm. John had often taken his horses there to be shod.

"Mr. Wallace," she acknowledged, blinking with emotion. "Thank you. John *was* a good man."

"Is there anything I can do?"

Fancy noticed that the younger Wallace's gaze was lingering on Fortune, who, as usual, kept her head bowed.

Fancy hesitated. There *was* something the Wallaces could do for her. "Would you tell my brother-in-law, Robert Marsh, about the service this afternoon?"

The elder Wallace nodded solemnly. "I'll ride over there right now." He paused, then continued slowly, "My son and I will finish our planting in a couple of days. If we can help you with yours, we'd be pleased to do it."

If only the offer had come two weeks ago, she thought, before John had been forced to travel to the horse auction, before he'd had to go to Chestertown to purchase Ian Sutherland's indenture. Before he'd worked and worried himself into his grave.

"I thank you," she said, "but we have someone helping us now."

"I heard," Wallace said, "but as late as you are in planting, you need more than one pair of hands."

Fancy was about to speak again, to politely refuse the offer, when Fortune placed a hand on her arm, stopping her. She looked at her sister, and Fortune nodded.

For an instant, Fancy was stunned speechless. Fortune had never—not once—encouraged the notion of having near strangers come to the farm.

"It would pleasure us to help," Little Tim said. He was a strapping youth with a gentle manner and a shy smile. Fancy remembered his mother, a sweet soul who had died two years ago.

Still she hesitated, her gaze going from Little Tim back to Fortune. Her back ached from two days of planting, and she knew the Scotsman's body must ache, too. Working from dusk to dawn, they had barely been able to drag themselves from the field to their beds last night. Yet the Scotsman had still fed and watered the horses. There'd been no question of him reading to them before bedtime; even if he could have stayed awake, she'd have fallen asleep listening.

Yet more than half of the tobacco plants remained to be moved. And the earth was drying quickly, making the planting even more difficult.

The offer of more help was tempting.

But what if Robert retaliated against them—against anyone who would help her keep him from getting the farm? Could she draw anyone else into her battle? The Wallaces, like so many of the small farmers, were barely surviving. If Robert had their credit cut, they could be ruined.

Amy was pulling at her dress, eager to leave. Other small farmers were already departing, several of the wives casting backward looks of sympathy toward her.

"Mrs. Marsh?"

She met the elder Wallace's gaze directly and made her decision. Her family was the most important thing. "We would appreciate your help," she said. "Thank you."

He nodded formally. "I'll take word about your husband's service to Mr. Marsh," he said. "And as soon as my son and I are finished with our tobacco, we'll be over to your place."

They said good-bye, and Big Tim walked away.

The younger Wallace smiled again at Fortune, who blushed slightly. Then he followed his father toward their horses.

Fancy watched the youth's retreating back. She couldn't blame Tim for being attracted to Fortune. Her sister was beautiful, and she did look especially pretty today. She had combed her wild hair and tied it back neatly, and her dress was, amazingly, still clean.

Then again, as she thought about it, Fortune had been different all week. She'd been staying much closer to home and helping take care of Amy. And she'd found a way to communicate with Ian Sutherland, who, thank God, seemed to have the sensitivity and understanding to handle timid, frightened creatures.

The change had started with Ian's arrival.

And John's death.

Death, as Fancy had learned long ago, had a way of forcing change upon the living. Whether or not they were ready for it.

Ian kept his distance from the group of people gathered around the grave.

He had worked all morning transplanting the tender tobacco plants. The horses had not been exercised in days, and they scolded him impatiently whenever he neared the paddocks or went into the barn. The fences needed mending. The house needed painting. The entire farm was a disaster.

Yet Fancy Marsh showed no sign of giving up.

The minister was bowing his head. Ian was far enough away that he heard little. He had not wanted to be a part of the group, a participant. Still, he'd been drawn to the service, to the haunting sound of hymns and the compelling voice of the minister.

Robert Marsh had appeared late and stood apart from the others. Ian thought about the look Marsh had given him upon his arrival. Their gazes had locked, and Ian had known instantly that Marsh was now aware of his indenture, of his lowly place on the farm.

The service ended, and the mourners headed for the Marshes' house. The other farmers had brought food with them, but only Robert Marsh and two other men—one young, one older, but both with clear blue eyes and proud stances—lingered.

Finally, after speaking briefly to Fancy, the two men left, and only Robert Marsh remained.

As Robert began talking, Fancy's face grew strained. Ian moved closer.

"You cannot stay here with a convict," he heard Robert say. "He could kill you and the children. John—"

"John wanted me to stay here, on our farm," Fancy said. "And Mr. Sutherland has no intention of hurting anyone."

"How do you know that?" Marsh said harshly. "He's just waiting for his chance."

"He's already had ample chance," she said softly.

Robert glared at her. "People disapprove."

"Be honest, Robert. *You* disapprove. You disapprove because you want this place. But you can't have it. John worked hard to have something to give to his children. You've tried your best to take it away, though God knows why, when you already have enough to satisfy ten men. But you can't have this farm. It's Noel's."

"Marsh's End will be Noel's," Robert said. "I can give him a good education. I can give you and the children a fine home."

"We have all the home we need."

He picked up her hands and turned them over, and Ian knew what Marsh was seeing. The effects of days of planting would not have been removed by scrubbing.

"Is this what you want, Fancy?" Robert said. "Dirt?"

Ian took several steps forward. " 'Tis honest dirt."

Robert swung toward him. "Keep out of this."

"Nay, I donna think I will."

Robert's lips curled. "I know all about you. You're a convict, a traitor."

"Only in the eyes of the Sassenach," Ian said contemptuously, not bothering to translate the term.

Robert turned back to Fancy. "I heard that John paid forty pounds for him. I'll buy his indenture for a hundred. Enough to send the boy to Chestertown for schooling and to give your sister a dowry."

Ian tried to control his anger. He felt his hands clench into fists at the idea of being sold again. But a hundred pounds would mean a great deal to Fancy Marsh. It would see her through this winter and another, even if the tobacco crop failed.

"No," Fancy said flatly.

Robert looked as stunned as Ian felt. But it was anger, not shock, that infused the other man's face with its brick-red color.

"I would like to know why," Marsh said, his tone barely controlled.

"I would never sell anyone to you," Fancy replied with a vehemence that Ian hadn't heard from her before. His admiration for her spiraled upward as she continued, "I've seen the way you treat your bond servants and slaves. I wouldn't give you control over an animal, much less a human being."

Amazed at her nerve in the face of someone he knew she feared, Ian watched Marsh's face turn even redder.

The man's eyes narrowed, his gaze flickering to Ian, then back to Fancy. "Are you sure there's not another reason?" he asked. The innuendo in his voice was unmistakable.

Fancy paled, then suddenly she slapped Robert Marsh with such force that the man stumbled backward several steps. Recovering quickly, he put a hand to his cheek and, with an angry growl, started toward her.

Ian stepped forward. "I wouldna be doin' tha'."

"Get out of my way," Robert demanded.

"Nay, I willna. And I suggest you leave. Now."

"You're a convict! A danger to this community. I'll have you jailed for threatening me."

"I didn't hear a threat," Fancy said.

Robert shook with fury, but Ian saw in the man's eyes that he feared him, feared what Ian might do to him. And well he should.

Ian willed Marsh to strike him. He wanted a fight. Bloody hell, he'd been wanting to vent the fury inside him ever since Culloden. If Robert Marsh gave him half an excuse, by God, he'd kill him.

But Marsh seemed to know that. He took one backward step, then another. Then he turned to Fancy. "This isn't over. I had hoped you'd be reasonable. But there are some papers you may not have seen. Soon enough this convict—and the farm—will be mine."

He turned, stalked to his horse, and climbed into the saddle. He didn't look back as he gave the horse a cruel slash with his quirt and galloped away.

Ian turned to Fancy, who remained tense and still, her face ashen.

"Why did you refuse to sell the indenture?" he asked.

She tore her gaze from her brother-in-law's retreating form to look at him. "Few of Robert's bondsmen live long enough to see their freedom," she said. "He treats his slaves slightly better because he owns them for life, but he doesn't spare the lash."

It was an answer, but Ian still didn't quite understand. Why should she care what happened to him? He was none of her concern. And he knew very well that she needed the hundred pounds.

"What papers could Robert have? What would your husband have given him?" he asked.

She shook her head quickly, with confidence, but her forehead was creased with worry. "John didn't trust Robert. He would never have given him anything."

"Then . . . ?"

"Robert would say whatever he thought suited his purposes," she said, adding with what appeared to be embarrassment, "I've told you that John didn't read, though he could sign his name. Still, Robert could easily put John's signature on a paper and bribe someone to say he was a witness. And, since I can't read, either, I wouldn't know if he was lying."

Ian was silent for a moment, his thoughts churning in an uncomfortable direction.

She had asked him to teach her and the children to read. She'd done it that first day he'd arrived, and she'd asked again several days ago. He'd refused, believing it would involve him even more in her life. But it wasn't merely enjoyment she sought to gain; it was a weapon. A weapon to protect herself and her family from her manipulative, dishonest brother-in-law, and from whoever else might try to rob her of what was rightfully hers. Ian realized that she had seen in him a means to acquire that power.

And how could he refuse to give it to her?

The answer was quick and sure: he could not.

Suddenly it became very important to him to give Fancy Marsh what she had asked: reading lessons. She had turned down what to her must have seemed like a fortune to save him from the cruelty of Robert Marsh. It didn't matter that he would not have stayed on Robert's farm any longer than he intended to stay here, that he would have found a way to escape. She had committed an act of courage and sacrifice on his behalf, and he owed her a debt. 'Twas as simple, and as painful, as that.

But he bloody well would repay the debt as quickly as possible.

She had turned away from him, had started toward the house.

"I willna owe any man or woman," he said.

She stopped and turned back to give him a puzzled frown.

"I'll be starting reading lessons this evening."

Her eyes widened, and her mouth actually dropped open. But she closed it quickly.

"Ha' the children there, and your sister too, if she'll come."

A smile played at the corners of her mouth. It was the first smile he'd seen from her since her husband's death.

She nodded. "All right."

Ian gave a single nod. Then, angry with her and himself and the whole bloody world, he turned and stalked off toward the tobacco field and the work that needed to be done.

Chapter 9

He started with the alphabet.

Watching Fancy's and Noel's expectant faces, Ian said a few letters, then had his rapt pupils recite the letters back to him. He repeated the process several times with the same letters before moving on, expecting at any moment that one of them would balk at the tedious repetition. But neither did.

Amy sat beside her brother and tried for a while to pay attention; Ian thought she might have learned quickly if he'd had pictures or some other way to make the lesson interesting for her, but as it was, she soon grew bored and went to play with her doll. Fortune, on the other hand, flitted nervously about the room, clearly interested, yet, for some reason that he could not fathom, unwilling to apply herself to the task. Still, he caught her a few times mouthing the letters that her sister and nephew were reciting aloud.

The evening was warm and humid, but a pleasant breeze came through the open windows, drifting over them as they sat around the table. He had eaten supper with the family, much against his better judgment, and he would have gone back to the planting if Fancy hadn't insisted on starting the reading lesson as soon as the table had been cleared.

Seeing the hope in her face, Ian felt inadequate to the task of meeting her expectations. There was so much to learn, and he didn't have time to teach them even a fraction of it. The best he could do was to give them the basic tools.

They worked until Amy fell asleep on the floor with her doll and Noel's head was nodding toward the table-top.

" 'Tis time we stopped," he said with a glance at the lad, and when Fancy Marsh nodded her agreement, he added, "We need paper and pens. And a reader."

"We'll go to Chestertown tomorrow," she said. "I have to go, anyway. I need . . . to see someone there."

"What about the tobacco?"

Her brow furrowed for an instant, but it quickly cleared. "It can wait."

If he'd needed any further proof of her desire to read, here it was. He had learned, only too well, how important the tobacco crop was to her.

Looking at Noel, he said, "You're a fast learner, lad."

"So is Mama," Noel said proudly.

"Aye, she is."

Rising from his chair, Ian crossed to the door, aware that Fancy was following him. He paused with his hand on the latch as she came up beside him.

"Thank you," she said softly.

"Donna be thanking me yet. And donna be expecting too much. I'm just going to get you started."

But her eyes held a genuine sparkle, along with gratitude. Gratitude he sure as bloody hell did not want.

Ian walked out of the house and started across the yard toward the barn. Halfway there, he stopped. The moon was full, and in its bright light, he saw the open furrows waiting for the tobacco crop to be transplanted.

With a deep sigh, he squared his jaw and headed for the fields.

* * *

After the Scotsman left, Fancy sent Noel up to his bed in the loft and retrieved one of her precious books from the mantel shelf. Opening it, she studied the patterns of ink on the page, hoping they would somehow magically come together and suddenly make sense to her. When they did not, she made a frustrated sound and slammed the book closed.

She remembered the letters he'd pounded into her. A start. But such a small one. Maybe she would be like John. Maybe she could never learn, never translate the letters into words. The thought pierced her to the core.

Putting the book back on the shelf, she turned her attention to the supper dishes, which she had set aside in favor of the lesson. As she poured hot water from the fireplace into a bowl and began washing the dishes, she continued to repeat the alphabet that Ian Sutherland had taught her. She was pleased when she got all the way through it three times in a row without making a mistake. At least she didn't think she'd made one. And to think she'd learned the entire alphabet in one evening—it seemed a miracle.

No, she corrected herself, the miracle would be when she understood how all those letters came together to form words.

Noel would learn quickly, she knew. What surprised her, though, was that Fortune had shown an interest in the lesson as well. She'd stayed with them all evening, mostly in the background but sometimes perching nervously on the edge of a chair.

Fancy understood her sister's nervousness, why she'd found it difficult to take part openly in the reading lesson. Fortune considered herself incapable of learning. She'd been told so often that she was dim-witted that she believed it was true. Fancy didn't know if anything could be done to give Fortune back the confidence that had been stolen from her. She'd been so young. . . .

With the dishes finished, Fancy climbed the ladder to the loft to check on Noel. She lit the candle next to his bed and saw that he was sound asleep, one arm wrapped around Unsatisfactory. So small, she thought, looking at him. So innocent. Leaning down, she kissed him, her throat constricting with love.

Oh, how she wanted to keep him safe. To see him, always, with a smile on his face. To give him the world. To make sure he never knew fear such as she had known.

Blowing out the candle, she climbed down the ladder and looked in on Amy. Moonlight lit the room well enough for her to see that Amy and Fortune were both asleep in the big feather bed. Amy was curled up in her aunt's arms, as always. Her expression, like her brother's, was a study in sweet, blissful innocence. And for once, Fortune looked content and peaceful, her forehead clear of the slightly anxious frown that usually marred it, even in sleep.

Her family. Her home.

How could she give it up for Robert's cold house? And his questionable attentions? She shivered just thinking of it.

Fancy kissed Amy, then went to her room and changed into her nightdress. Still restless, she walked to the window and held the curtain aside to look at the yard, bathed in the glow of the moon high in the clear night sky.

As her gaze wandered farther, she saw him. A lone figure silhouetted against the starlit sky. As he bent to work the ground, she could see how thin he still was, yet he moved with a grace and a purpose that was becoming familiar to her. His first efforts at planting had been awkward, but it hadn't taken him long to find the rhythm in working the soil.

Ian Sutherland. Her bondsman. A bondsman who was going far beyond what was expected of him to help her and her family survive.

Fancy watched the Scotsman for another moment. Then she took off her nightdress and put on the dress she wore to work in the fields. Too stained to ever come clean, it was plain, with long sleeves and a high neck. Leaving the top two buttons undone and pushing the sleeves up above her elbows, she went to join the Scotsman.

He looked up as she approached, carrying a flat of seedlings. Without a word, he took the plants from her, and she returned to the small field near the house to dig up more. When they had as many seedlings as she thought they could plant, she joined him in the large field, and together they began working their way down two parallel rows.

Time passed. The moon rose to its zenith. Still, Fancy remained determined to work as long as the Scotsman worked. After all, these were her fields. If he lost sleep over them, so must she.

Finally, when they had planted most of the seedlings she had dug, he rose to his feet and looked down at her.

" 'Tis time you went to bed," he said. "I remember the trip to Chestertown as a long one."

He was within a yard of her, standing tall and straight. It was too dark to see his expression, but the stark lines of his face were plainly visible. He smelled of fresh earth and sweat, and looking up at him, she felt a whisper run between them—an unspoken message that was nevertheless quite clear. The interchange created an immediate physical reaction within her, a fluttering, tingling sensation in her middle unlike anything she'd ever felt before.

The sensation was followed swiftly, though, by a wave of guilt. How could she be feeling such things with John barely cold in his grave?

Yet she was, and she could not deny it. Nor could she credit it to her imagination. In the still, warm hours of early dawn, she looked at Ian Sutherland, and he returned her gaze. She felt their awareness of each other grow stronger.

Staring at him, she spoke quietly. "You didn't have to do this."

"Aye, I did," he said. "But donna think more of it than wha' it is."

"What is it, then?"

"Payment of a debt. Nothing more."

"Still," she said, "I don't know what we would have done these past days without you."

"Your husband paid for me," he replied bluntly. "Ye best go in and get some rest."

"What about you?"

He shrugged. "I've gone days withou' sleep. 'Tis none too welcoming tae me."

Sleep was none too welcoming to her, either. Nor was the empty bed.

She didn't argue further, simply sank back to her knees, picked up the next transplant and the trowel, and began digging.

With a sigh, he too went back to work.

The moon slowly sank in the western sky. As it dipped below the trees on the horizon, taking most of its light with it, they planted the last two seedlings that Fancy had carried from the small field.

Sitting back on her heels, she looked over the planted rows. Many seedlings remained to be transplanted, but they had done well this night. Satisfaction ran through her, replacing some of her deep weariness.

The Scotsman stood and offered his dirt-encrusted

hand to her. She took it, and he pulled her to her feet. Both of them were covered in dirt and, she knew, tired beyond caring, but as she stood next to him, swathed in the moon's last beams, she knew a deep pride.

She could do anything. She could survive without John. Even the flash of guilt that accompanied the thought didn't lessen the relief she felt, knowing it was true.

She knew she should go to bed. And yet she didn't want to surrender the moment.

A rough hand pushed a lock of hair from her face, and she looked up at the Scotsman standing beside her.

" 'Twill be a long day tomorrow," he said, his burr rippling through the word "tomorrow" like little waves at ebb tide washing onto warm sand. "Ye best be getting some sleep."

He spoke softly, gently, in a way he hadn't spoken to her before, and the companionship of hard work shared radiated between them.

Companionship and something more.

Suddenly she was frightened. Frightened of the feelings she should not be having so soon after John's death. And certainly not for a man who had made it clear he would be leaving, no matter the cost to him, or to her.

She should flee. His mere presence was doing startling things to her body. Worse still, the look in his eyes told her that he knew quite well what she was feeling and that he was feeling it, too. She should run as fast as she was able for the safety of the house.

Yet she couldn't make herself move.

Her heart pounded when he raised a hand to lay it against her cheek, and for a brief instant a smile touched his lips. "You have dirt on your nose," he said, and his fingertip touched it. "Still, you are a pretty woman, Mrs. Marsh, and never prettier than now."

Then he abruptly dropped his hand and walked away, heading toward the well.

Fancy let the pent-up breath rush out of her lungs. Her legs felt weak, and her cheek burned where he'd touched her. His voice and the words he'd spoken had sent a river of warmth flowing through her.

Confused and slightly horrified by her uncontrolled—and unexpected—reaction, she hurried toward the house. She had to forcibly avert her gaze as she neared the well and saw that he had stripped off his shirt in preparation for washing. Once inside, she quickly filled a washbasin and scrubbed away the worst of the dirt on her hands and face. In her room, she put on her nightdress and climbed into bed.

The sky was still black. She might get an hour of sleep before dawn.

She might. But she really didn't think she would.

Any sense of companionship or warmth that had grown between them the night before was gone when Fancy saw the Scotsman the next day.

He did not come in for breakfast, and she thought he might have overslept, since they had worked so late. But when she went to wake him a short time after dawn, she found him working in the barn. A quick glance around told her that he had already fed and watered the horses and cleaned the stalls, and she wondered whether he had slept at all.

His eyes, though, as he looked up at her approach, were clear. Cold. She didn't see the man she'd worked with last night. She saw a stranger, who eyed her with indifference.

So much for the notions she'd entertained in that sleepless hour before dawn. She'd thought—hoped— that last night had made a difference, that now perhaps Ian Sutherland wouldn't be so reluctant to stay. She hadn't forgotten that he'd said there were others who needed him, but surely he must see that her family's need was desperate.

"Do you want to take the wagon or ride?" he asked.

"We can get back tonight if we ride," she said.

He looked at her skeptically. " 'Tis a difficult ride for a day."

"I know," she said, "but the horses will need tending in the morning. Noel can't do it alone, and . . . well, I don't want Fortune to be alone overnight."

Something flickered in his eyes, and she knew he wanted to ask why her sister, almost a full-grown woman, couldn't manage by herself for one night. He didn't ask, though.

Instead, he said, "Mayhap we shouldna go. Paper and pen can wait."

That paper and pen were more important to her than gold; they were the keys to her freedom.

Equally important were Ian Sutherland's indenture papers; she had to get them from Douglas Turner, as John had instructed her to do. Robert had made it clear that he intended to take control of the Scotsman's life, but before she'd let that happen, she would destroy the papers or sign them over, giving Ian Sutherland his freedom.

Best not say as much to him, though. Despite the guilt she felt at holding a man's freedom hostage, she didn't know how else to protect her sister, her children, or herself from what surely would happen to them if the bondsman left before the tobacco was planted. Only a few more weeks, she told herself, and perhaps he would agree to stay on his own. Then she could tear up the papers.

Or maybe not. The cold indifference in his eyes said there was no bond between him and her family. Indeed, his look was empty. Lifeless. As if any flame of hope that might have lived inside him had been quenched.

How? And by whom? The questions begged to be asked, but she didn't have the nerve to risk the flat refusal she was certain he'd give in response.

"Saddle the mare and the black," she said. "I'll pack some food to take with us."

"Aye," he said.

She stood for another moment, wanting to say something else, wanting to reestablish that brief connection they'd shared last night. But she could think of nothing to say, nothing that would melt the wall of ice he'd erected between them. And she wasn't really sure she wanted the wall removed, wasn't at all sure she was ready to face the consequences.

Biting her lip, Fancy whirled and headed back toward the house.

The nightmare had been bad. One of the worst yet. Only an hour of sleep and even it had been beset by the grisly images: Derek dangling from the scaffold, his body twisting in the air; Patrick lying on Culloden Moor, blood spurting from his chest; Katy standing on the ramparts of Brinaire, tears streaming down her face, her arms stretched out toward him, beseeching him.

That last picture stayed fixed in Ian's mind as he saddled the horses. He couldn't bear it any longer. He had to do something. And he had to do it now.

Yet his common sense warred with his driving need to take the sleek gelding he was saddling and ride like the devil toward a seaport. The maps in the book would help, but they wouldn't solve all the problems he faced. How would he know what ships were sailing, and at what time, from which port? How could he gain a berth on such a ship? And before he even tried, he had to burn the brand off his thumb and invent some plausible explanation for the scars on his wrists. No ship's master would take him as he was.

Knowing he must bide his time a bit longer, Ian thought about asking Fancy Marsh for the money to mail a letter. Mayhap he could get word of Katy. If there was any chance . . .

But letters seldom reached the Highlands. And he didn't know to whom he could write. Who had survived Culloden, and who had died? Who had turned traitor and who had not?

He could crawl on his belly and ask the Macraes, the family that had saved him from the noose, if they knew of Katy's fate. But they had done nothing to save Derek, and they had allowed Ian to be sold like a horse to the highest bidder. Worst of all, when it appeared they might lose their estates and title, they had betrayed Scotland and their fellow Scots. He had little expectation that the bloody traitors would do anything for a Jacobite, even a child, if doing so might offend the Crown and the king's minions.

No, there was no one he could trust, not where his sister's life was concerned. He had to return to Scotland himself. And he had to do it soon.

Leading the saddled horses from the barn, he found Fancy Marsh waiting for him on the porch of the house. She wore a black dress and bonnet, and her tawny hair was held back in a severe knot. But her drab garb only emphasized the fine structure of her facial bones and her vibrant amber brown eyes. And she looked so bloody defenseless.

She was the kind of woman who survived, he told himself, thinking of her persistence and determination the previous night in the field. Hell, she could endure far better than his sister.

She descended the porch steps to meet him, bulging

saddlebags in her hands. The crow—Trouble—flew
from its perch on the fence post to sit on her shoulder,
cawing anxiously. Leaving Fortune standing on the
steps, Noel and Amy trailed after their mother. As she
reached the horses she stooped and handed the crow to
Noel before hugging him, then Amy, who had tears
swimming in her huge eyes.

"Be good," she said to both of them.

"When will you be home, Mama?" Noel asked.

"Now, what did I say?" she replied gently.

"Tonight," he said, yet his tone and expression were
unbelieving.

"That's right," she said. "It might be late, but I will
be here. I promise."

"I want to wait up for you."

She hesitated for a moment, and Ian could almost
see her practical nature battling with her soft heart.
Finally she nodded. "If you can stay awake."

Only half satisfied, the lad turned to Ian. "I'll practice the alphabet. That'll keep me awake."

Ian's first impulse was to tell the lad that he was sure
he would practice very hard, but he bit back the words.
The effort it took to ignore the boy caused his hands to
tighten on the gelding's reins, and the horse, sensing
his tension, took several sideways steps.

"We'd better be going, Mrs. Marsh," he said.

Noel looked hurt, but he accepted another hug from
his mother. Then he took Amy's hand and held on to
the crow with the other.

Ian helped Fancy settle onto the sidesaddle, releasing her hand the second she gained her seat. He turned
to his own mount, lifted a foot into the stirrup, and
vaulted into the saddle. Lucky, who had followed him
from the barn, started limping behind them down the
lane.

"Stay," Ian said.

The dog gave him a bewildered look, then limped back to the house to sit beside Noel, looking as morose as an animal could manage.

Bloody hell, but it was going to be a long, long day.

They stopped briefly at midmorning to rest and water the horses. The Scotsman ate some of the bread and cheese she'd brought, but he'd limited his conversation to ayes and nays until Fancy finally gave up.

Still, she couldn't ignore this impossible awareness between them. Did he feel that same surge of lightning every time their gazes met?

Why had she never felt this way with John? Her guilt magnified with every glance.

She had heard tales of great loves, of Indian maidens throwing themselves off cliffs when their warrior died. But those were just tales. Weren't they?

Her father and his wife, Little Fawn, had been friends, as she and John had been friends. And wasn't respectful, loving friendship enough? She had thought so before. Before Ian Sutherland.

Fancy was still trying to rein in her feelings at noon, when they reached Chestertown. She directed the Scotsman to a general store and gave him some coins.

He took them with a raised eyebrow. "You're not going with me?"

She shook her head. "I have other business. Purchase whatever you think is necessary for our lessons; then you might want to get a glass of ale. I'll meet you here in an hour."

He looked at her strangely. "You trust me?"

"Yes," she said simply.

"You shouldn't," he said.

"Perhaps not, but I don't have much choice."

He stared at her for a moment longer, then dismounted. "Will you be dismounting here?"

She shook her head, then repeated, "I'll meet you here in an hour." She turned the mare and headed up the street.

Feeling Ian Sutherland's gaze bore into her back as she rode away from him, she tightened her grip on the reins. She truly wasn't sure she could trust him, but neither could she keep him on a chain.

After passing a row of office buildings, she dismounted in front of Douglas Turner's office. She looked back down the street, but she didn't see the Scotsman. Good. She didn't want him to know where she was going.

Fancy hesitated a moment, then opened the door, hearing the jingle of a little bell as she entered. She stood in the foyer for a moment, her eyes adjusting from the bright sunlight to the dim interior of the building. Bookshelves laden with volumes lined the walls on both sides of the entryway. The leather bindings smelled sweeter to her than any perfume.

Douglas Turner appeared in one of the inner doorways. She had met him several times and had always liked him. Usually his smile came easily, but when he saw her now, his face creased with concern.

"Mrs. Marsh? Are you here alone today?"

She bit her lip, for a moment unable to say the words. Finally, she managed, "John . . . John died two weeks ago."

Turner closed his eyes for a moment, then met her gaze. "I'm so sorry. I knew he didn't look well when I saw him last." He sighed. Then, motioning her into his office, he added, "Come sit down and tell me what I can do for you."

Fancy let him guide her to a high-back cushioned chair in front of his desk. Settling herself, she folded her hands in her lap, waited until he was seated behind the desk, then cleared her throat.

"John told me to come to you," she began. "He trusted you. There should be a will and some . . . indenture papers."

"Yes." Turner nodded. "He left an envelope with me that contained both documents. Naturally, you are to receive everything, to hold until your son comes of age."

"There's no . . . doubt of that?"

His brow furrowed. "None that I can see."

She hesitated. "Robert, my brother-in-law, might try to claim otherwise."

Turned shook his head. "He won't succeed, my dear. John made his wishes quite clear to me. I'll file the will immediately."

She released the air she had held in her lungs. "Thank you."

"I can give you the indenture to take with you," he said. "And my advice, Mrs. Marsh, would be for you to sell it. You won't be wanting that kind of man out there, not with you all alone."

"I'll consider it," she said softly, knowing she would do no such thing.

Turner disappeared into an adjoining room and, a minute later, returned with an envelope in his hand. "If there is anything I can do," he said, handing her the envelope, "let me know. I can see to the sale of the indenture, if you wish. There's a good market for bondsmen now, with planting season here."

She fingered the envelope. "I will remember that. Thank you."

"The sooner the better, Mrs. Marsh," he advised.

"I haven't decided," she finally said. "We need the help right now."

"Surely your brother-in-law can help you."

Her fingers clutched the envelope. "Thank you, Mr. Turner," she said. "I must go."

With a resigned shrug, he showed her to the front door, opening it for her. His eyes widened as he saw the horse. "You didn't ride here alone, did you, Mrs. Marsh?"

"Mr. Sutherland accompanied me," she said.

"Mr. Sutherland?"

"An acquaintance." True enough, she thought. When Turner showed no sign of recognition, she assumed that either he didn't remember the name on the indenture papers or that he hadn't actually read them.

After Turner helped her mount, she looked down and gave him a brief smile. "I do thank you," she said, tucking the envelope into one of the saddlebags.

He waved off her gratitude. "It's no trouble at all. Just remember, if I can do anything . . ."

Saying good-bye, Fancy guided the mare back toward the general store. Perhaps she could find some small things for Amy and Noel while she waited for the Scotsman. When she reached the store and dismounted, she happened to look up the street in time to see Robert Marsh's carriage roll to a stop in front of Douglas Turner's office.

Her breath caught in her throat as she watched her brother-in-law's substantial figure climb out of the carriage, then stride to the office door and enter the small building. Hoping he hadn't seen her, she hurried into the store. Robert certainly wasn't wasting any time.

The Scotsman's horse wasn't tethered outside, so it didn't surprise her when she didn't find him inside. How long had she been at Turner's? No more than thirty minutes, she judged.

He'll be back, she told herself, fighting the impulse to ask the store clerk whether he had sold a book and some writing implements to a tall man with short dark hair.

She looked at some dolls but they were all more

expensive than she could afford. Finding a music box displayed on a shelf, she opened the ornate top and listened to the tinkling notes of a waltz. At any other time she would have thought the music box beautiful, and she would have delighted in the cheerful music it played. But each note seemed to tick off the seconds, then minutes, that passed with no sign of Ian Sutherland.

The waltz played again. And again.

She looked out the window. Robert's carriage was rolling down the street, the black driver flicking a whip against the back of one of the two matched horses. The carriage passed the store, the tavern, then moved faster onto the road leading south, toward Marsh's End.

Fancy felt sick. What had Robert wanted with Douglas Turner? And where was the Scotsman? What if she had been wrong about him? What if he had taken the gelding and run?

Had it been an hour?

She went to the door.

"Ian Sutherland," she whispered. "Where are you?"

Chapter 10

Ian found the tavern he wanted. The Mermaid was small and poor, lodged between two shipping companies, and brimming with seamen.

He made his way inside, holding the package containing his purchases firmly. The Mermaid was the sort of establishment where things disappeared in the blink of an eye. He judged he had at least an hour before Fancy Marsh would start looking for him—two or three before she would report him. He needed information; he wasn't going to leave Chestertown until he'd found it, and he wasn't above spending what was left of the widow Marsh's money to obtain it.

The tavern was dark and smelled of unwashed bodies and cheap ale. All the tables were taken, which suited Ian. He merely looked around for a group of men who might welcome a fellow Scot.

He pulled on the gloves that covered the brand on his thumb. John Marsh's riding gloves, just as he wore John Marsh's clothes. The reminder that he had nothing, not a pence of his own, choked him. But he still had his wits, and with any luck, they would get him what he needed.

He listened intently to the ribald conversation. Soon enough his ear picked up a familiar cadence and he headed toward a rowdy bunch of ale drinkers in one corner. The five men were dressed in the rough clothes of sailors, and at least two spoke with a thick burr.

"Countrymen," he said as he approached the table. "Can I be joinin' ye?"

One man's face lit up at his accent. "Aye, ye may."

Another looked at Ian's ill-fitting but quality clothing suspiciously.

Allowing his burr full rein, Ian asked, "Wha' ship do ye be coming from?"

"The *Elizabeth*," said the one who had welcomed him. "Came in two days ago."

Ian sat down and took out several coins when a barmaid came to get his order. "An ale," he said, ignoring the curious looks cast his way.

He listened to the conversation as he sipped the bitter brew. It was poor stuff, but in the past year he'd tasted far worse. After several minutes had passed, he asked, "Where are ye bound?"

"The Indies, fer rum."

"Ye ha' enough hands?"

The friendly sailor looked at him sharply. "Ye donna ha' the look of a sailor aboot ye."

"I'm no' much of one," he admitted, noting other eyes falling upon him now.

"We always lose a few 'ands in port," one of the other men broke in, looking him over more carefully.

Another man chuckled. "Usually ha' to volunteer a few souls from some tavern. Captain Jacks is an 'ard master."

Ian felt his heart begin to race. Could it really be this easy? He had thought he might have to go farther, but if the ships were hard-pressed for hands, few questions would be asked of a willing body.

"From the West Indies, can a mon get a ship tae France?" he asked.

One shook his head. "Nay, no' from the British colonies."

Ian's heart started to sink, but then the man explained.

"The best way tae get tae France is tae go tae Canada, but 'tis a long way."

No way was too long. Ian finished his ale and ordered another. His companions were already well on toward drunkenness, except for the one who continued to study him.

"How do ye find Chestertown?" Ian finally asked, turning the conversation to safer matters.

"Not enough willin' women," one muttered darkly.

"Speak for yerself," joshed another. " 'Tis yer ugly face, for sure."

Suddenly a fist was raised, then another. Ian grabbed his mug and stepped back. The last thing he needed was to become involved in a brawl. He inched toward the door.

The sailor who had been studying him did the same. As they reached the door, the entire tavern erupted into shouts, curses, and flying fists.

Ian backed outside. It was time to return, in any event, or Mrs. Fancy Marsh might be calling the law.

The sailor followed him, though, and Ian stopped, turning to face him. The man's eyes went to his gloved hand as if he could see through the cloth.

"We sail in five days' time," he said. "I'm the second mate on the *Elizabeth*." He paused. "The ship's master will ask no' questions, and ye can find a ketch in the West Indies tae take ye tae one of the French ports. From there ye can go tae France."

Ian found himself holding his breath. *Five days.*

"Why are ye telling me this?" he asked.

The sailor turned over his hand to reveal a brand on his thumb. "Fer poachin' a rich man's rabbit," he said. "I served me seven years in the tobacco fields, and 'twas a hellish time. I wanted no more part of farmin' so I decided tae try the sea. I like it well enough. Cap'n

Jacks ain't a bad master. Work hard fer 'im, and 'e 'as no quarrel wi' ye."

The man's gaze swept Ian from head to toe. "Ye look strong enough, though ye need some meat on yer bones."

"I still donna know why you're tellin' me this," Ian persisted.

"I'll not be lyin' to another Scotsman. I'll git coin for findin' a willing 'and. The cap'n, he donna take much tae forcibly taking 'ands, bu' he wouldna' balk at smuggling ye aboard if ye be runnin' from somethin'."

Was his need that obvious? Mayhap only to a man who'd had similar thoughts in the past.

He simply nodded. "I'll be keepin' tha' in mind."

"I'll be 'ere every night till Friday. We sail Saturday at dawn. Tom Jarvie's my name."

The man thrust out his hand, and Ian took it, sealing their pact. The sailor nodded to him, then turned back to the tavern, a look of glee on his face in anticipation of joining the melee inside.

Five days. Five days and he could be starting his journey home. Mayhap he had finally gotten lucky.

Excitement coursed through him, and his step was lighter as he walked to his horse. Mounting, he tucked the package containing his purchases into the saddlebag. Paper and ink that wouldn't be used. A reader that wouldn't be read.

It was too bad, and perhaps he would feel a stab of guilt at abandoning Fancy Marsh in her hour of need. But it was nothing compared to the guilt he'd feel if he did not find Katy. Or if he found her too late.

Squeezing the gelding's sides with his knees, he urged the animal into a trot. Mrs. Marsh was waiting for him at the store.

And Katy was waiting for him a sea away.

* * *

Fancy refused to give up.

She knew the storekeeper was keeping an eye on her. He had asked several times if there was anything he could do for her. How could she explain that she had foolishly trusted a convict?

Her eyes hurt from unshed tears. Not only because she felt betrayed, but because it seemed the world was falling down upon her. How was she going to manage without Ian Sutherland? How would she run the farm?

It would break her heart, but she would have to sell one of the horses. It was too soon. They would be worth much more after one of them won a race. Still, with the money she could get for Gray Ghost or Sir Gray, they could survive the winter.

But what about next year? She couldn't keep selling the horses until they were all gone. To do so would be to risk her family's best hope for the future.

Her anxious gaze swept the street for the hundredth time. He was an hour late. Maybe more. She had told him to get an ale. Maybe he was a drunkard. Maybe he had met another Scotsman and they were commiserating in their cups over the loss of their country to the "bloody Sassenach." Then again, maybe he was . . .

She saw him. He was still far down the street, but she would have known him from an even greater distance by the way he sat a horse; his posture was natural and graceful, radiating the inborn confidence of a nobleman. As he drew closer, she was disappointed to see that he appeared just as stoic as when she'd left him. She had hoped he would find some pleasure in his time alone in town.

He pulled his mount to a halt in front of the store, and she stepped outside to meet him. When their gazes met, his expression didn't change, yet Fancy suddenly felt inferior. Ian Sutherland was an educated man, a man accustomed to wealth and power, and his eyes seemed to say to her, "How dare you think you can own me? What gives you the right?"

I have no right, she thought. Only need. Yet at that moment she despaired of being able to hold him for even a month, much less a year.

He dismounted and held out his hand to her, offering his help in mounting her mare. He didn't offer to explain why he was so late.

"Did you get the reader?" she asked.

"Aye, two of them." His tone was clipped. "And a slate, pens, pencils, and some precious sheets of paper."

Any excitement she might have felt at the idea of actually learning to use the things he'd purchased paled in the face of his hostility. It was hopeless, she thought. He hated her, hated this place, hated what he perceived as his captivity, and nothing she could say or do was going to matter.

She approached him as she might a mean-spirited horse and, reluctantly, half afraid he might bite, put one hand on her mare's sidesaddle and placed her other hand in Ian Sutherland's. The tension sizzling in the air between them seemed to gather and focus on the spot where their hands met. Her palm burned against his, and her legs felt suddenly weak. She might have pulled away, but his fingers tightened around hers and all she could do was stand there, self-conscious, flustered, and utterly confused.

A moment or two passed before Fancy regained her senses. She couldn't look at him. Finally, with her heart pounding, she braced herself and vaulted up onto the saddle.

Without a word, the Scotsman turned, mounted the gelding, and started down the road out of town.

Her gaze focused on his defiant back, and, her thoughts in turmoil, Fancy trailed after him.

* * *

They arrived home long after dark. By the time they drew to a halt in front of the house, Ian was nearly frantic to get away from his feminine companion. Neither of them had spoken a single word throughout the ride, but he had never been as conscious of another person's presence as he was of hers, every step of the way.

Bloody hell, Fancy Marsh didn't *need* to speak. All she had to do was *be* there beside him, and he could feel his defenses weakening. What was it about her that affected him so strongly? Was it the way she looked? He'd known more beautiful women. Mayhap it was her unwavering kindness. Hell, for all he knew, it could be the way she smelled, the light flowery scent that tantalized his senses whenever she was near. Regardless of the source of her power over him, he could not deny it existed. Although he'd set out from Chestertown with a clear sense of purpose and a resolve to be gone from this place before another week was out, he now felt torn, and his conscience was raw with indecision.

When he helped her down from her horse, it didn't surprise Ian to feel again that sudden and intense warmth flash between them—between the places where their skin touched. He knew she felt it, too, because she quickly pulled her hand away. She seemed as distressed by the experience as he was. The difference was that she appeared bewildered, whereas he knew exactly what was happening.

"Good night, Mrs. Marsh," he said formally as he took the reins of both horses.

"Good night . . . Ian."

He stopped in his tracks. It was the first time he'd heard anyone use his given name since Derek had said good-bye to him to walk up the steps of the scaffold. After months of being treated like an animal, snarled at, and called every foul name on earth, the sound of his own name came as a shock to his senses.

It sounded warm and soft, falling from her lips. A tender caress, a reminder of friendship and intimacy.

He turned to look at her. She looked lovely in the moonlight. She had taken off her bonnet, and her golden brown hair shone bright against the black of her mourning dress.

As they stood there, Trouble cawed loudly, diving down to settle on her shoulder.

"She will go to people she knows," Fancy said, stroking the bird's breast with her finger. "I used to send her to fetch John from the fields. She would go right to him, and he would know that supper was ready and it was time . . ."

She trailed off, and he saw her bite her lower lip, a habit he'd noticed before.

"I wish . . ."

"You wish what?" he asked, knowing he shouldn't.

"I wish I had given John more," she said, her lips trembling slightly.

He realized then, for the first time, that she was burdened by guilt. He knew guilt, too. Only too well. If only Derek hadn't stayed behind to help him after Culloden. If only he had gone on and saved himself. Not a night went by that the thought didn't occur to Ian, and then he would suffer the tortures of the damned for having survived when it should have been Derek who was still alive. Guilt was a terrible, crippling thing, and he couldn't bear to see her tormented by it.

"John Marsh seemed to me to be a happy mon," he said.

She raised her gaze to meet his briefly, then looked away. "He didn't ask for much."

"He had two foine bairns, a bonny wife, a fair piece

of land, and good horses. 'Tis arrogance to ask for more."

She was silent for a moment, her finger still stroking the bird on her shoulder. "What did you have, Ian?"

His name again.

" 'Tis best not remembered," he said.

"But you do remember, don't you?" she replied. "You think about it all the time."

"Aye, but they are nightmares, Mrs. Marsh, and not something you would be wanting to know about."

She dropped her hand from the crow and met his gaze fully. "Why did you come back?" she asked.

It was the question he knew she'd been wanting to ask since he'd met her at the store in Chestertown.

"There were no ships leaving today," he replied frankly.

He saw her shoulders slump, and he wondered if she had expected a different answer.

Well, that was no fault of his. She had known from the beginning what his intentions were. He had never lied to her.

"You are still set on . . ." she began.

"Escaping servitude? Aye, mistress."

"There's no way . . ."

"As bonny as ye are," he said, forcing a note of offensiveness into his voice, "ye canna change my mind."

"But the punishment—"

He shrugged. "I've already seen hell. Nothing scares me after tha'."

Nothing except his growing desire for her. Nothing except the heat welling up from deep inside him as he stood here, simply looking at her.

She started to say something, then hesitated. Finally she merely nodded, saying, "May God be with you tonight."

Ian snorted softly. "God left me long ago, mistress."

He emphasized the last word to mark the difference between them.

Then, before he could change his mind and do something very foolish, he turned and led the horses toward the barn.

Fancy was up at daybreak. Dressing hurriedly, she started breakfast, first opening the door to get a look at the dawn.

She stepped outside, in time to see Royalty racing across the pasture at a flat gallop with Ian Sutherland clinging to his back. Watching man and beast disappear into the woods on the far side of the pasture, Fancy slowly shook her head. The Scotsman was, if possible, a better rider than John. He had more power, more will, and seemed to communicate those qualities to his mount. Royalty was fast, and she'd never seen him in better form.

Immediately on the heels of that thought, the gnawing guilt set in once more. Why did she keep comparing Ian Sutherland to John? Especially when it came to horses? John had been wonderful with the horses, had always had an intuitive sense of their strengths and weaknesses. Others had envied the way the animals responded to him.

"Where is he going?"

Fancy started at the sound of Noel's voice, and she looked down to find him standing beside her.

Greeting him with a one-armed hug, she replied, "He's just taking Royalty out for some exercise." At least she hoped that was all he was doing.

"I wish he had taken me with him," Noel grumbled.

"I wouldn't want you to ride that fast," Fancy said, cocking one eyebrow at him in warning. Just the thought of losing him, too, was enough to panic her.

"I'm a good rider," Noel insisted. "Mr. Sutherland said so."

"I still don't want to see you riding that fast," she countered. Then, to change the subject, she asked, "How's the fox? Did you feed him yesterday?"

"Yes," Noel replied, clearly reluctant to let the argument go. "He's not limping at all, but . . ."

"But what?"

"Well . . . he tore an awful big hole trying to get under the fence."

"Hmm." Fancy sighed. It was time—past time—to let the fox go. She'd meant to free him last week, but she hadn't had time to carry out the task properly. "I'll look at him after breakfast," she said. "And then you and I will start planting more tobacco."

"And Mr. Sutherland?"

"I imagine he'll plant with us when he's finished with the horses."

Noel's eyes were full of hero worship, and Fancy knew his heart would be broken—again—when the Scotsman left.

And after yesterday, she thought his departure would occur sooner rather than later. Taking him to Chestertown with her had been a mistake. Something had changed during the trip, and she wasn't sure what it was or how it had happened. She knew only that since they'd met at the general store, he'd been colder and more distant than ever.

"Do you think he'll teach us more letters tonight?" Noel asked.

Fancy started to bite her lip, then stopped herself. "I don't know if he'll have time," she said.

"Yes, he will," Noel said confidently.

If he comes back, she thought.

But this had to stop. She couldn't wonder every waking minute of every day if he would be there the next time she looked for him—or if he would be gone, and one of her precious horses along with him.

Enlisting the children's aid, Fancy prepared mush with molasses for the morning meal. But all the while, she couldn't rid her mind of Ian Sutherland's determined face. She had to decide what to do about him, but in considering the choices available to her, limited as they were, necessity warred with conscience.

Her needs or his? Her family's security or his freedom?

She could simply let him go. She could sign the papers that were, at this very moment, hidden beneath her mattress and give them to him. Then she could sell the farm and the horses, as he had suggested, and buy a small house, perhaps in Annapolis or somewhere else far away from Robert. And when the money ran out, she'd . . . she'd what?

She didn't know what she would do.

The only alternative Fancy could see was to prevent Ian Sutherland from leaving. And the only means she had available was to exercise her legal power over him. She couldn't stop him from trying to escape, but she could make it nearly impossible for him to succeed.

And if she did that, what would he think of her? Would they ever again stand in a dark field and share a moment of genuine companionship? Would he ever look at her and say she was bonny? Would he still be willing to teach her to read?

And did it really matter how he felt? Or did it matter only that he plant the tobacco and tend the horses and do whatever else was necessary to keep her family together and secure?

The sound of hooves pounding into the yard brought Fancy's torment to crisis.

Noel ran toward the door, and Amy wasn't far behind him.

Fancy took a deep breath. "Noel, stop." When he halted, hand on the door latch, ready to bolt, she said, "You stay here with your sister." Tearing off her apron, she dusted her hands on it and crossed to the door.

"But, Ma . . ." Noel complained.

"Stay," she said in a tone she was well aware she'd never used before.

Clearly surprised, Noel let go of the door and took a step away from it. With his eyes wide, he gave her a reluctant nod.

She smiled down at him. "Thank you, sweetie. I won't be long." Then, giving both him and his sister a quick kiss, she headed out the door.

Ian had already removed Royalty's saddle and was rubbing the horse down when she entered the barn. The rich aroma of leather and sweat tantalized her senses as she approached him. His shirt was wet and clung to his lean body, and she could see that he'd not yet shaved. His cheeks were dark with stubble, and his green eyes glittered in the sun filtering through the open doorway.

He didn't speak, didn't even acknowledge her presence, but the strokes against the horse's side seemed to come faster as she stopped beside the stall. And that muscle in his cheek was jumping, as she had noticed it sometimes did.

"Ian?"

"Mrs. Marsh." He hadn't looked at her as he spoke, but at least he hadn't called her mistress in that mocking tone.

"You've been avoiding me."

"Difficult to do, since you own me."

"Can't you please forget that?"

"Would you?"

No, she would not.

Silently she watched him groom the stallion,

watched the hard muscles ripple beneath the fabric of his too small shirt as he drew the brush across the stallion's flank.

"Not many men can ride him," she observed.

A moment passed before Ian replied, the cold indifference in his tone giving way slightly to admiration. "He's a fine animal. I've seen none better."

"John's father said the same. The horses were his heart, as they were John's."

"I think you and the children were your husband's heart."

"Perhaps," she said. "But he did love these horses, and he never wanted Robert to have them. Robert . . ."

Giving her a glance, the Scotsman raised one dark brow to encourage her to continue.

"My brother-in-law mistreats his horses," Fancy admitted. "That's why John's father left them to his younger son. He knew Robert would do anything to win a race, even whip a horse to death."

Ian's hands stilled on the stallion's back. The muscle twitched again in his cheek. A moment passed. Then, abruptly, he returned to his task. "Sell them to someone else."

"The three-year-olds haven't raced yet," she continued, "and the two-year-olds aren't saddle-broken. The only thing I have to recommend these horses to anyone is John's faith in Royalty. And no one will pay me for that. I'd only get as much as they think the horses *look* like they *might* be worth. Why, two weeks ago, John got only forty-five pounds for one of the yearlings." She stopped suddenly, and she felt heat creeping into her cheeks.

Ian's gaze bored into her. "Five more than what he paid for me. A horse for a human being. He should have kept the horse."

"Does that mean you still intend to leave?"

"I never lied to you about that."

"But I hoped you would . . . like it here."

" 'Tis no' a matter of liking or not liking."

"Then you *do* like it here?"

His reply seemed, to her, deliberately evasive. "The land is fair enough. Gentler than the Highlands, if a bit too warm for my taste, though tha' could be a blessin' in the winter. But tha' is no' the point." He gave his head a quick shake. "I couldna stay if I thought this the bonniest land on earth. I must go home, to Scotland." The burr thickened as he spoke of his home.

"We both know the penalty you'll face if you return," she said. "They will kill you."

"They already have. There's bloody little left of me worth havin'."

"You're wrong, Ian Sutherland."

"Mrs. Marsh, you are fooling yourself."

Drawing a deep breath, Fancy gathered her nerve. Then, as her father would have said, she played her best card. "I can't let you go."

He snorted. "Neither God nor the devil can keep me here."

"You asked about ships in Chestertown," she said.

He didn't deny it, merely gave Royalty's neck a final pat, then walked out of the stall, past her. "You'll want the horses put out to pasture, I imagine," he said.

"I'll send word to the sheriff," she said. "It could mean another seven years."

"Aye, it was all explained to me. Several times." He turned on her. "I was born a free man. No English king will change that. Nor will you."

His voice was so cold, so unyielding. But if she gave up now, who would fight for her children's future and that of her sister? Who would fight for *her* future?

"I will have you chased down," she said. "If you leave here, I'll have every ship searched."

"Ah, the sweet Mrs. Marsh bites," he said sardonically.

She glared at him, hating him, hating herself.

"One year is all I'm asking, and then I'll tear up the papers. If you leave, I *will* see to it that you're caught and years added to your indenture."

Quickly she turned and started for the door, before he could see the tears in her eyes—but not before she heard his soft-spoken words.

"Oh, no, you won't."

Chapter 11

Ian worked through the day with the horses. He knew horses, sturdy Scottish ones, but these big, sleek creatures of Fancy Marsh's were something else again. Still, in many respects, a horse was a horse. They all had to be fed and watered and exercised. And they had to be broken to a saddle.

He rode each of the three-year-olds, cantering and trotting and galloping them. As he put them through their paces, he couldn't help but catalog their strengths and weaknesses, though he knew it was foolish. He wouldn't be here long enough to apply the knowledge to their training.

As he rode in and out of the yard, taking each horse in turn, he was able to observe the progress of the tobacco planting. Fancy Marsh had her brood out in force, all hands helping to plant, though he guessed Amy was doing more digging in the dirt than actual planting. And each time he caught a glimpse of the woman who was trying, by force of sheer will, to bind him to her family, he thought about their last meeting.

He didn't blame Fancy for threatening him. Indeed, that she'd felt compelled to do so only increased his guilt over abandoning her. He'd heard the anguish in her voice. He knew she was only trying to protect her family, as he was trying to save what was left of his. The tragedy was that their needs were simply, and irrevocably, incompatible.

Noel brought some bread and cheese to the barn for

him at midday. Without invitation, the lad perched on an upended barrel and watched him eat.

"Mama says I have to take Joseph back to the woods."

"Who is Joseph?"

"You know Joseph. He's my fox."

"Ah, the beastie who lives in the pen behind the house."

"Yes, that's Joseph. Fortune found him in a trap when he was little, and Ma made him well. I want to keep him, but Mama says he will go after the chickens."

Ian cocked an eyebrow. "Your ma is right."

The lad frowned for an instant, then sighed. "I guess so. Anyway, now that he's old enough to hunt, we're going to take him back to the woods where we found him." He paused for a moment, then asked, "Will you go with me?"

"Your ma can go, or your aunt," Ian replied. Bloody hell, he could not encourage the lad. It would do neither of them any good in the long run.

When Noel didn't respond, Ian glanced at him. Disappointment was stamped into his young features, but Ian held his ground, as hard as it was. He kept eating in silence.

Still, Noel tried again. "I bet you know a lot about foxes," he said. "You know about everything. Mama says you're as good with horses as my . . . as my pa was." Some of the light faded from his eyes, and he ducked his head quickly.

Hiding tears, Ian suspected.

He couldn't do it. He simply could not reject an innocent child who'd so recently lost his father and who'd done no harm to him or to anyone. What if the child were Katy? What if, at this very moment, her need for love and affection—even her very survival—

was dependent upon the kindness of some stranger? As it might well be. Would he not pray to all the saints that the stranger give her what she needed, even if it meant putting his own needs aside? Aye, of course he would.

"All right," he said. "We'll free Joseph tomorrow. Now you'd best go back to helping your mother."

Noel's head came up. "Will you give us a reading lesson tonight?"

"Aye."

"And read *Robinson Crusoe*?"

"For a little while. Then I have to plant."

The lad frowned. "But when will you sleep?"

Ian shrugged. "I donna need much rest."

"I don't think I do, either," Noel said very seriously. "But Ma says I need more sleep 'cause I'm growing. She doesn't realize I'm nearly grown."

Ian had to resist the urge to chuckle. In truth, though Noel was only seven—and not a very large seven at that—he had seen the lad work, had seen him milking the cow before dawn and carrying armloads of firewood and planting tobacco seedlings all day in the fields.

"Aye," he said. "You do a mon's work."

Noel beamed at the praise.

"Now go and help your ma and your aunt," he added, "and let me get back to the horses. Sir Gray is still waiting for his turn at a little exercise."

"Can't I help you?" Noel asked.

"Nay, your mother needs you more than I do."

Taking the dismissal in stride this time, Noel started toward the doorway. When he reached it, he turned. "I'm glad you came to help us," he said shyly. Then he spun around and darted out of the barn.

Rising, Ian moved to stand by Royalty's stall, his gaze following the lad as he sped across the yard toward the tobacco field, where Fancy and Fortune were still busy planting and Amy was diligently mounding dirt into a two-foot-high pile. Beyond the tobacco field, he could see acres of hay rippling in a light breeze.

'Twas hay that would have to be cut. Then the tobacco would have to be picked. Then there were the fences that needed mending. And the mare that, if he was any judge at all, would be ready to be bred in a few days. And God knows what else there was to do that he, not being a farmer, didn't yet know about.

How could a woman, a timid and mute fifteen-year-old girl, and a seven-year-old boy manage?

The answer was patent: they couldn't. But he knew as surely as he knew his name that Fancy Marsh would die trying.

Turning his back on the scene framed by the barn doorway, Ian folded his arms along the top rail of Royalty's stall and buried his head in them.

Fancy scrutinized her name on the paper, then carefully copied it. It was beginning to make sense, those figures on paper. Letters.

She couldn't restrain a smile as she wrote her name again and again on the slate. Never again would she sign her name with an *X*.

She recognized other words, too: "cat" and "dog." They were simple words, but she didn't care. She would learn bigger ones. If only she had more time. If only she could spend as many hours learning to read as she spent planting tobacco. Three days had passed since they'd made the trip to Chestertown, which made four evenings of reading lessons, and she already felt like a different person.

Noel was also grinning as he wrote his name. He looked at Ian as if the Scotsman had handed him the world. Fancy knew it was truer than he realized.

She also realized that the Scotsman was a natural teacher. He had the patience of Job and a way of correcting his pupils' mistakes without ever making them feel inadequate. Moreover, he praised each small success, which drew grins from the children and even enticed Fortune, who continued to hover just outside the circle, into joining them for brief stretches.

Ian was always careful to leave a space for her at the table, and once in a while she would perch on the edge of the chair and mouth the alphabet, as Ian insisted they do at the beginning of each lesson.

Even Amy would try. "*A, b, thee,*" she would say. Fancy would see Ian's lips twitch before he caught himself.

"*C,*" Noel would correct his sister.

"I said that," Amy insisted indignantly each time. "*Thee.*"

And the lesson would continue.

Ian wrote words on the slate, then Fancy tried to read them. It was always something simple like "Fancy sees Noel." Then Ian wrote something for Noel to read.

He had never asked Fortune to do anything, and so Fancy was surprised when, that night, he wrote "Fortune" on the slate and handed it to her sister.

"Fortune," he said, emphasizing the two syllables of the word. Holding out the piece of chalk, he asked, "Do you want to write your name for me? Just like I did?"

While Fortune only stared at him, Fancy held her breath.

"You *can* do it, lass," he said gently. "I know you can."

Fancy remembered the taunt that was tossed so cruelly as her bruised and bleeding sister had stumbled into her arms so long ago: "She's jest a stupid Injun."

Fortune hadn't spoken since that day.

"You can do it," Ian said again.

Slowly, her hand trembling, Fortune took the chalk from him. She looked at the slate with the three names—Fancy, Noel, Fortune—written on it, then raised her gaze once more to Ian.

He nodded his head. "Go on."

Drawing a shaky breath, Fortune applied chalk to slate and began to write. When she'd finished, she studied her work for a moment, then turned the slate to Ian.

He nodded. "That's right." Then he took a cloth and erased the writing, and handed the slate back to her. "Now do it again."

Nothing to copy this time. Suddenly Fancy wondered if this was such a good idea. Even she and Noel hadn't yet written their names without having something to copy from. And the last thing Fortune needed was to fail.

But her sister seemed to have found some hidden well of confidence. Or rather, Fancy thought, Ian Sutherland had found it for her, and for some reason Fortune trusted him enough to try. Slowly, very slowly, she began to write. It took her several minutes, but when she finished, she looked at the word she'd written, seemed satisfied, and handed the slate to Ian with less hesitation than she had shown on her first attempt.

He took it from her, glanced at it, and grinned. Actually grinned. Seeing his pleasure, the first Fancy had seen him display, was like seeing sunlight glittering on the water.

"Aye, tha' is verra gleg," he said.

"Gleg?" Fancy asked.

"Smart. Quick-witted," he replied.

Fortune's face glowed, her eyes sparkling in a way Fancy had not seen them sparkle in many, many years.

"Am I gleg, too?" Noel asked.

"Aye, you are, lad. And your sister and mither, too."

Fancy gathered that she was the "mither." She rather liked the sound of it.

"Now," he said, rising from the chair, "you all can be practicin'. I ha' some tobacco to plant."

"What about *Robinson Crusoe*?" Noel exclaimed.

The Scotsman hesitated. "You'll be able to read it soon enough if you keep practicing and reading the primer. Ye know the letters now, and the writing of your names."

It wasn't enough. Fancy knew it wasn't, but he was telling her something, something she didn't want to hear. He was telling them not to depend on him.

"Please," Noel begged.

Lucky, who had accompanied Ian inside for supper, took that moment to whine, and the cat meowed.

"See, they want to hear it, too," Noel added.

The Scotsman looked at Fancy helplessly for a moment, but she couldn't bring herself to aid his cause. He was right; he ought to be planting tobacco. But she wanted to hear *Robinson Crusoe* too. And so, in answer to his silent appeal, she simply shrugged.

He sighed. "Half a chapter. No more."

Noel sprang from his seat to fetch the book.

Ian took it from him and returned to his seat at the table. "Let's see. We were on chapter seven. . . . Ah, here we are." He began to read, and his rich baritone filled the room.

Fancy felt a ripple of warmth run up her spine as she listened to the tale of a man who awakened on a beach after a storm and found himself all alone. She heard Crusoe's loneliness, his despair, in Ian Sutherland's voice.

" 'It was in vain to sit still and wish for what was not to be had,' " he read, and he imbued the words with such depth of emotion that she thought it was not about Crusoe's loneliness and despair but about his own that he spoke. And he made her feel it, too.

They had both lost a great deal; and they were both trying to reach for things that were probably impossible to gain—or regain.

A tear stung the corner of her eye, and she looked away. She wanted to bolt from the chair and run outside to cry the tears she hadn't yet shed. They were there, bottled up in her heart, but she hadn't been able to release them. Punishment for her sins of omission.

Oh, how she missed John and his steady presence. He had tried so hard to provide for his family, to make sure they would be able to manage without him. But in buying Ian Sutherland's indenture, he hadn't been able to buy a man's loyalty. Perhaps he had planned to earn what couldn't be purchased. He had simply not been granted the time.

How would they manage without the Scotsman? Without this man who, in only a few weeks and against his will, had made himself indispensable?

Ian read half a chapter, then closed the book and stood up, shaking his head when Noel begged for more.

"Mrs. Marsh." He acknowledged her politely, distantly. And without waiting for a response, he left the house.

After everyone was abed, Fancy looked out her bedroom window and saw his shadowy form in the tobacco field. She thought briefly about joining him. But tonight, as she had the previous three nights, she resisted. The memory of the night she had worked beside him, of his touch on her face and the warmth that had spread through her, was still a living thing in her mind. All it took was seeing him, being in his presence, to rekindle the sensations.

She understood now why he had avoided being alone with her since that night. He knew as well as she did that the attraction between them was impossible. She dishonored John's memory every time she so much as acknowledged it to herself.

But, oh, it was hard to pretend that attraction didn't exist—or to convince herself that she didn't want to feel it.

"Ian Sutherland," she whispered in the hush of her room. "What am I going to do when you're gone?"

Ian woke, as always, at dawn. He'd had less than four hours of sleep, but he felt better than he had in months. Tonight he would leave for Chestertown, and by this time tomorrow he'd be aboard a ship, on the first leg of his journey home.

He'd worked out the details in his mind. He would leave after dark, taking the gelding and leaving a note for Fancy, saying that the horse could be found in a Chestertown stable. He still had one of the coins she had given him the other day, and he would use that for food. He needed nothing more.

As he'd worked last night, he'd made peace with himself. Most of the tobacco was planted. Fancy could sell two of the horses and keep the stable going. The sale would allow her to hire a man, mayhap two, and the proceeds from the tobacco would see them through the winter. The oats needed cutting, but one of the neighbors should be able to help with that. At the very worst, she could always purchase another indenture.

Today he would exercise the two gray three-year-olds and the black filly.

Royalty, indignant at being passed over, pawed restlessly as Ian passed his stall. The stallion, he knew, would be Fancy's greatest problem. She couldn't control the spirited animal herself, and Royalty required more exercise than he could get simply by being turned out into the small pasture.

Ian didn't know how she would solve that problem, but he refused to feel any guilt over it. He didn't owe her a solution to every dilemma she faced. He didn't owe her anything. John Marsh had taken a risk when he purchased a human being. He had gambled. He lost.

Ian collected Gray Ghost from the pasture. The most promising of the lot, the three-year-old was the same color as his sire and already had much of his power, along with a far better disposition. Ian slipped a halter over Gray Ghost's head and led him back to the barn, where he quickly saddled him, then rode out.

He'd enjoyed the morning rides. Moments of blessed freedom. Rare times when he could forget the reason he was here. Only God knew when he would find as fine a mount again. Or such productive land. He was not a farmer, but even he saw the glory and promise of the rich Maryland earth.

Indeed, this new country had much to offer a man. Land for the taking, an abundance of sun and water to nourish it. Freedom from poverty for the multitudes who were trapped in England's class system. Aye, were it not for the circumstances under which he'd been brought here—and were it not for Katy—he could have been persuaded that the American colonies were a good place for a man to fulfill his dreams and find freedom . . . and contentment.

Not that America didn't have its ills, he reminded himself. Aye, slavery was an insidious disease, and this new land was infected with it. He would never be able to forget that.

Touching his heels to Gray Ghost's sides, Ian felt the surge of power beneath him. He knew little about racing as it was practiced here, as a sport. He knew about speed and power and control, though, and this horse had it all. If trained by someone who knew what he was about . . .

Ian dismissed the thought. That someone would not be him.

He took Gray Ghost along the woodland path toward Tuckahoe Creek. When he reached the creek, he turned the horse, planning to head back to the farm, but at the sound of rustling coming from the bushes along the creek bank, Gray Ghost whinnied softly and took a few sidesteps.

"Ho, there, laddie," Ian said. "What is it now?"

In the next instant, Fortune stepped out from behind the bush, a bucket in her hand, her untidy braids hanging down to her waist, the hem of her dress dusty from the earth.

"Lass!" he exclaimed. "What are you doing so far from home?"

She raised an arm to point, and he followed the direction of her finger to a cluster of mushrooms.

"Ah, gathering ingredients for your sister's stew."

She gave her head a vehement shake.

"Nay?"

She shook her head again and made a face.

"Poison?"

She nodded.

"So what do you have there in your bucket?"

When she beckoned him, he dismounted, looped Gray Ghost's reins over a low-hanging branch, and followed her. She took his hand and led him down the bank of the stream to a thicket of bushes heavy with berries. Telling the story with her hands, Fortune explained what she was about.

"I see," he said. "Fancy wants berries for a pie."

He was astonished when, instead of simply nodding, she smiled at him. He'd never seen her smile at anyone, not even Fancy, and he felt deeply honored. But what had he done that was so extraordinary to earn her precious trust? Nothing. Nothing but treat her as he would have treated any wounded creature. How anyone could hurt such a bonny fey lass he didn't know, but hurt she had been. He'd recognized the terror in her eyes the first time he'd seen her.

"Katy," he said, and, at Fortune's quizzical look, he explained. "Katy is my sister. You remind me of her. She has your dark hair."

Fortune reached for his hand and squeezed his fingers in a gesture of comfort.

And why shouldn't he accept that comfort? He'd been living for a year without being able to tell a soul about the pain inside him. Fortune had given him her trust, and somehow it seemed fair that he give her his, like returning her gift in kind.

"She has dark hair," he said. "But her eyes are green, like mine."

Holding a hand parallel to the ground and level with her own head, Fortune raised her eyebrows in query at the same time she moved her hand slowly downward to about shoulder height, then back up again.

"How old is she?" he guessed.

Fortune nodded.

"She would be almost eight now. About the same age as young Noel."

Fortune's eyes widened in surprise, and he realized she had expected his sister to be older, perhaps closer to his own age.

She spread her hands, palms upward, and looked around, then frowned in puzzlement.

"I donna know where she is," Ian said. He closed his eyes, struggling to speak past the ache in his throat. "I donna even know if she is alive."

When he opened his eyes, Fortune was gazing at him with such compassion that he felt himself start to break. He had thought the walls he'd built between himself and the pain were impregnable. He'd thought enough time had passed so that the profound grief he'd felt a year ago would have faded.

He'd been wrong. The wall was made of sand. The grief was still enough to bury him, if he let it. But he couldn't let it, not before he'd done what had to be done.

" 'Tis time for me to get back to the farm," he said. "I still have horses to exercise today." Then, not wanting to leave her alone—even though she spent half her time wandering the woods—he gestured toward the bucket she carried. "Let me help you pick; then you can ride back with me."

Fear flickered in her eyes, but it passed quickly. She nodded, and together they set about filling the bucket with plump, ripe berries.

Ian rode Gray Ghost back to the farm with Fortune sitting behind him, the berry bucket between them, her hands clutching his waist. When the house came into view, he saw Fancy. She was washing clothes in the side yard, and as they approached, she looked up briefly—then looked again.

Straightening her back, she kept her gaze on them, eyes wide with astonishment.

Ian pulled up a short distance from her, swung his leg over Gray Ghost's neck, and jumped down, then turned to take the bucket from Fortune and help her dismount.

Handing the bucket back to her, he said, "Thank you, lass, for such a pleasant morning. I haven't picked berries in years, and 'twas a pleasure."

Fortune gave him a fleeting half-smile and, with the bucket clutched to her middle, hurried into the house.

Ian looked up to find Fancy standing with her hands on her waist, still gaping at him.

"How did you do that?" she asked.

"Do what?"

"Get her on a horse with you?"

"I asked her."

Fancy's brow furrowed. "She never lets anyone touch her."

"I'm no one to fear, Mrs. Marsh."

"I know," she replied, "but—" She stopped abruptly.

Ian wanted an answer to one of the many questions that had been nagging him. And he wasn't going to let Fancy wriggle out of it this time. "When did she stop speaking?"

Fancy hesitated, and he wasn't sure she would answer. Then she gave him a single nod. "She spoke until she was six. That's how old she was when our father died. A friend of his—at least we thought he was a friend—said he would take us to a fine house in Boston where we would be safe and cared for. Instead he . . . he attacked her."

Ian felt sick, though he wasn't surprised. God knows, the English troops had done the same to many Scottish women and children, and the thought that such violence might have befallen his own sister . . . well, it was enough to drive him mad if he let himself think about it.

With a muttered curse, he looked at Fancy, hesitant to pry further yet unable to contain his fury. "And you?" he finally had to ask. "Did the bastard harm you as well?"

She gave her head a quick shake, her hand flapping in a small, helpless gesture. "I was in another room. I heard Fortune scream and tried to get to her, but the door was locked. When she came out . . ." She closed her eyes briefly, and he saw her draw a slow, deep breath. "I knew something terrible had happened, and I wanted to kill him. I *tried* to kill him. But he was too strong, and I succeeded only in getting myself beaten."

He heard the guilt in her voice that what she'd done hadn't been enough.

Quietly he asked, "Wasn't there anyone you could go to?"

She shook her head. "Cranshaw . . . that was his name . . . he threatened to have me arrested for theft if I told anyone. No one would believe a half-breed child and a fifteen-year-old girl who'd been living with the Indians. He said . . . he told me he wouldn't have me arrested if I signed some papers."

Lifting her chin in that determined look he was coming to recognize, she added, "I wouldn't sign something I couldn't read. But in the end it didn't matter. He had himself appointed our legal guardian, and then he arranged the paperwork himself so he could sell us as indentured servants."

Ian's lips parted in shock. Still holding Gray Ghost's reins, he took slow steps toward her, listening intently as she continued.

"He took us to Baltimore, far enough away so that we could never tell his wife what had happened. The auction was . . ." She waved her hand again, shaking her head.

"I know how it was," he said roughly, coming to a stop an arm's length away from her.

She squeezed her eyes closed, nodding. Then, meeting his gaze directly, she said, "John bought us, just as he bought you, not because he approved of slavery or indenture but because he had a good heart." She was silent for a moment, then added, "He bought your indenture because the other man who was bidding for you is known for working his servants to death. We really wanted a redemptioner, someone who was willing to work for his passage from England."

Ian's hands flexed, his fingers curling into his fists at his sides for want of something to take his anger out on. He thought of the taunts he had thrown at her, and at her husband, about people who traded in human beings. He thought of all the times he'd been hostile, blaming her for his circumstances.

He thought about the ship leaving on the morrow—and a knot began to form in the pit of his stomach.

Suddenly Fancy's breath caught in her throat. Her gaze was directed past him, down the road leading into the farm, and her expression had changed.

Ian turned to see what had disturbed her.

Robert Marsh.

The crow, which had been resting on the roof of the house, flew off, cawing. Lucky let out a string of menacing barks. The cat scooted through the door of the house when Fortune opened it to step outside. The girl's face turned to stone as she saw Marsh approaching.

Marsh, Ian observed, eyed Fortune with ill-disguised distaste. Whirling, the girl scurried back into the house, out of harm's way.

Marsh pulled up short a few yards away but did not dismount. Ian got the distinct impression that he intended his position to be one of superiority, that he wanted Fancy to know he was looking down on her. His gaze swept the newly planted tobacco field, and his lips thinned. Then, with a long, contemptuous look at him, Marsh focused his attention on Fancy.

"I see you got your tobacco planted," he said.

"We did," she replied.

"I talked to the sheriff. He agrees that you should not be living out here alone with this convict."

Fancy spoke with studied calm. "I am not living *with*

anyone other than my sister and my children. Mr. Sutherland stays in the barn."

"*Mr.* Sutherland?"

"Yes."

"The community won't stand for it."

"I don't care what the community stands for or against," she said. "No one has been able to help us, and don't pretend you haven't had anything to do with that."

"You slander me, Fancy," Marsh said. "You know I offered John my help."

"Only if he agreed to mortgage his land to you. And when he refused, you made sure he couldn't get the help he needed from anyone else."

Marsh shook his head slowly. "Ah, but you're *wrong*. John wanted me to have his land, and I have the papers to prove it. Of course, I was expecting you to *want* to come to me, and then I would gladly have taken the burden of this farm from your back. But for your own good, if you don't start listening to reason, I'll have to take the matter to court."

She was frightened. Really frightened. Ian saw it in the trembling of her hands, clasped together at her waist, and in the drawn look around her mouth. Still, she held her ground.

"I don't believe you," she said. "John would have told me if he did something like that."

"Now, Fancy . . ." Marsh heaved a condescending sigh. "A man doesn't tell his wife everything."

Ian's gaze snapped to her face. He knew what she was thinking as surely as if she'd told him. She was certain that her husband hadn't wanted the land to go to his brother, but she wasn't certain that Robert Marsh wouldn't forge papers that said he had—and since she still couldn't read anything Marsh might produce, she wouldn't be able to prove the papers were false.

But there wasn't enough time. . . .

"You lie," she said to Marsh.

"We'll see. But really, Fancy"—he shook his head—"I don't want to go to court. For God's sake, you're my brother's widow. It's my moral and spiritual duty—my *right*—to take care of you."

Bloody hell, Ian thought, the man actually believed what he was saying. He couldn't simply admit he wanted to take her land away from her. No, Robert Marsh had his cause all neatly rationalized in terms of moral duties and God-given rights. Which, to Ian, meant that Fancy had all the more reason to fear her brother-in-law. The righteous, as any Scot knew, never gave up.

"And how do you intend to take care of me?" Fancy asked.

He gave her a shallow smile. "I'll give you a home at Marsh's End. Or if you insist on staying here, I'll take this man's indenture and send you two reliable men each day."

"I told you before, Mr. Sutherland is not for sale."

Marsh cocked his head, and his voice was silky and full of insinuation as he asked, "Is there a reason you won't take two for one?"

Ian heard her suck in a quick breath.

"Get off my land, Robert!" she demanded, outrage making her voice quaver.

"We'll see whose land it is," he said. "And who this man belongs to."

"Get off *now*!"

Glaring, Marsh urged his horse forward, toward her, and Ian took three quick strides, putting himself between Fancy and the horse.

"You heard Mrs. Marsh," he said. "She wants you gone."

Marsh's face turned red with rage. Yanking on the reins, causing his mount to let out a whinny of complaint and lift its front hooves a foot in the air, he forced the animal into a quarter turn. The horse continued to paw the ground in agitation as its master fixed his angry gaze on Fancy.

"This isn't over," he warned. "If you keep this man here, I warn you, you'll be ostracized. Shunned. And in the end the land will all be mine anyway." Raking both of them with a final glare, he added, "I'll give you a week to see reason, Fancy."

Then, with a jerk of the reins, he turned the horse toward the road and gave it a vicious lash with his quirt. When it reared, he hit it again, and the animal took off down the road.

Ian spun to face Fancy. His thoughts were racing, and the knot that had begun to form in his stomach before Marsh's arrival was being tugged tighter and tighter. Or mayhap it was a noose, and it wasn't in his stomach but around his neck.

Desperate to find a way out before he found himself swinging, Ian asked, "Why don't you tell him you want to stay here and that you'll give him my papers for the two men he says he'll send?"

"He would kill you," she said simply. "You wouldn't escape from him."

"I can take care of myself."

"You don't know how ruthless he is. If you ran away from him, he would hunt you down to the ends of the earth."

Not if I leave tonight! he nearly shouted at her. Robert Marsh would not find him aboard a ship on the Atlantic. So close. He was so close to going home.

"Besides," she continued, "turning your papers over

to him wouldn't be the end of it. He won't be satisfied until this farm is part of Marsh's End again and the horses are back in his stable. In Robert's mind, getting you out of the way is the first step toward the real goal."

And if he left tonight, Ian realized, he'd very obligingly be taking that step all on his own, leaving nothing and no one—no one but Fancy—standing between Robert Marsh and what he wanted.

God! What had it come down to? His sister—or Fancy Marsh and her family. Was he actually going to have to make this choice? When had he allowed Fancy Marsh to take on enough importance in his heart and mind that she could rival his sister, his own blood, for his loyalty?

He was burning inside and didn't see any way out of the fire.

Chapter 12

I n the end, Fancy made the decision for him.

After he finished his evening lesson, he left for the barn, ready to begin the wait until the house was dark. He had nothing to pack, nothing to take. Only hope. And guilt.

But then the barn door opened, and Fancy entered. "Come with me," she said, turning back to the door. She obviously expected his compliance and, though resentful, he followed. He would do nothing to raise her suspicions now.

The main room of the house was deserted; the children and Fortune had evidently gone to bed.

"Wait here," she said, then disappeared into another room and returned carrying paper, a quill, and ink. He recognized the parchment immediately. His indenture papers.

Puzzled, he waited as she fetched the pen he'd purchased several days ago. "I want to give your freedom back to you," she said. "How do I do it?"

He stared at her in astonishment.

"Robert will find some way of getting you," she said. "You have made an enemy, and he won't forget your coming between him and me. He has power, and he will not stop at forgery. I can't let that happen."

He stood there for a moment, trying to comprehend the enormity of what she was saying. "You want to free me? Without conditions?"

She looked down at the table, and he knew she was remembering their recent conversation—and her threat. "Without conditions. I will not risk Robert getting your indenture."

In that moment she tied him to her more securely than any chain could.

That she would so easily surrender her hold on him put him in debt to her. Incalculably. Honor, which meant more than life, demanded no less.

Still, he knew a moment's hatred for her as his dream died, as he slowly released his plan to leave tonight. She had found the one key to holding him even if she hadn't been looking for it.

"What must I do to free you?" she persisted.

And to take him into another kind of captivity. The devil must be chuckling.

The terms of his indenture had been explained to him. Many of the convicts had not understood them, but Ian had. He had studied law at Edinburgh as well as other subjects. He knew that his indenture was meant to be for fourteen years without exception.

He picked up the papers he'd not had a chance to read before. Whoever had prepared them had either been sloppy or was used to a different kind of indenture after which to model them, for they did not prohibit his purchase of his own freedom.

He had no money, but legally a pound would suffice.

Freedom! But at a price far greater than any sum of money.

He looked up from the paper. She was biting her lip, obviously unaware of the torment she was causing within him. "I can buy my indenture," he said finally.

"Then I will sell it to you for whatever is in your pocket."

"You were willing to send the law after me," he said slowly. "Why did you change your mind?"

She shook her head. "I never would have. I just hoped you would learn to . . . like it here."

He sighed. He didn't want to talk about Katy, the last unbroken piece of his heart. "It isn't that I didna like it, Mrs. Marsh. 'Tis just that no man wishes to be traded or sold or to have his freedom taken from him."

She looked down. "Now that—"

He knew what she was thinking, hoping. "Nay, Mrs. Marsh," he said after a long silence. "I told you I have an obligation in Scotland. I have a sister, Katy, who is not so much older than your Noel. I found out while I was in prison that she disappeared. I don't know if she's safe. I have to find her."

Understanding flooded her eyes. At the same time, he saw the hope die.

One of her hands reached out, touched his own. "I'm so sorry," she said, and he flinched at the compassion in her expression.

"I was going to leave tonight," he said. "You should be knowing that. There's a ship leaving at dawn for Jamaica. From there, I planned to sail to a French island, then to France, and finally to Scotland."

She looked up at him, acceptance in her calm brown eyes. "Tell me where to sign my name on the papers." Then her gaze sharpened. "*Can* you go back?"

"Not if the Brits know about it," he said.

She looked down at his hand, and he knew she was thinking of the brand that marked him. "I planned to burn it off."

"I don't have much money," she said finally, "but you can have what there is." She hesitated, then set her jaw stubbornly. "You can sell one of the horses in Chestertown."

In the entirety of his life, he had never witnessed such generosity. She asked for nothing in return, just stood there willing him to take her offer, even when he knew how desperate her own situation was.

"And you, Mrs. Marsh? What will you do?"

"Because of you, I have the tobacco. Maybe I can get young Tim Wallace to help us harvest it. If not, I will sell the yearlings and try to find a redemptioner, someone willing to work for his passage from England."

"And what of Robert Marsh?"

"He is lying. He has no such papers. I know he doesn't. He just tried to frighten me."

He wished he was so sure. Her hopes and dreams were tied up in this land and the horses. "You offered to give me my freedom in a year," he said, feeling trapped. "I'll pledge you that year as a free man."

"And your sister?"

Hopelessness weighed down his heart. Honor extracted a heavy price. "I will write letters to every family I know, if you can spare me the money for it. 'Tis the only thing I'll ask of you."

"What about the rest of your family?" she asked.

"My older brother was killed at Culloden, my younger was hanged afterward," he said shortly. "There's bloody few left of my clan, and God only knows where they be."

She was chewing on her lip again, but he wanted no compassion from her, no sympathy. He wanted to fulfill his debt, nothing more. A year! What if a year was too long?

She seemed to know what he was thinking. "I think you should go," she said, "or you'll never forgive yourself."

"Nor could I forgive myself if something happened to you and the wee ones," he said. "I canna leave you at the mercy of tha' mon."

And he couldn't, although the obligation choked him. The irony of his arguing to stay and her arguing for him to go did not escape him. The taste was bitter.

She didn't say anything more, obviously convinced he wasn't going to change his mind, not at this moment, anyway. "I don't think we should risk not making you a free man," she said, picking up the indenture papers. "Where do I sign this?"

He shook his head. "It must be witnessed. By someone you trust."

"Fortune."

He shook his head. "She isn't old enough."

"The reverend," she said. Then her face fell. "But he won't be here for another week. I think I should do it now. I don't trust Robert."

Those papers lay between them. To him, they were a high, strong wall, keeping him from Scotland, making a different kind of prisoner of him.

But she was right. Something was better than nothing.

Her name was meaningless, though, unless she could prove she knew what she was signing. That meant more lessons. More intimacy.

Bloody hell, but the devil had set him dancing.

He hesitated, knowing that what he was doing would seal the agreement. Then he wrote, "In recognition of payment in full, the indenture is redeemed." He watched as she proudly wrote her name, looking to him for approval. She took such pride in the accomplishment that his heart ached.

She folded it. "I will have Reverend Winfrey sign it at the next meeting."

He nodded. The bargain was complete.

But he didn't know how in the devil he was going to live with it.

Robert left his sweating horse with a groom and quickly strode to his house and into the library, where he poured himself a drink. He tried to control his rage as he considered his options.

His bluff hadn't worked. He had no papers, nothing

that said John wanted him to have the farm. He didn't think Fancy knew that—men didn't discuss business affairs with women. She was just plain stubborn.

But he could forge a new will. He had hoped it wouldn't come to this, but no matter. He would say he had not presented his copy of the will immediately because he hadn't really wanted to dispossess his sister-in-law until it became readily apparent to all that she could not manage her own affairs. He would appear both magnanimous and concerned. In the meantime he could create so much outrage about a single man living at a new widow's home that the will would be readily accepted as prudent on John's part.

It would not be difficult to have the document forged, but forgers had little more integrity than liars. If he was betrayed, and word leaked out that he was trying to cheat his brother's widow, his reputation would be ruined forever. Still, he would risk it.

And then there was that cursed Scotsman. Everyone knew that bond servants had to be kept in their place. And their place was not living alone with a young widow and her children.

Robert truly believed that. He also believed that Ian Sutherland was a dangerous man and most likely had eyes for his mistress. He couldn't believe that Fancy would return any such favor, but the mere possibility angered him. She had repeatedly turned a cool shoulder to him; he couldn't bear to think that she would take up with a man who could not even call his person his own.

He had to make sure that didn't happen. It would be intolerable. And he would be helping her, even if she didn't understand that just now. He *would* take care of her, and he would remove her from the influence of the Scotsman.

And then he would "take care" of the convict. No

one treated him with contempt and got away with it,
nor did anyone thwart him with impunity. He knew
how to season slaves. There were ways to tame them.

He poured another drink and downed it. He would
start his campaign tomorrow with the Anglican priest,
then with the county officials. He would start them
worrying about the Scotsman.

It shouldn't take much more than a few days to convince his sister-in-law that it would be best for her family if she sold the Scotsman to him. Then he could
persuade her to move into his home. Perhaps he could
still avoid the trouble of having the will forged.

Robert smiled, savoring the thought of having the
Scotsman at Marsh's End, where he would teach him
to respect his betters.

Never-ending work should have made the days fly
faster. But every moment was agonizing for Ian.

He wrote his letters, and he took them into Chestertown two days after he had thought to meet the
mate of the *Elizabeth*. He rode alone this time. He rode
with Fancy's trust. And it was like riding to hell.

Avoiding conversation with anyone, he posted the
letters, then briefly tortured himself with a stop at the
waterfront. He stayed long enough to see that the *Elizabeth* was indeed gone and another ship was berthed in
its place. No visit to the tavern this time. He didn't
want to hear about other sailings, afraid he'd be
tempted to break his pledge.

His heart, as he turned Royalty onto the road back
to the farm, felt as if it were breaking apart. A year!
How in God's name would he live through it? The past
year of relentless anxiety about Katy had already taken
a heavy toll on him. He honestly didn't know if he
could survive another.

He did know that his need to take positive action

was overwhelming and that writing the letters hadn't helped much. In fact, the exercise of writing to friends he thought most likely dead had been excruciating. Even more excruciating was riding this deserted road alone, with all the time in the world to wonder whether those letters would even reach Scotland.

He felt better when he was working. Exhausting himself in the tobacco fields brought a measure of relief from his worries. So did hours of intense concentration on the horses' training. Teaching the Marsh family to read, though it put him in proximity to Fancy more than he feared was wise, also served as a distraction. For the past few days, he had driven himself like a man possessed—God knows, there was no shortage of work to be done—and in doing so, he was able to divert his thoughts for minutes at a time from the waking nightmares about Katy.

Ian had been encouraged yesterday by the appearance of the boy named Timothy Wallace, the son of one of the men who had attended John's funeral. He was a good-looking lad with a pleasant face and sharp, intelligent eyes. He was called Little Tim, Fancy explained; his father was Big Tim.

He and his da, the boy said, had finished planting their corn and tobacco, and he had some time to spare. Could the Marshes use another hand?

"Are you sure?" Fancy had asked him. "Robert—"

"No one tells a Wallace wha' to do," the boy said boldly, his eyes going to Fortune, who stood shyly by the door.

The boy's father had been a bondsman himself, Fancy had explained later, and he had a rough pride that refused to ever again take orders from anyone. Tell him to do one thing, and he would do the opposite, she said.

So Little Tim had set to work, and after two days, he

showed no sign of leaving anytime soon. If he stayed long enough, Ian thought, they could cut the oats and repair the pasture fences. Ian himself would be able to spend most of his time preparing the three-year-olds for the fall races.

He understood clearly that a winner would spell success.

Patting Royalty's neck as they traveled the road home, Ian mused over that possibility. "What do you think, laddie? If one of your sons wins a race, will your stud fees double to match your pride?" No doubt they would. And the selling price for the younger horses could easily double, too.

Fancy would not be able to say then that he had not kept his promise. He would give her everything he could for the next year. And at the end of it, by God, she would have a thriving farm and stable, and he would have a clear conscience. He would make certain she hired a competent manager and trainer for the horses, as well as someone to help with the farmwork. Then he could be on his way.

He could only pray that, by then, it wouldn't be too late for Katy.

Ian reached the farm after dark, despite the long summer day. He saw the light from the house, and it beckoned to him. He knew the people inside were waiting for him. Knew he could open the door of that house, and he would be welcome.

It was painful—and dangerous—to admit that the small, unassuming farmhouse had a warmth to it that the huge pile of stones called Brinaire, his birthplace, could never have, merely because of its age and size. Brinaire had held another kind of warmth, though. He remembered his mother's beaming smile and his father's gruff pride in his accomplishments, the bear hugs from his brothers, their affectionate taunts about their studious brother. And he recalled other trips home, later trips, when Katy had come running and jumping into his arms, covering his face with kisses.

Gone. It was all gone. And he wasn't ready for substitutes. Maybe he would never be ready.

Riding directly to the barn, Ian put Royalty into his stall, then began rubbing the animal down. He ran his hands down the neck of the stallion. Royalty. He was well named.

He took his time watering the horse. He knew Fancy would be waiting for him to make an appearance, even if only to say he had returned. But he wasn't ready to face her. Today he had made the final commitment to stay here for a year, and it hurt. Bloody hell, but it hurt.

He heard the barn door open, and though he neither glanced up nor heard her approach, he knew when she came to stand behind him, on the other side of the stall rail. The faint scent of flowers, drifting on the breeze let in by the open barn door, told him that it was Fancy.

"I'm sorry," she said softly.

He drew the brush down Royalty's neck in a steady rhythm. "About what?"

"You missed that ship."

"Aye."

A few moments of silence passed; then moving opposite him, on the other side of the stallion, she put her hand on Royalty's neck. Ian was grateful that the horse was tall enough to block their view of each other.

"Royalty was John's favorite," she said.

"Aye, I see why. We had horses in Scotland that could travel all day like this one, but none ha' his speed." He heard the hollowness in his own voice. He was talking just to talk, to fill the emptiness in his heart.

"I didn't know if you would come back," she said.

"Aye, you did," he said bitterly.

Another moment of silence.

"Yes," she admitted after a long pause. "I should have said I wasn't sure I wanted you to."

He wasn't going to ask what she meant. Mayhap she was only expressing concern for his sister. Then again, mayhap she feared his presence in the same way he feared hers.

"How did Tim do today?" he asked.

He heard her sigh. "He's a hard worker. I think he's sweet on Fortune."

"And Fortune? How is the lass taking it?"

"Cautious as always, but she did agree to take him milk and bread at noontime."

Their voices were toneless, without emotion. Mindlessly, he kept brushing the stallion's neck, and every so often he saw her fingertips appear above the animal's mane as she continued to stroke him.

"I'm too tired to give lessons tonight," he said. Not tired, but heartsore.

"I thought you would be," she replied. "I brought you some food."

"I'm not hungry."

"You're still much too thin."

"I can do the work," he said tersely.

"I know."

The stallion lowered his head to his water bucket, and unexpectedly, their gazes met, their hands, suddenly both stroking air, came together. His hand felt scorched at the contact, and his heart ached at the bleakness he saw in her eyes. Her look should have been triumphant; instead, it was filled with sorrow. And he knew that sorrow included his losses as well as her own.

Infuriated at himself and at her, Ian walked out of the stall, stopping by the central post of the barn, beneath the lantern he'd lit. A second's glance, a bare instant of his skin touching hers, and he was aroused to the point of pain. He needed too much from her, and the need was of both his body and his heart. A craving for tenderness as well as lust.

Behind him he heard the squeak of the stall gate as it was closed, the click of the latch.

"Noel wanted to wait up and say good night," she said. "He finally fell asleep."

"More likely he wanted to hear more of the tale."

A smile colored her reply. "Yes, that too. I said I would say good night to you for him."

Groaning inwardly, he squeezed his eyes closed, willing her to leave now, before it was too late. Strange how the smell of flowers mellowed the other odors in a barn until it and it alone filled his senses.

Opening his eyes, he turned to find her leaning against the stall gate. Mayhap eight feet separated them, but it might as well have been eight inches.

Nor could he take his eyes off her. "Isn't it time you were abed?"

She lifted one shoulder in a shrug. "I will be. Soon." When she brushed a lock of hair back from her face, the lantern light caught in the tawny strands, turning them to gold.

She motioned to a pewter tray she'd placed on the upended barrel he used as a table. The tray was laden with food and a full tankard. "You really must eat," she said again.

He nodded, his gaze never leaving her face.

Blast it, why didn't she leave?

But then, he couldn't make himself turn away from her, either.

He wanted to touch her, wanted to feel her hair curl around his hands, to caress the soft skin of her cheek with his fingers . . . and his lips. He wanted to hold her. He wanted . . . too much.

As they stared at each other, neither of them able to break away, he knew they were standing in the center of a storm. It was quiet, motionless, with scarcely a breath being drawn that could be heard. Yet the calm was deceptive, for he knew that mere inches—seconds—away, the storm raged out of control. All it needed was a step in the wrong direction and . . . disaster.

They'd made all the gestures to leave. They had exchanged all the pleasantries. And yet . . .

They moved at the same time, each taking a single step toward the other. She hesitated, then took another one. And another.

With a muttered oath, he closed his eyes and held out his arms to her, and when she stepped into them, he wrapped her close, a long, groaning sigh escaping him. Her head came to rest against his chest, and he knew she must hear the quickened beat of his heart.

Without lifting her head, she raised her arms, her hands creeping around his neck until he felt her fingers clasp together, binding him to her as he had bound her to him. Only then did she look up at him.

He returned her gaze for a moment, letting himself drown in the warmth and yearning he saw reflected in her lovely brown eyes. Then, lowering his head, he fitted his lips to hers.

Need. He was instantly awash with it. Part was pure lust, but the greater part was the compulsion to join with another living person, to feel alive again. It had been so long. . . .

And for her, too. Aye, it was the same for her. She was telling him so with the clutching of her fingers in his hair and the small, whimpering, needful sounds coming from her throat.

He didn't care what it was or why either of them felt this way. As the storm broke over them, he let his instincts take over. His mouth opened over hers, and she responded, her lips parting as his tongue swept in to explore, then plunder, his desire for her rising swiftly to dizzying heights.

He felt her back arch and her body melt into his. He felt her fingers move from his hair to his back, raking it with long strokes. He shuddered at her touch, his hands traveling up and down her body, exploring it as if her clothes were a mere inconvenience. She was as soft as a woman should be, yet he felt her strength, and it inflamed him beyond anything he'd ever known.

Cupping her buttocks, he pulled her tightly against the aching ridge of flesh inside his trousers. She gasped, and her hands stopped moving, clutched his shoulders, her body trembling. Releasing her mouth, he trailed his lips and tongue over the delicate planes of her face, and he felt her shudder.

He also tasted tears.

His body was agony—a pulsating, painful core of nerves demanding relief. He could have that relief; her body was ready. But the tears told him her mind and heart weren't.

He raised his head then, brought his hand up to hold her head against his chest, under his chin. She clung to him, her body shaking with the silent tears, tears she refused to let fall. Tears held in check for weeks now by that same iron will that could slice through all obstacles and prejudices.

Her breath caught on a sob, and she went utterly still.

" 'Tis the only way, lass," he said. "You canna carry it inside you forever. You must let it out."

She hesitated another instant, then, with a racking shudder, she let her breath escape and she began to cry.

Her sobs were muffled against his shoulder, but she was no longer trying to restrain them. With his chin resting atop her head, he held her close, his hand gently stroking her back.

Time passed. He had no idea how long he stood there, holding her, murmuring soothing sounds and Scottish words that she wouldn't understand. Finally the tears began to subside. Slowly the shudders faded to an occasional tremble. He continued to support her until she straightened, her hands going to his shoulders to push herself back far enough to look up at him.

"I'm . . . sorry, so sorry," she said, and started to turn.

His lips brushed her forehead. "You have nothing to be sorry for, lass. Nothing at all."

She stared at him for a moment. Then, breaking free of his embrace, she gathered her skirts in her hands and ran out of the barn.

Following slowly, Ian stopped in the doorway and watched her run toward the house. She ran as if all the fiends in hell were chasing her.

But he knew that some of those fiends had stayed behind to torment him, and no doubt the torment would continue for months . . . and months to come.

Chapter 13

ancy had never been so ashamed in her life. John had not been dead a month, and she was acting like a mare in season.

Burying her head under a pillow, she tried not to remember the feelings that had overtaken her sense of right and wrong. "Forgive me, John," she whispered.

Her hand crept across the bed, through the empty place where he used to lie. When their lovemaking dwindled with John's health, to her everlasting guilt, she had not missed the act. It had been a duty, not an unpleasant one but not something she had craved.

Not as she had craved it moments ago.

Swallowing hard against the tears that rose once more to blind her, she thought of John's kind face, his integrity, his honesty. "I did love you," she said into the silence.

Still, the question begged asking: why did her body—and her heart—respond so readily to Ian Sutherland? She couldn't deny that her feelings toward the Scotsman went beyond the physical. An inexplicable connection existed between them, and it had been there almost since the first moment they'd met, despite her efforts to pretend it did not exist.

Her attraction to him was not only inappropriate; it was also impossible. Ian Sutherland had made it plain again and again that he wanted no attachments in this country. He intended to return to Scotland, regardless of the danger to himself, to find his sister. Moreover, it was foolish to believe that he would ever simply *want* to stay with her. He had a been a lord in Scotland, and he was well lettered, a man of breeding and power. And who was she? A foolish, illiterate widow with two children, a mute sister, and a small struggling farm that offered nothing but endless physical labor.

Fancy tried for a long while to beat back the demons enough to fall asleep. But they would not be silenced. At last she gave up, throwing back the twisted covers and rising from the bed. Lighting a candle, she wandered aimlessly through the house until finally her meanderings took her to the door.

She stepped out onto the porch and took a deep breath, filling her senses with the rich aroma of freshly turned earth. She loved that smell. It spelled renewal, life. The sky was bright with light from the moon and so many stars that they looked like grains of sugar spilled across a dark blue blanket.

The yard was plainly visible in the unearthly light, and her gaze moved slowly over it, drawn inevitably to the closed barn door. Was he asleep?

Sighing, she took a few steps into the yard, away from the barn, and began walking toward one of the pastures, where some of the horses stood silhouetted in the moonlight. One of the mares was nuzzling her colt, which fumbled under her, looking for a late meal. The youngster was all legs and had a gangling charm that, even in her state of distress, brought a smile to Fancy's lips. The others—two mares and their older offspring, a colt and a filly—were sleeping, standing perfectly still with their heads bowed.

Looking at them made tears sting her eyes yet again. She loved them all. She loved the farm, loved watching it change through the seasons and seeing the miracle of birth repeated over and over, year after year. She loved the new, struggling plants and the budding roses that colored a small bed in front of the house.

Did *he* see the peace here? The beauty? Did it affect him at all?

Wiping the tears from her cheek with the back of her hand, she turned and walked slowly into the house.

Sheriff Tom Vaughn paid a visit to the farm the next day.

Fancy was washing clothes when she saw three riders approaching. Apprehension knotted her stomach. Fortune, who had been watching Amy, grabbed the child and disappeared inside. Noel, who had been pulling weeds in the vegetable garden, quickly moved to his mother's side.

Ian was in one of the paddocks, exercising Sir Gray. She saw him pull the horse to a halt, watch the riders for a moment, then go on with his business.

Sheriff Vaughn and his two deputies rode up to her and took off their hats. But while the sheriff dismounted, the other two men remained on their horses, and she saw them turn their heads toward the paddock where Ian was riding.

"Mrs. Marsh," the sheriff said. "I was sorry to hear about John's death. He was a good man."

"He was," she agreed.

"Is there anything I can do for you?"

She shook her head, noting that he too was glancing toward the paddock. The knot in her stomach tightened.

Directing his gaze at her again, Vaughn said, "I heard you had a bondsman. A convict."

"My brother-in-law talked to you," she said flatly.

"He is worried about you."

"It is none of his business," she said, immediately regretting her sharp tone.

The sheriff looked at her with disapproval etched into his features. "It's his duty."

"I appreciate your concern," she said, "and Robert's. But Mr. Sutherland is no danger to my family."

Vaughn scowled. "That's not what the Crown thinks," he said plainly, his lips thinning. "They thought him dangerous enough to condemn him. There's talk. People remember what happened in the past when convicts rebelled agin their masters. And you, a widow woman, out here alone—people don't like it."

She thought about telling him that the Scotsman could go where he wished, that he was free, but something held her back. The papers were not witnessed, and she did not trust Sheriff Vaughn.

"It's simple," the sheriff added. "You cannot live here alone with this man. There's already talk of charges agin you."

"*What* charges?"

"Fornication."

Stunned, she could only stand there, staring at him. The disapproval in his face deepened into contempt, and outrage filled her. Robert, damn him. She could guess what lies Robert had told him.

Shaking with fury, Fancy tried to control her voice as she spoke. "If my brother-in-law claimed there is anything improper happening between Mr. Sutherland and me, he lied."

The sheriff's expression of disbelief made spots of fury appear before her eyes, and for an instant she had the urge to hit him.

"It's not only Mr. Marsh that's saying things," Vaughn pointed out. "Nobody understands why you don't go and live under your brother-in-law's protection, where you ought to be."

"Oh, I see." Fancy gritted her teeth. "I can live under the same roof with Robert Marsh, but I can't live in my own home as long as there's a bond servant staying in the barn. Is that right?"

"Mr. Marsh is yer brother-in-law," Vaughn replied. " 'Tis fitting and proper for you to live in his house. That bondsman is an outlaw and no kin of yours." He turned toward one of his deputies. "Go bring the convict over here."

With her hands clenched at her sides, Fancy watched as one of the men rode over to the paddock where Ian was riding. She knew a moment of relief when, after a brief exchange between the two men, Ian rode Sir Gray over to the fence, dismounted, and came toward them. She could only pray that he would not do or say anything to provoke the sheriff. Her prayer gained momentum as she noted his swaggering walk and the arrogant set of his jaw.

As Ian reached them, the sheriff poked him in the chest with the horsewhip he carried. "Yer name?"

"Ian Sutherland."

The sheriff grabbed his hand and turned it over to reveal the brand. "Address yer betters with more respect."

When Ian didn't reply, the sheriff flexed the whip and hit him across the palm. Ian didn't so much as flinch. He simply glared at Vaughn.

"Yer crime?" the sheriff said.

"The Sassenach called it treason," Ian said contemptuously. "I called it fighting for my rightful king."

Vaughn turned to her. "Where's his papers?"

Fancy hesitated, glancing at Ian. He was watching her closely, and she knew that he expected her to tell Vaughn that he had purchased his freedom. But something was wrong. She felt it in her bones. She knew Tom Vaughn, and she knew he did what Robert told him.

"I don't have them here," she lied.

The sheriff's eyes narrowed. "Where are they?"

"Safe."

"I advise ye, Mrs. Marsh, to sell this man's bond. He's nothing but trouble."

"Is that so?" She waved an arm to encompass the tobacco field and the pastures. "None of this would have been done without Mr. Sutherland. My husband trusted him, and *I* trust him."

The smile Vaughn gave her was perhaps the most patronizing look Fancy had ever seen. "Beggin' your pardon, missus," he said, "but you *are* a woman, and women are fools about men."

"Women including your wife?" she grated, rage overtaking her natural politeness.

The sheriff's face darkened to a vivid purple. "I'll tell you right now, missus, that people here won't stand for this. You best get rid of him while you can."

Noel chose that moment to speak up for the first time. "I don't want Mr. Sutherland to go."

Vaughn looked down at him. "He's a criminal, boy. He might kill you all."

"He would *not*," Noel shot back.

The sheriff dismissed him, his gaze returning to Fancy. "Get rid of him."

Then, without waiting for further argument, he mounted his horse, and he and his deputies rode away.

Ian stood with his back to Fancy, watching the three men retreat. Why hadn't she told the sheriff that he was a free man?

Or *was* he free? Her signature on the indenture papers had yet to be witnessed. And she had stood there talking to the sheriff as if he were indeed her property. Mayhap she had no intention of freeing him. Mayhap her heart-wrenching act over the signing of the papers had been just that: an act designed to win his loyalty, while she planned to find one excuse after another not to have her signature witnessed.

Familiar bitterness welled up inside him. Without a backward glance, he strode toward the barn.

"Ian."

He heard Fancy's voice behind him, but he paid no attention.

"Ian!" she said again, and then she was beside him, trying to match his steps.

He ignored her, but she followed him to the barn and showed no sign of stopping at the door.

He turned to confront her in the doorway. "Why didn't you tell him?"

Her eyes, as they pleaded with him to understand, were large and luminous and truly beautiful. For a moment they distracted him from his anger, but the rage soon rose up again to blind him to all else.

"I couldn't let Vaughn have the papers," she said. "I don't trust him."

And I do not trust you. He nearly said the words. Instead, he spun away from her, heading toward the pasture.

"Ian!"

"You ha' wha' you want."

"Not if you think I lied, I don't."

"It doesna matter wha' I think."

He whistled for Sir Gray, who came to meet him at the pasture fence. Slipping between the fence rails, he vaulted into the saddle and urged the horse into a trot.

Once, twice, three times, he circled the paddock, and with each round, he pressed the horse for more speed. At the beginning of the fourth circuit, he looked toward the yard, fully expecting to see Fancy standing there.

But she was gone.

* * *

A week later Fancy knew upon arriving at the camp meeting that Robert had already done his work well. No one other than the Wallaces would speak to her.

She stood alone as the reverend baptized a babe and married a young couple. She felt a tear roll down her cheek as the minister asked the young couple whether they would love each other in sickness and in health, keeping unto each other as long as they both lived.

Then there was the kiss, awkward and uncertain, but tender. Her own marriage ceremony had been like that—awkward and uncertain—but it had turned into something fine. She had watched other marriages performed: some out of convenience, some of necessity, some of love.

She swallowed hard as a thought struck her. She tried to dismiss it, but it wouldn't go away. It kept flitting around her mind like a pesky fly, and its buzzing became louder and louder. She sat stone still through the remainder of the service, almost paralyzed by the enormity of her wayward thoughts.

After the service, only Reverend Winfrey approached her as she stood with Fortune, Noel, and Amy.

"Mrs. Marsh," he acknowledged, smiling down at Amy, who grinned happily at him.

When his gaze returned to hers, Fancy saw no censure in his eyes, only kindness.

"Can you have supper with us?" she asked.

He hesitated.

"I need your help," she said.

He nodded. "I've prayed for you and the children. And Miss Fortune," he added with a smile aimed at her sister. "Supper would be fine."

She waited while he visited with the other families who'd attended. Some, who had cast angry looks toward her when they'd arrived, looked ashamed as they walked away.

When the minister returned to their group and tied his horse to the back of the wagon in preparation for riding with them, Fancy spoke to him quietly.

"Maybe you should ride over later," she said, wanting to spare him the criticism he might receive for visiting a loose woman.

"And miss the pleasure of your company?" he said.

She smiled. She had always liked him, and never more so than at that moment. He was a man whose thin, sallow face would probably be called homely. His hair was untidy and lank, and his body was all legs and arms attached to a stick form. His clothes were of poor cloth, and his stock untidy. But the compassion and love that radiated from his clear blue eyes made a person forget all the mismatched parts. His God was a kind, unthreatening one, and as His minister, Rufus Winfrey had a courage and dedication that drew people to him. He was defying his small congregation for her, and she was grateful.

But how far would he go in defying that congregation? How much would he ask of his God?

With Fortune and the children settled in the bed of the wagon, Fancy made room on the seat beside her for Reverend Winfrey. As they started the ride home, she wondered how to begin. Before she could decide, he asked about the crops.

"Tim Wallace is helping us," she said. "But . . . Ian did most of the planting, and he is working with the horses."

"Ian. That's your bondsman?" Reverend Winfrey asked. "I noticed him at John's funeral. He seems a bitter man."

"He has reason to be bitter," she said.

"Can you tell me why?"

"No," she said. "But perhaps he will."

"Do you feel safe with him?"

"Yes, and the children like him."

"Children are good judges of character," he said approvingly. "And you? How do you feel about him?"

She hesitated, then admitted, "I like him." Then after a moment, she added, "I want to free him. I asked you to supper in part to witness my signature on the indenture papers."

The reverend was quiet for a moment. "I don't believe in slavery, Mrs. Marsh," he replied finally. "Not of any kind. You're doing the right thing."

"There's something else," she said slowly, lowering her voice. "You've heard the rumors. I'm sure they are coming from Robert. He will make it impossible for Ian Sutherland to stay, and if Ian leaves, I will lose the land."

"Does he want to stay?"

"He will stay for a year," she said, avoiding a direct answer.

Reverend Winfrey sighed. "A bargain? His freedom for a year's labor?"

If only it were that simple. "Not exactly," she said. "I offered to give him his freedom without conditions, but he insists on staying a year."

"He's an honorable man, then?"

She nodded.

"You realize there's already talk," he said carefully. "Several families wanted me to condemn you today during the service."

She looked down at her hands. They clasped the reins so tight they were white. "Why didn't you?"

"I told them not to judge lest they be judged," he replied. "But it is a strong wind blowing. I might have weakened it today, but it will strengthen again."

"Robert," she said quietly. "He wants my land. He

knows I cannot manage it without help. And he has frightened off almost everyone."

"You said the Wallaces will help."

"And they will, as much as they can, but they have their own farm to tend."

"Aye," the reverend said.

"The sheriff came several days ago. He said some people have accused me of . . . of fornication. I'm sure Robert set him to it."

"Dear child!" the minister exclaimed.

"He hasn't . . . I wouldn't . . ."

He put one creased hand on her arm. "Of course you haven't," he said.

Fancy twisted the reins in her hands. The horses responded impatiently and she forced herself to relax. How to phrase her question? How to even approach it? It was blasphemy, pure and simple, but she could think of no other way out of her dilemma. She could think of no other way to protect her family. It was a wild idea, and Ian would probably never agree to it, nor would this man of God. But she had to try—it might be her only hope.

She tested the words inside her mind, but they wouldn't come out. Instead, she changed the subject. "Ian is teaching us to read," she said, aware of the defensiveness in her tone. "And he works hard."

"He's a teacher?" New interest—even excitement—touched the minister's voice.

She shook her head. "He was a lord in Scotland, though he doesn't talk about it. He's very well read, and . . . well, yes, he is a good teacher. A wonderful one, in fact. Noel can already read sentences." And so could she, but she thought it might be bragging to say so.

The clergyman looked thoughtful, but remained silent.

"He's not a criminal," she added hurriedly. "He fought for his king." They were nearing the farm. She had to mention it now. "Reverend," she said. "If Ian Sutherland and I were to wed, it would stop the talk, wouldn't it?"

She expected an outburst, but it didn't come. After a moment he asked, "Has he suggested it?"

She felt red stain her face. She shook her head.

"Do you think he would agree?" Reverend Winfrey asked. "This . . . lord?"

Humiliation swept through her. She was so afraid Ian would not. But she had to see this through. She would lose everything if he was taken away from her now. He *had* to agree. Even though he had made it clear he wanted no attachments in this country.

"He might," she said tentatively, "if it were in name only, if he could annul it later." She watched the minister's face closely, but it had shuttered and she couldn't see what he was thinking. At least he hadn't said no. He hadn't told her she blasphemed.

But even if he did agree to do this thing, would Ian?

They rode in silence the rest of the way. When they arrived at the farm, he helped her down first, then the children.

"Where is your Scotsman?"

Sir Gray was gone from his paddock. "Riding, I imagine," she said. "He's readying Sir Gray for the races in Chestertown."

"Where are those papers you want me to witness?"

Fancy went to her room and pulled the indenture papers from under the feather mattress. Reverend Winfrey had seated himself at the table to wait for her. She handed him the battered parchment, and he read it over as she located the pen and ink.

"This is your signature?" he asked.

She nodded.

He scribbled his own signature and the date below her name.

"Thank you," she said, and he nodded, smiling.

She looked down at the papers in his hands, the precious papers that represented a man's freedom. It had hurt more than she wanted to admit that Ian thought she had betrayed him—and she knew that was exactly what he thought. She supposed he had just cause not to believe in anyone. But she so wanted him to believe in her. Maybe now—now that she had done as she promised—he would begin to trust her.

But would he trust her enough to marry her? Would he believe she would honor the arrangement and agree to an annulment after a year's time? Or would he suspect another trap?

Indeed, would he agree not to consummate the marriage?

She wondered how she could bear it herself. Whenever she saw him now she felt something clench inside her, something fierce and burning and needy. Yet it was the only way he could leave free and honorably. She already sensed how important that was to him.

Excusing herself, Fancy returned the papers to their hiding place, then went about making supper.

Ian cantered into the yard on Sir Gray, exhilarated by the progress the three-year-old was making. He would rub the horse down, then get something quick to eat before taking Gray Ghost out for his exercise. He came to an abrupt stop, however, when he saw the tall man in the ill-fitting black suit, sitting on a bale of hay in the barn.

Lucky ran to greet him as he dismounted, and he gave the dog a distracted pat, his gaze focused on the stranger.

But then, the man wasn't quite a stranger.

"Reverend," Ian said cautiously, remembering the face—and the clothing—from John Marsh's burial service.

The minister spoke as Ian led Sir Gray into his stall. "I don't believe we were introduced at Mr. Marsh's funeral, Mr. Sutherland. My name is Rufus Winfrey. Mrs. Marsh has been kind enough to invite me to supper. She wanted me to witness the signing of some papers."

Ian stopped cold, his hand reaching for the grooming brush. So Fancy hadn't lied to him. She'd had Reverend Winfrey witness her signature, just as she'd said she would. In that instant he realized that he'd never really believed she wouldn't, had known all along that she would not betray him. He'd used her lie to Sheriff Vaughn—a lie she'd told to protect him—as an excuse to distance himself from her and the feelings she evoked in him.

He didn't have to think for long to know why he had done such a thing: it was easier to convince himself that she was duplicitous than it was to live with the memory of the tender moment they'd shared, when he knew that moment was all there would ever be for them.

"Have you thought of marriage?"

The question, put matter-of-factly by the plain-spoken clergyman, shocked Ian to the quick. Turning slowly, he stared at the older man, who had come to stand at the corner of Sir Gray's stall.

"I see I've surprised you," Reverend Winfrey said.

Ian started to speak and, to his embarrassment, found he had to clear his throat first. "I assume you're speaking of Mrs. Marsh. 'Tis sacrilege. She just lost her husband."

Winfrey shrugged. "Widows often remarry swiftly on the frontier. 'Tis for their protection."

"I ha' no intention of marrying."

"She just gave you your freedom, man."

"And now you want to be taking it away?"

"She told me you agreed to stay a year."

"Aye, I did."

Reverend Winfrey raised one scraggly eyebrow. "Robert Marsh is already spreading a rumor that you have an unhealthy influence over her and that there might well be something indecent going on between you." Pausing, he added, "She was shunned at the meeting today."

Ian swore under his breath.

"Marsh intends mischief. A marriage would nip it in the bud."

"No." Ian snatched up the grooming brush and applied it to Sir Gray's sweaty coat. "I plan to return to Scotland."

"In a year?"

"How ca' you encourage a marriage without love?"

"Is there liking between you?"

The brush strokes grew more vehement.

"Marriages are made on a lot less, Mr. Sutherland."

And more vehement still.

"Robert Marsh will make good his threat. He will ruin her."

Ian whirled on him. "I willna do it."

Reverend Winfrey smiled. It was, Ian thought, a sly smile. He didn't trust it.

Gesturing broadly, Ian nearly shouted, "She *canna* be expecting me to—"

"She does not," the minister said. "*I* think it is a solution."

"Hmph." Turning back to the horse, Ian went on with the grooming. "'Tis a bloody bad idea," he growled.

A moment of silence passed before the minister

spoke again. "If the marriage is not consummated, it can be annulled."

Ian turned his head and stared at the man. The clear blue eyes didn't waver. "You are daft."

Mr. Winfrey spread his hands in a palms-up gesture. "It could solve both your problems. A marriage would protect both of you, legally and otherwise, from outside interference by anyone, including Robert Marsh."

"Nay," Ian said. And again, louder: "Nay. 'Tis a price I'm not willing to pay."

"Not even for Mrs. Marsh and her family?"

"*Damn* you!"

Throwing the brush to the floor, Ian stomped out of the stall and began to pace, his long, angry strides taking him to the far end of the small barn and back again. The Reverend Rufus Winfrey was no man of God. He was a devil, sent by Lucifer himself. And he knew exactly where to stick the knife and how to turn it. Already Ian could feel the guilt twisting inside him, eating away at his resolve.

How could he refuse to consider what the minister was suggesting? How could he refuse to help the woman who, with the signing of her name, had single-handedly thwarted the Crown's plan for his punishment and—they no doubt thought—his ultimate demise? She had given him back his freedom.

Coming to a halt a yard or two from the minister, who still stood calmly by Sir Gray's stall, Ian met the man's direct gaze. "She would never agree to it," he said.

A small smile played on Reverend Winfrey's lips. "Perhaps not."

Ian swallowed past the lump in his throat. He was a Catholic; marriage was forever. But an unconsummated marriage could be annulled. Exactly how much did he owe Fancy Marsh?

A year. Only a year.

But would a marriage certificate turn that year into two years . . . or three?

It didn't matter. She would never agree to marry a penniless convict, anyway. Why would she when, if he could get the farm going, she would have her choice of suitors?

Somehow *that* idea did not please him at all.

"I'll think about it," he said. "But I'll not be doing the asking."

The minister's expression brightened, but Ian gave the man credit for having the sense not to gloat outright.

"I'll talk to her," Winfrey said as he began walking—calmly and with a studied lack of haste—toward the door.

"She'll say nay," Ian warned.

Reverend Winfrey tossed a final word over his shoulder as he exited the barn. "Perhaps," he said.

And perhaps not, Ian thought. And then what would he do?

Scowling, he retrieved the grooming brush and got on with his work.

Chapter 14

The Reverend Rufus Winfrey murmured a prayer before he entered the farmhouse. He knew he would have to have a very long conversation with his Maker later this night, but now was not the time for lengthy soul-searching. At the moment he could only hope that Fancy's quiet, uncertain proposal had been God speaking through her.

He wasn't sure it was proper, using God's sacraments as an instrument of convenience. But then, he had been chided many times for his liberal interpretation of God's will.

Besides, he'd liked the Scotsman immediately, having recognized the man's rock-solid integrity under the bitter surface. He discounted entirely the label of convict. The Scotsman's crime, after all, was no crime to many; he'd fought for a cause he considered right: his country. One man's traitor was another man's hero.

The children obviously looked up to the Scot. And most important of all, Fancy Marsh's eyes sparkled noticeably when she spoke her bondsman's—her *former* bondsman's—name. Ian, she called him.

Yes, indeed, the minister thought, if he were a gambling man, he would wager his prayer book that an annulment would prove unnecessary.

Still, did he have the right to condone such a marriage? He wasn't sure. Yet the idea seemed so *fitting*. Noel and Amy needed a father. Fancy needed a husband. And they all, including Ian Sutherland, needed a sturdy defense against Robert Marsh. Rufus knew how dangerous Marsh could be. He was a man without conscience.

With every step he took, Rufus felt Fancy's idea, which he had now taken on as his own, grow in righteousness. He'd halfway convinced the Scotsman. He'd nudged the truth a bit by claiming the proposal was his idea. But indeed he *did* think it was a solution to both Ian's and Fancy's problems, and it was better, he thought, for Ian Sutherland to believe the idea came from a third party.

He prayed again that his deviousness would not offend the Lord.

Sniffing the delicious aromas wafting from the open doorway of the house, Rufus stepped inside. An instant later he felt a whoosh of air passing his shoulder and, with a gasp of surprise, saw a huge black crow settle on Fortune's shoulder as she was preparing the table. She gently nudged it away, and it cawed loudly, then took a flying hop to perch on the back of a chair.

"That's Trouble," Fancy said, crossing the room to set down a large covered bowl. "She thinks she's a member of the family."

"She is," Noel interrupted from his seat on the floor in front of the hearth. "And so are Lucky and Unsatisfactory," he added with a grin.

"I know Lucky," Rufus said. "Now, who is Unsatisfactory?"

"You are about to sit on him," Noel said.

Rufus whirled to look at what had been an unoccupied seat only a few seconds earlier. A calico cat sat there, languidly waving its tail and acting as if it had been there all along.

Rufus moved to another chair, and Unsatisfactory was there, too.

"It's a game he plays," Noel explained as he came to pick up the cat.

"I see," Rufus said, though he didn't see at all. Why would the Marshes keep a cat they felt compelled to name Unsatisfactory?

Amy was seated at the table already, her arms crossed in front of her on the tabletop and her chin resting on them. "Unsat'sfact'ry likes mice," she said, staring at him.

"But not to catch," Fancy added, her tone warm with amusement. "He's a peaceable cat."

The more he saw of the family Marsh, the more comfortable Rufus felt about his matchmaking role. He'd watched the Scotsman with the horse; though the man had been in an obvious state of agitation, he'd treated the animal with affection as well as authority. In those few moments, Rufus felt he had measured the essence of the man. There was pride and integrity in him, but also gentleness. He would fit perfectly into this family.

The only question remaining in Rufus's mind was how he could get Ian Sutherland to see what, to him, was as clear as the light of day.

"Mrs. Marsh," he said, "may I speak to you alone?"

She looked at him nervously, knowing that he had talked to the Scotsman. The question shone bright and clear in her eyes. She glanced toward Fortune. "Will you finish for me?"

Fortune nodded and went to the fireplace, where a Dutch oven was emitting a wonderful aroma.

Rufus stood aside for Fancy to precede him through the open doorway, waited—unrattled this time—while the crow flew out as well, then followed in the crow's wake.

Fancy sat on the top step of the porch, next to a rosebush, and he did the same. Her hands entangled themselves in her apron. "I'm sorry, Reverend Winfrey," she said. "I should never have suggested . . ."

"No, my child," he said. "I think it is a splendid idea."

She stared at him blankly, and he realized she had taken his earlier silence as disapproval. "You do?"

"Yes, indeed." He didn't add that he already felt these two people had qualities that made them an excellent match and that he doubted very much there would ever be an annulment.

"You spoke to him?"

"Aye. He did not say no."

"And he did not say aye," she said, but the smallest pinprick of hope glimmered in her eyes. Her dry tone held amusement as she mimicked the Scotsman's "aye." She knew him well. That was good.

"I let him believe it my idea," Reverend Winfrey said. "He does not believe you will consent to it."

Her golden brown eyes grew large, and it came to him that she never thought the plan had any hope of success. Now that it did, he saw pain—and grief—fill her eyes. He realized then how much courage it had taken for her to make the proposal, how much love for her children and for what her husband had tried to build. He could almost feel the agony burning within her. "He is right. I should never have mentioned it. I just buried my husband."

"I know. And I know, too, that you loved your husband. But many women in the colonies are faced with your problem and they solve it by remarrying quickly. You know this is true." He gave her a wise look. "Farming is a hard life, Mrs. Marsh. You need a man."

She frowned, her gaze darting to the barn, then back to meet his. "He doesn't care for me. And I don't love him."

"Did you love John when you married him?"

She hesitated long enough to make an answer unnecessary.

"Many couples come together for reasons other than love, and they find happiness." He hesitated a moment, then continued to crush the last of her doubts. "A marriage would protect both you and Mr. Sutherland, and it would quiet the talk that your brother-in-law has started."

"Protect both of us?"

"A marriage would protect him, too," he said gently. "No one could say he forced you to sign the papers freeing him."

Her face paled as she considered his words. Then she said, "You really think it would not be . . . disrespectful to John?"

"I think John would want you to be protected. Is that not why he bought the Scotsman?" He paused. "I see two people who can help each other, and there is nothing wrong or sinful in aiding a fellow human being."

She was silent for a moment, then said cautiously. "My property would become his property."

Rufus smiled to himself. He had feared she might have second thoughts about the proposal, as well she should. She should be sure. But now, after talking to both of them, he truly felt this marriage was the right thing.

Treading carefully, he said, "We could draw up papers that would protect your holdings. But I do not believe, in my heart, that Ian Sutherland is a man who would take advantage of a woman."

Her expression told him that she didn't think so either. Still, she shook her head again and repeated her previous statement. "You said he did not agree."

"I think he will. For you and the children."

She met his look with a troubled gaze. She caught her bottom lip between her teeth and worried it for a moment or two. Finally she heaved a sigh. "If he agrees . . ." Her voice trailed off.

What was she thinking? It was daft. Marriage was a holy thing. Not something to be undertaken because it was the most expedient way to solve a problem.

Why had she ever mentioned it?

What would John think?

Fancy shuddered. How *could* she marry Ian Sutherland? She still felt John's presence in the house. Dear Lord, the bed still smelled of him. How could she even consider allowing another man to take his place?

And yet . . .

John himself had brought Ian Sutherland to their home. He'd sat at the table and looked at her and said that he hoped the Scotsman would become part of their family. A shiver raced up her spine at the notion that John might have known he was going to die, not six months or a year from that fateful day but very, very soon.

She served the food to Reverend Winfrey, Ian, and her family. Troubled, she wanted to run and hide when she saw Ian's gaze following her. His expression was unreadable. Could Reverend Winfrey be right? Would Ian be willing?

The very idea sent her into a panic, putting knots in her stomach that made it impossible to eat. But she had set this in motion herself, and she had to remember why.

She toyed with her food, watching as the stew disappeared, then the bread and vegetables and, finally, the pie. Thank God, the children chattered with the minister throughout the meal; otherwise, there wouldn't have been a sound in the room.

When the meal was over and there was no more avoiding the subject, Fancy spoke quietly to her sister.

"Fortune, would you please take the children outside to play?"

Fortune looked at her, then at Ian, then at Reverend Winfrey. Her eyes darkened, and for a moment Fancy saw an unaccustomed flash of rebelliousness in her gaze. But she took Amy's hand and led her outside.

Noel gave them all a puzzled look, then followed Fancy, with the cat in tow. Lucky had come in with Ian, but even the dog seemed to sense that he should leave.

Reverend Winfrey rose from his chair, hesitated a moment, then said, "I think this is something you two should discuss. Alone." And he disappeared through the door with the restless dog at his heels.

Hands folded tightly in front of her, Fancy stared at the table. She couldn't bear to look at Ian.

It was he who finally broke the awkward silence. "Mrs. Marsh, the minister has proposed a devil's bargain. I agreed to stay a year. He believes the only way to do that is if we . . . wed."

No hint of tenderness in his words, no sign that he thought a marriage with her would be anything more than what he had called it: a devil's bargain. He had never even called her by her first name. To him she was just "Mrs. Marsh." It sounded so cold. So foreign.

Could she hand her life, and the lives of her children and her sister, over to this man about whom she knew so little? Married women had almost no power in the colony. No matter how Reverend Winfrey tried to protect her, she would be dependent on Ian's Scottish honor.

Honor. Lord knows, she'd seen the worst and best of men. She'd trusted a man who had betrayed her and her sister. Then she'd handed her trust to John, who had never failed her.

Fancy raised her gaze to look at Ian, sitting across

from her. His emerald-green eyes were cool, watchful, neither encouraging nor discouraging. His dark brows were arched in question, but his face gave nothing away.

Could she trust him? With everything? The children, the farm—her heart?

Reverend Winfrey obviously did. So did Noel and Amy . . . and Fortune. Lord above, the *dog* trusted him. So why shouldn't she?

Still holding his gaze, she asked a question to which she absolutely had to have an answer before going forward. "There's . . . no one in Scotland?"

"A wife, you mean?" he said sardonically. "I would not commit bigamy, Mrs. Marsh."

She bit her lip in embarrassment. "No, I meant . . . Well, I wouldn't want you to . . . to do anything that might hurt someone you cared about."

A glitter passed across the calm, cool surface of his eyes. "Why should it matter to you? You would be getting what you wanted."

The room was suddenly cold. He was striking out at her, and she didn't know why. Had she somehow inflicted pain upon him?

Fancy rose, trying to retain a shred of dignity. "It was a poor idea. I'll tell Reverend Winfrey."

Ian's chair scraped the floor as he rose and came around the table to catch her hand, stopping her. He pulled her to him roughly, but his fingers, when they touched her face, were gentle. Hot green flames darkened his eyes and made them appear dangerous.

"A marriage in name only," he said, "is not an appealing prospect."

She felt her body tremble. She knew he could feel it, too, for a moment's satisfaction reflected in his eyes. For some inexplicable reason, he wanted her to fear him. But she didn't fear him. She feared her body's reaction to him, the irresistible pull between them.

"Nay, 'tis not appealing at all," he said.

She tried unsuccessfully to pull away. "I do not like games," she said, her own wrath starting to rise.

" 'Tis no game we are playin'," he said. "I ask in dead earnest—do you truly think we can live together as husband and wife *in name only*?" His emphasis on those last words made the blood pound throughout her body.

His eyes glowed with a fierce, hungry heat, and his lips came down on hers. The kiss was angry and needy, and she felt its power to the marrow of her bones. Then, slowly, as she responded to his passion, she began to understand his anger, came to see what he was trying to show her. He felt as trapped as she did.

How could they possibly put on a charade of marriage? How could they share the intimacy of a house? How, and not destroy themselves?

Their bodies sought each other, hungered for each other, desired each other. The pull was so strong she couldn't tear herself away even though she knew everything depended on her having the strength to do so.

His lips ravished hers; then his tongue invaded her mouth. She knew she should deny him such liberties, but she could not. Dear God, he was awakening needs inside her that she hadn't even known existed.

In the end, it was Ian who tore himself away. His face was a study in pain, his breathing ragged, and tension radiated from his body. "I am a Catholic, Mrs. Marsh," he said, "and while my ancestors have shifted from one religion to another, I canna. Scots are fine at fighting, but too often lacking in principle. They find it easy to compromise with the winning side. I canna do that. I gi' my oath, and I will die wi' it."

His burr thickened, and it resonated inside her as he

continued. "I vowed to find my sister," he said. "And then I vowed to help you for a year. If the only way I can do that is to marry you, I will do it. Bu' I will abide by the terms of the agreement. I willna lie wi' you. And tha' will be hell on earth, because I want you. I would be lyin' to say otherwise."

Fancy swallowed hard. A great hungry craving had settled in the pit of her stomach. She had never known such wretched need.

A marriage of convenience? The notion was almost laughable. It seemed to her this was going to be a marriage of great *in*convenience. And how she would live through it she didn't know.

Yet she held his gaze, and when he asked sharply, "Do you agree?" she gave him a wordless nod.

" 'Tis done, then," he said. Then, abruptly, he went to the door and opened it.

Reverend Winfrey was sitting on the porch, watching Amy and Noel trying to summon the crow from Fortune's shoulder. They were holding out pieces of corn, but the crow didn't move until Fortune placed her fingers near the bird's feet. It hopped onto them, then flew to Noel and daintily pecked at the corn.

"It's amazing," Reverend Winfrey said.

Coming through the doorway to stand behind him, Fancy said, "She used to fly to John in the fields and let him know when supper was ready." When the minister looked up at her in disbelief, she added, "Trouble likes men, so we decided she must be a female. In another week she'll be fetching Ian."

Ian. She had said the name with such ease. Her gaze darted toward him. His jaw was set, his gaze hard. It was as if he were being led toward an execution rather than a marriage.

But he was the one who stepped forward and spoke

to the minister. "I've asked Mrs.—I've asked Fancy to be my wife, and she has accepted."

A broad smile spread across Reverend Winfrey's homely countenance. "We will need a witness. Two, if possible."

Fancy thought a moment. "The Wallaces?"

Reverend Winfrey nodded. "A fine choice."

Ian stepped off the porch. "How do I get there?"

"Noel can show you," she said, then beckoned to her son.

Noel came over to the porch. "What, Mama?"

Fancy knew she had to tell her family, had to explain the unexplainable. How did she tell a boy who had just lost a father that he was getting a new one—and yet he wasn't? Should she tell him it would be for a year only? Would he grow too attached to Ian otherwise? Would he anyway? Her son's eyes already glowed when he looked at the Scotsman.

She looked helplessly at Reverend Winfrey for guidance, but he looked as much at a loss as she was. Sighing, she stepped off the porch and gathered Amy and Noel and Fortune together in a small circle.

"I'm going to marry Mr. Sutherland," she said.

"I like him," Amy offered instantly.

Noel frowned. "Is he gonna be our papa?"

"Not exactly," she said slowly. "He's going to help us for a while, but then he will have to go back to Scotland."

Noel looked confused. So did Fortune.

She tried again. "People don't approve if an unmarried man and unmarried woman are . . . together without another adult. So Ian and I will get married, but everything will stay the same as it is now."

"Will he move into your room?" Noel asked with innocent curiosity.

Fancy had not thought that one through. In truth,

she hadn't thought anything through. "No," she said. "He will continue to live in the barn."

Fortune didn't say anything, but Fancy knew she often understood far more than was obvious.

"Fortune?"

"Fortune likes him, too," Amy said helpfully.

Fancy kept her gaze on her sister, waiting for a response. Fortune took her hand and gave it a quick, gentle squeeze. It was a simple gesture of support.

Fancy clasped her sister's hand tightly. "You understand, don't you?"

Fortune nodded.

Fortune might, but Fancy knew that neither of the younger children did. Not really. She dropped to her knees and looked Noel directly in the eyes. "You understand that Ian will stay for only one year."

Noel nodded.

"You have to pretend that he really is your new father," she said, relieved that she didn't have to explain this to Amy, as well. Her daughter, at three, wouldn't have to pretend anything; she would simply assume that Ian was with them for good, until he wasn't there any longer.

Noel's chin drooped slightly at this, however, and Fancy knew he was thinking of John, and whether he was being disloyal. She knew it because she felt the same way.

"Papa wanted Ian to stay and help take care of the farm," she said gently.

"I know," Noel said.

"Can you show him how to get to the Wallaces'?"

Noel nodded, his eyes still full of confusion.

"And you won't tell Mr. Wallace and Little Tim what we just talked about?"

He shook his head.

She drew him to her and held him for a moment. He

was so dear to her. So young and yet, in many ways, far older than his years. She wasn't sure she really wanted him to understand everything she'd just told him. She didn't want him to be deceitful or to think his mother capable of lies. Of such a big lie.

"You go now," she said.

He hesitated, then went toward Ian, and together they headed for the barn. Noel was already imitating Ian's walk. Before long, he would be saying nay and aye. Fancy wondered whether he'd truly absorbed the fact that Ian would be with them for only a year.

To a boy, a year was forever. To her, it was tomorrow.

She had heard the words before. She had said them before, when she was a frightened fifteen-year-old. Now she was saying them again in the same monotone in which she'd spoken them the first time.

She had not loved then, nor did she now. Emptiness filled her as she thought of another marriage undertaken for reasons other than love.

Her eyes moved to the Wallaces, father and son, standing in the corner of the large room, wide grins on their faces. They didn't know the truth.

But she did, and she feared that what she was doing was an offense to God.

Glancing briefly at Ian, standing rigid beside her, she wondered if he thought so too. She only hoped the Lord would understand the desperation of her need. Their need.

"If any man can show just cause why they may not lawfully be joined together, let him now speak, or else hereafter forever hold his peace."

She half expected Robert to jump out from behind a wall, or even that lightning might strike them all, but there was only a flat, empty silence.

Reverend Winfrey turned to Ian. "Wilt thou have this woman to thy wedded wife, to live together after God's ordinance in the holy estate of matrimony? Wilt thou love her, comfort her, honor and keep her in sickness and in health and, forsaking all others, keep thee only unto her, so long as ye both shall live?"

A muscle moved in Ian's cheek, but after a second's hesitation, he replied firmly enough. "Aye."

She whispered her assent to the same question when it was posed to her, and Ian looked down at her, his green eyes unreadable and his lips in a thin tight line. She sensed that he wanted to bolt from the room, and only massive self-control was keeping him there.

Reverend Winfrey bent his head in prayer, and his words burned into her: "Send thy blessing upon these thy servants . . . that they, living faithfully together, may surely perform and keep the vow and covenant betwixt them and may ever remain in perfect love and peace together." And finally: "Those whom God hath joined together let no man put asunder. . . . Forasmuch as Ian and Fancy have consented together in holy wedlock . . . I pronounce that they are man and wife, in the Name of the Father, and of the Son, and of the Holy Ghost."

It was over, this mockery of a ceremony, and she breathed more freely. Only then did she realize that her hands, clasped in front of her, were pinched white.

"You may kiss the bride," Reverend Winfrey said, and Fancy had a sudden, unholy urge to kick him. He knew this was to be an arrangement in name only, yet when she looked at him she saw a twinkle in his eyes and a smile on his lips that could be called nothing if not mischievous.

Ian leaned down and kissed her—a light, quick kiss, yet she felt it burning down to her soul. Then he stood tall and accepted congratulations from the Wallaces, a

grown-up handshake from her son, and a hug from
Amy. Fortune held back, her gaze filled with uncertainty.

The younger Wallace moved closer to Fortune,
placing his body between her and the rest of them as if
trying to protect her from some unknown but sensed
trouble. Fortune didn't try to slip away from him, and
Fancy relaxed.

Big Tim did not seem to notice the tension and
stalked over, stretching out his hand to Ian. "You got a
good woman here," he said.

Ian nodded. "Thank you for coming."

" 'Tis a pleasure knowin' that Miz . . . Sutherland
is in good hands. My Timmy thinks a lot of you."

"He's a good worker."

"Aye," Big Tim said with a smile. Then, with a
glance at Little Tim and Fortune, he added, "And I'm
thinkin' there's another reason he wants to be here."

Fancy stood as if rooted to the floor. She almost felt
like an interloper. Wallace obviously liked Ian—they
were countrymen, after all. He'd entered the house
with all the energy of a howling wind thirty minutes
earlier. And here he was now, grinning at them, clearly
unaware that their marriage was a sham.

"I've brought a spot of cheer with me," Wallace
said. "For luck."

Reverend Winfrey beamed.

Ian allowed a small, contained smile.

Mildly relieved to have something to do, Fancy went
to get some cups. A celebration for an event that deserved none. And yet the Wallaces could not know the
truth of it. They wouldn't intentionally hurt her, but
something might slip out—an offhand comment to a
friend in Chestertown, perhaps—that would make its
way back to Robert. And he would use whatever information he gleaned against them.

Fancy handed each of the men a cup and kept one for herself. Big Tim poured a healthy measure of rum into each, a smaller one for her.

"May your home be filled with laughter, and may the wind always be at your back," Big Tim said.

The men drank long drafts while Fancy barely sipped hers.

When Reverend Winfrey had finished his rum, he took her hand, saying, "I must go. But I wish you all well, and I'll see you in two weeks at the meeting." He hesitated, then added, "It might be well to keep this quiet until I can file the marriage certificate on my return to Chestertown. No one can question it then."

"Thank you," she said softly.

Leading her away from the others, he lowered his voice. "Ian has signed a paper giving up any claim to your property." He patted her hand in an attempt at comfort. "Fancy, you've done what you must to protect your family. Try to be at peace with the decision. I'm sure John would have approved."

"I wish I believed that," she said.

He smiled sadly. "My dear, he may have known exactly what he was doing when he purchased that indenture. He told me himself that he was going to find someone who could take care of the farm *and* his family."

She swallowed and blinked back tears. "He couldn't have imagined this."

Reverend Winfrey hesitated. "God moves in mysterious ways."

God's ways might be mysterious, she thought, but they were also powerfully painful.

The minister gave her hand a final pat, then released it. "If you need me, my wife will know where to find me."

She nodded.

Minutes later he was gone. The Wallaces left shortly afterward.

While Ian went to feed the horses, Fancy fixed a late meal. Noel hovered around her skirts, chattering about the wedding, but Amy was unusually quiet and busied herself with the raccoon, who had padded inside after everyone else had left.

Fortune helped set the table, then unexpectedly came over to her and hugged her tightly. Also unexpected was the tear that wandered down her own face at her sister's uncommon gesture of affection. When Fortune leaned back to look at her, Fancy wiped the tear away and tried to smile.

Fortune pointed toward herself, and her eyes phrased the question. Fancy knew what she was asking. Had she married again to protect her?

"Not only for you," Fancy said. "For all of us."

Fortune hesitated and crossed her arms. *I love you.*

"I love you, too," she replied.

Fortune looked at her for another moment, then finished setting the table.

Fancy placed a fresh loaf of bread on a cutting board. It would be a simple supper, this wedding meal. Stew and bread. Ordinary food for such an extraordinary day.

But it was not the day that occupied her thoughts as she sliced the bread. It was the night—and all the things she and Ian would not be doing.

Chapter 15

Ian tried to eat, but with four pairs of eyes watching him, he found it impossible.

His wedding supper.

The food nearly choked him.

He recalled the grand banquet held at Brinaire when his brother Patrick had wed. The hall had fairly vibrated with the sounds of revelry, and every clansman in attendance had shared his family's joy.

But tension, not joy, permeated the air this night, and no one was laughing. Why should anyone be happy? Happiness for a marriage was built upon expectations for the future, and his marriage to Fancy had no future. After supper he would return to his own narrow bed, alone. Life would go on as before.

And there was no point in delaying it.

Ian pushed away from the table, preparing to take leave of his new family. But before he could rise, Amy hopped down from her chair and up into his lap.

"Are you my daddy now?" she asked.

Noel focused on him intently, clearly interested in his answer.

Ian looked at Fancy, seated at the opposite end of the table, but she appeared to be as much at a loss as he was.

He sighed deeply and gave Amy a smile. "No' exactly, lass," he said. "But I like ye very, very much."

Apparently satisfied, she snuggled against him.

"Will you teach us tonight?" Noel asked.

Why not? This night was no different from any other.

And yet deep in his gut Ian knew it *was* different. Something subtle had changed between Fancy and him. The attraction between them, always strong, had reached the breaking point, like a string pulled taut at both ends. A few words had changed everything. A few words, and a kiss.

He wanted her. He wanted to run his fingers over her cheek. He wanted to kiss those lips, and he wanted to bury himself in her. He wanted to know that peace she seemed to carry within her, to savor her gentleness, to share the steadiness that was her courage. He'd never wanted any woman so badly in his life. And now both the church and the law had sanctioned their union. All that kept them apart was the oath he'd taken that would force him to be gone at the end of the year.

Never, he knew, would an oath be so tested.

But he must not fail. As he felt Amy's chubby, trusting arms around him, he was aware of how much damage he could do to this family. He could not let the children look upon him as another father. Better to be someone they could easily forget.

Yet even as he gently put Amy down and watched her toddle over to climb into Fortune's lap, Ian knew that forgetting was already impossible. He would never forget these people, nor would they forget him.

Rising from his chair, he fetched the slates and reader. But as he turned back to the table, he caught Fancy's gaze and saw tears hovering in her eyes as she looked at him. Aye, she knew what he was thinking, understood exactly how difficult this was for him. It was the same for her. Her tears were for herself as much as for him, and he wanted to flee before they etched themselves into his heart for all time.

Noel picked up the reader and started haltingly to

sound out words. Ian battled against the pride he felt in Fancy's and Noel's, and even Fortune's, progress. He tried to be detached, tried to make himself an outsider.

All the while, in his heart, he knew he was failing. Miserably.

The next few days passed in a whirl. It seemed that Ian never stopped working. He refused to eat supper with the family, choosing instead to eat alone in the stable, although he appeared each night for their reading lesson.

Fancy felt his simmering impatience, his reluctance to spend one moment more with her than necessary. It hurt, even though she understood. She understood because she ached every time he was near her. She understood because the yearning inside her, the same yearning she saw flare in his eyes when he looked at her, was growing stronger by the day, the hour . . . the minute.

She had not heard from Robert, which she assumed meant that he had not yet learned of her marriage. As soon as it was registered with the county, she knew she could expect the full force of Robert's considerable rage. The mere prospect sent shivers up and down her spine.

Noel came running in, his face flushed with excitement.

"You should see Sir Gray," he said, grabbing her hand. "He's the fastest horse I've ever seen. Come on."

Fancy's heart sang at the happiness on his face. There had been so little since John had died. He'd been too serious, had taken too much onto his slender shoulders.

She thought of the loaves of bread in the oven built within the fireplace—they needed another twenty minutes at least—and allowed her son to pull her out the door, Amy following behind, a thumb in her mouth.

Fortune was sitting on the fence, watching as Ian raced Sir Gray around inside the paddock. Resting against the fence a few feet from her sister, Fancy watched as Ian leaned over the neck of the colt, his body in perfect rhythm with the horse as its hooves pounded the ground. They were incredibly handsome together, the large gray colt and the lean, controlled Scotsman.

Ian. She thought of him that way now. He was, after all, her husband. That thought combined with the sight of him, so bold and strong as he rode, sent new waves of heat through her. Faster and faster he urged the horse, though he used neither quirt nor whip and she saw no obvious signals. Only a master horseman, John had once told her, could develop that special intuitive communication between himself and a good mount.

Ian, Fancy realized, was such a horseman. And her body was trembling with the heat of arousal at the power and beauty she saw.

The horse slowed to a trot when Ian straightened in the saddle. Catching sight of his audience, he rode over to where they all stood watching. But he looked only at Fancy.

He ran a hand down the horse's neck and spoke with pride coloring his tone. "He's rare."

She nodded, thinking she could say the same of him. "Will he be ready to race this fall?"

"Aye," Ian said, "and then some. He's a foine braw lad."

She couldn't turn her eyes away from him. Sweat glistened on his face and drenched his thick, short hair, causing it to curl slightly. He was wearing one of John's white shirts. It was too small and stretched tightly across his shoulders; damp from his exertion, the material clung to his body, outlining every muscle. Though he was still too thin, the hard labor of planting the tobacco, working the fields, and training the horses had carved intriguing lines in his body.

Her heart continued its painful contractions as he dismounted and came to stand in front of her with only the fence between them. He smelled of leather and soap and sweat, and she found the combination intoxicating.

"He can win any race," he said, his eyes glittering with victory, an appealing smile curving his lips.

"He runs well for you," she said, unable to keep the breathlessness from her voice.

She didn't want to lose the moment, the excitement she felt simmering inside her. She wanted to reach out and touch him, to throw her arms around him and kiss him. She wanted to share his triumph.

Instead, she tried a small smile. "I think this deserves an outing."

He cocked an eyebrow.

"A picnic," she explained. "There's a beach we like to go to on special occasions." Actually, they'd only been there twice, and the special occasions had been the outings themselves.

"Can we?" Noel said. Then he gave Ian a hopeful look. "Maybe we can go fishing."

"Are you a fisherman?" Ian asked.

"Pa took me once, before he got sick. But we've still got the poles and the hooks."

The one time John had taken Noel fishing had been two years ago, Fancy thought with an ache. John simply hadn't had the energy to do anything except what had to be done; even before his illness began, he'd never enjoyed such luxuries as picnics. He'd never known how to relax, how to be satisfied doing nothing of import.

"Ian?" she asked.

"There's work to be done."

"You've done nothing but work since you set foot on this farm."

"I thought that was why I was brought here."

The remark hurt, and she wondered whether it was meant as a reminder to her—or to himself. As the light faded from his eyes, she saw the prospects for a special day together grow dim. When his jaw took on that stubborn angle she'd come to recognize, she was sure his answer was going to be an uncompromising nay.

For once Amy picked the right moment to intervene. Reaching for Ian's hand and looking straight up at him, she said, *"Pleeease,"* in her most appealing fashion.

"Bloody hell," Fancy heard him mutter.

"Is that an aye?" she asked, imitating the word he didn't use often enough.

His eyes glittered with amusement for a second. Then he heaved a sigh. "Aye, I suppose it is. I have to cool Sir Gray first, though, then rub him down."

"I'll help you," Noel said eagerly.

"Me too," chimed Amy, who knew very well that she wasn't allowed near the horses.

"You can help *me*, sweet pea," Fancy said, and, taking her daughter's hand from Ian's, she led the skipping child toward the house.

She felt a little like skipping herself. Silently she prayed: Please, God, don't let this be a disaster.

Sitting beside Ian on the wagon seat, Fancy gave him directions that took them west, across Tuckahoe Creek, toward the Chesapeake.

Behind her, Noel and Amy bounced with excitement, and, though she was as quiet as always, even Fortune was smiling. Lucky was hanging over the side of the wagon, his tongue lolling out of his mouth and his tail in perpetual motion. Meanwhile, Trouble, who would not be left behind, perched—a little nervously—on the back of the wagon seat.

The picnic basket was packed with sliced ham, fresh bread, cider, and the first ripe peaches of the season. The day was hot, but not unbearably so, and the sky was a cloudless blue.

All the right ingredients, Fancy thought, for what she hoped would be a grand day for all of them.

She couldn't help but notice that Ian had washed and changed his shirt. She had changed, too, though only into another plain dark dress; after all, despite her remarriage, she was still in mourning. She was glad, though, that she'd given in to the moment of rebellion that had made her free her hair from its tight knot and tie it back loosely with a blue ribbon. That simple act alone made her feel young again.

As they got closer to the Chesapeake, gulls circled and shrieked overhead, and the woods thinned. Fancy had to pay close attention to the road, looking for the spot where the ruts made by wagon wheels indicated their turnoff. Noel spotted it first, and at his direction, Ian turned the horses onto the narrow lane. When the ground became too sandy and the wagon too difficult for the horses to pull, he stopped.

The beach lay just ahead, visible through the tall loblolly pines and the low shrubs. Fancy could smell the salt in the air.

Lucky was first out of the wagon, taking off after a squirrel, surprisingly fast for a dog with only three legs. With a beat of his wings, Trouble flew off to perch in a wax myrtle bush, awaiting the moment when the food would be unpacked.

Noel scrambled over the side of the wagon and headed directly for the beach, while Ian jumped down to help Fortune and Amy. Fancy waited until he came around to stand in front of her.

When he reached for her, she leaned down to grasp his shoulders, and his hands spanned her waist. Those strong, worked-roughened hands lifted her easily and lowered her gently. Her body brushed against his, the contact causing her heart to skip a beat. With her feet safely on the ground, though, her fingers did not want to let go of his shoulders. Nor did his hands relinquish their hold on her waist.

Raising her gaze, she found his face only inches from hers. The same soft breeze that caressed her skin was ruffling the dark curls of his hair, and the warm sunshine seemed to wrap itself around them, for a moment blocking out the rest of the world. Standing there, so close, their gazes locked, she felt as if she were humming inside with the beauty of life.

He lowered his head an inch . . . two inches . . . and for an instant she was certain he was going to kiss her. She willed him to do it, to let them both have a taste of the desire that ran like a shifting river-current between them. When, instead, he released her and took a backward step, disappointment made her release a tiny sigh.

Ian lifted the picnic basket from the wagon and handed it to her. "Go on ahead. I'll bring the blankets when I've taken care of the horses."

"I'll wait for you," she said.

He shrugged. "Suit yourself."

She watched as he unhitched the team—two geldings that John had decided were never going to be fast but who had stamina to spare—and staked them within reach of a bucket of fresh water.

He joined her once more, and they walked together along the short, narrow path lined with bayberry and myrtle, to the beach. Low-growing salt-tolerant grasses soon gave way to an open stretch of sand perhaps fifteen or twenty feet wide.

The beach curved inward around a large cove, one of thousands of such inlets in the ragged shoreline of the Chesapeake. There, inside two long, narrow strips of land that jutted out into the bay, sandbars were visible as much as two hundred feet from shore, and the relatively protected waters looked inviting and warm. Beyond the headlands, sunlight glinted off whitecaps that rose from the deep, cold waters farther out.

Noting that the tide was out, Fancy asked Ian to set the basket far back from the water. Then she spread the blanket she had brought to sit on. They all removed their shoes, which were already filled with sand, and Fortune took Amy to look for shells. Ian joined Noel at the water's edge, where small waves broke onto the sand in an endless cycle of ebb and flow.

Fancy knelt on the blanket and sat back on her heels, watching her new husband with her son. They were both squatting, knees spread, examining a sand crab that Noel was holding. The scene was almost too painful to watch. It should have been John, talking with Noel, sharing his excitement, teaching him about this land that was their home. But she couldn't help being glad, for Noel's sake, that Ian Sutherland was willing to give him what he needed and deserved to have.

Fancy spent the morning indulging in the rare pleasure of unproductive activity. She built a sand castle with Fortune and Amy. She collected some pretty pieces of driftwood. She showed Noel and Amy how to dig for buried treasure, tying up her skirts, wading into the shallows, and burrowing with her toes in search of oysters, some of which, when cracked open, proved to harbor tiny pearls.

Later she merely rested on the blanket, content to watch the others. Fortune and Amy chased waves and added to their shell collection while Ian and Noel retrieved the long fishing poles they'd brought along, rolled up the legs of their trousers, and waded out a short distance to a sandbar "to catch supper," Noel announced optimistically.

She watched them, occasionally letting her eyes drift down the bank. At one point she saw something move in the stand of trees above them, and thought it might be someone else seeking fish on a sunny afternoon. But as she concentrated on the disturbance, the movement stopped. She thought she saw a face, but then the sun hit the trees in a dazzling rain of golden rays, and she lost sight of it. Who could possibly be up here? And why would anyone hide? She tried to tell herself it was her imagination, nothing more. Perhaps it was only a deer. Yet . . . she couldn't rid herself of the apprehension prickling the back of her neck.

She started to say something, then decided against it. She'd never seen Ian and Noel so content. She didn't want to spoil their pleasure now.

Sometime after midday, Fancy decided it truly had been her imagination. She'd seen no sign of another human being, and she pushed the nagging disquiet away. She opened the basket and unpacked the food, arranging the dishes on the blanket. That was the signal Trouble had been waiting for. With typical perfect timing, the crow landed beside her, looking for a handout, her beady black eyes scrutinizing every tidbit Fancy uncovered.

As a sudden thought occurred to her, Fancy studied the bird. Then, supposing she had nothing to lose by trying, she called to Ian, beckoning him to her with a wave, and he waded out onto the beach and came toward her.

"It's time to eat," she said. "But first I want to try something. Take this." She held a piece of bread out to him, and, though his expression was puzzled, he took it. "Now go stand over there by the fallen tree and put the bread on your shoulder."

"May I ask why?" he inquired.

"You'll see. I hope."

With a shrug, he complied with her strange request, standing by the loblolly pine that lay toppled onto the beach, roots to the sky and needles brushing the water's edge.

Fancy looked at Trouble, who, she knew, had been watching her exchange with Ian with great interest—particularly the part where she'd handed Ian the bread. "Trouble," she said, "go to Ian."

The crow cocked her head and looked at Fancy.

"Go to Ian," she repeated slowly, and pointed.

Cawing loudly, Trouble took off, circled a couple of times, then swooped down to land on Ian's shoulder. Instead of snatching the bread and flying off, though, the crow kept her perch and delicately pecked at the food.

Fancy grinned, both at her success and at the startled expression on Ian's face. He didn't jump, though, or make any loud sound that might startle his visitor.

After a few moments she called the crow back to her. Taking what remained of the bread with it, the crow returned and landed on the blanket beside her. She took the bread away and spoke again.

"Ian," she said. "Go to Ian."

Indignant at having its meal stolen, the crow eyed her for a moment or two.

"Ian," she insisted. Without the bread to tempt the bird, Fancy wasn't sure the trick would work. "Go to Ian," she repeated.

Trouble surprised her by taking off and flying directly to Ian's shoulder.

"Walk over to me," she said to the Scotsman.

"Slowly." As Ian neared the blanket, she held out the bread again. "Good bird," she said, offering the crow its prize.

Trouble accepted the offer, though this time the now wary bird took her treat and hopped onto the sand several yards away before she began to eat.

Ian dropped to his knees on the blanket beside her, astonishment etched into his features.

Fancy laughed. "Trouble used to go to John in the fields. The first time it happened, John was as shocked as you are now. Then we figured out that it was because John always carried an apple or a piece of bread with him."

" 'Tis an amazing thing, even so," Ian remarked. "I've seen many a hawk that was trained to hunt and fly back to its master, but I've never seen a bird behave like a pet."

"Trouble has been with us since she was a baby, when she fell out of the nest," Fancy said. "Fortune taught her to trust us. I can help heal critters when they're hurt, but my sister is the one they love."

"My sister was . . . is like that," he said quietly. "She had a pair of ferrets."

"Ferrets?"

He gave a brief, soft laugh. "Aye, they look like over-long mice. At least, I always teased her that they did." A light flickered briefly in his eyes, then was gone.

Fancy felt as if a light inside her had also been extinguished. Part of him, she realized, would always be across the ocean. Best to accept that once and for all. And foolish to be disappointed over and over again.

Sighing, Fancy asked Ian to fetch Noel while she finished setting out the meal.

They ate together on the blanket—after Fancy made them dust the sand off their feet. Lucky and Trouble, who were forbidden to set foot, or talon, on the blanket, hovered nearby, making sure they got their fair share.

Afterward, Amy fell asleep, covered with blackberry jam and clutching a smooth pink stone she'd found. Fancy spread another blanket a few yards back from the sunny part of the beach, in the shade of a stand of loblollies, and Ian carried the sleeping little girl to lie on her makeshift bed.

As he laid her gently upon the blanket, Fancy caught Ian's gaze lingering on her daughter. She saw a hunger in his green eyes, a hunger for home and family and all he had lost and feared he would never find again.

Because of her, she thought. How could he ever forgive her for keeping him here?

Unable to put aside her troubled thoughts, Fancy set about packing the remaining food into the basket. Fortune wandered off to explore the beach beyond the cove, and Noel stayed on the blanket, finishing his peach.

"Did you go fishing in Scotland?" he asked Ian.

"Aye," Ian replied. "My brothers and I used to catch salmon in the rivers."

"Will you fish some more now, with me?"

"Aye, I can do that. But you shouldna get your hopes up for catchin' anything at this time of day. The fish are most likely lying in deeper water, waiting for the water to cool before they come into the shallows again at dusk to catch their own supper."

Noel's face fell. "But we can *try*, can't we?"

"Aye, we can always try, lad. And mayhap we'll get lucky."

With a happy shout, Noel picked up his fishing pole, grabbed the pail of worms he'd brought along, and ran toward the water.

As Ian bent to retrieve his fishing pole, Fancy spoke quietly.

"Thank you," she said.

Straightening, he met her gaze and held it for a moment, then nodded. Then, without a word, he followed Noel out to the sandbar.

Finished with her task, Fancy lay on the blanket, propped up on her elbows, and watched them fish. Their backs were to her. Her son's tawny hair glinted in the sunshine, and his young body, usually in motion, was still for once. Copying Ian, she imagined.

She could scarcely believe how long Noel was willing to stay with the task at hand. Over and over he and Ian cast their lines out into the water, then slowly reeled them back in. She herself would not have had the patience, she was certain. Smiling, she thought it must have to do with that odd communion that seemed to form between males united in the pursuit of fish.

At about the time when Fancy was sure that even Noel would give up, she saw Ian lean toward him and point to the end of her son's fishing pole. A second later she saw the tip of the pole bend, bounce back up, then bend again—and stay bent.

Noel's first reaction was to be overcome with excitement, and he jumped up and down in the water. Then Ian spoke to him again, and the boy quieted and nodded his head.

Fancy sat up to watch the action. She expected to see Ian take over, or at least help Noel land his catch, but he didn't even put his hands on the pole. Rather, he encouraged the boy with a hand on his back and, from what she could see, a steady stream of words, all accompanied by animated gestures indicating how Noel should handle the fishing pole and the catch at the other end.

After several minutes of careful maneuvering, Ian

reached below the water in front of them and lifted the fish out by its gills. Their faces—the boy's and the man's—were alight with the joy of victory.

So was hers. It nearly made her cry, seeing her son so happy. Because of John's illness he'd been asked to grow up quickly, asked to take on chores more suited to someone twice his age. But he was still a little boy, and in the space of a few hours, Ian had helped him remember what it felt like to be one.

But this was a mistake. The whole day was a mistake. She knew it now as she hadn't known it when she'd so impulsively suggested the outing. She'd wanted to give Ian something special, something to remember, something to take his mind away from tortured thoughts of his sister and of the brothers he'd lost. And, too, she'd wanted all of them to have a day of rest and play. But she could see now, as the attachment between her son and Ian grew deeper before her very eyes, that the price they would pay for this day would be a heavy one.

Perhaps too heavy to bear.

"Look, Mama!" Noel came running up the beach with his fish, a yellow perch that Fancy estimated to be about two pounds. "Can we have it for supper?"

"I think it would make a wonderful supper," she replied.

"Especially if you catch another," Ian said from behind the boy.

"You get to catch the next one," Noel said generously.

"Nay, lad, you can do it by yourself now," Ian said. "I'm going to sit for a spell."

To Fancy's amazement, Noel didn't even look disappointed.

Carrying his precious fish, Noel ran to retrieve a bucket, which Amy had left at the sand castle construction site. Filling it with water and plopping the fish inside, he carefully set the bucket back from the rising tide before he splashed toward the sandbar, calling over his shoulder, "I bet I can catch an even bigger one!"

"Aye, I bet you will, too," Ian called.

Dropping to the blanket, he stretched out lazily on his back, one knee bent and the other leg lying flat, his eyes closed against the sunlight. Fancy sat perfectly still, no more than a foot away. She was afraid to speak, almost afraid to breathe, lest she disturb him. The lines of worry around his eyes had eased, and he looked content for the first time since she'd met him.

Letting her gaze drift over him, she took in the hard lines of the muscles in his arms and legs, stretching tight against the fabric of his clothing. His skin had darkened from laboring in the summer sunshine; conversely, the dark springy hair on his arms, beneath his rolled-up cuffs, was a shade lighter.

She wanted to touch him, to stretch out her fingers and touch that silky-looking hair on his arms, run them over the sharp planes of his face. Resisting for all she was worth, she clasped her hands together in her lap.

"Noel is a smart lad."

The sound of Ian's voice came as a small shock. She had thought he was asleep already.

"Y-yes," she replied. It was all she could manage.

"He has a fisherman's touch."

"Mmm."

His eyes remained closed, his expression relaxed. She could see that he was enjoying the sun on his face, and it made her think about all the months he must have spent in prison and in the hold of a ship, with no sunshine and not even a breath of fresh air. She wished he would open the lacings at the neck of his shirt a bit farther to capture more of the bright rays. And she couldn't believe how improper her thoughts were. Or were they? Was he not her husband?

When he opened his eyes, squinting against the sun, and glanced toward her, she looked away quickly, embarrassed to be caught staring.

"Tell me about your mother and father," he said.

It was the first time he'd ever asked her about herself, and for a second or two she was too stunned to answer.

"My . . . da?" she finally managed.

"Aye. And your mother."

"Well . . ." She took a steadying breath. "I don't remember my mother. I think I was little more than a year old when she died and my father brought me to the colonies with him."

Rolling to his side, Ian propped his head on his elbow. "Where did your father come from?"

She hesitated, afraid of his reaction.

"He came from England," she said, finally. "He was like you—the second son of a lord."

"That explains it, then," Ian said.

She glanced at him, puzzled. "Explains what?"

"Your speech," he replied. "You speak very well, like someone who has been tutored."

"I do?"

"Aye. Which is why I've been puzzled that you do not . . . or rather *did* not know how to read or to write even your name."

Aware of the bitterness in her voice, she murmured, "My father didn't believe women needed to know how to read or write. When I was young, I asked him to teach me, because I'd seen him read and write and I wanted to be able to do it, too. But he said, 'Girls do not need book learning. It corrupts them. Just like it corrupted your mother.'"

Ian frowned. "Do you know what he meant by that?"

Fancy stared at her fingers, laced together in her lap.

She'd never told anyone—not John, not even Fortune—nor did she want to tell anyone the answer to the question he'd asked. Yet must they remain virtual strangers for an entire year? If they could not share a bed, at least they ought to be able to share themselves and their lives.

Gathering her courage, she said, "Yes, I know what he meant. One night not long before my father died, he got very drunk. He drank quite often, but this particular night was very bad. He was crying, saying all sorts of things that didn't make sense at first. But then I understood. I learned a lot of things about him that night."

She drew a shaky breath. "My mother was the daughter of a noble family, and she'd had tutors and was well educated. My father loved her, I think, very much. He must have, or else I don't think he would have been so angry when he came home one night to . . . to find her in bed with his brother."

Ian muttered an oath, and she raised her gaze to meet his directly.

"He killed them both," she said. "He killed his brother and his wife—my mother. Then he took me and fled England."

"And the Crown did not track him to the colonies?"

She shook her head. "No, we never lived anywhere one might expect to find a nobleman. Father loathed any reminder of his background. We stayed away from cities and towns. He was a trapper, and we lived in the forests. When I was seven, he met Fortune's mother, and we went to live with her people."

"The Cherokee," Ian murmured.

"Yes. I learned a great deal about the land from them, about planting and hunting and healing. But I never learned to read, because my father believed that my mother had betrayed him because she'd been educated and made to feel that she deserved better than the second son of an earl."

Ian snorted softly. "Now, that's one I have not heard. Infidelity blamed on the ability to read and write."

"It was foolish," Fancy said. "But he'd convinced himself it was true. That night, when he got so drunk and started rambling, he said to me, 'You don't need to learn to read. You just learn to take care of a man. Be loyal to him. Be good to him.'" She shook her head. "He even changed my name because it was hers. I don't know whether it was to protect himself or whether he just despised it so."

He was silent for a moment, then asked, "Do you know what it was?"

"Eleanor. But all I ever remember being called is Fancy. I wouldn't even know it had been changed if he had not warned me once that if anyone should ever ask about an Eleanor I should deny it. I don't know whether he thought I might remember it, even as small as I was, or if he even realized I had been too young to remember." She shook her head slowly. "He was a very unhappy man."

"What happened to him?" Ian asked.

She sighed heavily. "The English attacked our village. Fortune's mother was killed, and Father was mortally wounded. He knew he was going to die, and so he sent us to his friend, another trapper, who promised him he'd take care of us."

"The man you told me about before?"

She nodded. "Father really wasn't a bad man. He did his best to take care of me and, later, of Fortune. But he trusted the wrong people."

"Mayhap that is why you learned to trust the right ones."

Startled, she looked at him.

But he had rolled onto his back once more. When he spoke, his words were slightly slurred and the burr was beginning to creep back into his speech. "Your da was no judge of men—or of women—so you learned to judge them to protect yourself. You knew John Marsh to be a trustworthy man. And you know that his brother is no'. And though I was bu' a stranger, and a convict, you knew I wouldna hurt you or your sister or your children."

Ian closed his eyes and let out a drowsy sigh. "You will ge' your wish, Fancy. You will learn how to read and write." Yawning hugely, he murmured, "Indeed, at the rate you and Noel are both learning, it willna be long before we will need to make another trip to Chestertown to buy a more difficult reader."

She smiled, blushing at the praise. "Thank you."

"Donna be thankin' me yet." He yawned again. "Wait until . . . until we start havin' . . . spelling tests and . . ." His voice trailed off into an unintelligible mumble.

For a long while, Fancy indulged herself in the pleasure—and the torture—of watching him sleep. She would have loved to lie down beside him, to put her head on his shoulder and feel his arm close around her and hold her. But she didn't dare.

Instead, she glanced around again, at the stand of trees where she'd thought she'd seen someone. There was no movement except the brush of wind against the leaves. Surely that was all she'd seen earlier.

And yet she couldn't rid herself of the feeling of being watched, of something . . . sinister waiting to pounce. Then she dismissed it as her own guilt pricking her. How could she be so content? *I haven't forgotten you, John. I'll never forget you.*

With bittersweet longing, she sat beside Ian, lost in her thoughts of the past . . . and the uncertain future.

Chapter 16

It was nearly dusk as Ian hurried the horses homeward. Noel was sitting in the back of the wagon, accompanying the three fish he'd caught. Amy was sound asleep next to Lucky, and Fancy, sitting beside Ian, was humming quietly to herself, a soft smile on her lips.

And he was . . . God, for the first time since Culloden he felt human. He was coming alive again in a way he once believed impossible. The simple act of watching pride cross a boy's face as he caught fish gave him pleasure. Or mayhap 'twas Amy, running up to him with her little hands full of shells and stones, saying, "Look, Ian, look at my treasurers!" Mayhap it was simply the sun and the water and the wide-open feeling of freedom and possibilities that this land inspired. Most likely, he thought, it was Fancy, who, in her quiet, persistent way, had made certain the day was a success for everyone.

Whatever the cause, he felt good and whole, and he was not going to dispute the matter. For this day, at least, he was putting guilt and grief aside.

As he drove the wagon, he kept his gaze averted from Fancy. He didn't need to look at her to see her, anyway. Her image danced in his mind: her hair blowing in the wind, soft laughter tumbling from her throat, her skirts billowing out as she ran barefoot through the foamy surf after her daughter.

The wagon hit a rut, Fancy's thigh pressed against his, and despite the layers of cloth separating them, he felt the familiar jolt of awareness. His gaze flickered involuntarily toward her, and for a moment he was captured by the glow in her rich brown gaze. Her cheeks were pink from the sun, and her hair was a tangle of long curls. He had to tamp down the sudden rush of possessiveness he felt, the overwhelming need to pull her to him and hold her and protect her and, God help him, love her.

She looked away first, her hand brushing his arm before falling naturally to his thigh. It slid away almost instantly, dropping to the wagon seat, but that split second of white-hot contact set his heart to pounding. For a moment he couldn't breathe, and he was powerless to stop the hardening of his body inside his trousers. He jerked his gaze back to the road ahead, flicking the reins and clicking his tongue to the horses, telling them to hurry.

The perch were delectable. And so were the oysters. Ian savored every morsel of the unfamiliar foods, wondering if the pleasure he now found in every meal, after months of near starvation, would last—or if he would eventually come to take food for granted again. He hoped he would not. Yet even without the incentive that involuntary fasting had given his appetite, he was certain he would have appreciated these new delicacies.

The others at the table seemed similarly impressed. Well, most of them. Fortune ate more than he'd ever seen her consume at one meal, and Noel glowed with pride over every mouthful of fish he ate. Amy, however, took two bites of her supper and promptly fell asleep again.

And Fancy . . . well, she ate a decent portion of Noel's fish and made enough sounds of approval to satisfy the lad, but Ian could see that she was having a difficult time getting through the supper. She was avoiding his glances, and her face was flushed from more than the sun. And he knew why.

When Noel pressed for a reading lesson, she shook her head. "We're all tired. And I think Ian deserves a respite tonight."

"Ah, Ma . . ."

"Ah, Ma . . ." She echoed his plaintive tone perfectly, patting the cowlick that sprouted from his head. "It's late, Noel Marsh, and time for bed."

Noel began another protest.

She raised one eyebrow sternly.

The lad sighed. Then, to Ian's surprise, Noel rose from his chair, came to stand beside him, and held out his hand. "Thank you for taking me fishing."

Ian took the lad's small hand in his and shook it. "You are welcome, lad," he said in a tone every bit as serious as Noel's. "Thank you for providing such a foine meal."

Noel hesitated a moment longer, then headed up to the loft.

Fortune gathered up the sleeping Amy and glided over to him to touch his sleeve and smile. Ian felt the power of that smile, for she gave it so rarely that it glowed like a priceless jewel. Before he could say anything, she disappeared into the room she shared with the little girl.

Which meant that Fancy and he were left at the table. Alone.

The fire was already fading, reduced to a pile of glowing embers. The night breeze, coming through the open windows, carried the scent of her wild-rose-and-honeysuckle fragrance to his nostrils.

He had to leave. Now. If he didn't, he would kiss her again. And this time he feared neither of them would end it. They would find themselves in bed together, their marriage would be consummated and irrevocable, and he would be committed to her as deeply and as surely as he was to anyone else, living or dead, on either side of the ocean.

And then what would he do? Cut himself in two equal parts, one to remain here while the other went in search of Katy?

Without a word, Ian rose and stalked out of the house.

He was too restless to sleep. Indeed, he was burning with the need for activity. One particular activity most of all. As that was not an option, he walked to the pasture fence and whistled.

Royalty came over to him, sniffing for a treat.

"Sorry," he said, stroking the stallion's neck. "I dinna bring you anything."

The stallion tossed his head, but seemed to forgive him, whinnying softly and butting his shoulder with his velvety nose.

He would go to the barn and get a saddle. A good ride would provide at least a partial distraction from his carnal thoughts. It was a good night for riding: as warm and soft as the day had been. A few wispy clouds drifted between the moon and stars, spinning a web of lace across the dark blue sky. . . .

When he felt her presence behind him, he stiffened, but he didn't turn. His hand continued its unconscious stroking of the stallion's neck as seconds ticked by in silence.

Finally he spoke in a low rumble. "You shouldn't be here."

Her voice, a mere whisper, came from close by. "I know."

Another eternity of silence. And then . . .

"Bloody hell." It was too much to resist. He was a man, dammit, not a bloody saint. Letting go of his pent-up breath, he turned to her.

She was only an arm's length away, and he reached for her, bringing her to him. She came willingly into his embrace, and his arms closed around her. She melted against him, her arms sliding around his waist, her face burrowing against his neck. Whispering her name, he pulled her closer, his arms tightening until he felt as if she'd become a part of him.

She *was* a part of him. Somehow, without his planning it or even wanting it, in these few short weeks she had become essential to him. As essential as the air he breathed.

He looked down at her. "Why did you come out, lass?"

"I didn't want the day to end. I didn't want you to be alone. *I* didn't want to be alone." She caught her lower lip between her teeth, then buried her face against him once more. Her breath was warm against his throat as she spoke in muffled tones. "I will go if you wish."

His lips touched her forehead, then her temple. "Nay, I do not wish it."

She tilted her face upward, and he raised a finger to trace the line of her cheek, the slope of her neck, the sweet curve of her lips. He thought he could touch her exactly like this forever; she was that exquisite.

"If we lie together, it willna change my mind about leaving," he warned her.

She closed her eyes briefly and nodded. "I know." And when she looked at him again, her eyes, in the moonlight, reflected no hint of doubt or hesitation. They were full of passion.

God help him, he didn't have it in him to refuse her—or himself.

Cupping her face in his hands, he kissed her briefly, then took her by the hand and led her into the barn, toward his cot. Drawing her down to sit beside him, he held both of her hands in her lap and spoke quietly into the darkness surrounding them.

"Fancy, there is something you must know—now, before we do this thing that we both seem bound to do."

She went very still.

He drew a ragged breath and forced himself to speak of things he had never expected to reveal to another living being. "I told you that my brother Derek was hanged."

"Yes," she whispered.

"I didn't tell you that I was there, that I witnessed it."

He heard her breath catch, at the same time her fingers tightened around his.

"We were captured together," he continued. "But he could have escaped. I was wounded, and they took Derek because he stayed to help me. His reward was a British rope." Pausing, he added, "I was meant to hang with him."

"Why . . . why didn't you?" she asked.

"The family I fostered with . . . Scots often send their children to other families to be raised and trained, and I was sent at age eight to the Macraes, as they were good friends of my family. But when war came, they sided with the Crown. After the battle at Culloden Moor, the Macraes heard I was to be hanged, and they convinced the Crown that one of their rewards for fighting against their own countrymen should be my life." Bitterly he added, "But they dinna save Derek. And the Brits waited until I had seen Derek and mayhap thirty other friends hang before telling me that I was to be spared."

"Oh, Ian . . ." It was a ragged whisper, full of pain, and he felt her compassion, but that was not what he wanted. He had to make himself absolutely clear.

"Fancy, I dinna want my life," he said, speaking past the tightness in his throat. "The fact that I was still living and breathing was a betrayal of Derek, and of Patrick, who fell at Culloden. 'Twas a betrayal of *all* Scots who died at Culloden and after. And the only reason I dinna force the soldiers to kill me then and there was that I had to live to find Katy."

Pausing, gathering himself to tell her what he knew she would see as the worst, he willed himself to finish. "The last words Derek said to me were 'I'll see ye soon, brother. In heaven or in hell.' And he is still waiting. I'm on borrowed time, lass. Enough time to find Katy and see to it that she is safe. You must understand tha'. You must see tha' when I leave here I most likely willna be back. And ye will be a widow once again."

Her body went still. He couldn't see her face, for he had not lit the candle next to his bed. But he felt the tear that splashed on his hand as it lay in her lap with hers.

He touched a fingertip to her cheek and discovered it wet. Gently wiping her tears away, he said, "Donna cry for me, lass. Tha' was no' my intent in tellin' ye. I only thought ye ha' a right to know."

"Oh, Ian, I can't even imagine—"

"Hush. 'Tis over now."

But her tears kept falling.

"Ah, Fancy," he sighed, "ye ha' too tender a heart." He leaned toward her, his lips brushing her cheeks, tasting tears. Her head tipped upward. Their lips met and clung, and he thought how odd it seemed that, though it was the salt of her tears he tasted, 'twas the sweetest kiss he had ever known.

But the sweetness soon gave way to passion. It rose between them swiftly, and soon they were clutching each other in a tight embrace. Fueled by her tears and by the truths they'd shared that day, he felt them both swirling in a maelstrom of desire, yearning, and expectation.

Need burst inside him, clawing to get out. His tongue found its way between her lips to explore her mouth, soundlessly urging her to join him, to give herself to him completely and . . . oh, God, he wished it could be forever.

Fancy felt her body turn molten under the onslaught of Ian's passion. She clung to him, her fingers digging into his back, a river of sensation coursing through her. She felt his vitality flowing into her, igniting her, calling to her.

Her body answered, melding to his, her curves fitting themselves against the length of his hard-muscled frame. His mouth left hers, and his lips and tongue moved down her neck, leaving a trail of fire in their wake. His hands were everywhere, stroking and kneading her through the fabric of her clothing. Her body was changing under his touch, her breasts tightening, her skin tingling, and a warm, throbbing pressure building in her very core.

His fingers tugged at the laces that held the front of her dress closed, then she felt the sleeves being pulled down to reveal her shoulders. With one fingertip, he traced a pattern across the upper curve of her breasts, above her chemise. Then, with a tug of the ribbon, he pushed the thin cotton downward, baring her breasts to his touch.

She whispered his name on a sigh as he gently pushed her down to lie on the cot. Leaning over her, he kissed one hard nipple, then the other. He cupped her breasts, lifting one to take the nipple into his mouth, nibbling and sucking on it.

She gasped, arching against him as his mouth created a delicious, hot pulsation deep in the innermost part of her. It was new to her, this feeling, and shocking and wondrous. And she never wanted it to stop; she only wanted more.

The desire turned to need, and the need became desperate. She was desperate to touch him, to feel him against her, to join with him. Her hands shook as she untied the leather thong holding his shirt together at the neck. Then her fingers delved inside, running across his shoulder muscles, then downward along the slight indentation along his spine. She felt him shudder.

Groaning, he pulled off his shirt, then her dress and chemise, and together they undid the thongs to his trousers. He shoved them down, kicking off his shoes, then rolled toward her to pull her full-length against him.

A sound escaped her, a whimpering moan, at the first exquisite meeting of his bare flesh and hers. His mouth came back to hers, and her hands clutched at his back, sliding up and down over smooth skin and work-honed muscles. But her hand came to a sudden stop and her breath caught in her throat when she felt the long, jagged scar down his side.

His words came back to her, haunting her: "I was wounded, and they took Derek because he stayed to help me." In her mind's eye, she saw him lying on a field littered with death and destruction, urging his brother to go. But his brother had stayed and, as a result, was hanged, leaving Ian with a well of guilt as deep and as vast as the ocean. Leaving him alone.

She wanted to tell him that he was *not* alone, that he would never be alone again. She knew, though, that he wouldn't listen to any words she might speak, and so she tried to tell him in the only other way she could, with her body.

She moved against him, her legs twining with his, her hands traveling over the planes of his body. Turning her head, she went in search of his mouth, and finding it, she kissed him with all the ardor and tenderness she possessed. He responded with a deep, rumbling groan, his mouth slanting over hers in deeper possession. The kiss became searing, full of need and promise yet to be fulfilled.

She knew a deep ache, an intense craving such as she had never known before. Of its own accord, her body strained toward his, arching into him, moving shamelessly in unmistakable invitation against him.

He dragged his mouth away from hers, gasping. "Fancy . . . are ye sure, lass?"

"Yes . . . Oh, yes," she said.

He kissed her breasts again; then his tongue trailed downward to her stomach, and she quivered.

"Ian," she whispered urgently. "Ian."

He moved, positioning himself above her, and she felt his manhood begin to probe, slowly, seductively, deeper and deeper each time until she was mindless, whimpering with need and desire.

Then, in a smooth, gliding thrust, he filled her completely, and she cried his name, her legs tightening around him. He moved sensuously, creating fireballs of heat that careened through her. His rhythm increased, and pleasure rolled through her like thunder, each rumble more powerful than the one before. The momentum mounted until, suddenly, unexpectedly, she came apart, the tension inside her exploding in long, pulsing bursts of pleasure.

She heard herself cry out. Heard him growl against her neck. Felt the shudders that racked his body as he drove into her a final time. And when the explosion was over, for several long, luscious minutes, they lay in each other's arms, quivering with the aftershocks.

"Fancy." He said her name like a prayer, his voice

raw and breathless and filled with something that sounded like awe.

Lying there, wrapped so tightly against him, still joined in the most intimate of ways, she had never felt so complete or so cherished.

Finally he moved away from her, to the side of the bed, and she heard him strike a flint to light the candle. She almost told him not to, that she didn't want light, but when she saw him, she changed her mind. She had felt him, the muscled planes of his body, but in the candlelight, she could see that he was beautiful—lean and hard with incredibly broad shoulders and a chest covered with a dusting of silky dark hair.

Her gaze swept over him, then halted at the sight of the scar she had touched that carved a path down his left side. A sword stroke.

When her gaze moved upward again, she caught him looking at her, just as she had looked at him.

"You're so bonny," he said.

She loved that word on his lips. She loved the way he looked at her, as if he didn't see the calluses on her hands or her too thin body or her skin that was indelicately brown from the sun. For the first time in her life, she felt beautiful.

Also for the first time, she felt at ease with her body, unembarrassed to have him looking at her so intently. She and John had always undressed in the dark, and he'd engaged in none of the preliminary lovemaking that Ian had. Thinking about it, she couldn't remember a time when John had ever seen her totally naked, nor had she ever seen him.

She should feel ashamed, or at the very least, guilty. But she didn't. Instead, she felt a terrible sadness for John. She had never known, nor had he, she guessed, how truly splendid lovemaking could be. The act had been a duty for him, a necessary function performed upon rare occasions in order to bring children into the world. She had known no differently. Until now.

She didn't realize that her expression had changed until Ian spoke and it became clear that he was misinterpreting her silence as a moment of regret. She had so many regrets—but not about him. Not about this.

"I'm sorry," he said. "I should not have allowed tha' to happen."

Her expression cleared. "Why not? We are married."

"Aye, we are."

"I wanted it to happen as much as you. I'm not sorry."

He paused, reaching out to stroke her stomach. "And wha' if there is a bairn?"

"Then I will love it, as I love Noel and Amy."

He frowned. "I know you would, but I wouldna want to leave you with that extra burden. We canna let this happen again."

She put her hand on top of his much larger one. "I know."

"Lass . . ." He broke off, sighing raggedly. "We canna get an annulment now."

"I'll lie," she said.

"Nay." He shook his head. "I would not have you lying to your God."

"He's your God, too."

"Nay, He and I abandoned each other as I watched Derek climb the gallows steps."

So much desolation clung to his voice that she could feel her heart breaking for him. "Ian," she pleaded, "don't give up. Your letters will find your sister, and you can bring her here to live with us."

His frown deepened. "Seeing Katy safe is no' my only reason for returning to Scotland."

"But—"

"Nay." He shook his head. "You donna know. They took my land, lass. They took my heritage, my children's heritage. You canna know what tha' means if ye ha' no' grown up hearing stories about wha' it means to belong to your clan. What it means to be a Scot." He paused, fixing her with a solemn look. "Both my brothers died for tha' land. They honored it."

And he had not, because he had lived. He didn't have to say the words for her to hear them. They were there, in his eyes, along with the hopelessness that had colored his voice.

Sighing, wondering if he could ever learn to live with the guilt he felt, she ran a hand down his arm in a tender caress. Then, rising from the cot, she picked up her discarded clothing and began to dress.

He rose too, and pulled on his trousers. As she watched him, her gaze went again to the scar on his side.

" 'Tis none too pretty," he said.

And it wasn't. The wound had not healed well, and the scar was thick and still ugly. The wonder was that the wound had not killed him.

Reaching out, she touched it lightly. "I only hate the pain it gave you."

He shrugged. "Many suffered far more."

"I don't think so," she said softly.

His eyes closed, and his arms went around her, clasping her to him tightly. "You're a candle in the darkness," he said hoarsely. "I fear I'll snuff it out. I donna want to destroy you like—"

She stopped his words with a finger over his lips. "You have given me gifts I will always treasure. You've opened the door to reading and given *all* of us a world we never had before. And you've given me tonight."

A muscle worked in his cheek for a moment; then he dropped his arms. "You had best go."

"Yes," she said. But it took all the strength she possessed to walk away from him.

A year. She had a year. He had promised her that, and she knew he would keep his word. She also knew more than just Katy was calling him. He thought he had to return to Scotland to die, as his brothers and countrymen had died. It was a matter of honor. But perhaps locating Katy would change his mind. And *she* had a year. A year to convince him that there was as much honor in living as there was in dying.

As she left the barn, Fancy looked upward, toward the sky, and said a quick, simple prayer.

"Please, Lord, let him find Katy."

Chapter 17

ancy woke to the rhythmic sound of wood being chopped. When she opened her eyes and saw the sunlight flooding the room, she sat up with a start, realizing it was late—much later than she usually awakened.

Another angry, shattering noise came to her from outside and she went to the window. Ian was chopping wood as if he were slaying a legion of British soldiers. And perhaps, in his mind, he was, she thought, for each stroke of the ax had a peculiar viciousness to it.

Well, she didn't blame him. She hadn't slept well at all, and thinking about the problem that had kept her awake made her want to smash something, too.

She dressed quickly and went into the main room to find that her family hadn't waited for her to begin the day. Fortune had started a fire, and the aroma of johnnycake filled the room. Her sister had also dressed Amy, who was playing with the cat.

"Should I fetch Ian?" Noel asked.

Fancy hesitated, then nodded. The sound of chopping had stopped. "Have you milked the cow?" she asked him.

He gave her a sheepish look. "I'll do it now."

"Sarah can wait until after you eat."

"All right." He barreled out the door to call Ian for breakfast.

Fancy watched him run, her thoughts in chaos. She wasn't quite sure how to act this morning or how she would manage to meet Ian's gaze without giving herself away. The simple fact was, she loved him. Yet if she told him, she would only be adding to his burden. And he was already carrying enough weight on his shoulders, as broad and strong as they were.

But how could she act as if nothing had happened when her body still trembled from last night? When her blood warmed at the very sound of his name? Odd, but she realized that the shame she had felt over her attraction to him had faded. Somewhere in the deepest part of the night, as she'd lain awake thinking thoughts she'd never dared admit before, she'd become convinced that John had somehow planned this, that he was smiling in approval.

Fancy wasn't surprised when Noel returned alone. "Ian is saddling Royalty," he said. "He said he doesn't want to eat."

"Royalty needs exercise," she reasoned in the face of his obvious disappointment. Now if she could only comfort herself as easily.

"Why don't we take the fox back to the woods today?" she said.

Noel frowned. "Ian said he'd go with me."

"I wanna go, too," Amy chimed in. "With I'n."

"Ian has work to do," Fancy said more sternly than she intended.

Noel's gaze fell.

Amy, on the other hand, decided to be stubborn. "I want I'n."

Fortune gave her a helpless look, then went over to Amy, soundlessly urging her to the table.

"I think you had better eat, young lady," Fancy said, "before we do anything."

"Don't want to eat. Want I'n."

"After breakfast," she promised. He would be back by then, surely, by which time it was likely that Amy would have forgotten her demand.

Fancy finally got both children to the table, but she only toyed with her own food as moments from the previous night sprang unbidden into her mind to be relived in glorious detail. Was it the same for Ian? What was he thinking this morning? Did he regret last night? Could it possibly have been as wonderful for him as it had been for her?

Forcing food past the lump in her throat, she made herself eat a few mouthfuls. Then, with Fortune's help, she quickly cleared the table. When all was put away, she looked toward the barn. The door was still closed, and Royalty was not back in the paddock.

"All right," she said, "who wants to go with me to the woods?" Truly, it was way past time for the fox to be returned to his natural home; his leg was well, and he was old enough to hunt for himself. It simply hadn't been possible, with all that had happened in the past month, to spare the time to take care of the matter.

"I still don't understand why we have to take him all the way to the woods," Noel said. "Why can't we just let him go?"

Fancy raised one eyebrow. "You know why. If we just let him go, he'll stay around the farm, and then he'll start eating our chickens."

Noel nodded, still reluctant to relinquish one of his friends.

Fancy looked at her daughter. "Amy?"

Tears gathered in Amy's eyes. "Don't want him to go."

"But you want him to be happy, don't you, sweet pea?"

The tears fell, though Amy remained silent.

"Amy?"

"Don't want I'n to go."

"Ian?" Startled, Fancy hurried to correct her daughter's assumption. "Amy, we're talking about the fox, not Ian."

"Ian's not leaving," Noel stepped in.

Amy looked from her mother to her brother and back again. "Really?"

Fancy nodded. "Really. Ian's not going any time soon, sweet pea. He's out now exercising Royalty, but he'll be back."

"He didn' read us a story las' night."

"He was tired, and so were you. You went right to sleep."

"He didn' say good night," Amy accused.

"You were asleep," Noel put in, trying to help.

She frowned. "I woke up."

"He didn't know that," Fancy said soothingly.

"I don' care," Amy said, tears still spilling from her eyes.

At a loss, Fancy wondered what had caused her daughter's sudden concern. Perhaps the thought of saying good-bye to the fox, combined with the vague notion that Ian, who wasn't "really" her new papa, would be leaving them in the unknown future, frightened Amy more than she'd realized. And, too, maybe Amy had detected some of her own fear.

Leaning down, Fancy picked Amy up and held her close. "No one's going away any time soon, darlin'," she whispered.

Amy allowed herself to be hugged for several moments, then started wriggling free. "Can I tell Samuel good-bye?"

"Samuel?"

"The fox," Amy said in an impatient tone.

"I thought you were calling him Joseph." And both children had been told it would be best not to name the fox at all.

"His name *is* Joseph," Noel said, correcting his sister.

"No, it isn't. It's *Samuel*," Amy stated with great authority.

While the two argued, Fancy smiled. Telling them not to name the animal had been like instructing the wind not to blow.

Interrupting her children's disagreement, she told Amy, "Of course you can tell him good-bye. And you can ride in the wagon with him and Noel and Fortune while we take him home."

"Do you think he will find his fam'ly?"

"Hmm . . ." Fancy hesitated, choosing her words carefully. "I'm sure he'll have a very fine family."

"Aw right," her daughter said sorrowfully. "I'll go wif you."

"We have to go a long way into the woods," she said, "so I'll hitch up the horses. Noel, you get the wire cage that your father made for Lucky when we first found him. It's in the barn. Fortune, why don't you help Amy put some peaches in a basket for us, in case we get hungry before we get back?"

They all went to do their tasks, and Fancy headed for the barn. There she noted that all the horses had been fed and watered and that there was a pail of milk outside of Sarah the cow's stall. Ian must have milked her when Noel hadn't appeared.

A part of her wanted to wait for him, wanted to linger there in the barn, perhaps even sit on his bed, and daydream about the night they'd shared. Simply *looking* at the bed where they had lain together made her legs a little weak. Indeed, her whole body was humming. She felt warm and trembly and alive in a way she'd never felt before. And it was all because of him.

But it wouldn't do, feeling this way. At least it wouldn't do to let him know it. He thought they should go on as they had before, acting as if they weren't aching to touch and kiss and hold each other. And perhaps they could. But she very much doubted it.

After Fancy finished hitching the two geldings to the wagon, she helped Fortune and Noel coax the fox from his large pen into the smaller cage John had insisted upon making for the various animals that always seemed to be touching their lives.

Once the fox was safely in the cage, Fortune and Fancy lifted it into the back of the wagon, and they all climbed on for the fox's last ride with them.

"Can we pet Joseph through the cage?" Noel asked.

"His name is Samuel," Amy insisted.

"Joseph."

"Whatever his name is," Fancy replied over her shoulder, "you can't pet him. Remember what I've told you about handling a wild critter. That makes it harder for them to return to their natural home." As she said the words, she realized she could be issuing the same warning to herself about Ian.

The sky was as clear and bright as it had been the day before, but without the breeze coming off the bay, the air was stifling. Hot and humid, oppressively so, without even a hint of a breeze stirring.

As the wagon rolled past the crop fields, heading for the woods on the far side of the farm, Fancy's gaze swept over the acres of tobacco. It had grown quickly and was green and sturdy. It looked as if it would produce a good yield. She wished her vegetable garden looked as healthy. The more sensitive plants were suffering badly from the lack of rain.

They rode down the path, then veered off onto an old track through the trees. The going was slow and difficult, as the track wasn't much used and so was overgrown with weeds. Fancy's eyes kept sweeping the fields and the woods beyond; she couldn't rid herself of that moment at the beach when she thought she saw someone watching them. But today she saw nothing, only a flock of birds taking wing at their approach. Yet the prickling feeling of being watched remained, growing stronger with every jolt of the wagon.

They'd been traveling for about an hour and had reached a small clearing when Fortune touched her shoulder.

Fancy glanced at her sister, who nodded, indicating that she thought they had gone far enough. All around them, tall pine trees mingled with oaks and sycamores and maples to form a dense green canopy. The creek was less than a quarter of a mile ahead. The woods were full of squirrels, and the creek was home to ducks and geese and several kinds of fish, which meant the young fox should have an ample and varied diet.

Fancy let Noel help Fortune unload the fox in his cage. But when she would have opened the cage and let the animal go, Fortune stopped her. She gave her sister a questioning look.

Fortune's gaze slid to Noel.

She was right, Fancy thought. Noel had spent hours sitting on the ground outside the fox's pen, talking to him. He deserved to be the one to let him go. And it was time for him to learn the hard but valuable lesson.

"We have to be careful not to scare him," she said. "Noel, what if we all get back in the wagon and you take him behind those trees and open the cage for him?"

Noel looked up at her, and for a moment his solemn expression reminded her very much of John. "All right," he said.

"I want to say good-bye too," Amy chimed in.

Fancy stooped beside her. "You can say good-bye right now, sweet pea. But it's been a long time since"— she gave Noel a wink—"since Samuel has been out of a cage, and he might be too scared to come out if we all stand around watching him."

Amy thought hard about that, and Fancy exchanged a look with Fortune, both of them aware that this momentous occasion could become very unpleasant for everyone—particularly the fox—if Amy chose to make it so.

To Fancy's great relief, Amy said, "Aw right," and grabbed Fortune's hand to tug her toward the wagon.

Fancy gave her sister a thoughtful glance. Fortune was growing up, she realized. Since John had died, she'd been disappearing from the farm less and less often. She was helping out more, too, with Amy and with chores. But the real changes had begun the night that Ian had taught her to write her name. In the few weeks since that night, Fortune had smiled more than Fancy could remember her smiling in all of the past nine years combined. Since the horrible day when Cranshaw had attacked and abused her, then discarded her, calling her a stupid half-breed.

A few minutes passed before Noel reappeared. Fancy studied his expression carefully. He looked unhappy, and yet he looked as if he'd done something that he knew was right. There'd been too many such lessons lately, but she was as powerless as any other mother to protect her children from all of life's harsh teachings.

With everyone loaded into the wagon, Fancy turned the horses, and they started toward home. It was almost noon, she realized, noting the golden beams of sunlight filtering through green leaves from directly overhead. Ian would be back and, most likely, hungry after missing breakfast.

They had gone only a short distance when Noel climbed from the back of the wagon onto the seat beside her. She patted his arm and smiled at him.

"I think he was happy to be free," he said.

"Everyone wants to be free," she replied.

"I'll miss him."

"I know, but I imagine you and Fortune will find other critters. And you have Trouble and Unsatisfactory and Lucky and Bandit."

"Lucky likes Ian better."

Relieved that he didn't seem too upset by what had become obvious to all of them, Fancy said, "I think Lucky knows that Ian needs him more than we do."

Noel gave her a puzzled look. "He does?"

She nodded. "I think so. Remember, Ian lost his home and his family and, for a long time, his freedom."

"But he has us now," Noel argued.

He spoke with such assurance that apprehension tingled inside her. No matter how many times she warned him, he would go on believing that Ian would stay with them forever—until it turned out not to be true.

Perhaps it was time he knew the reason that he would be forced to let Ian go.

"Ian has a sister who was lost in the war his country fought against England," she said.

"I know," he said.

"He doesn't know where she is or if she's even safe, and he must find her." She looked at him. "How would you feel if someone took Amy and you didn't know what had happened to her?"

Noel didn't reply, and Fancy thought it best to let him ponder the question in silence. He stayed beside her on the wagon seat while, behind them, Amy chattered happily to Fortune.

Fancy spent the remainder of the ride through the woods trying not to think about Ian. She planned supper. She made a list in her head of clothing that needed mending. She recited the alphabet.

But then, where the lane ended at the farm road and

they left the dense woods, all of those mundane thoughts fled.

Smoke. Rising in billowing clouds above the trees. And it was coming from the farm.

"Ma!"

"I see it! Fortune, hold on to Amy!"

Fancy slapped the reins, urging the horses to quicken their pace. It took enormous restraint not to whip them into a gallop, but such speed with the wagon, on this road, would have been dangerous. All the same, she encouraged them to go much faster than was wise.

Within seconds it became clear that it was not the farmhouse or the barn that was on fire. It was the tobacco. As the horses raced along the road by the field, the wagon rattling behind them, Fancy's gaze took in the horrifying sight. The far end of the field, the side farthest from the house, was ablaze.

And there was Ian, racing toward the well with a bucket in either hand and Lucky at his heels.

Warding off panic, she gave the horses another flick of the reins. At the same time, she reminded herself that not a breeze was stirring. Without wind, perhaps the fire could be contained.

Yet as she drew the wagon to a halt in the farmyard and jumped down, she could see that her hope was in vain. Even without wind, the fire was spreading over the dry field at a frightening pace.

Gathering her wits, Fancy grabbed Noel by the shoulders. "Take Amy inside," she told him. "Watch her. Don't either of you leave the house." And as Lucky came tearing up to them, she added, "And take Lucky, too. Don't let him out—for any reason!"

Noel opened his mouth to protest, then shut it.

Fancy didn't wait for him to argue. She raced toward

the barn with Fortune beside her to get more buckets. Ian came running up to them at the well.

"The south side," he said, panting. "Concentrate on the south side."

"How did it—"

"I donna know," he interrupted her. "But 'twas no accident."

His expression was grim, and his face was already dark with soot. How long had he been tearing back and forth?

"Here," she told Fortune. "You fill buckets for us." She waited until two were full, then dashed after Ian, who had refilled his own buckets and raced off.

Her heart sank when she realized he had given up on the back half of the field and was soaking the plants and ground in a line, starting about halfway to the house, intent on saving the front half of the field. But she knew in her heart that they weren't going to make it. Fingers of flame were streaking toward them from the left, right, and center as the fire consumed the back half of the field and went searching for new fuel.

She handed Ian her buckets, took his empty ones, and ran back for more water. At the well she grabbed the two buckets that Fortune had filled and took off again. Back and forth she ran. While she was in transit, Ian used a water-saturated blanket to try to snuff out the encroaching flames.

Again and again Fancy made the trip from the well to the field and back again. She did it until she could barely breathe. Smoke filled her lungs, the muscles in her legs burned, and her arms ached from carrying the full buckets. Ian worked quickly but with almost frightening calm, she noted, as he struggled to lay down his barrier. More buckets of water—and still more. Then the Wallaces appeared and added their rough, strong hands to the desperate work.

"Saw the smoke," Little Tim called to her, and that was the only explanation needed.

When she couldn't run another step, Fancy stayed with Fortune, whose arms were giving out from turning the heavy crank to lift the water barrel from the deep well. Together they filled buckets, and then Fancy would meet one of the men a few yards from the well, handing him two full buckets and taking his empty ones.

From an ever-shrinking distance, she kept her eye on the fire. She lost sight of Ian and the Wallaces for long stretches of time when their forms disappeared behind clouds of smoke and fire. Whenever she thought they were making progress, the fire rose up again in another spot. Embers and fragments of dry leaves floated from plant to plant, starting new blazes. When she saw flames shoot up from the area where she'd last seen Ian, she couldn't contain herself any longer. Grabbing two full buckets, she ran into the field.

She found him and the Wallaces surrounded by fire.

"Ian!" she shouted above the crackling blaze.

"Get out," he yelled back.

She didn't even consider obeying him. Throwing the water she carried onto the blazing plants between the men and her, she turned to run back for more. But Fortune was right behind her with two more full buckets. And behind Fortune, Noel came stumbling with a huge pot filled with water. Fancy dumped all of the water onto the fire that separated her from her husband and the other two men, and, amazingly, it quenched the blaze—at least for a few seconds. Enough time for Ian and the Wallaces to escape.

Ian ran through the narrow passage between the flames, took one look at Noel, scooped him up, and kept running. "Get out!" he called to her again as he ran.

This time she listened. Snatching up the empty buckets, Fancy left the doomed tobacco field with Fortune and the Wallaces running beside her. She could feel her heart breaking.

They gathered at the well to watch the destruction. The fire crackled and popped, spreading with spectacular speed through the field.

Fancy laid a hand on Noel's shoulder, and she looked down at him. "I thought I told you to stay with Amy."

His expression was a painful mix of shame and defensiveness. "She promised to stay inside. And, Ma, I just couldn't! I wanted to *help*."

Fancy sighed. She knew she should be angry with him, but she didn't have it in her. She wouldn't have been able to sit idly by, either.

Fortune turned and ran toward the house and in a few moments came out carrying Amy. Fancy put one arm around her sister's waist and draped her other hand over Noel's shoulder, drawing him back against her. She felt Ian's presence as he came to stand behind her, and together they all watched as their future went up in smoke.

It didn't take long. The fire consumed the entire field of tobacco in an astoundingly short time. When the last orange flame died and only a few wisps of smoke and fading embers remained, Fancy heaved a ragged sigh.

Turning her head, she looked up at Ian. His clothes were black with soot, and singed holes in the fabric covering his arms and shoulders revealed patches of raw skin beneath.

He met her gaze with eyes that glinted dangerously, and she realized he was barely containing his rage.

"I'm sorry, lass," he said to her.

She gave her head a little shake. "You did what you could. It isn't your fault."

"I thought I could stop it."

Big Tim Wallace uttered a snort of disbelief. "Nay, 'twas hopeless, as dry as it's been this summer. The fields are all like tinderboxes, just waiting for somebody to strike a flint. Once a fire gets started in those dry plants . . ." He shook his head again. Then, frowning, he asked, "What happened?"

Fancy half turned to look at Ian as he explained.

"I was cooling down one of the stallions in the barn when I heard Lucky bark," he said. "I thought someone must be riding up the road, and I came out to see who it was. Then I saw flames shooting up from the two back corners of the field."

Wallace scowled. "That far apart?"

"Aye."

" 'Tis no doubt, then. 'Twas set."

"Aye, but I didna see who did it."

Wallace grunted. "I'd wager we could guess who did it."

Little Tim came to stand by his father and said the name that had popped immediately to Fancy's mind.

"Robert Marsh."

Ian frowned. "I can't believe he would dare—"

"I can," Big Tim said.

So could Fancy. Ian hadn't known Robert long enough to realize how ruthless he could be.

A muscle worked in Ian's cheek. He turned back to the well. "We had best wet the grass between the field and the pasture. There's no wind to speak of, but I wouldna want to chance one coming up and carrying an ember or two among the horses."

Fancy turned to Noel. "This time, stay with your sister."

Noel nodded.

"Promise," she said.

"I promise."

"Do that, lad," Ian said. "Your mother has enough to worry about right now without worrying about you and your sister, too."

Noel gave a brief nod. "I'll take good care of Amy." And he led a very subdued Amy back to the house.

Fancy unhitched the horses, who had been standing in their harnesses all this time, and led them to the barn. Then she went to help the others. Two buckets had been left in the field when they ran and were now, undoubtedly, cinders. The three men took whatever containers they could find, while she and Fortune filled the pails and pots, hoisting the big wooden bucket from the well over and over again until Fancy thought her arms would break.

The acrid smoke permeated the air, burning her lungs. She tried not to look at the source of the smoke. All of John's pampering of the tiny plants, all those nights of planting, wasted in a few horrific minutes. She had depended on the money from that crop to carry them through the winter. Her stomach knotted as she wondered if Robert would indeed stoop so low. Had he found out about her marriage to Ian and burned the tobacco as punishment? Her hands kept moving while her thoughts were in turmoil.

They continued for several more hours, wetting down large areas to prevent any errant sparks from starting new fires. It was well past suppertime, and the sun was sinking low in the western sky before Ian and the Wallaces thought it was safe to stop.

Fancy looked down at her hands. They were blistered from cranking the well handle and carrying the buckets. Every bone in her body ached, and she knew Fortune felt the same way. They were both covered

with soot, their dresses ruined. The men were in even
worse shape. Her gaze traveled over the three who had
dropped to the ground near the well. They were black
from head to toe, their clothing was full of holes, and
they all had burns, some of which looked serious.

On top of everything else, she was certain everyone
was hungry.

"Fortune, go tell Noel to start a fire in the hearth,"
she said, stifling the urge to laugh hysterically at the
notion of deliberately starting a fire. Then, walking
over to the men, she examined their burns to see what
she'd need to treat them. "Come inside," she ordered.

Beyond argument, they got slowly to their feet and
followed her.

The food that Fancy set on the table disappeared faster
than she would have thought possible. Amy wanted to
get onto Ian's lap to eat her pie, but Fancy pulled her
onto her own lap instead, whispering to her daughter,
"Ian has hurts."

"Ohhhh," Amy said, immediately ending her
squirming and looking sympathetically at Ian.

" 'Tis not that bad," he said, trying to smile. "I've
had much worse."

Thinking of the scar along his ribs, Fancy knew he
was right; still, the burns he'd acquired were bad
enough. The Wallaces had their share, too. Before fixing the meal, she'd given each of the men a glass of
brandy from the bottle John kept for special occasions.
Then she doctored their wounds with cloths soaked in
witch hazel. But she knew they were in pain, and there
was little else she could do for them.

The meal was nearly over when Ian's gaze met hers
across the table.

"How badly did you need that tobacco?" he asked.

She held his gaze as she replied. "We can't feed ourselves and all of the horses this winter without selling a hogshead of tobacco."

He was silent for a moment, his jaw clenched. "So without the tobacco, you have to sell some of the horses?"

"Yes."

"How many?"

"It depends on whether Sir Gray and Gray Ghost win any races this fall. If they do, we could probably manage by selling two—probably two of the two-year-olds. If they don't win"—she lifted a shoulder in a small shrug—"perhaps four."

"Which would mean selling at least one of the fillies," he concluded.

She didn't need to reply. Nor did she need to tell him that selling the fillies would mean a severe setback in building a line of racing stock. They needed those fillies to breed winners.

"Even then," she went on, "we wouldn't have enough money to plant next year's tobacco crop."

"That bastard Marsh . . ." Big Tim began, then, glancing at the company around the table, which included women and children, his face reddened. "Beg pardon, ma'am," he said, nodding to Fancy.

She waved a hand in dismissal. "You said it for me."

"I can help you with tobacco next year if my own crop prospers," he said.

"I wouldna let Marsh hear you say that," Ian said bitterly. "Yours might go up in smoke, too."

"If I catch him near my farm, I'll kill him."

Ian grunted. "He would be dead now if the barn or pastures had caught and any of those horses had been lost."

Fancy shook her head. "Robert wants the horses. Still, I keep wondering what prompted him to take such drastic action." Frowning, she looked at the Wallaces. "Could Robert know of the marriage?"

Big Tim shook his head. "Not from us. We haven't spoken a word about it to anyone."

Fancy's heart constricted. If Robert had planned this without knowing of the marriage, what would he do when he learned of it? The possibilities were terrifying, and she suddenly feared that it had not been a good idea, after all. Robert would kill Ian, or have him killed.

As her mind conjured up nightmare images, Ian spoke again.

"Somehow," he said, "I canna see Robert Marsh skulking around, setting tobacco fields on fire."

Big Tim nodded. "Nay, the man would not dirty his own hands."

"Could have been that overseer of his," Little Tim said. "Blackhearted soul if there ever was one. Whipped a slave to death last week."

Fancy's blood ran cold. She had met Robert's overseer, Cecil Martin, and she didn't doubt the tales she'd heard about him. He had the coldest eyes she had ever seen. Dark and flat, they were more reptilian than human, but unlike a reptile he didn't strike for protection; he attacked because he enjoyed cruelty and the power it gave him.

And she agreed with Ian and Big Tim: Robert Marsh would not do his own dirty work. If anyone caught the overseer, Robert would deny knowing anything about it.

"We had best be going." The older Wallace rose from his chair, wincing slightly. Removing the witch hazel compress that covered his left hand, he looked at Fancy. "You got any more of that?"

She nodded and rose to gather the requested items. Wrapping some witch hazel leaves in a piece of cloth, she handed him the bundle, saying, "You saw me make the potion. Just make sure you use clean cloths. Use it again tonight and in the morning."

When Little Tim rose to leave, Fortune followed him to the door. His eyes, Fancy had noticed, hadn't left her sister for more than two seconds throughout the meal.

"Thank you," Fancy said to both men.

"No need for that," Big Tim said gruffly. " 'Twas worth it for the meal. We get tired of each other's cooking. This was a treat, especially the pie."

"I'll send Fortune over with a fresh one for you tomorrow," she promised, noting that Little Tim immediately looked at Fortune, who smiled at him and nodded.

While Ian walked the Wallaces to their horses, Fortune took Amy to bed, and Fancy kissed Noel good night and sent him up to his loft. When she returned to the door to see what was keeping Ian, she saw him standing with the Wallaces by their horses. She tried to hear what the men were saying, but they were speaking too softly.

When the Wallaces rode off and Ian came back inside, she gave him a questioning look.

He shrugged. "They are going to ask around, see if they hear anything."

"I hope they're not harmed because they helped us."

Ian was silent for a moment, then asked, "Did John have a weapon—a pistol or a musket?"

She nodded. "He had a musket he used for hunting. But he didn't use it more than once in the past year." She remembered John telling her that the musket, a gift from his father, was one of the finest available.

" 'Twill need cleaning," Ian said. "What about powder and shot?"

"I know we have some." She frowned. "I think he had some paper cartridges."

"No pistol?"

She shook her head.

"Do you know how to shoot?"

"No."

"I will teach you in the morning."

She wanted to refuse—she didn't think she could ever actually shoot anyone—but after the day's horror, she feared he was right in believing that she should at least know how. "All right," she said.

He nodded. "Now, where is the musket, lass?"

Fancy led him into her room, realizing he had never been there before. She saw his gaze sweep over the modest but colorful chamber, taking in the flowered curtains, the rag rug, the rocker in the corner. It had always seemed like a palace to her, after living in Indian lodges so much of her life. But how would it look to the son of a nobleman? Less than grand, she supposed.

Still, he gave no sign that he disapproved, and when his gaze came to rest on the feather bed, she knew he wasn't thinking of how grand or modest the surroundings were. Last night his cot had sufficed quite well.

Ian's face reddened for a moment before his gaze went to a musket hanging in the rack above the bed.

Fancy reached for it and handed it to him.

He grasped the gun easily, comfortably, handling it as if he was familiar with that kind of weapon. He nodded with approval. "Aye, 'twill do."

Watching him, seeing the cold light that glittered in his eyes, she thought about the war he and his countrymen had fought. How many men had he killed? Seeing him as he was now, she realized that he had become a stranger again, a man who knew but didn't fear danger. And it occurred to her that if Robert had appeared at that moment, Ian would have been perfectly capable of killing him.

Although suddenly fearful of what she might be setting in motion, Fancy opened the chest at the foot of the bed, retrieved a box of paper cartridges, and handed them to Ian.

"I'll see you in the morning," he said as he turned toward the door, all his attention on the musket and the ammunition.

She followed him to the door, her heart leaden. The look on his face was one she had seen many times before—on the faces of Indians when they planned to attack another tribe. Affection, laughter, and smiles were replaced by a hardness that offered no mercy. It had frightened her then. It frightened her now.

She watched Ian walk to the barn. Then, sighing, she closed the door and turned, planning to clear the table before going to bed. When she caught sight of Noel, lying on his stomach at the top of the ladder and looking down from his loft, she stopped.

His eyes were huge and filled with curiosity. "I couldn't sleep," he said, climbing down to her.

Fancy put her arms around him, hugging him fiercely. She didn't want him to grow up. She didn't want to see a musket in his hands or the hard gleam in his eyes that she'd just seen in Ian's.

Noel wriggled in her embrace, embarrassed by the maternal gesture. "Do you think Ian will teach me to shoot Pa's musket?"

"He's too busy now," she said. But she knew that one day Noel would learn to handle his father's weapon. He would need to know how to hunt, how to handle arms. But, dear God, not now. Not yet.

"Go up to bed, and take Bandit with you," she said. "He's been ignored." And perhaps the cuddly raccoon would help him fall asleep.

Unsatisfactory had already been hauled off to bed with Amy, and the raccoon was curled up under a chair, his tail sticking out like a furry snake. She watched

Noel carefully scoop the animal into his arms. That was the Noel she wanted to see—caring, gentle. Perhaps he would even be a doctor. Now, that would be fine.

When he looked up at her, his expression was incredibly sweet. "I'm glad we have Ian," he said. "Do you think Papa knows he's taking care of us?"

"Sweetling, I know he does."

Chapter 18

Ian sank onto his narrow bed. Knees spread, elbows propped on his thighs, he buried his face in his hands. Bloody hell, but he was tired. And he hurt. Despite Fancy's doctoring, the burns on his skin felt as if they were still on fire. And the pain fueled his rage.

What kind of man would perpetrate such wanton destruction, endangering the lives of humans and animals alike?

There was only one answer: the kind of man who rode roughshod over his land and his clan, interested only in furthering his own selfish ends. Such a man did not care about the pain and hardship he caused others, did not even think about it.

If Robert Marsh were laird of a Highland clan, the act he'd committed today would be just cause for his clansmen to take action against him.

Ian picked up the musket he'd laid on the cot beside him. He had learned about the latest arms in Edinburgh, had taken a number of weapons home to Brinaire. His had been the best-armed clan at Culloden. In the end, that had meant nothing against England's greater numbers and weaponry. But this was not Culloden, and Ian did not have to fight an entire army.

It felt good to have a weapon in his hands. For the past year he had been unable to fight back against those who, like Marsh, thought they could bend him to their will. But circumstances had changed. By God, they had changed. He was free, and he would not allow Robert Marsh or any other man to threaten him or his own. He intended to fight the craven coward. And the devil himself would not stop him.

The indenture papers were gone.

Fancy ran her hands under her feather mattress for the third time but to no avail. The folded parchment simply was not there.

After Ian left, she had gone to her room, washed away the worst of the grime coating her face and arms, and put on her nightdress. Then a nagging voice in the back of her mind had prompted her to see that the papers were where she had put them. *The fire was set,* the voice said. *Ian and the Wallaces are convinced of it. You've lost an entire tobacco crop because someone violated your property.* The voice would not let her climb into bed until she had reassured herself that her home itself had not also been violated.

But it had been. The papers were gone.

Her heart pounded frantically as her gaze swept over the room. Nothing seemed out of place. Still, and though she knew quite well where she had put the papers, she searched every drawer and under every piece of furniture. There weren't many of either—the bed; a bureau with four drawers, on top of which sat a pitcher and bowl and above which hung a mirror; the rocker; and the chest at the end of the bed where she kept linens. It didn't take long to exhaust all the possibilities.

Frantic, she wondered what else might have been stolen, and that horrifying thought had set her to searching the entire room again. Her money box, containing all the cash she had, lay undisturbed in her top bureau drawer. The papers proving ownership of the horses were still at the bottom of the second drawer.

When she got to the chest, her hands were shaking

and her breathing was coming fast and heavy. Still, she willed herself to go slowly, to look carefully through the neatly stacked blankets and sheets. In the summer, she kept the blankets on the bottom, where they were hidden from view by the lighter-weight things on top of them; as she stared at the chest's contents, she realized that she could see a good three inches of the bottom blanket. Yesterday, when she'd put away the clean sheets, that blanket hadn't been visible. She was certain of it.

Despite the muggy heat of the evening, she felt icy cold all over. Someone had been in her room, going through her possessions. Someone had been watching her every move, waiting for the moment when the family was away.

She remembered the glimpse of a face she'd seen yesterday, at the beach, and the feeling she'd had for the past two days of being watched. Why had she not told Ian? Why had she not found a safer place for her most valuable possessions—the papers that meant Ian's life?

As for the culprit, she didn't think she had to look beyond her brother-in-law, Robert Marsh.

Fancy's heart froze at the realization that Robert now knew that Ian was a free man. She tried to think what he would do with that information—or what he could possibly do with papers that had been signed and witnessed. Nothing. Ian was still safe . . . unless Reverend Winfrey met with some kind of accident.

But surely . . . *surely* not even Robert would harm a man of God. Not when he spent so much effort backing up his every manipulative act with righteous words about his moral duty and God's will.

Still, if she was so certain that Robert would leave Reverend Winfrey unmolested, why did she have this knot of dread in the pit of her stomach? And why did her fear for the minister, as well as for Ian and, for that matter, herself, increase a hundredfold when she considered the possibility that Robert might also have learned of her marriage to Ian?

Had Reverend Winfrey recorded it yet? He was to have stopped at the county office on his return from his trip around the circuit. She didn't think there'd been time for him to do that yet.

And an even more immediate question presented itself: should she go to the barn now and tell Ian that the indenture papers were gone?

No, she thought. What purpose would it serve? They could do nothing about it tonight. She would wait until morning. Then she would have to tell him. He had to be warned.

He should leave. The thought was unbearably painful, but it had to be faced. She couldn't endanger his life. He had given up something vitally important to him by postponing his search for his sister, and he'd done it for her. She could do no less for him.

Tomorrow she would tell him to go.

She tried not to think about the possibility that he might be leaving one dangerous place for an even deadlier one.

Sleep eluded Fancy that night. She half expected riders to come clattering up to the farmhouse, with Robert in the lead. She could hear him ordering her to turn Ian over to him, and when she refused, issuing commands to the men he'd bribed into doing his dirty work to "find the convict and bring him here."

In her mind, she saw Ian boldly facing Robert, John's musket in his hands. She heard the shots that would surely be fired. She saw the blood that would surely be spilled. And she saw Ian lying dead on the ground.

As she lay awake, waiting for her nightmare to come true, every sound was exaggerated, every fear magnified.

Finally, just before dawn, she rose, washed away the sweat of a tortured night and the rest of yesterday's soot, and got dressed. By the time the others were awake and about, she had the morning meal on the table. She felt alone with her knowledge, though, until Ian appeared.

His hair was damp, his face neatly shaved, and his clothes clean. Still, he looked haggard and worn, with lines etched around his eyes and mouth, and his movements were slow and careful—in deference, she guessed, to his burns.

Last night, with the Wallaces joining them for a meal, he had sat in John's old place at the head of the table. She watched as he lowered himself into that same chair, opposite hers. When he met her gaze, nodding in silent greeting, she gave him a shaky smile.

Noel, in his usual seat to the left now of Ian's, said, "I let the fox go yesterday."

Ian's controlled expression softened a little. "I'm sorry, lad. I said I would be going with you."

Noel dropped his gaze, shrugging. "That's all right. I guess it's a good thing you were here when the fire started." He hesitated, then, with a quick glance in Ian's direction, added, "Maybe sometime you can take me back there to, you know"—he shrugged again—"to see that Joseph is all right. If I can find him."

Ian hesitated, his gaze flickering briefly to hers. "I'll try, lad," he said.

Fancy saw the disappointment in Noel's eyes. He'd wanted a positive answer, something he could count on. She hated knowing that his disappointment over something as minor as a trip to the woods would soon become devastation over a much greater matter. How

would she explain to him that Ian was leaving, not in a
year but that very day? She could barely tolerate the
pain herself.

Fancy wasn't able to eat the biscuits she'd made, nor
could she enjoy the bacon, despite the fact that it was a
rare treat. She noticed that Ian wasn't eating much either. Fortune, Noel, and Amy, however, were all de-
vouring the food, apparently unaware of the tension
swirling around them.

The meal was only half over when Ian rose suddenly. "I have to work Ghost," he announced. And he
walked out of the house before Fancy could stop him.

She half rose to go after him, then, when three pairs
of eyes focused on her, clearly questioning what she
was about, she settled back into her seat. The news
would wait until the meal was over. She didn't want to
upset Noel and Fortune and Amy before it was necessary.

Or perhaps she was being a coward, putting off the
inevitable. She had never been a coward before. But
then, she had never been in love before. Nor had she
ever been faced with having to tell the man she loved—
her husband—that he must leave her now, this very
day, before her former brother-in-law destroyed him.

Amy wanted to help her wash and dry the dishes,
which meant it took twice as long. Fancy would have
asked Fortune to coddle Amy through the procedure,
but her sister was intent upon baking the pie for the
Wallaces. And Noel had run outside to play Robinson
Crusoe.

When the dishes were finally clean and put away and
Amy's attention had been diverted to "helping" Fortune bake the pie, Fancy looked out the window. Ian
was astride Gray Ghost in the stallion's paddock.

Her heart beat erratically watching him. He was a
foreigner from a distant land, uprooted against his will

and plunked down in this unfamiliar environment without so much as a shirt or a pair of trousers that fit him. Yet, seeing him there, on the stallion's back, moving as if he were one with the horse, it seemed to her that he was exactly where he belonged. He looked at home, entirely. And she didn't know how in God's name she was going to tell him it had to be otherwise.

Gathering her nerve and the broken pieces of her heart, she went to the door and opened it, determined to do what had to be done. But as she stepped outside, a movement along the road caught her eye. She turned her head, and her breath caught at the sight of her brother-in-law galloping toward the house.

She stood rooted, her thoughts scattering wildly, as he approached, then pulled his horse to a halt at the bottom of the steps.

Turning in his saddle, he looked down at her, a bland expression on his face, though his eyes seemed to glitter with malice. "Fancy," he acknowledged politely enough.

She felt anger rise inside her. Oddly, it occurred to her that she wasn't afraid of him anymore. Not for her own sake. He couldn't trick her, couldn't steal her horses or her land. If he shoved false papers under her nose that said John had given the land to him, he would not get away with it.

Because she would know the papers were false. Ian had taught her to read and, in doing so, had given her the weapon she needed to defend herself against Robert's skulduggery. It gave her momentary pleasure to remember that Robert did not know that.

Robert's gaze swept over the burned tobacco field, then came back to her. "I heard about the fire. I came to see what I could do."

"I think you have done quite enough," she said.

"Meaning what?" he retorted arrogantly.

"I don't think I have to explain, Robert. The fire didn't start itself."

He managed to look surprised. "Then I would look toward your convict," he said contemptuously. "He found an easy way to avoid his rightful work."

Simple anger turned to blind fury inside her, yet she managed to speak calmly. "I do not believe so, since the work was already done and the tobacco was flourishing."

"Ah, sister, there would have been the harvest this fall. You are much too trusting." Then he abruptly changed the subject. "I heard the Wallaces tried to help," he said. "I'll convey my gratitude."

"That won't be necessary. I've already expressed my gratitude to them directly."

Robert shed his bland mask and scowled. "You must watch your association with them, Fancy. They're Scottish trash, just like that bondsman."

"Because you can't tell them what to do?" The words popped out before she could stop them, surprising her as much as they clearly surprised him.

"They don't know their betters any more than that damned convict."

There was no point to this. If it went on much longer, she was going to lose her temper and say something she would truly regret. Something like "That convict is my husband, and if you do anything to harm so much as a hair on his head, I'll see you arrested and charged."

"Thank you for your concern, Robert, but it isn't necessary."

Robert's scowl deepened. "He's dangerous, Fancy. This proves it," he said, waving an arm toward the burned field.

She bit her tongue to stifle any reply. Could he really believe that she would think Ian was responsible for the fire? Did he believe she was that gullible? Probably. She waited for him to take the next step.

"Now that the tobacco is gone," he said, "you might as well sell the place."

"To you, naturally."

"Of course. You can come to Marsh's End," he said, "and bring the horses. I'll find a trainer for you. You can still own them."

"How very generous."

Ignoring her sarcasm, he nodded. "I'll send over my people to get your belongings." He started to turn his horse to leave.

"No," she said sharply.

He turned back.

"I'm not going anywhere, Robert."

He rolled his eyes in exasperation. "Fancy, you're a fool. You can't trust that man. My God, woman! You're risking the lives of your children, not to mention your sister!"

"If I am, it is not your concern."

"Of course it's my concern! You are my brother's widow! God's law demands that I protect and care for you."

She laughed. She couldn't help it. The sound just came spurting out, brief and harsh and devoid of amusement. "You are very selective, aren't you, about which of God's laws you choose to obey? What about the one that bids you to do unto others as you would have them do unto you?"

He opened his mouth to answer, then closed it, swiveling in the saddle when he saw her gaze shoot over his shoulder.

Fancy's stomach clenched when she saw Ian striding toward them. She didn't want a confrontation. She didn't want Robert to believe he had to do something now, today. They needed time—time for Ian to escape Robert's grasp.

But from the look on Ian's face, he had no intention of waiting to tell Robert exactly what he thought of him. He walked straight past Robert's horse and mounted the two steps to stand beside Fancy. His stance was aggressive, his mouth set, and anger blazed in his eyes.

Fancy tried to ward off the inevitable. "Robert, I'm asking you to leave. Now. We have work—"

Ian cut her off. "Come to see whether your minions carried out your orders in a satisfactory manner?"

Robert's face reddened. "I don't know what you're talking about. I came to offer help—not that I need to explain anything to the likes of you."

"Ian—"

"Oh, I think you have a *lot* of explaining to do," Ian persisted. "The only thing that remains to be seen is where, exactly, you will be when you deliver this explanation—in a courtroom or in hell."

"Why, you insolent—" Shaking with rage, Robert lifted his riding crop and brought it down in a vicious slash aimed at Ian's head.

Ian's hand shot up and caught the whip, yanking it from Robert's hand. Before Fancy could speak, before she could do anything but gasp, Ian dived off the steps at Robert, knocking him off his horse.

"Ian! Oh, God . . ."

The startled horse reared, and Fancy stifled a scream as she watched the powerful hooves dance in the air above the two men struggling on the ground. A wave of relief rolled through her when the hooves landed without striking flesh, but the relief was fleeting. Though the horse trotted off to stand a short distance away, she saw disaster happening before her very eyes.

Helpless, she watched Ian haul Robert up from the

ground only to plow a fist into his stomach, then his jaw, sending him to the ground once again. Robert rolled away and managed to stumble to his feet, his fists striking out blindly. He landed a few solid punches, but none stopped Ian. Indeed, they did not seem to faze him at all as he moved deliberately forward, pummeling Robert with every step he took. Robert continued backing up, swinging impotently at his stronger, more determined opponent until a single punch from Ian's fist landed on his jaw and he crumpled.

Ian fell on top of him, but all of a sudden Robert kicked upward, sending Ian sprawling. Robert scrambled on his elbows and knees across the dirt, latched on to his whip, and brought it around in a backward arc toward Ian, who was approaching for another attack.

The whip caught Ian on the arm, and Fancy saw him wince. But whatever pain he felt didn't stop him from once again snatching the whip from Robert's hand and tossing it away. Then, grabbing Robert by one shoulder, Ian rolled him over, dropped to his knees to straddle him, and struck him in the face. Then he struck him again. And again. And again.

"Ian! Stop!" Rushing down the porch steps, Fancy ran to him.

Another fist to the jaw. And another.

"Ian!" She shook him by the shoulders. "You'll kill him!"

Blood was dripping from Robert's nose and mouth. At first he tried to protect himself, his arms flailing at his attacker, but as Ian continued to pummel him, his arms fell to his sides, palms upward.

"Ian, for God's sake . . ." Giving up, Fancy pressed a hand to her mouth and sobbed.

Finally Robert lay still. His face was dripping with blood, his eyes swollen shut. Fancy was enormously relieved to hear him gasping raggedly for breath.

Pushing himself to his feet, Ian stood over him for a moment, looking down, before staggering a few yards away to lean against one of the posts of the porch.

Only then did Fancy notice Noel. He was restraining Lucky, and the dog was growling, his teeth bared at Robert's helpless form. Hurrying to Noel's side, she stooped down to put one arm around him and one around Lucky.

The dog quieted, and the only sound that broke the terrible silence was that of Robert's labored breathing. For several minutes no one moved.

Then, slowly, Robert rolled to his side. He pushed to his knees, then his feet. He took several lurching steps toward his horse. Stopped, swaying. Took several more and reached for the stirrups of his saddle for support. The horse shied, trying to sidestep away, and Fancy rose with some notion of trying to help him mount. But Robert grabbed the horse's reins and gave them a cruel jerk to bring the animal's head down.

She watched as Robert hauled himself into the saddle, groaning. Lying along the horse's neck, unable to right himself, he brought the animal around.

His furious glance at Ian, Fancy noted, was hindered by the fact that he could only open one eye. "You'll regret this," she heard him mutter.

Ian ignored him.

Robert managed to summon the strength to give his mount a kick in the sides. The animal jumped forward and took off at a canter toward the road.

Fancy watched Robert's retreat until he was out of sight. Then she turned to Ian. He, too, was staring at the now deserted road, his expression hard and cold but for the slight satisfied smile that curved his lips.

She didn't know him, as he was at that moment. She knew the gentle, patient man who taught her sister how to write her name and whispered nonsense into the ears of the horses he rode. She knew the passionate lover who heated her blood and made her heart sing. And, yes, she knew the embittered, alienated Scot who'd been cast out of his homeland.

But this man, the warrior who could throw his fury into beating another man, then stand there looking calm and triumphant . . . no, she didn't know him at all. And he frightened her.

He did not frighten her anywhere near as much as Robert did, however. The thought of what her brother-in-law might do, having been so thoroughly humiliated—in front of a woman, no less—chilled her to the marrow.

"Ian, I need to talk to you," she said.

He met her gaze, then glanced at Noel, who was slowly walking toward them with Lucky. An instant later the front door squeaked, and Fortune's head appeared around the edge of it. She glanced around, seemed to think it was safe, then stepped hesitantly onto the porch. Amy was clinging to her skirts, her fingers stuck in her mouth.

When Ian looked back at her, Fancy added a single quiet word to her previous statement. "Alone."

He glanced once more at their audience, then said to her, "Go for a ride with me."

She nodded.

"I'll saddle the mare for you," he said. "Meet me in the barn."

He walked away, and Fancy turned to her sister. "I need you to watch Noel and Amy for a little while."

Fortune frowned, her gaze darting up the road, then back at Fancy, then up the road again.

"Robert will not come back," Fancy assured her. "He could barely sit his horse. And I won't be gone long, I promise."

"*I'll* take care of Amy."

Noel's voice brought Fancy's gaze down to him. He was looking at her with those wide, serious eyes. The fight had scared him, she was certain of it; she'd seen his fear when she helped him keep Lucky from tearing Robert apart. Yet he was doing his very best to act . . . to act like a man.

Lord, how many times could her heart keep breaking?

Before Fancy could respond to Noel's gallant offer, Fortune stepped forward and touched her shoulder. When Fancy looked at her, she nodded, then gestured toward the barn.

"You'll be all right?" Fancy asked her.

Again her sister nodded and even tried to give her a weak smile of reassurance.

"Will Ian have to leave?" Noel asked. "Now, I mean?"

Fancy opened her mouth to reply, but a quick glance at Amy, still clinging to Fortune's skirts, made her close her mouth. With a look and a nod of her head, she asked Fortune to take Amy inside. The last thing she needed right now was a three-year-old's tears.

Fortune lifted her niece into her arms and carried her back into the house, closing the door. Fancy took Noel's hand and led him to the porch step.

Pulling him down beside her, she said, "You're right, sweetling, Ian might have to go now."

"I don't want him to," Noel said.

"None of us do," she replied. "I'll miss him, too. But I'm afraid your uncle might do something to hurt him if he stays. And I would feel even worse if that happened."

Noel was silent for a moment. "So would I."

Fancy watched the competing emotions struggle for dominance on her son's young face. He had just lost a father, and now he was about to lose the man he'd come to love like another father. He was much too young for this second loss.

"Can I say good-bye?" he said finally, his voice breaking.

"Of course," she said. "And think of all the gifts he's already given us. We will always have those. And he'll stay in our hearts."

A tear slipped down his face.

"I have to go," she said gently. "You will look after Fortune and Amy for me, won't you?"

He nodded, ducking his head to wipe his cheek on his shoulder.

She stood. "I'll be back soon."

She forced herself to walk away from him, her little boy who was being forced to grow up much, much too soon.

She met Ian coming out of the barn with the mare. He handed her the reins, and she followed him to the stallion's paddock, where he had left Gray Ghost when Robert arrived. Fancy opened the gate for him, and he rode the stallion into the yard. Then he dismounted to help her into the sidesaddle.

His green eyes were wary, his hands more efficient than affectionate as he lifted her. He sprang into his own saddle, and they crossed the yard, heading for the riding path that led through the woods to the creek. When they reached the path, of one accord, they pushed the horses into a slow canter.

Fancy made no attempt to talk as they rode, nor did Ian break the silence. They rode to the creek, and then he helped her down from the horse, looping the reins of both animals over a couple of low branches.

Fancy looked across the narrow strip of water. It ran sluggishly, the water level low from lack of rain.

She felt his presence next to her, recognized the currents that always ran so strong between them. And she knew she had to do what would be the hardest thing she had ever done in her life.

She turned and looked up at him. His mouth was grim, his eyes still glittering from the recent encounter. He looked hard and capable. And that would kill him. A bondsman could not fight Robert and win.

Her hand went to his face. "Ian. You will have to leave. You cannot stay now." It was both plea and moan, and his expression softened. The glitter in his eyes faded, and he took her in his arms.

"Do you think someone like that craven dog can run me off?" His eyes burned into her. She felt the violence that still radiated from him, the aura of explosiveness that hung around him like a cloak. He was every inch a warrior, and to her dismay she was stirred by it, caught in the irresistible tides of danger and urgency. The now familiar fire flared inside her, a fire every bit as greedy as the one that had destroyed their crop. More dangerous. This one threatened to consume them both.

He muttered something she guessed was a curse. His fingers came up and traced the outline of her face.

Fancy found herself leaning into him when she should have been separating herself. She tried to swallow through the lump in her throat and forced herself to move backward. "Please listen to me," she pleaded.

His fingers caught her hand and pulled her back to him. "Ah, lass," he said. "You must be a siren, for I cannot think around you."

"A siren?"

"From a grand adventure, lass. The sirens would use their wonderful voices to call to sailors, then destroy them. No man could resist them."

Fancy looked up at him, her heart breaking. Would she be his siren?

"Nay, lass," he said as if he knew exactly what she

was thinking. "There was one who survived to conquer his enemies, and I *do* plan to survive."

But she was frantic with fear for him. She knew Robert's power; Ian didn't. She had to find a way to make him understand. But the mere prospect of his going left her feeling intolerably empty. She trembled as she looked up at him, her eyes begging him to heed her.

She felt the tension, the need, in his body as his arms tightened around her. She stood on tiptoe and lifted her head so she could touch his lips with hers. She wanted it to be a good-bye. She had to make him go.

Instead, his lips opened and his tongue probed her mouth as her body melded to his. And she was kissing him back, desperation and fear driving a passion that needed no goading. She wanted one last taste, one last memory.

She felt a hot wash of tears behind her eyes, and she tried to keep them from rushing out. His touches were sorcery, sending her caution flying like fall leaves in a heavy wind.

His lips hungrily caressed her cheeks, her lips, the warmth around her eyes, then slipped away, his tongue playing up and down her neck. Every nerve end cried out as her body tensed and moved under his touch, then arched against him in an agony of need. For the moment, nothing mattered but the two of them. Not the past, not the future, only the fierce sweetness of each touch, each look, each soft caress.

Her fear for him made her response primal and voracious as she felt the probing intensity of his body even through the cloth. Then they were fumbling with each other's clothing until the garments dropped to the ground, and she felt the rich, warm rays of the sun on her skin as he led her to a springy patch of grass under a grandfather oak. He guided her down with one hand

and knelt beside her, his hands moving over her lightly as if touching a fragile treasure. But she didn't feel fragile. She was all heat and tingling nerves and coursing need. She held her arms out to him, and their bodies touched, searing each other to their very souls.

Still, he hesitated for a moment. She felt the restraint in his body, saw the anguish on his face. "You are so incredibly bonny," he said brokenly. "I . . . God, I . . ."

She touched his lips, then the lines around his eyes. She laid the palm of her hand against his left cheek. She memorized the way he felt, the way he looked, the scent of soap and leather that surrounded him. Then she gently, so very gently, drew him closer until their bodies were locked together. Exquisite ripples danced through her as she felt his maleness hungrily probing her. Together they moved until she was on the ground, her back to the grass, his body poised above hers.

She felt as if the universe had suspended itself. Her world was Ian, and for the moment nothing else mattered. He lowered himself, his maleness arousing and seducing the most sensitive part of her until she was nearly mad with desire. He entered her slowly but seductively, moving deep inside her like a sensual dancer, awakening and teasing every particle of her being. She felt him love her inside, felt him reaching for more of her, and her body responded, her hips moving with his rhythm, becoming one with him in the most intimate way possible. Moving with a deliberate, savage grace, he prolonged every movement, incited each hidden feeling, exploited them until the dance turned wild and uncontrollable. His thrusts ignited hundreds of tiny explosions until her whole body erupted with sensations so great, so rapturous, she thought she would drown in them. Bursts of supreme pleasure spread like sun rays to warm every part of her body and soul.

She was filled with his seed, and she felt its warmth. She exulted in it, even as she felt the soft stroke of his fingers on her face, the whisper-light kiss of his lips, heard the murmur of unintelligible words in her ear.

She knew then, deep in her soul, that she'd just made a terrible mistake, that he would pay for her weakness. She already knew how divided his heart was, and now his sense of honor would be even more sorely tried.

And she still had to make him leave.

But just for this moment she couldn't let him go. She relished the feel of him in her, the quiver that sent little aftershocks of pleasure through her. Her hands played with the hair at the back of his neck and she felt the dappled rays of the sun on his back.

She treasured this time, engraving it deep in her heart. The physical feelings might flee but never this emotional bond, this entwining of souls.

He rolled over, his hand catching hers and bringing it to his mouth. He was so gentle, yet she saw the bleakness in his eyes, a blame that should have been hers. She clung to his hand.

She wanted to give him so much. She wanted to lighten the guilt he carried; instead she feared she had only deepened it through her own lack of discipline, a recklessness she never knew existed inside her.

She wanted so much to say she loved him, but that would be sentencing him to death. That would create the final obligation—the one that might well force him to stay. And then she, and she alone, would be responsible for what befell him.

She tried to even out her breathing, to prepare arguments she doubted he would accept. She tried to dissipate the golden glow that remained inside her. After a moment she gathered the words that would destroy it forever.

"Ian, you have to leave Maryland. Now."

He stared at her as if she were daft.

"Your indenture papers are gone," she said.

He jerked his head toward her, his green eyes focusing on her intently.

"I put them under my mattress," she continued. "But last night, after the fire and all the talk about Robert, I felt uneasy. I decided to check, just to make sure they were still there. And they weren't."

He didn't speak, he only continued to watch her, that muscle twitching in his cheek.

"I looked everywhere. They're gone, and"—she sucked in a quick breath—"there's only one reason someone would take them: to get his hands on you. And there's only one person who would want that: Robert. After today there will be no stopping him."

His brows came together in a frown, and she saw refusal in his eyes. He didn't want to run from Robert. That much was clear.

"Don't you see?" she said desperately, voicing words that tore her apart inside. "If Robert has those papers, he can forge a new document that says John deeded you to him or left you to him in his will. He's been trying to get you at Marsh's End since he found out you were a bondsman, but I wouldn't . . . sell you. And after what just happened, if he hadn't already planned to kill you, he surely will now."

"As powerful as he might think he is," Ian growled, "I doubt any court would let him get away with murder."

"The murder of a free man, no," she agreed. "But the accidental death of a bondsman who died being whipped for disobedience? He wouldn't even be charged."

He was silent, considering her words.

"Without those papers," she continued, "neither

you nor I can prove you bought your freedom back or even whether you were allowed to do so. And the sheriff is a crony of Robert's; he'll support any lie Robert tells."

"Reverend Winfrey can testify," Ian started. "He witnessed . . ."

His voice trailed off, and as he stared at her, Fancy saw comprehension dawn in his eyes. "Surely he wouldn't hurt a minister."

"Robert is very capable of planning an accident," Fancy said. "I've heard rumors before of accidents befalling farmers who wouldn't sell their land to him."

Ian's jaw clenched. "We have to warn Reverend Winfrey."

"I will warn him," she said. "*You* have to leave."

"Do you think I would leave you to the mercy of a man we both think might be capable of murdering a minister?"

"I can take care of myself and my family. I have done it for a long time," she reassured him. "I'm freeing you from your promise, Ian."

"To hell with the bloody promise," he shot back, stunning her. "Do you not remember the vows we took together?"

"But they were . . ."

"False? Lies?" He shook his head slowly. "I told myself that. And I think I believed it—until we lay together." His expression softened, his gaze raking her features. "Lass, do you truly believe that I could leave you, and mayhap an unborn bairn, to Marsh's mercy?"

She gave him the one explanation she knew would make him go. "If you don't go, you most certainly will be leaving us to his mercy."

He stared at her with disbelieving eyes. "I don't understand, lass."

"Robert can't touch me as a married woman. The

farm would be yours, since a woman's property goes to her husband. He can't get the property, nor can he harm you, if you're gone. You can look for your sister, fulfill your vow, and in a year's time return if you wish. In the meantime, if he tries to forge any papers disputing the ownership of your bond or of the land, I'll have time to prove them false."

Fancy's heart was cracking. She knew Scotland could be deadly for him, too. Yet she was convinced that Robert was by far the most immediate danger.

For a moment, indecision flickered across his face. Then he reached out, caught her hand, and held it, his thumb rubbing the backs of her fingers. "Katy is one," he said, "and you are four. She is my sister, but you are my wife by law. Your children are now my children, and your sister my sister. I willna abandon any of you to him."

By law. Not by heart. His duty. His responsibility. Not his love.

Even as the realization struck like a dagger to her heart, she put her finger to his lips. "Ian, I swear to you that Robert will convince the law that you belong to him, and he will kill you. You heard Little Tim say that Robert had a slave whipped until he died—and it wasn't the first time. He treats his bondsmen even worse than he does his slaves because he doesn't pay as much for them. How could you protect me then? Ian, you have to go. I can handle Robert. I can't handle, nor can my children handle, seeing you killed because of your damned pride."

"Ah, lass," he murmured, "in the past year I have been skewered through the ribs, almost hanged, beaten, starved, and shackled in irons. The English couldna kill me, so I donna think a pompous ass like Robert Marsh is likely to succeed where so many others failed."

Stunned, Fancy simply stared at him for a moment. She had given him what he'd professed to want more than anything in the world, and he was not going to take it.

"And what of your sister?" she said. "What if she needs you? What if she dies because no one came for her? Robert might continue to try to get my property, but he will not touch a hair on my head. Even if society disapproves of me, I'm his sister-in-law, and to harm me would bring censure on him. He thinks too much of his position to risk that. But if you die, who will look for Katy? She's a child, Ian. And she's alone."

He flinched, and she saw the agony in his face, the terrible conflict of loyalties.

"You wouldn't be leaving me, Ian," she continued hurriedly, sensing her advantage. "You will be looking for your sister. The Wallaces will help me. I'm protected by the marriage license. Even so, if anything truly threatens us, I can always take my family to the Cherokees. They are family and would protect us." She smiled. "In truth, I would like to see them again. They are good people. You would like them."

Ian's expression didn't change.

She caught his hand. "Please, Ian. For me, for Noel. Go." Her fingers touched the new cuts and bruises on his hands.

He looked down at them, then at her. "Hitting him," he said softly, "felt good, lass. No one will touch me with a whip again and live."

His low, hard tone sent tremors through her. But then he raised his hand to her face again, placing his index finger under her chin to tilt her head upward until she met his gaze. He touched her lips with his, lightly, tenderly—and all too briefly. "You will never know what you've given me, lass," he said. "You've given me back my faith. Faith and hope. And I was in sore need of both."

A good-bye? She fervently wished it, even knowing how much she would miss him. He must be safe, or she could not go on living.

"You'll go, then?"

"I canna go until I know that the minister is safe and that the marriage is recorded," he said.

Sighing deeply, Fancy forced her mind to practical matters. "I'll go into Chestertown tomorrow," she said. "I'll speak to Reverend Winfrey's wife and find out where he is. And I'll talk to Douglas Turner."

"The man you said you weren't sure you could trust?"

She frowned. "John trusted him, at least enough to give him your papers and his will."

"Then he must have had reason to think the man would not betray him—or you," Ian concluded. "But I should go with you."

She shook her head. "I cannot leave Fortune and the children alone at the farm, not after the fire. And if we take them all with us, the farm and the horses will be unprotected." She shook her head. "Robert will probably nurse his wounds for a few days before striking again. By then I'll be back, and you can be on your way to Scotland."

She had tried to sound convincing, but inside she was shaking with fear . . . for him and for her own loneliness when he left.

"I'll consider it," he said with a slight smile. But deep in her heart she was afraid that he'd already made up his mind. He stood and gave her his hand, drawing her lightly to her feet. "We'd best go, lass, before I do something more I'll regret."

Her heart sank even deeper. Did he regret their lovemaking because he was leaving? Or because it would bind him to her? Either reason produced hurt beyond bearing.

With Ian's help, Fancy mounted her mare, then watched as he vaulted onto Gray Ghost's back. She followed him along the path toward home, her battered heart aching as it had never ached before.

Chapter 19

Robert gingerly explored his face. His lip was split, his left eye swollen shut, his whole face a motley collection of purple and red patches, all of which hurt like the devil. Those were the superficial signs of the injuries he'd sustained.

Other injuries were not so obvious. His jaw hurt, but he didn't think it was broken. His ribs, however, were; he was certain of it, for he could barely breathe through the pain. In fact, there wasn't a part of his body that *didn't* hurt.

He poured himself a tall glass of whiskey and cautiously downed a quarter of it, swearing as the alcohol burned the cuts on his lips and the insides of his cheeks. He paced back and forth, too angry to stay still even though every movement was agony.

The Scotsman would pay. He would pay for every bruise, for every ache, every cut, every labored breath. That the man had attacked him in front of Fancy only deepened Robert's fury. She would be his wife, by God, and now she'd seen him on the ground, bleeding . . . beaten. The humiliation was beyond endurance.

A tentative knock sounded at the door.

"Come in," he commanded.

A parade of three servants entered: Hannah, his housekeeper; Darlene, his maid and mistress; and Silas, his manservant. Hannah carried a box of medicines and powders; Silas brought two buckets of hot water; and Darlene held several strips of cloth. Darlene's hands, Robert noted with satisfaction, were shaking; it helped his battered ego to know that, even in his present state, he instilled fear in the hearts of his inferiors.

"Took you long enough," he said, taking another gulp of the whiskey.

"Had to heat the water, Massa Marsh," Silas said.

Robert glared at him. "You arguin' with me, boy?"

"No, suh."

"Better not. I'm in no mood for insolence." Robert wanted to strike the servant. He probably would have, had he not realized it would hurt him more than Silas. "Help me get these damnable clothes off."

Silas set the water down and hurried to undo his master's cravat, unbutton his shirt, and ease it off his body. The slave sucked in a quick breath as he caught sight of the damage. When his eyes narrowed, Robert could see him wondering who had done this to him, but he wasn't about to tell Silas or anyone else the truth.

"My horse fell," he said, wondering why he bothered to offer any explanation at all. But he didn't want speculation. He knew the grapevine that ran from plantation to plantation, and he couldn't bear the thought of his neighbors learning of his beating at the hands of that Scottish scum.

His anger deepened. He had to get a new will forged, and as soon as possible. Damnation. He had sent a man to snoop around Fancy's house and find John's will—if there was one. He'd told him to look for any papers with a seal on them, but the man returned without the will; instead he'd brought the Scotsman's indenture papers. Robert had been enraged to find that the man had manipulated Fancy into allowing him to purchase his freedom. Of course it was no matter to him; the hand of a skilled forger would create a will that showed the indenture had belonged to Robert since his brother's death, and thus Fancy would have no authority to sell the miserable cur his freedom.

And he'd already waited too long to visit the forger. But there had been problems on the plantation, and he'd been sure he could convince Fancy that she would be best served by coming to him. And she would have, had it not been for the interfering Scotsman.

Now he could wait no longer. Robert would write detailed instructions and send the same man who'd visited Fancy and burned her tobacco to Edward Hays in Baltimore. He'd used Hays before to change the boundaries of land grants. Hays was skilled, he worked fast, and as he feared Robert, he would never betray him.

It would take three days at most to get the forged documents, and then Robert could submit them to the local magistrate, a man he paid well enough that he expected no problems. He would say, to satisfy public curiosity, that he had hoped Fancy would simply accept his generous protection, and so he had delayed the unpleasant legal proceedings for as long as possible.

Unfortunately, John had died only two days after purchasing the Scotsman. Not much time to make a new will. But if Robert said that John had anticipated this very situation because of his poor health, he was sure people would believe that John, like any prudent husband, had wisely planned ahead by naming his brother his beneficiary—in return for caring for his family, of course. And given that he ended up with an arrogant and violent convict, it would be seen as a very good thing that he'd had the foresight to take appropriate measures.

The bondsman's feeble attempt to gain his freedom would be for naught—and the Scot would become, along with all of John's other possessions, Robert's property. To do with as he would.

Reverend Winfrey, as witness to the purported sale, might try to cause trouble, but Winfrey was only an interloper who didn't know his place. His new religion encouraged people to defy their betters. The county would be far more peaceful without his presence. . . .

But now he had to tolerate the clumsy attentions of his servants. His ribs felt like hot pokers as Hannah probed his chest. After one particularly painful jab, he exploded, "Do that again and I'll have you whipped."

"You got bad ribs there, Massa Marsh. I'll have to wrap you tight. It's gonna hurt."

Robert felt the pain deep in his bones. He should send someone for a doctor, but a doctor would recognize a beating when he saw one. Damn quack would probably tell everyone. No, Hannah would have to do. She took care of the slaves and bondsmen.

"You know what you're doing?"

"Yessir."

He downed the remaining whiskey in one gulp as the woman started to wrap a cloth tight around his chest. Pain rippled through him, then grew in waves. Muscle spasms gripped him until he thought he couldn't bear it.

His hand whipped out, catching Hannah across the face and throwing her nearly across the room.

"You did that on purpose," he accused. "You didn't have to pull it so tight. Get out of here before I have you whipped within an inch of your life."

Hannah rose quickly, wiping blood from a cut on her face. The other two servants stood still, obviously petrified. Robert took some satisfaction in the fear in their faces. It made his own pain more bearable.

He thought again about sending Silas for a doctor, but his pride won. Besides, a doctor would probably tell him he should go to bed for a week, and he had things to do that wouldn't wait.

"Get me another bottle of whiskey," he said to Silas. He looked at Darlene, pretty Darlene with skin the color of gold and a lush body. She trembled before his gaze, and he felt himself growing warm in the belly. But there was no way he could bed her, not for days. Not with pain radiating throughout his body every time he moved.

"Get the hell out of here."

Without a word, she scampered from the room with the speed of a fox being hunted by dogs.

He sighed, deciding that he was tired of her. It was time to sell her and find a new mistress. Perhaps he would wait until after he and Fancy were married and she was carrying his heir.

He didn't love Fancy, but she was quite comely and, more important, she was fertile. Not like that sickly thing he'd married first or the frightened little bitch who'd been his second wife; the two of them had convinced him that the gentry bred weak women. Fancy's speech and deportment were acceptable, and at this point her fertility made up for her unfortunate background.

Of course, he still had to overcome her reluctance. And as he watched Silas cautiously pour him another glass of whiskey, he knew he must put his plan in motion. It was clear that Fancy cared what happened to the Scotsman, so once Robert had the man here, at Marsh's End, it would not be so hard to force Fancy to marry him.

Then, after the marriage, he could kill the bastard.

The crow seemed to fly out of the setting sun. Tucking her wings close to her sides, she landed on Ian's shoulder as he bent over the young tobacco plants. Trouble. A fitting name, he thought. Trouble was something he didn't seem to be able to avoid.

He was still in turmoil from the . . . ride with Fancy earlier that day. His heart and mind were so bloody confused. His body warmed every time he thought of their lovemaking, but his heart had taken a beating.

Loving Fancy had surpassed his wildest dreams. He'd felt consumed by the warmth, which filled him so completely that he never wanted to let it go. Or let her go.

But she was right. Katy was a child. Was she all alone? Starving? He wouldn't even let himself think of other things—worse things. If Fancy could take care of her own, could he do less for his family?

But could she really take care of hers—without his help? That was the crux of the matter.

He'd had little time to consider it. They had returned from their private ride to find that Little Tim Wallace had arrived with a load of surplus tobacco plants, a gift from his father. Ian had spent the rest of the day with Tim and Fortune in the field, planting the seedlings. They would be late but with luck, rain, and sun, they might have a small crop. Not enough, but it would be something.

Trouble cawed again as she perched on Ian's shoulder. Ian rose to his feet and stretched, expecting the bird to fly away, but Trouble kept her perch, digging her claws in to hang on. He tolerated the discomfort. Fancy seemed to hold a special place in her heart for the bloody creature. And Ian was coming to hold a special place in *his* heart for Fancy.

A feather batted his cheek as Trouble flapped her wings and uttered a loud "caw" directly in his ear.

"Bloody hell!"

At his exclamation, Fortune straightened and gave him her gentle smile. He had to wonder what was so amusing until he realized that her gestures indicated that it must be time for supper. At her next communication—a graceful movement telling him to praise the bird—Ian rolled his eyes. Nevertheless, he ran his hand over the sleek black body, calming Trouble's restlessness.

Like Patrick's hawks, he thought. His older brother had loved to hunt. Ian himself had never enjoyed the sport, but he had relished the hours spent riding the hills with Patrick.

He closed his eyes for a moment, pushing aside the painful memory. Would his memories ever be anything but painful? Would he ever be able to recall pleasant times without the pain of loss overwhelming the goodness of the memory itself?

Trouble dug her talons into him and pecked impatiently at his hair. No wonder, he thought, the Marsh clan believed the creature was a female. She actually seemed to be nagging him.

"All right," he said. "Keep your feathers on. I'm going."

Ian looked at Little Tim, who was staring in disbelief. Ian gave him a crooked smile as if being summoned by a crow were an everyday experience, then started toward the house. Only then did the crow leave his shoulder and fly on ahead.

As he approached with Tim following behind, he saw Fancy feeding the crow a tidbit. A reward for pecking holes in his head, no doubt.

She spoke as he drew closer. "Trouble found you, I see."

"It always does," he said, coming to a stop in front of her. "I admit, though, having a crow nesting in my hair is a unique experience."

"Oh, she groomed you, did she. That means she likes you."

"I would rather she did not." God, in a year, he'd be

bald. Or worse. "Mayhap you can make her like your brother-in-law."

"Robert would make crow stew."

"I might do the same."

The crow flapped her wings, as if she had understood him, and Fancy giggled.

The sound easily made up for whatever discomfort the crow had caused him, Ian thought, watching the golden light of sundown dance in her eyes.

"Well, we won't be eating crow," she said, "but supper *is* ready."

"I'll be in as soon as I wash."

When she turned and went inside, Ian walked over to the well. Pulling up the large bucket, he splashed water onto his face and hands, rubbing vigorously, enjoying the icy-cold shock against his sun-heated skin. Despite his burns and blisters and the minor bruises he'd acquired that morning in his fight with Marsh, he felt as fit and fine as he ever had.

He'd done little physical labor at Brinaire, though he had trained in arms both as a boy and as a young man. On his return from Edinburgh University, he had kept the estate books for Patrick, and except for riding, which he'd always pursued for pleasure, he hadn't really made use of his strength until it had become clear that war was coming and he'd started training again.

He'd never suspected that he had a farmer's heart, that he would enjoy the texture of earth between his fingers. He wouldn't have dreamed he'd feel such pleasure in watching what he planted grow. Or that he'd feel such pain in watching it being destroyed.

Damn Robert Marsh! *Damn* him!

He splashed more water on his face, then strode toward the barn to change.

Standing next to his cot, he pulled off his sweat- and

dirt-stained shirt, took a freshly washed one from a hook, and pulled it over his head, leaving the leather thongs at the neck untied. Then he picked up a comb from the small table that held the few personal items he'd inherited from John Marsh. As he ran the comb through his damp hair, he glanced at the mirror he used for shaving, and something about the way he looked made him stop—and look again.

His skin was bronze now, and his face had filled out, although it was still leaner than it had been when he left Brinaire to join Prince Charlie. And there were lines around his eyes and at the corners of his mouth that hadn't been there two years ago. He looked hard at his reflection, searching for the man he had once been, the Scottish scholar who had stood first in his classes.

But that younger man was no more. Scotland was an ocean and a lifetime away. And the home that he had known and loved was gone forever.

With sudden fury, Ian swept the contents of the table onto the barn floor. Candleholder, book, razor, porcelain washbasin. The basin shattered as it hit the leg of his cot, breaking into large, thick pieces. He stared at them, trembling with the violence that filled him, the rage he felt toward himself.

"I'll . . . help you pick it up," a small, timid voice said behind him.

Ian swung around to see Noel standing a few feet inside the barn doorway, looking unsure whether to run or to hold his ground.

"I want to do that sometimes, too," the lad admitted quietly.

Ian held himself absolutely still, trying to control the roiling emotions inside him. After a moment he asked, "When have you wanted to?"

"When Papa died," Noel said in a low voice. "I didn't think it was fair."

"But you didn't break anything?" Ian asked carefully.

"I was afraid to," Noel murmured. "Mama was . . ."

Ian walked toward him and stooped to bring his face level with the lad's. "Your mother was . . ."

"She was so sad," Noel whispered, his voice cracking a little.

"Sometimes it helps to smash things," Ian said.

"It does?"

"Aye, but only in dire circumstances."

Noel's gaze slid past him to take in the broken basin, and when he looked back at Ian, his look was questioning.

"I was thinking of Scotland," Ian said, "and my sister."

Noel thought about that a moment. Then his small throat moved as he swallowed. "Mama told me that you don't know where she is."

" 'Tis true," he replied. "My brothers and I left her at home when we went off to the war. But when we lost the war, our home was stolen from us, and I donna know what happened to Katy."

Noel hesitated, then asked, "How old is she?"

"About your age," Ian replied.

"And you want to look for her? That's why you want to leave us?"

"Ah, lad . . ." He put a hand on Noel's shoulder and squeezed gently. "I donna *want* to leave you. But my sister is all alone. Our parents have been dead several years, and my brothers are dead now, too. Most of our clansmen—mayhap all—were killed in the war. So Katy has no one . . . no one but me. And I have to find her. Can you understand that?"

Noel heaved a sigh, then nodded reluctantly.

"I willna leave, though," Ian added, "until I know that you and your family are safe."

The lad's lips quivered. "Will you ever come back?"

Ian couldn't lie to him. Still, he couldn't bring himself to dash his hopes entirely. In the end, he managed a compromise. "I'll try," he said.

Noel was silent for a moment. "Before you go," he began slowly, "will you teach me to hunt?"

Ian couldn't suppress a smile. First it was reading, now hunting. Doubtless some other thing would crop up that only he could do. He could see Noel's brain churning. He was a natural born schemer.

"Aye," he said, "I'll teach you. I'll take you tomorrow if we get enough planting done."

"Can I ride Gray Ghost?"

"Nay, he's still too young and headstrong. But you can take the gelding if you do exactly what I tell you."

Noel beamed.

"Did your father ever take you hunting?"

Noel shook his head. "He said I was too young."

The lad *was* young. But then, Ian thought, he had learned to hold a gun almost before he could walk. And Noel might well need to know how to handle firearms when Ian was gone.

Gone . . . The word sent a chill racing through him that was followed by a sudden sense of loss. God, he'd barely survived the loss of one family. How in the name of all the saints would he survive the loss of another?

Shaking off the dread that filled him, he gave Noel a nod. "We'll go in the morning."

"And you'll finish *Robinson Crusoe* tonight?"

"Aye." Standing up, he added, "Come now. If we are going to do all you want, we had best start."

Noel stood for a moment, then held out his hand. Ian hesitated for only an instant, then took the small hand in his large one. Together they walked from the barn.

Robinson Crusoe quelled a mutiny that night and made his way home to find a fortune waiting for him.

Amy fell asleep in Ian's lap, while Noel leaned forward in his chair and listened intently to the end. Fortune and Tim Wallace, who had decided to stay over and finish the planting in the morning, tried not to look at each other. Fancy guessed they missed nearly every word.

She closed her eyes and let Ian's Scottish burr wash over her, let it seep into her heart, her soul, her being. She wanted to store every word, every nuance of his voice in her memory. When he closed the book, she felt at once deeply satisfied and horribly disappointed that it was over. She wanted more. More stories, more memories. More of him.

The silence lengthened in the aftermath of the tale. Finally Fortune rose, took Amy from Ian's lap, and carried her to their room. Noel was awake—barely—and his lashes were fluttering in his effort to ward off sleep. He made no protest when Ian picked him up, balanced him over one shoulder and climbed up to the loft.

Tim said an awkward and reluctant good night and left for the barn, where he would spend the night.

Fancy stayed in her chair, waiting quietly, until Ian climbed back down the ladder.

"He was asleep," he told her, "from the moment his head hit the pillow."

"He said you promised to take him hunting."

"Aye, it's time he learned."

She hesitated. "You're staying?"

"Until that tobacco is planted," he answered.

"I'll help," she said.

"You should warn Reverend Winfrey."

"He won't be back in Chestertown for several more days. If I leave the day after tomorrow, we can finish planting first. Robert will probably be abed all week." She hoped. She prayed.

Two more days with Ian. Two more days to love, to want, to make greater the loss. Even now she felt the heat rising in her again.

"Do you really think it's time to take Noel shooting?"

"He needs to learn, lass."

She wanted to say no, that Noel was still too young. And she was also worried that Noel was becoming too dependent on Ian, so soon before he left. But she couldn't deny Noel these last few days. Both she and her son needed Ian Sutherland—for different reasons, but they needed him all the same.

She watched as Ian picked up *Robinson Crusoe* and returned it to the shelf over the mantel. Rising, she moved to stand beside him. She raised a hand to touch the bruise on his cheek, and his head turned, his gaze meeting hers. The flame from the oil lamp seemed to flare, the light in the room intensifying . . . or was it the flames that rose between them that intensified?

"I wish . . ."

He smiled slightly. "You wish what?"

"That you had not been hurt."

" 'Twas little enough for the pleasure I had in hitting him." He shrugged a little, then added, "I admit that I gave to your brother-in-law a share of what I have wanted to give many others in the past year but couldna because I was in irons. 'Twas the first time in a long while that someone has hit me and I have been able to strike back."

Her hand found the mantel, and her fingers clutched the edge of it to keep from touching him. "Tell me about Scotland . . . where you lived. Unless," she added quickly, "you'd rather not."

He looked at her for a long moment, then sat a few steps away on the edge of the table, facing her. "I lived at a place called Brinaire."

"It has a lovely sound," she said.

" 'Twas a beautiful place—in the Highlands, not far from the sea and bordered by mountains."

"Was?" she asked softly.

"The Sassenach took it, along with the hereditary title that would have belonged to my son. I have nothing to offer anyone, not you or the bairns, or even my sister."

"Oh, no . . ." She took a step toward him. "You have so much!"

He snorted softly, a low, bemused sound. "Aye, mayhap you are right. I find that I am becoming a farmer and a horse trainer and a storyteller."

"Can you . . ." She trailed off, hesitating. "That must be difficult . . . after being a lord, I mean."

He shrugged. "I cared little about the title, but I do regret having it stripped from my family, my . . . heirs. It has been in my family for centuries." He hesitated, then added, "I never wanted to be laird. I loved books. My years at Edinburgh University were some of the happiest I've ever known."

His gaze held hers steadily as he continued, "Fancy, you know why I have to leave. It is not because I miss Scotland. Aye, I miss the sea and the heather and the mountains with their wild waterfalls. I miss my family, and I miss my friends, and I think it will always be thus. But I have found something fine here in Maryland. And when I leave, I will miss it."

She was having difficulty swallowing, and she was very much afraid she was going to cry. The distance between them suddenly seemed intolerable. Ian had

volunteered to stay a year because of his honor, because—for her own sake—she had forced him into
marriage. He had never said he loved her. He had
never said he wanted to stay. He had only said he
would miss this land, and despite his kind words, she'd
heard the pain in his voice when he spoke of Scotland.

"Lass?"

Her eyes must have reflected the anguish she felt,
because he stepped over to her and put his arms around
her. One of his hands stroked her hair for a moment
before he abruptly let her go. Folding his arms across
his chest, he sighed heavily. "I donna know how long I
can bear this, lass. I want you, but my future is uncertain. The English will kill me if they find me in Scotland."

Was she sending him to his death? She could bear
that no more than if Robert harmed him. Would she
know what became of him? Was she doing the right
thing in urging him to go back? She felt so helpless
against the forces that controlled him.

"Lass?" he said again, into the silence.

"Would you consider going south with me, to the
Cherokee?" She asked the question suddenly, head-
long, without letting herself think about why. "We
could live safely there."

"And hide, like your father?" he said gently. "Your
husband wanted this land for you and the children. And
I'll always need to find Katy."

She felt herself trembling. She wanted so much.
More than he would ever be able to give her. She
wanted his heart. "You'd better go," she said, blinking
back a tear that she would rather die than allow him to
see.

She heard the sound of his steps crossing the floor,
then the thick, heavy sound of the door opening and

closing. Going to the window, she watched him stride toward the barn. He didn't look back.

But she knew he looked back to Scotland. He lived for the moment when he could return, and she could not fault him. His sister was a helpless child, like Amy and Noel. If either of her children were missing, she would hunt for them forever.

And if someone tried to stop her, for whatever reason, she would grow to hate him. She never wanted to see hatred in his eyes—hatred for her for keeping him here.

Turning away from the window, she went to her room. But she knew she wouldn't sleep that night any better than she had the last.

Chapter 20

Ian was feeding the horses in one of the paddocks when he sensed Fancy's presence. It was the smell of flowers, the scent she mixed into soap, that alerted him. Or perhaps it was just instinct; he just *knew* when she was near him.

Two days had passed since Robert's visit, and she had been cool toward him, always careful to make sure they were not alone. While he ached to hold her, he knew she was doing the wise thing.

But now it was all he could do not to carry her into the small room that was his. Especially now.

He didn't want her to ride to Chestertown alone. It was frightening how much he cared about her, how protective he felt. And yet he knew she had to go. Reverend Winfrey had to be warned.

He turned around slowly and saw that she was watching him. He wondered how long she had observed him muttering inanities to the horse as he poured oats into the feed trough. He felt heat rising in his cheeks as he met her gaze.

She was wearing a worn but pretty amber-colored riding dress that nearly matched her light brown eyes. It was plain, but it fit her trim waist perfectly; with the matching bonnet tied becomingly under her chin, she looked very bonny indeed.

And discomfited under his perusal. "I had only the one mourning dress."

"I like it," he said. Indeed, he liked it too much.

He turned back to the mare, busying himself with a

careful—and unnecessary—examination of her right foreleg. He was afraid of what his face might reveal this morning—his longing for her. He had spent the whole bloody night aching and was afraid he might simply take her in his arms and to hell with the bloody consequences. Dammit, she was his wife.

"Would you saddle her for me?" Fancy asked in a calm tone.

He faced her then, his eyes on the dress again.

"I still don't like you going to Chestertown alone," he said. Instantly he knew he had said the wrong thing. Her chin rose determinedly and fire sparked in her eyes. Her back straightened as if someone had put a steel rod in it.

She regarded him steadily, and he wondered where the gentleness had gone. She looked formidable, ready to do battle with him or anyone else who tried to stop her. "*I'll* saddle her, then," she said, heading for the tack room.

"*I'll* saddle her," he said, "and Royalty. I'll go with you."

"No," she said flatly. "You promised to teach Noel to shoot, and he was disappointed when you didn't have time yesterday. And there is the last of the tobacco to be planted and the horses to be exercised."

He felt his own temper rising. For the first time, she was treating him like . . . a bond servant. "I'll ask Tim to stay," he said.

She shook her head. "He said his father needed him today. And besides . . ." She hesitated, frowning slightly. "I'm afraid Robert might send someone to cause more mischief. I worry about the horses."

He couldn't really argue with her judgment in the matter. But still . . . "I don't want you going alone," he persisted stubbornly.

"Ian . . ." The look she gave him was mildly exasperated, but her tone was very serious as she said, "When you leave, I'll be going to town, and to auctions, on my own. I had best start taking care of myself. And mine."

Trapped—and he had done it to himself. She was right. What was the point of guarding and insulating her from the world now when he had every intention of leaving? Yet his desire—nay, compulsion—to protect her was growing at a staggering rate.

"I will be fine, truly I will," she said, "and I'll be back by nightfall."

"At least take the buggy. I don't think you should ride sidesaddle alone."

She stared at him for a long, silent moment. Then, calmly, she said, "It would slow me."

Ian recognized that he had lost. And it was like a kick to his stomach. Of course he could not tell her what to do. Despite the sham marriage, he was little more than a convict her husband had bought. He was not *truly* her husband. He could not ask her, much less tell her, to do something only to please him.

"As you wish," he said gruffly, then brushed past her to fetch her sidesaddle from the tack room.

As he saddled the mare, he told himself that she would be safe enough. She was a fine rider, and the road to Chestertown was well traveled. Yet anxiety ran down his backbone, for reasons he couldn't explain. It wasn't as though she would be alone at night in an Edinburgh slum, and Marsh was probably still nursing his wounds. Moreover, her brother-in-law had never threatened her with physical harm.

"Ian," she said, breaking the tense silence that had fallen between them.

He turned, hoping that she'd changed her mind.

"When you take Noel hunting . . ."

"Aye?"

"He loves animals, but he does so want to be with you. The idea of you teaching him to shoot appeals to him, but the reality of shooting . . ."

Ian knew what she was trying to say. Hunting was a necessity; a man learned the skill in order to provide food for his family and to protect his livestock. But he remembered his own first hunt—the building excitement, then the stunned sadness when he'd watched his first stag fall to the ground. It was a rite of passage, but not necessarily a kind one.

"We will only practice shooting today," he said. "He should learn how to use the musket."

A real smile broke across her face, and he felt as if he had done something heroic. It required more discipline than he possessed to quash the warmth that flooded him.

Reluctantly he helped her into the saddle and watched as she rode out.

After breakfast, Ian saddled two horses, Royalty and the gelding named Tuck—short for Tuckahoe—with Noel watching his every move. He helped the lad onto the gelding casting an approving eye at the innate skill and confidence with which Noel took up the reins and settled onto the large animal's back.

They walked the horses to a quiet place in the woods, where Noel slipped down from the saddle on his own. Holding the musket, Ian dismounted. He had brought several pieces of parchment, and he nailed one to a tree.

"Did your father ever show you how to load a musket?"

Noel shook his head. "But I watched him."

"The first thing to remember is that you must be very careful. Keep the musket clean and your powder and cartridges dry." He gave the musket to Noel and showed him how to hold it.

"When you fire it," he said, "it's going to kick like a yearling being saddled for the first time."

Noel nodded, but Ian could see he wasn't concerned in the least about being kicked. He was too busy with the previously forbidden object.

Ian took him through the loading procedure step by step. "Wipe the pan," he said, "with the thumb of your right hand. Then bring the musket to the right-hand side."

The gun was as tall as Noel, and he was awkward with it. Ian smiled inwardly at the lad's earnestness, remembering his own eagerness to learn what all men had to know.

He handed a cartridge to Noel. "Take hold of it and open the cartridge with your teeth."

Noel followed his directions, but a trace of powder evidently got in his nose, and he sneezed, dropping the cartridge and spilling the powder.

Dismay and embarrassment flooded the boy's features.

"I did the same the first time," Ian said. He handed Noel another cartridge. "Take a gentler bite."

Noel attacked the cartridge gingerly this time.

"Good," Ian said. "Now pour the powder into the barrel and push the ball into the muzzle."

Noel had to angle the musket to do it. When both were done, Ian handed him a ramrod.

"Tamp both down," he said, watching carefully.

Noel finished, then handed the ramrod back to him.

"Before these paper cartridges were invented, you had to measure out the powder. If you use too much, the musket will backfire. Remember that if you ever use plain powder."

"Aye," Noel said.

He had to smile outright that time. The lad was doing his best to sound like a Scotsman.

Putting a hand on Noel's shoulder, Ian said, "Are you ready to try to fire now?"

Noel nodded eagerly.

"Hold it tight against you. It doesn't kick as badly then. I would suggest that you lie on the ground and brace the musket against your shoulder."

Noel frowned. "How can you shoot something lying down?"

"Are you sure you want to shoot something?" Ian asked.

Noel thought about it for a moment, his expression turning serious in that way he had. Ian was deeply impressed when the lad raised his troubled gaze to him and spoke words that many men who were thrice or even four times Noel's age had not learned.

"I don't think I'm ever going to *want* to shoot something. But I know I will have to someday, and I want to do it right. I don't want any animal to suffer."

Ian felt as proud of Noel as he would have felt of his own son. It struck him that, in the weeks that he'd been with Noel and Amy, he'd had many occasions to feel such pride. He'd barely been able to contain himself the night Amy had snatched up the writing slate, stuck out her lower lip, and written the first three letters of the alphabet.

But it was Noel's quiet, instinctive compassion for life that made him reexamine his own life, that turned his heart into something resembling warm, sweet pudding. It had not been adventure that Noel sought today; it had been a knowledge he knew he needed despite the hurt it might cause.

Noel Marsh was going to be a fine man.

At the moment, though, he was still a young lad, and

he had a hundred questions in his eyes that Ian felt inadequate to answer.

Instead, he led Noel over to a fallen log. "Lie down facing the target."

Noel obediently lay on his stomach, facing the log, and propped himself up on his elbows. Ian positioned the musket, balancing the barrel on the log, then told Noel to aim for the piece of paper fluttering against the tree.

"Now, remember," he warned Noel, "the musket will kick back. Be prepared."

Noel nodded. He aimed toward the fluttering paper, then waited.

"Fire," Ian said.

Noel pulled the trigger, and his body promptly rolled to one side as the musket rebounded against his shoulder. He got to his feet immediately and picked up the musket.

Ian wordlessly handed him another cartridge, and the boy confidently bit off the end, poured the powder into the barrel, then stuffed the ball into the muzzle. Without prompting, Noel used the ramrod to push the ball in, then flopped down in front of the log again.

"You forgot something," Ian said.

He watched as Noel visibly ran over each of the steps. "The pan. I didn't clean the pan first."

"Aye," Ian replied. "Remember that. Sometimes you may not have time to . . ." His voice trailed off. He had not had time at Culloden. He'd had to load, fire, then load again. And again, and again, until his hands were black with powder and his fingers burned with the heat of the barrel. He saw the faces and bodies dissolve in blood, some still coming toward him. He saw . . .

"Ian?"

He glanced down to find Noel giving him a worried frown.

"Try again," he said, pushing the memories back where they belonged, in the dark pits of his mind.

Noel got into position, aimed carefully, and pulled the trigger. The acrid smell of gunpowder permeated the air, and smoke drifted upward from the musket. The lad had held his position, but Ian guessed that he would have a substantial bruise on his shoulder.

He watched Noel load and fire three more times. On the last attempt, the lad hit the piece of paper and shouted triumphantly.

"You have a good eye, Noel," Ian said quietly. "We'll come back in a few days and try again."

Noel nodded and handed the musket to him. "Thank you," he said.

Ian reached down and pushed a shock of tawny hair away from the lad's face. Noel grinned at him, and they walked back to the horses together.

Fancy did not want to linger in Chestertown any longer than she had to. She went to the government building and found that Reverend Winfrey had not yet filed the marriage certificate. Then she paid a brief visit to the minister's wife and was disappointed when the kindly woman reported that she didn't know exactly where he was at the moment or how he could be reached. He was due home the next day, but . . . well, he was often late.

As Fancy headed for Douglas Turner's office, she took some comfort in knowing that if she couldn't find Reverend Winfrey, then it wasn't likely that Robert could either.

Turner greeted her cordially. "Mrs. Marsh! Why, it's good to see you looking so well." Escorting her into his office, he handed her gallantly into the high-back chair, then took his own seat behind his desk. "What can I do for you today?"

"Those papers I got from you," she began. "The indenture papers. They've disappeared."

The congenial smile left Turner's lips. "Are you having trouble with the fellow?"

"No, no." She shook her head. "In truth, he bought his freedom back and agreed to stay with us of his own will."

Concern deepened the lines in his forehead. "Was that wise?"

"It was what John wanted," she said. "Ian has already started to teach us to read. He's a fine horseman and trainer, and he has worked through the night, more nights than I can count, to get our tobacco planted, and . . ."

Turner raised an eyebrow. "And . . . ?"

"I married him."

He started up out of his chair, caught the desk with his hands as if for balance, then sank back into the seat, his mouth actually dropping open. "You *married* him?"

She nodded, taking a steadying breath. "I . . . we . . . Ian and I thought Robert might cause trouble. He wants my land. He thinks it should have been his, and he's determined to get it. He threatened to spread rumors of fornication if I didn't sell Ian's indenture to him, and he even got the sheriff to ride out and threaten me, saying that the law wouldn't tolerate Ian living at the farm with me."

"I see." Turner rubbed a hand across his face. "Um . . . when did this marriage take place?"

"Almost two weeks ago," she replied. "Rufus Winfrey, the Methodist circuit rider, conducted the service, and two neighbors served as witnesses."

"I see," he said again.

Fancy understood that Turner was having a difficult

time adjusting to the idea, and she was certain his difficulty lay not in the notion of her remarrying but in the
fact that Ian had been a bondsman and was a convicted
traitor. The widow Morrow, who lived downstream
from her, had married a week after her husband died.
Women were dependent on men in this society; if they
had no children of an age to help, they were generally
forced to find a new husband quickly.

She hated that fact, just as she hadn't liked Ian's
attempt earlier that day to protect her. From the time
she was fifteen, John had taken care of her, looked after
her, protected her. Then he'd died and left her to cope
with more troubles than she'd ever imagined—including a recalcitrant bondsman. Even if Ian had been planning to stay with her, she would have fought to be
independent. She never wanted to be vulnerable again.
Never.

Her hands clenched together in her lap.

Slowly, Turner seemed to come to grips with the
situation. Giving her a puzzled frown, he asked, "Why
are you worried, then? If your, um, new husband is so
capable—"

"Our tobacco field burned yesterday."

Turner's puzzlement turned to shock, his eyes
widening as he stared at her.

"It wasn't an accident," she said. "The fire started in
two separate places at the back of the field. Afterward, I
discovered that Ian's indenture papers, the ones I
signed to give him freedom, were missing."

She knew what Turner would say, knew the conclusion he would instantly reach.

"Have you considered the possibility that the fire
was started by . . . your husband?" he asked.

"No," she said.

To his credit, he didn't indicate that he thought she

was being simple. He simply asked, "Then who do you think set it?"

"Robert," she said.

Turner's brows came together in a deep scowl. "That is a serious accusation against a man like Robert Marsh."

Fancy felt her heart start to sink. If Robert had bought off Turner, too . . . But, no, she wouldn't give up yet.

"Robert says that John wanted him to have the farm," she continued. "I know he did not. John didn't trust his brother."

Turner hesitated, then gave her a nod. "I know that to be true. He said so several times. And he worried about you."

"Will you . . . *can* you help me?"

She watched reluctance war with duty on the lawyer's face, and she had to acknowledge that she was asking a lot of him; siding with an unknown Scottish convict against a well-known and highly regarded planter would be an unpopular, possibly even dangerous, position to take.

Finally Turner let out a heavy sigh. His eyes narrowed as he regarded her thoughtfully. "I would like to meet this man of yours," he said.

"I'm sure he would like to meet you," she assured him. "He wanted to come with me today, but we couldn't leave the farm unattended—not after the fire. But is there anything you can do for me . . . for us now?"

He thought for a moment, then nodded. "I'll write a statement in which you swear that your husband has bought his indenture back from you. As for the marriage . . ." He hesitated. "I would advise you to obtain a copy of the marriage certificate, or have someone remarry you. If you are absolutely sure . . ." He trailed off, obviously still in doubt about the wisdom of the union.

"Thank you," she said. "How long will it take you to prepare the statement?"

"I'll do it now," he said, opening the drawer of his desk to remove a piece of paper. Taking up the quill lying on the desktop, he dipped the tip into the inkpot and began to write.

Fancy tried to curb her impatience as she watched him. When he finished, he blew lightly on the page to dry it, then let his gaze skim over it. "I'll read it to you," he said.

"Thank you, but I can read it," she said proudly.

He handed it to her without another word. She looked at it, and some of her confidence faded. She did see a word or two she knew, but many were unfamiliar. How long would it be before she could read a document like this?

Turner seemed to understand. He backed his chair away from the desk and came to stand beside her. He read the page aloud, and she followed along, picking out words she recognized. The longer ones were completely beyond her, but she understood enough to know that he had written what she asked.

Reaching for his quill, she signed the page where he indicated. When she'd finished, she clutched the paper for a moment before returning it to his care.

"I'll keep an eye out for the marriage registration," he said kindly as he retreated behind his desk. "And bring that Scotsman in to see me."

Fancy looked into his eyes and saw only concern. "I will," she said. "And thank you."

She had worried about Douglas Turner, had wondered if his past relationship with John and his loyalty to her would be strong enough to overcome any fear he

might have of Robert. But she left his office feeling that
he was a man of integrity whom she could trust.

Turner helped her into the sidesaddle, and she urged
the mare toward home. She felt almost light-headed
over her accomplishment. She had come to Chestertown alone. She had conducted business on her own,
and she had been taken seriously by Douglas Turner, a
respected lawyer. Most of all, she felt she now had an
ally in her fight against Robert.

She couldn't wait to get home and tell Ian. She'd
already forgotten her resolve to keep him at a distance,
to make it easier for him to leave.

Ian felt the power of Sir Gray as he raced around the
paddock, the colt's hooves pounding against the hard-
packed ground that now ringed the track just inside the
fence. He leaned lower, asking for more speed, and he
felt the colt's response. He was fast, bloody damn fast!
Pleasure born of accomplishment spread through Ian.
And a sense of euphoria.

Satisfied, he started to slow the horse, pulling back
gently on the reins until the horse broke from the gallop into a canter, then a trot, and finally a walk. Ian
patted his neck. "Fine braw boy ye are," he crooned.
The horse tossed his head as if understanding and ac-
cepting the praise as his due.

Ian continued to walk the horse, cooling him down.
The momentary euphoria of a fine run faded. He
looked toward the house and wished again that Fancy
would return, even though he knew it was unlikely she
would arrive before nightfall. In the hours since dawn,
he had not stopped worrying about her. Not during the
shooting lesson. Not during the planting he and Tim
had finished before the younger Wallace left for home.
It took every ounce of discipline he had to resist the
urge to saddle the stallion and go after her. Only the

galling fact that she was right stopped him. He would leave her, and she would have to cope on her own. He just hadn't realized how deeply that would hurt him, how much he had come to care for her, for the whole Marsh family. Nor had he expected to enjoy farming and finding such intense satisfaction in working with the horses. He would be cutting out his heart by leaving, but he still heard his sister calling to him in his nightmares. She needed him, and he felt it soul deep.

He was about to dismount when he heard riders. He turned and watched as eight men on horseback approached.

As they drew closer, he recognized the man who had visited a few weeks ago. Vaughn. Sheriff Vaughn. And Robert Marsh was astride the horse next to him.

Apprehension prickled along his spine. Reluctantly he turned the horse toward the gate, opened it, and walked the horse through to meet the oncoming riders. He didn't think about running, though he knew Sir Gray, even as tired as he was, could outrun any of the animals in the bunch now pounding down the last stretch of road to the yard. He would not run from the likes of Robert Marsh.

Nor would he leave his family . . . yes, *his* family . . . to face whatever trouble Marsh had in store for them.

They were close enough now so that Ian could see the sheriff motion to his men, then thrust out an arm, pointing at him.

Ian's gut clenched as one of the men took a pistol from his belt and aimed. Directly at his heart.

He forced his voice to remain calm. "What do you want?"

At that moment Marsh rode up behind the sheriff, and Ian saw his face—purple, swollen, cut—mottled to a dangerous shade of scarlet.

"You," Marsh said.

"You have no authority here, Marsh."

"I am *Mister* Marsh to you," he barked.

From the corner of his eye, Ian saw Fortune edge out onto the porch. Noel was right behind her, and . . . bloody hell, he had his father's musket in his hands. Trying not to draw attention to the lad, he motioned with one hand to Noel to put the musket down.

But either Noel didn't see him or he was intent on protecting him. He lifted the musket.

Oh, God, no . . .

One of the men saw the gun and yelled something. They all turned to look, and the man yanked a pistol out of its holster and fired before Ian could even take a breath to scream.

He watched in horror as Noel dropped the musket and sank to his knees, a circle of blood forming on his shirt.

"Ye bastard!" Ian launched himself off the horse and ran toward the boy. In his single-minded purpose, he took little note of Lucky racing from the porch to attack the man who'd fired—or of the other man who hit the dog with the butt of his musket, knocking him to the ground, where he lay silent and still.

"Take him," he heard the sheriff say, and he kept running even as he saw that he wasn't going to make it.

A bullet grazed his side. He stumbled slightly, and, in the next instant, a sharp, agonizing pain shot through the back of his head as the butt of a rifle struck him.

He tried to go on, but his legs didn't work. The world went black, closing out the sight of the wounded boy and the circle of pale, angry faces looking down at him.

Chapter 21

ancy felt the mare tiring beneath her as they neared the farm. She, too, was exhausted, her earlier euphoria having given way to weariness. She had not slept well the past few nights, and she caught herself nodding several times, jerking upright as she realized she was on the verge of falling.

Yet when the last bend in the road appeared up ahead, still visible in the last minutes of twilight, her energy seemed to renew itself. The evening was warm and close, the air still muggy from a day of baking in the summer sun, but the heat that flowed through her with the thought that she'd soon be seeing Ian had nothing to do with the sun.

She tried to quell her need, knowing it would come to naught, but it was hopeless. She wanted him so badly. She wanted to hold him and to feel his touch on her skin. She wanted the intimacy of his body against hers. Even the prospect of a baby—a bairn—did not frighten her. She would, at least, always have a part of him.

Treasuring that possibility, Fancy felt her excitement building as the farmhouse came into view. But her excitement turned to puzzlement, then to anxiety, as she saw the light of a lantern moving on the porch, then recognized Fortune, holding the lantern in one hand as she waved frantically with the other.

Heart suddenly pounding, Fancy kicked the mare into a fast canter. When she reached the porch, she slid out of the saddle, flung the reins over the railing, and ran up the two steps to meet her sister. Fortune's eyes were red, her hair in more disarray than usual.

"What's happened?" Fancy asked, her tone edged in panic.

Fortune's lips moved, her mouth opening and closing, but no sound came forth.

Fancy forced calm she didn't feel into her voice, knowing she wouldn't get anywhere if she frightened her sister. "Fortune . . . here, let's hang the lantern so your hands are free. Now show me. What is it?"

Fortune's hands fluttered helplessly, at the same time her lips twisted. "I . . . an. I . . . an."

Fancy's astonishment at hearing her sister's voice was quickly swept away by the fear that flooded her. Grabbing Fortune's trembling hands, she fixed her with an intent look. "What happened to Ian?"

"Took . . . took I . . . an. Sh . . . shot Noel."

"*Shot* him! Dear God, where is he?"

Fortune pointed to the door, and Fancy brushed past her, racing inside. Her gaze scanned the main room, found it empty, and she started for the loft. But Fortune grabbed her dress, pushing her toward her bedroom.

Noel lay on the bed, his small form nearly swallowed by the feather mattress. He was very still, but she knew immediately that he was alive by the pain etched upon his face.

As she flew to his side, Fancy nearly tripped over Lucky, lying on the floor beside the bed. Vaguely, she noted the stitches in the dog's head before she sat on the bed and focused her attention on her son.

Noel, her precious son. Her life.

She looked quickly around the room and saw little Amy curled up in the rocker, asleep, with a blanket wrapped around her, and the cat and raccoon tucked under her arms. Tears had painted dirty streaks down her face.

Turning back to Noel, Fancy placed the back of her hand against his cheek. His skin was warm, thank God, and his breathing was natural. She pulled down the bedclothes and saw the large bandage holding his arm close to his chest. Dried blood had turned the white cloth to rust, but bright red mingled with the rust, telling her that the injury was still seeping.

"The bullet . . ." she said, looking at Fortune.

Her sister made a circle with her thumb and index finger, then poked the index finger of her other hand through the circle: the bullet had gone through. She gestured toward the table.

Fancy saw the empty glass and a familiar jar of powder and knew that Fortune had given Noel something to make him sleep.

"And Ian?" she asked. "Where is he?"

Fortune's lips twisted again, her entire face contorting in her effort to speak. Then finally: "Sher . . . iff, R-Robert . . . took him. Sh-shot . . . Noel."

"*Robert* shot Noel?"

Fortune shook her head violently. "Sheriff's . . . man."

"But Robert was here?"

A nod.

"And he left Noel like *this*?"

Another nod.

Fancy's blood seared her veins, boiling with fury. "How many men were here?" she asked.

Fortune thought for an instant, then held up eight fingers.

"Was Ian hurt, too?"

She hardly needed her sister's frantic nod to tell her that he had been; he never would have allowed anything to happen to Noel unless he'd been unable to prevent it.

Fortune held up a hand in an unmistakable gesture: shooting a gun.

"Ian was shot *too*?"

Yes.

"Badly?"

A desperate shrug. Fortune didn't know.

"But they took him with them?"

Fortune nodded.

Fancy closed her eyes. She could feel herself on the edge of screaming. Her palms were clammy, her insides shaking with fear, but at the same time she was so completely enraged that when she opened her eyes everything seemed to have black and red spots in front of it. She had to get control of herself or she would be of no use to anyone.

Taking several slow, deep breaths, she turned and took Fortune's hands. "I know it's dark," she began, "but I need you to go get the Wallaces, then fetch the doctor."

Fortune's gaze flickered to the window. Beyond the wide panes, the sky had turned a deep purple. In a few more minutes it would be very dark indeed. Still, Fortune's nod of agreement was determined, if a bit shaky.

"Are you sure?" Fancy said. "I know you're afraid, but truly there's nothing to harm you between here and the Wallaces' farm. And it isn't a long ride."

Fortune nodded again.

"Good." Fancy squeezed her sister's hands and forced what she hoped was a reassuring smile. "We'll saddle Tuck. He'll get you there safely."

Fancy went with Fortune to the barn, taking the mare, who'd been waiting patiently at the porch railing, with her. She helped saddle Tuck, then watched as Fortune mounted and rode out, heading for the Wallaces'.

Fancy's heart pounded furiously and she had to consciously steady her hands before unsaddling the mare and giving her oats and water. She was gripped by worry for Ian, for her Scotsman, as well as for her son. She looked down at her hands. They were shaking again.

Then the impact of Fortune's stumbling words struck her. Her sister had spoken—actually spoken words—for the first time in over nine years. Out of dire need, she'd overcome her terror. If the circumstances weren't so utterly appalling, Fancy thought, she would be crying for joy.

Instead, the tears she brushed from her face, as she ran back to the house, were born of fear.

"Dear God, please let Noel be all right," she prayed. "And please, please, don't let Robert kill Ian. Please . . ."

"Burn it."

Ian heard the words through a gray fog of pain and confusion. He tried to move but couldn't, and he desperately tried to gather his wits to fight whatever was restraining him. Images spun in his head. Men. Horses. Shots ringing out. Noel falling to the ground . . .

"He's awake."

Ian didn't recognize the second voice, but he knew the first. Robert Marsh.

"The knife ready?"

"Not yet. A few more moments."

"Dammit, I don't want to stand here all night."

"You can go if you want. I know what to do."

"I want to hear the bastard scream."

"I don't understand why you don't just kill him."

"And lose a strong body?" Marsh said. "And an even better weapon? No. I want to see him in my fields, working like the convict he is. I'll teach him his place."

Ian remained quiet. He didn't want to give Marsh the pleasure of seeing him struggle. Besides which, his side hurt like bloody hell. Any movement would make it worse.

As his mind started to clear, he realized he was in a horse stall, in a barn. Opening his eyes a slit, he could see that the stall had been outfitted as a prison, doubtless for rebellious slaves. The sides were equipped with rings, and his ankles were linked by a chain, which in turn was fastened by a padlock to a ring in back of the stall. His arms were stretched out and bound by rope to rings on one side of the stall.

He'd been stripped of all but his trousers, and he could smell the stench of his own blood. Focusing on the source of his greatest pain, he allowed his hooded gaze to travel downward until he saw the wound—a graze—on his right side.

The sound of metal scraping against metal came from behind him, and somewhere close a fire burned. He could smell it as well as feel its heat. A moment later a pair of boots appeared in his line of vision. Deciding that there was no point in putting it off any longer, he looked up to meet Robert Marsh's gaze.

"I don't waste money on doctors for my slaves," Marsh said. "Martin here is my overseer. He'll close that wound, though it isn't much more than a crease."

"I'm not . . . your slave."

"You think not? I have a will that says I inherited you the moment John died." Marsh stooped and put a piece of wood into Ian's mouth. "Wouldn't mind if you bit off your tongue, but you might swallow it and choke. I don't want that happening . . . yet."

Ian knew what was coming. He'd endured it before at the much gentler hands of his brother. The memory hadn't faded over time. Still, he spit out the wood.

"Noel?" he asked.

"Barely a scratch," Marsh said, picking up the piece of wood again. "The cub shouldn't have lifted a gun against a deputy." He pushed the wood back into Ian's mouth. "Spit it out again and I'll shove it down your throat and gag you."

This time Ian was grateful for the piece of wood as a big man stopped next to him and held a white-hot blade against his raw flesh. He bit down on the wood, his body arching in agony as the smell and sound of his flesh sizzling filled his senses. For the space of one . . . two . . . three seconds, the fires of hell raced through him. Then he fell back into welcome blackness.

Rufus Winfrey had only three miles to go before reaching Chestertown. He had declined an offer to spend the night with the family of one of his parishioners so that he could surprise his wife by being a day early. In his pouch were several documents announcing momentous events to be registered with the government: two marriages, three deaths, and three births. *A time to be born, and a time to die.* Three lives gone; three lives just beginning. The miracle of it all never ceased to amaze him.

It had been, he thought, a more successful trip than usual. He loved marriages, and he loved babies. He enjoyed the outdoor services, and he liked the farmers who made up his flock. They were hardworking, honest, and generous.

His wife wanted him to ask for a church, but he had been told not to expect one. He was too outspoken, and often his judgment was questioned by his superiors. He was very aware that his actions would be scrutinized even more closely if the bishop learned of the Sutherland marriage.

A sham marriage would never be approved. Yet if he was any judge of people, he didn't think it would be a sham for long. He had seen Ian Sutherland and Fancy Marsh look at each other. No matter how the two tried to pretend otherwise, Rufus knew the seeds of love lay there between them.

He let himself slump in the saddle. The plodding of his aging horse nearly put him to sleep. But a figure sitting on the side of the road brought him upright and alert. Perhaps someone required assistance.

He pulled his mount to a stop, and the man rose and took a few steps into the road to meet him. He looked tired, Rufus thought, as if he had been waiting for a long time, and his eyes, as he raised his gaze, were dull. Rufus tried not to form immediate opinions about people, but, looking at this man, something cautioned him. He was sure he had never seen the fellow before, but there was coldness in his eyes that bothered him.

"Can I be helping you?" he asked.

"You can if you are Reverend Winfrey."

"I am," Rufus said. He was used to strangers knowing his name, and he rarely, if ever, feared them, if for no other reason than the fact that this poor mount and worn clothing held little appeal for a thief.

"I was told you were nearby," the man said. "My ma, she's dying. She wants a man of the cloth to give her ease. I was going into Chestertown, but I met a tinker who said a preacher had just said words over a dead man and might be coming down this road. Would you come with me?"

Rufus did not want to go. His mare deserved a rest, and so did he. And his wife was waiting for him. Yet he could not refuse a dying woman.

"Which way?" he asked.

"Just follow me," the man said, and started toward the woods.

Feeling duty bound, Rufus followed.

* * *

Robert strode into his study and closed the door. Pouring himself a drink, he stood by the window and looked across the well-tended yard, toward the barn. A smile formed on his still swollen lips.

He felt better. Oh, he still ached, but the fact that the bondsman was surely hurting one hell of a lot worse was better medicine than any doctor could have given him.

He'd almost killed the bastard. He'd wanted to. And no court would have convicted him for the death of an insolent, disobedient bond servant condemned by the Crown. But he'd realized that Sutherland could be of use to him. No one cared about the man, a convict, scum transported by the English to clutter up the colonies. No one cared, that is, except Fancy.

And exactly what would Fancy do to save her precious bondsman?

Robert intended to learn the answer to that question at the earliest opportunity.

But first . . .

Holding his drink in one hand, he went to his desk, opened the middle drawer, and removed Ian Sutherland's indenture papers. A candle stood on the corner of the desk, and he moved it closer, then held the papers over the flame until one corner was burning nicely. Then he crossed the room and tossed the papers into the fireplace, standing back to watch them burn.

In his mind, he went over his plan again, ticking off items, assuring himself that he had taken care of every detail: the forged will; the destruction of the indenture papers that had freed Ian; the disappearance of the minister who had witnessed them.

Robert also had the testimony of the man who sold Ian to John, along with the will handing all of John's possessions to him. According to the forged document, the Scotsman had been his since the moment John died.

Satisfied that he had covered all eventualities, he smiled. Soon now, very soon, Marsh's End would be restored to its original, intended glory. The horses would be back in his stables. And Fancy would be his to do with as he saw fit.

Ian Sutherland . . . well, once he'd served his purpose, he would be dead.

Seeing the last of the parchment curl, then crumble into ashes, Robert took a long swallow from his cup.

Life was good.

Chapter 22

"I should have been there," young Tim Wallace said.

"There's nothing you could have done," Fancy insisted.

"The bastard," his father growled, then added quickly, "Beggin' your pardon, Mrs. Sutherland."

Fancy was pleasantly startled by the form of address. It was the first time anyone had called her Mrs. Sutherland. But the momentary jolt faded immediately. If she didn't do something quickly, she would be a widow for the second time within a few weeks.

It was past midnight, and they were standing beneath the lantern on the porch. Fortune, who had returned with the men, had gone inside to sit with Noel. The nearest doctor was unavailable, birthing a child ten miles away.

Fancy looked from one man to the other. The anxiety straining her features was reflected in her tone as she spoke. "I'm so afraid Robert will kill him."

The older Wallace shook his head. "Not likely if he's trying to claim Ian as his bondsman. But he'll work him. Hard. I don't see how he thinks he can get away with this."

Fancy tried to believe him. If only Reverend Winfrey had filed the marriage certificate. Inside, she felt as if she were dying. Outside, she struggled to maintain her calm, contain her fear—but it was a losing battle. She could hear Noel's whimpers of pain. Lucky had whined in bewilderment as she examined the vicious cut on his head. And she kept visualizing Ian's face.

Dear God, keep him safe. Please, just keep him safe until I can do something.

She would free Ian by whatever means were necessary. Neither the land nor the farm nor the horses nor anything else mattered any longer. Nothing mattered but keeping her family safe. And her family included Ian. Her husband. Her heart. When had it become so? She didn't know. She simply knew it was true.

And another truth was now very clear: Robert was capable of anything to get his way. Even murder.

"How is Noel?" Little Tim asked.

"Hurting now that he's awake," she replied, "but the ball went through without hitting a bone. If there's no infection, he should be fine."

"Son of a bitch," the elder Wallace muttered. This time he didn't beg her pardon.

He didn't have to. She seldom got angry, but when she did, John used to say he would rather face a hurricane, a tornado, and a cyclone. Together.

And now she was angrier than she'd ever been in her life. Robert had hurt her child and kidnapped her husband, a man who had sacrificed everything he held dear to help her. All because Robert wanted her farm.

Pigs would fly before he harmed another hair on a loved one's head.

"We need Reverend Winfrey," Fancy said. "He must go to Sheriff Vaughn—or perhaps a magistrate— and say that he married us and witnessed my signature on Ian's indenture papers. Ian is a free man. I'm sure Douglas Turner would go with him if it would help."

Wallace nodded. "I'll go into Chestertown and find out what cause Marsh gave the sheriff to take yer Scotsman. Then I'll try to find Rufus." He gestured with a nod toward his son. "Young Tim will stay here with you. He can check on our animals each morning, but I do not want to leave you alone fer long." He hesitated. "Now, don't you go doing anything on your own."

She forced a smile, but she didn't reply. She was not going to make promises that she had no intention of keeping.

After saying good-bye to Big Tim, she went inside while Little Tim went to stable Tuck and his own gelding.

Catching sight of her through the open bedroom door, Fortune came to join her in the main room.

Fancy smiled at her sister—a genuine smile, even if it was frayed with exhaustion. "Fortune—" She broke off, searching the young woman's striking features. "You spoke!"

Fortune swallowed. "I . . . Ian."

Fancy hugged her tightly, then drew back to meet her gaze. "Can you say *my* name?"

She managed a few broken syllables. "Fa . . . Fan . . . cy. Sor . . . ry . . . so sorry." Then she burst into tears.

"Oh, Fortune, no!" She squeezed her sister's hands. "It wasn't your fault. It wouldn't have made any difference if I'd been here." She knew that was true. Not even she could have predicted the speed and the savagery with which Robert had acted.

Fortune looked at her through a veil of tears. "I-Ian," she whispered.

Fancy hugged her again. "Don't worry. We'll get him back, and Noel will be all right. I swear it."

Fortune held on tight, sobbing quietly. Fancy didn't tell her sister that Noel's first words upon awakening were questions about Ian, or that Amy had cried for him, too, as she'd squeezed poor Unsatisfactory nearly to death. In only a few weeks' time, Ian had earned a place in everyone's heart. He was essential to them, to their happiness, to their lives. Even the Wallaces were willing to take great risks on behalf of their fellow Scotsman.

Did he know? Was he aware of how much he had come to mean to all of them?

Was he even still alive?

"Don't cry," she soothed Fortune. "In the morning I will go and see Robert."

Fortune looked at her. "I'll . . . go, too."

Fancy knew then the extent of Fortune's fondness for Ian. She was uncommonly afraid of Robert and always had been.

"Someone has to look after Noel," Fancy said gently. She saw the tears still glistening in Fortune's eyes, and the despair—the same despair she herself felt. "You did well with him," she added.

Fortune was not to be comforted, not even when the door opened and young Tim came in, Trouble startling the young man as she flew in behind him. Moving to stand beside her sister, Fancy saw a small smile break across Fortune's face as Trouble perched on Tim's shoulder.

"She likes you," she said quickly, the words running together this time rather than being stuttered, and Fancy saw she was having a hard time picking up the rhythm of speech.

Tim stared at her in astonishment. "You spoke."

Fortune ducked her head, and he crossed the floor to stand in front of her. Lifting her chin with his hand, he beamed at her. "Say something else."

She was silent for a moment, her lips twitching. A minute went by, and she made no sound. Finally, Fancy saw her face begin to crumple and something like panic flash in her eyes.

Realizing instantly that being asked to perform on request was putting more strain on her sister than she could bear, Fancy intervened. Slipping an arm around Fortune's waist, she reassured her. "It's all right. You don't have to speak if you don't want to. Neither Tim nor I would ever try to force you."

"Of course not," Tim said. And his neck turned slightly pink as he added, "I like you just fine whether you talk or not. We do all right without words, don't we?"

Fortune dropped her gaze again, her own cheeks turning pink.

"I know you're scared," Fancy continued. Indeed, terror was the very thing that had caused her sister to stop speaking all those years ago. To escape the torture inflicted on her, she'd gone silent, and over the years she'd taken on the qualities of a shadow—there one minute and gone the next, fleeting and unobtrusive. Always silent. Until now—a miracle.

"You're safe," Fancy said softly. "Nobody is going to hurt you. I won't let them. I promise."

And that was a promise she intended to keep.

"I'll keep you safe too," Tim said boldly.

Fortune's gaze flickered to him, and Fancy could see her fighting the ghosts that haunted her. Her sister had lived in fear for so very long. Could she let it go now?

"T-Tim." The word was a mere whisper, but it was clear and true.

Humbled, Tim held out his hand, and Fortune took it in hers.

Faith had won over fear, and it gave Fancy renewed hope. If Fortune could conquer the powerful demons that had lived inside her for so long, then surely Fancy could conquer her brother-in-law. After all, he was only human.

Although at that moment he seemed like the very devil himself.

* * *

Waking the second time was little better than it had
been the first. Ian groaned, unable to suppress his response to the intense, searing pain that enveloped him.
For several minutes he could think of nothing else. His
right side was on fire, and his head felt as if hammers
were pounding inside it. Moving even an inch sent every muscle in his body into an agonizing spasm.

He fought through the fog of pain to open his eyes
and was gradually able to take in his surroundings. He
saw the walls of a stall. Heard the whinny of a horse.
Smelled hay and sweat and dung.

Cautiously he raised a hand to wipe his eyes, then
glanced down at his body, trying to find the source of
his greatest pain. A piece of cloth covered his side, held
in place with narrow strips tied around his ribs. Slowly,
an inch at a time, he pushed himself to a semi-upright
position, leaning against the side of the stall. What had
happened to him? And why were his legs so heavy and
difficult to move?

Then he saw the irons and the chain.

He remembered everything. And he was filled with a
sense of urgency.

Noel! God, was the lad alive? He closed his eyes
briefly and saw again the blood exploding across Noel's
shirt.

Ian struggled to sit up, dizziness keeping his movements slow, labored, uncertain. His hands were free
now, which surprised him. But then, Marsh had no reason to consider him a threat. At the moment he
couldn't have swatted a fly.

He checked the iron manacles around his ankles, the
length of chain leading to the ring fastened to the wall,
then the ring itself, trying futilely to pull it out. It occurred to him that stronger men than he had probably
pulled at these same chains to no avail. He could feel
the lingering despair of past occupants.

But still he fought against it. He had come too far to permit a strutting coward like Marsh to stop him. He intended to keep his pledges—to Fancy and to his sister. He would survive this as he had survived everything else that had been thrown at him over the past year.

The nervous movements of horses nearby alerted him that someone else was in the barn. The door to his stall opened, and a dark-skinned youth entered cautiously, staying out of his reach. The lad held something in his hands.

"Mistuh Martin didn' think you be awake so soon," he said. "You was hurt bad."

Ian tried a smile but knew it was nothing more than a grimace. He needed friends at the moment. He needed allies. "I'm still hurt bad," he agreed wryly. "What do you have there? Might it be water?"

The lad leaned over and handed him the cup. "Mistuh Martin told me to check on you. Tell him when you be awake. I thought you might need some water. But doan tell him I brung you some."

Ian drained the cup, his tongue fishing for every last drop of liquid before he handed the cup back to the lad. "Thank you."

"I have to tell 'im you be awake."

Ian nodded.

The lad cast a fearful glance around the stall. "They brought my brother here after they whupped him. Said he weren't working hard enough. He told 'em he was sick, but they didn' listen."

"Where is your brother now?" Ian asked.

The lad regarded him for a moment before replying. "He dead."

Then, with another glance at the cell, he turned and left, locking the gate behind him.

* * *

Tim left at sunrise to see to his own farm. Fancy waited until he had disappeared down the road before she and Fortune went to the barn and saddled her mare.

She had dressed carefully, choosing her best go-to-meeting dress. It was modest and suitable for mourning—a soft gray color—but it was made of good material and fit her to perfection. It had been John's favorite.

Fancy led the mare to the pasture fence, where she handed the reins to Fortune. Then, as Fortune kept the mare still, Fancy used the fence as a ladder to climb into the sidesaddle, muttering all the while about how inconvenient the ridiculous thing was.

Once settled on the mare's back, she looked down at her sister and swallowed hard. She hated leaving Fortune alone again.

"Tim will be back soon," she said.

Fortune nodded and managed a tremulous smile.

Fancy returned the smile, then signaled to the mare that it was time to be under way.

It took her nearly two hours to reach Marsh's End, and though it was still early, the slaves and white bondsmen were already out in the fields. She shuddered as she saw a burly man riding through the rows of tobacco on horseback reach out and strike a man with his whip. She didn't see Ian.

As she approached Robert's house, a young slave ran forward to take the reins of her mare. She dismounted on her own, then ascended the steps to the columned porch, squaring her shoulders.

The door opened almost immediately at her knock. She recognized the dignified woman who opened it.

"Mrs. Marsh," the woman said without a smile.

"Good morning, Hannah," Fancy said. "Is my brother-in-law in?"

"Yes, ma'am, he is."

"I would like to see him."

Hannah ushered her into the parlor, then disappeared down a hallway into the recesses of the manor house.

Fancy went to a heavy velvet chair and sat down. She wanted to look relaxed, at ease. Her heart, though, was beating erratically, and her stomach was tied in a dozen knots.

Her surroundings did nothing to ease her nerves. She hated the room and always had. It was suffocating, with dark wood and deep red draperies. The furniture was as uncomfortable as it looked, the chairs straight-backed and the stuffing skimpy. It was a room designed to chase people away, not to invite them to linger.

"Ah, sweet sister-in-law." Robert's voice floated to her, as sweet as sugared pastry.

She turned and watched him approach, noting that his back was a little stiffer than usual. Ian's work, she thought. But what price had her husband paid for the fury he'd vented on Robert Marsh?

"Robert," she said.

He took her hand, raising it to his lips but watching her eyes. "To what do I owe the pleasure of your visit?"

"I understand you paid *me* a visit yesterday."

"Ah, sister." His smile deepened. "I merely sought to fulfill John's wishes."

She congratulated herself on limiting her reaction to a raised eyebrow. "And what wishes would those be?"

"Didn't you know?" He drew back in feigned surprise. "Just before he brought that convict to your home, John had second thoughts. He knew he wasn't well, and he didn't want to leave you at the mercy of some renegade. So he made a new will, leaving me all his property in return for looking after you."

Fancy was stunned. The implications of his words almost overwhelmed her. He could claim everything, and her signature on the indenture papers would mean nothing. Neither would the marriage. A bondsman could not marry without permission of his owner, and Robert would claim he had owned all of John's possessions since the moment of his death.

Her chest tightened with desperation. Fancy managed—barely—to speak. "You lie. John's will was with Douglas Turner."

"But the new one is dated the day before he died," he said smoothly. "And it's a good thing, too, given the bad piece of refuse John brought home with him."

"Then why haven't you presented it before now?" she asked. "Mr. Turner is already filing John's will with the Crown."

"As I explained to the magistrate, I didn't want to take your land," he said loftily. "I wanted you to come to your senses and accept my help. If you had, I never would have filed that will, my dear sister-in-law."

"There wasn't time for John to make a new will," Fancy said, hating the note of fear in her voice. "He died the day after—"

"After he bought the Scotsman? He came by on his way to the sale and said he wanted to protect you. Said he wasn't feeling well, and was going to purchase a bondsman to help. But in case anything happened—"

"John didn't come here before going to Chestertown. When he died, he hadn't seen you in months."

"Hadn't he?" Robert asked silkily. "My servants will say otherwise."

Rage threatened to overtake her, and Fancy fought to curb it. Everything depended on her remaining calm. She couldn't prove John had not visited Robert the day he'd bought Ian's indenture. Who would believe her, especially if all of Robert's servants swore otherwise? "I wonder what Douglas Turner would say about all this," she said, "considering that John visited him *after* purchasing Ian's indenture and said nothing about a new will."

The briefest flash of uncertainty crossed Robert's face. Then he smiled. "Well, while the courts are deciding the matter, I feel duty-bound to honor John's express wishes, the primary one being not to leave you with the bondsman. Of course, I don't know how long the man will last in my fields. Scotsmen are not used to heat, you know. They have to be seasoned."

But she saw the nervous tic in his cheek. He wasn't quite as sure of himself as he was pretending to be.

Backing off—for the moment—Fancy tried another approach. "You haven't asked about my son," she said. "I didn't think even you would stoop low enough to hurt a child, especially your own nephew."

Robert's face reddened; then he blustered, "I had nothing to do with the shooting. The boy raised a musket against an officer of the law. He needs bridling. Discipline."

"He's seven years old!"

"He's old enough to raise a weapon."

"For God's sake, Robert, you're John's brother! How *could* you come to our house and leave your nephew with a bullet in him?"

"Everything I've done has been for your own good," he said, ignoring the question. "John wanted me to look after you. That bondsman is dangerous. He could turn on you at any time."

Fancy gaped. "Shooting my son is for my own good?"

He waved a hand in dismissal. "I knew he wasn't hurt badly. And when he comes to live here, I'll make sure he becomes a young gentleman. I'll make it all up to him."

Fancy's plans were falling apart, and she couldn't

halt angry words. "*You'll* make sure he becomes a gentleman? How, when you don't have the vaguest idea
what the word means? I would rather see Noel raised
by the Indians than by you. At least they understand
concepts like family and honor." Taking a step toward
him, she allowed her voice to rise. "I want Ian returned—now. You have no right to keep him here."

Scowling, Robert replied, "The magistrate says I
have every right."

"You bribed him!"

"That's a seditious charge."

"I wonder whether the governor will agree when I
explain to him that there never was another will. The
magistrate may say he believes you because you paid
him, but even you, Robert, can't bribe the governor."

"But by the time you see the governor," he came
back icily, "your Scotsman will be dead."

So that was his ploy. Fancy felt sick. He had Ian, and
he would kill him if she made any move to contest the
will. But at least he was still alive. For a brief second,
relief flooded through her.

But Robert noticed the change. "Yes, he's still alive,"
he said, "but he will stay that way only if you do as I
say."

"What is that?"

"Marry me."

Her jaw dropped. "*Marry* you? You dare to ask me
that after shooting my son? I would rather die."

His eyes narrowed. "But would you rather Ian Sutherland died?"

She couldn't answer. He had her trapped. And he
knew it.

"It could be arranged," Robert continued. "Sutherland attacked the traders who brought him here. He
attacked me. No one would doubt my word if I were to

say he attacked me again. The penalty for a bondsman attacking his owner, as you know, is hanging."

At that moment she hated Robert Marsh to the very depth of her being. She wanted to say that she was already married—to Ian Sutherland. But that surely would bring about Ian's immediate death. Robert wouldn't wait for a hanging.

She needed time. She had to prove that the will Robert had produced was a forgery. And she had to get Ian away from him, perhaps send him to the Cherokees. He would be safe with them.

Keeping her mind focused on her goal, she spoke in harsh but not overtly hostile tones. "If I agree to marry you, will you free him?"

"No. He will work out his term," Robert said. "But he won't hang. Not if you are a dutiful wife."

Her fingers knotted into fists. If she married Robert, she wouldn't be able to testify against him. And he would continue to use Ian to control her. How could John and Robert have come from the same blood, the same family? Did power always corrupt? But it couldn't have been power alone that had twisted Robert. Ian came from wealth and privilege, as did John, and both were strong and decent.

"Why do you want to marry me?" she asked. "You always believed John married beneath him."

Robert lifted one shoulder in a slight shrug, then winced when the movement seemed to pain him. "John taught you manners and speech," he said. "And you are fertile. I want heirs."

A broodmare. He wanted her to be his broodmare. She shuddered at the very thought of his touch.

"I must have time," she said. "My son is gravely injured. And I'm still in mourning."

He searched her face as if judging her intent. "Sutherland goes into the fields tomorrow. I don't know how long he'll last out there with his wounds. As for hanging him, I can wait a few days. But don't try my patience, Fancy."

She shook her head. "There will be no marriage if he doesn't stay alive. And if he dies, I'll fight you in court. I will make sure everyone knows that you're responsible for the wounding of my son and that you are a thief."

Robert cocked his head, considering the matter. "A bargain, then? The man lives if you marry me."

"As I said, I need some time." She hesitated. "Why do you want a reluctant wife when you could have a willing one?"

He gave her a smile that sent a river of ice up her spine. "I tame my slaves and bondsmen," he said. "I can tame a wife, too. In fact, I rather enjoy the process."

And all at once Fancy understood. A man had total control of a wife, but angry fathers and brothers could destroy his reputation. And a woman of good family surely would have fathers, brothers, uncles, and other relatives to come to her defense. She, on the other hand, had no one to offer even a modicum of protest if she was mistreated.

Robert Marsh was a member of the planter class, a respected, if disliked, gentleman. Instead of being criticized for marrying his brother's unlettered widow, he would be praised as a compassionate Christian.

She thought of his wife, Emily, gone five years now, the way her eyes had been dead even while she lived. What kind of hell had he put her through? Fancy realized that, while she'd long distrusted Robert, she had never truly understood the evil in him.

She was suffocating in his presence, barely able to get air into her lungs. She had to get outside, away from the corruption that permeated the room.

"I will give you an answer soon," she said. She turned and started for the door.

His hand touched her shoulder. "I look forward to our marriage, dear sister."

She forced herself not to run; she wouldn't give him the pleasure of seeing her fear. She merely nodded and continued toward the door, her back ramrod straight. She was relieved when he didn't follow her.

Hannah opened the door for her. Outside, the boy who had taken her horse stood in the same place, still holding the reins tightly.

"Thank you," she said.

He looked away as if embarrassed, even afraid, of such a small courtesy.

Fancy hesitated, then asked, "Do you know where they are keeping the new bondsman?"

The boy gave her a furtive, fearful glance, then looked toward the house. Turning to face the other way, he whispered, "Yes'm. He in the barn. He be chained there."

"Is he . . . ?"

"He hurt, but he still livin'." At the sound of the door opening behind him, the boy thrust the reins into her hands and slipped away.

Fancy looked up. Robert was standing there, watching her. He moved slowly, with attention to his injuries, down the steps. "You must forgive me, Fancy. Of course, you need help in mounting."

Everything in Fancy wanted to draw away, but she set her jaw and accepted his lift into the sidesaddle. Nor did she feel any compassion at the obvious pain the effort cost him.

His hand caught hers, and when she tried to pull back, he held on firmly.

"You should be honored, Fancy," he said. "All this will be your domain." He gestured with his free hand, a grand sweeping motion that encompassed all of Marsh's End.

Fancy let her gaze sweep over the fields and the barn and the large house, all that made up the large plantation. She saw the bodies of the men and women stooped low as they toiled. She recalled the frightened face of the boy who'd held her horse. The stoic, wary manner of the housekeeper.

This was a place of unhappiness and fear—fear that permeated everything. She could never bring her children or her sister here. Never. Not even if it meant Ian's life.

But it wouldn't, she swore to herself. Robert would not stop her.

This time when she pulled her hand away, Robert released it, but he smiled at her. It was a smile that turned her heart to stone, so confident, so sure.

"I'm sorry you couldn't see your convict today," he said, "but he is recuperating. We gave him good care. He *might* live a long life."

Another warning. Yet she knew that Ian would not live a long life at Marsh's End, even if Fancy accepted Robert's bargain. If he was forced to remain here, he would goad Cecil Martin or Robert into killing him.

She didn't have long. A day, maybe two. After that she wouldn't bet a farthing on Ian's chances of survival.

Giving Robert a curt nod, Fancy flicked the reins, and the mare cantered down the road toward home.

Chapter 23

Ian tried to sleep, but the image of blood spreading across Noel's shirt gave him no rest.

Anger was fruitless. He thought about praying for the boy, but he no longer had faith in prayer. The last time he'd made a request, he'd asked God to spare Derek's life. Instead, his own had been spared. He did not want that to happen again. He could not bear to think of Noel's life being forfeit because of him.

Lying in the prison stall, irons digging into his already chafed flesh, he thought about Derek as well as Noel. And he thought about Fancy. He felt in his bones that she was in graver danger than either of them had realized.

And it was *his* fault. He could see that now. Because of him, his brother had died, a boy lay wounded, and Fancy and her brood were in danger. He and his temper had spurred Robert to take destructive action.

Now he had to survive at least long enough to ensure Fancy's safety and that of her family. He had to survive long enough to kill Robert Marsh.

Ian made the vow knowing that it meant all the other vows he'd made would not be kept. But he would be giving the woman he loved . . . his wife . . . the only thing he could give her, the only thing he had left to give to anyone. His life. And he would give it to her gladly.

With renewed purpose, Ian tried once more to sleep. He needed it to regain his strength.

Day passed slowly into evening. The light coming

through the cracks in the barn walls moved from the east to the west side of the large structure. Despite the pain and his tortured thoughts, Ian dozed sometime in the early evening, waking when he heard the click of a key in the lock.

He sat up as the gate opened. The man who had cauterized his wound stepped inside. Robert Marsh stood behind him.

"I'm Cecil Martin, Mr. Marsh's overseer," the man said. "You'll do as I tell you from now on." He stooped, tore the cloth from Ian's side and examined the wound. Then he looked back at Marsh. "I think we should wait a day or two before sending him to the fields."

"He goes tomorrow," Marsh said flatly.

Martin nodded. "So be it."

Marsh grinned down at Ian. "Work him hard, but don't kill him. Not immediately. My sister-in-law seems concerned with his welfare."

Ian braced himself as Marsh took a few steps toward him. Still, he was unprepared for the booted foot that shot out to catch him in the ribs. Shards of pain streaked through him, each one greater than the last.

Marsh stepped back quickly. "Feed him tonight. I want him clearing the south pasture tomorrow."

The two men backed out, leaving Ian alone again. Marsh's kick had sent him backward, jamming his wounded side into the wall. The pain was white-hot, and he thought he might pass out again.

One thought kept him conscious—a question: what had Marsh meant when he said that his sister-in-law seemed concerned with his welfare? Had Fancy been here? Or had Marsh paid her another of his pleasant social calls?

Several hours passed before the gate opened again, and the lad who had brought him water stepped hesitantly inside. He lowered a tin plate, and Ian looked without interest at the unappetizing mush. The cup of water in the lad's other hand, however, looked better than a pot of gold.

After he set both items down, the lad lingered. "Mistuh Martin said I was to watch you eat and bring back the plate."

Even as his stomach growled, Ian ignored the food. But he drank some of the water.

"A lady ast 'bout you," the lad said. "She was here this mornin'. Wanted to know where you was."

Ian stopped, the cup halfway to his mouth, and fixed his gaze on the lad. "Mrs. Marsh?"

The lad nodded.

"She looked . . . well?"

The lad nodded again.

"Marsh didn't hurt her?"

The lad shook his head. "I gotta git back. Please eat, or Mistuh Martin will hit me."

Ian took another sip of water, savoring it. He was still intolerably thirsty. Then he looked back at the plate. "There's nothing to eat with."

"Mistuh Martin, he said not to give you no spoon or fork."

So Marsh was intent on inflicting every possible humiliation on him. Yet Ian knew he must eat.

Using his fingers, he forced the tasteless food into his mouth, then made himself swallow. He ate methodically, ignoring the pain that still hammered at him. Then, silently, he handed the plate back to the lad.

"I'll bring you some more water," the lad whispered, "if you doan tell nobody."

Ian nodded. "Thank you."

The lad ducked out of the stall without locking it. It hardly mattered, Ian thought. His ankles were chained to the wall, and even if they hadn't been, he was too weak to go far.

In seconds the lad returned, carrying a full cup of water. Ian drank slowly, and again the lad waited until he'd finished, taking the cup with him when he left. This time he locked the gate behind him.

Feeling only slightly better after this sustenance, Ian was nevertheless determined to see if he could stand up. Using the side of the stall as a brace, he struggled to his feet, straightening slowly, not trying to stretch to his full height for fear of tearing open his cauterized flesh. He could take only a step before the chain stopped him short.

Breathing hard, he leaned against the stall. He was in agony. But he had to find a way to endure the pain. Tomorrow morning Cecil Martin would set him to work the south field. And work he would. Marsh was looking for any excuse to kill him. And he wasn't ready to die.

Not yet.

Fancy had a plan, but she would require help and luck—a lot of both—to carry it out.

Could she ask it of Fortune?

She would have to.

As she approached the farm, the door opened and her sister stepped onto the porch with Amy. Fancy slipped down from the saddle, but before she could ask Fortune to walk with her to the barn, Noel came outside. Surprised, Fancy looked him over, taking in the unhealthy pallor of his face and the white sling supporting his arm.

"Noel," she said sternly, even as she hugged him, "what are you doing up?"

"I'm fine, Ma," he said. "Honest. It's my arm that hurts, not my legs."

Exchanging a look with Fortune, Fancy sighed. She was about to tell him to go back to bed when Little

Tim came running from the stable, his face pinched and sweaty.

"Mrs. Sutherland, I was about to come after you. You shouldn't have gone anywhere alone," he scolded.

She smiled at his earnestness. "I'm sorry if I gave you cause for concern, but I simply had to—"

"How's Ian?" Noel interrupted, his voice cracking with anxiety. "Did you find him?"

"He's alive," she said.

The pained look of Noel's brow eased.

Tim muttered an oath that managed to express his relief.

Fortune took her hand and gave it a squeeze.

"I wan' Ian," Amy said, pulling on Fancy's dress.

"I know, sweet pea." *So do I.*

They all looked to her for answers, and she dreaded their reaction to the only solution she'd managed to find. Her plan was so full of potential pitfalls that it seemed doomed to failure.

"Come inside," she said, tying her mare to the porch railing.

"T . . . Tea?" her sister asked, following her up the steps.

Each time Fortune spoke, Fancy's heart jumped. Her intonation was odd, clipped and even a little harsh, as if each syllable was produced only with great effort. Yet every word Fortune uttered reminded her that miracles did happen. Now if only she could ask for one more. . . .

"Let's talk first," she replied.

Inside the main room of the house, Fancy was met with the delicious aroma of baking bread. Fortune gave her a nervous smile, as if she thought her sister might be displeased. She had never baked bread on her own before. Indeed, she'd never taken full responsibility for anything, and Fancy was delighted at the change. Fortune was growing up. And healing.

"Hmmm, smells good," she said. "But if we could . . . For heaven's sake. Sweet pea, I almost stepped on you." Bending down, Fancy disentangled her daughter from her skirts—to which she seemed determined to cling—and picked her up. "Why don't you go see how Lucky and Unsatisfactory are? I think they both need some extra sweetness."

Amy thought about it for a moment, then nodded. "Awright. I'll go pet them. But I won' pet Lucky's headache."

"That's a good girl."

Fancy set her down and watched her skip her way to her room. She considered sending Noel back to bed to remove him from the conversation, too, but she discarded the notion; until Ian came back, Noel was trying to be the man of the house, and he would not accept a dismissal lightly.

Taking her seat at the table, Fancy decided she might as well get the worst over with first. In a flat, matter-of-fact tone she said, "Robert asked me to marry him. He says he will hang Ian if I do not."

Fortune's and Noel's faces turned white, while Tim's went red with anger.

"You . . . can't," Fortune said.

"No, of course I can't," Fancy replied. "I *wouldn't*, even if I weren't already married to Ian. But I might have to let Robert think I will. Until we can help Ian escape."

"But how are we going to do that?" Noel demanded.

Fancy turned to Tim. "Do you have a pistol?"

"Pa does, but I know how to use it."

"I don't want you to use it. I want to smuggle it to Ian."

"How?" Three voices chimed in at once.

Fancy took a deep breath and started telling them her idea.

When she had finished, Tim Wallace shook his head. "Mrs. Sutherland, no offense ma'am, but that's about the wildest plan I've ever heard."

Rufus Winfrey knew he'd been a fool to go with the stranger—a man his intuition had warned him was no good. And yet how could he have refused?

He pondered that question as he lay in the old, blessedly dry well. His head ached. He was thirsty and hungry, and he knew he would feel a great deal worse before his ordeal ended.

The man who had stopped him on the road had led him to the ruins of an old farmhouse that Rufus knew was once the home of a family named Adams. The father and all seven children had been killed by Indians and the mother carried away. Local legend had it that the ghosts of the children haunted the place, looking for their mother. The small piece of land had been purchased several times, and each time it had been abandoned after crops died and fires destroyed one barn after another. All the occupants had left swearing they had heard the Adams children crying.

So Rufus had been surprised when the man led him there; he hadn't heard of anyone living in the place for a very long time. And when he had turned around to ask the stranger his name and how he'd come to live in that particular house, the man pulled a pistol.

Rufus knew the man had meant to shoot him dead. But he had mumbled something about hell and not shooting a man of God before hitting him over the head. He had awakened in the well.

Rufus supposed he should be grateful that the well was not very deep, and he had survived the fall. But the reluctant murderer had done him no favor. A quick death was preferable to a long, lingering one. Yet he clung to life. He shouted until he was hoarse, then decided to conserve what remained of his voice until he heard some evidence that humans were close by. Something deep inside him kept telling him that no one was going to approach this land, that no one would come in time. Still, his wife would miss him and perhaps send her brothers looking for him before it was too late.

He spent hours listening for friendly voices. Finally he started listening, too, for the sound of children crying. But he heard only the wind and the soft sigh of leaves rustling in the trees. If there were indeed ghosts, they were not helpful ones.

But the greater mystery to him was why he had been attacked. The man had asked for him by name; otherwise he would have thought the stranger was a horse thief.

He prayed awhile. He wasn't sure whether he should pray for deliverance. He'd never thought God looked favorably on self-serving prayers. Still, he hoped his flock needed him. He knew his wife needed him. Maybe God would understand this once.

His wife. Dear Margaret. She was long-suffering, and bore seeing him only a few days a month with gentleness and good humor. She'd hoped for a child, but they had not been blessed. Her sweet face fell each time her monthlies came, and yet she always greeted him with a welcoming smile.

So he said a prayer, asking that God's will be done, if indeed His will was to save him.

Night fell, and above the walls of his circular prison, he could see the stars. The moon was out of his view, but he pictured it in his mind. He made a respectful request for rain because his mouth was so dry. His stomach, which was rumbling from emptiness, he could ignore.

He tried not to think about who had sent his attacker, and why. He did not believe in hate or revenge. All men were God's creatures, and Rufus knew he should accept them as they were. Still . . .

He forced the "still" to the back of his mind. It was not for him to question. Not for him to judge.

Yet as the hours passed and his mind wandered, he could not help but think about the men who, in the course of his travels, he'd come to know personally or through their deeds or through the eyes of other men. And of all those men, only one struck him as wicked enough to murder a man as harmless and powerless as he was. Only one who might wish to harm him.

The man's name was Robert Marsh.

Ian slept for several hours despite the pain. He had experience sleeping through pain and hunger and thirst—too much. Yet his sleep was haunted by nightmares that lingered in his mind when he awoke in the darkened stall.

His brothers faced him, one covered with blood, the other with a noose around his neck. And in the background, a child beckoned to him frantically as a pack of wild dogs closed in on her. He heard his own voice shouting, "*Katy!*" But as he said her name, she disappeared, and in her place, he saw Fancy. The dogs drew closer, snarling at her, crouching as they prepared to leap. . . .

Struggling, unwilling to visit that dark place again, he pushed himself up to lean against the side of the stall. Sweat dampened his face and bare chest. He was still sitting there when the gate opened and the overseer came in.

"Git up," Martin said, standing over him. "You goin' to clear a new field today." He leaned down and unlocked the chain that linked the leg irons to the wall.

Ian stood and managed to move several steps, but he was hobbled by the irons, which remained on his ankles.

"Better git used to 'em," Martin said, pushing him toward the opening. Ian fought to stay on his feet. He bloody well was not going to give this bastard the satisfaction of seeing him fall. His pride wouldn't allow it.

Martin walked him to the yard outside the barn, where he pushed him toward a group of men and women, some barely old enough to be called such. Most were dark-skinned slaves, but several were white men. Bondsmen, Ian guessed. Two of them also wore leg irons. They had probably tried to escape. Now their eyes were dull, without hope, as they shuffled forward at the overseer's command. Not one so much as glanced at him as he joined their ranks, their curiosity long since beaten out of them.

A thin white man ordered him to walk with a group of six slaves. By the brand on the man's hand, Ian judged that he was either a current or former bondsman. He carried a whip and strutted back and forth, snapping it self-importantly.

Ian followed him without comment, stumbling frequently as he tried to accustom himself to the leg irons. He was the only one without a shirt, and his skin was already glistening with perspiration.

They walked a mile or more, sapping what strength Ian had. The pain in his side increased with every step, and he could only imagine what new agony the day would bring. He tried to think of other things, tried not to worry about Noel, tried not to wonder if he would ever see Fortune's smile again, tried not to miss Amy's plump little body curling up in his lap.

Most of all he tried not to think of Fancy and of all the moments they would never share, of all the things he would never say to her—one thing in particular that he wished he had said and now could not.

He stumbled again, and this time he did fall. The whip cracked across his back.

Lying face down in the dirt, Ian gritted his teeth and slowly pushed himself to his feet. He thought he'd left hell when he stepped ashore in Maryland. But he knew now that he'd been wrong.

Chapter 24

ancy sat at the table, struggling with the note that was such an important part of the plan. While she could read, and even write some words, she soon discovered how limited her skills were. She brushed a tear away from her eyes. She'd always desperately wanted to learn, and now it was life and death, and she was powerless.

Tim might be able to help, but he had left early that morning to fetch his father's pistol and, Fancy hoped, to persuade the widow Phillips to stay with the children. They would tell the woman that Fancy had business in Chestertown and hope she asked no further questions.

While they waited, Fancy and Fortune had seen to the livestock, and Fancy had asked Noel to help weed the garden. He could do that with one hand, and he needed something to do; he was unusually quiet, and she was certain he was chafing at not being part of the plan to rescue Ian.

At noon, Fancy was immensely relieved by the arrival of Mrs. Phillips. She came in a buggy driven by her youngest son, Tom, a strapping young man of seventeen. Tom helped her down, and she bustled over to Fancy, patting her arm comfortingly.

"Tim said you had to go into Chestertown on business. I'm real pleased I can help out. You just go and stay as long as you must. The young 'uns and I will get along just fine."

Noel, still upset that he was not trusted to care for

his sister alone, gave Fancy a betrayed look and walked off to sulk. Amy, however, warmed up to the woman immediately, especially after Mrs. Phillips uncovered a basket of cookies.

Fancy's gratitude was equaled by her astonishment. She had never expected any help from her neighbors because of John's connection to the feared and hated Robert Marsh. It occurred to her now that perhaps the neighbors had avoided her and her family because of John's own almost painful shyness, which, she knew, stemmed from being the target of his brother's verbal abuse for so many years.

In any case, Fancy was pleased to have Mrs. Phillips sitting at her table, chattering away as if they'd been friends for years. She would have enjoyed the social time had she not been so on edge, waiting for Tim's return.

He appeared an hour after Mrs. Phillips's arrival, his father's pistol in hand. Fancy joined him in the barn, away from the children's and Mrs. Phillips's curious eyes.

"It's loaded," he said. "I'll show Fortune how to hold it."

Fancy went out to the paddock and whistled. In a moment, Trouble flew to her shoulder. "Can you do your part?" she asked her pet. She knew this was the most difficult part of the plan.

The crow flapped her wings, craning her neck to look around at them. Fancy took it as a good sign. But there were so many ifs, so many things that could go wrong. Still, this was her only hope—and Ian's.

Fancy went to the house to gather her writing materials, then returned to the barn, where Tim and Fortune were waiting for her, and where Noel lurked, still hoping, she knew, to be told he could join the adventure. She set the quill, ink, and tiny pieces of parchment on Ian's table, then looked up at Tim.

"Can you write the note?" she asked humbly.

Nodding gently, he knelt down beside the table to pick up the quill. He knew about the reading lessons, and he must have known how hard she had tried before asking for help. "What should I write?"

"Put 'pistol,' 'barn,' and 'closest hay' on one note," Fancy said after a moment. "The other should say, 'today,' 'horses,' and 'creek.' "

Tim looked doubtful. "Will he understand?"

Fancy wasn't sure. But giving Tim what she hoped was a confident look, she said, "He'll have to."

Fancy reached over and touched Fortune's clenched hands. They were white and cold, but Fortune looked at her and they exchanged brief encouraging smiles as Fancy turned their wagon into Marsh's End. She saw Robert almost immediately in an uncultivated field; no one else at Marsh's End sat a horse with such arrogance.

Fancy noted the workers scattered over the field; they were clearing rocks—bending, lifting, carrying their burdens to a wagon. She also saw Cecil Martin riding from worker to worker, cracking his whip in the air in a bullish display of power.

She shuddered as she saw the whip land on a bare back. When the figure straightened, her blood froze in her veins. Ian. Even from a distance, she recognized his tall, lean form.

With tremendous effort, she managed to force her lips into a false smile as Robert cantered up to them.

"An unexpected pleasure," he said, looking at her carefully chosen dress with approval. Then his gaze flickered toward Fortune, and Fancy saw distaste in his eyes as he took in her sister's disheveled appearance, then focused on her budding breasts. "And my sweet . . . simple sister."

Fancy's fear-chilled blood began to simmer with anger, and she moved her hand a few inches to give Fortune a touch of reassurance. But her sister only gave her a blank stare. She prayed Fortune would not be too frightened to do what needed to be done.

"I hope you have good news for me," Robert said to her.

"It depends," she said. "You also made a promise."

"And I am keeping it. Your Scotsman is working in that field, alive and well."

"He was wounded."

Robert shrugged. "I don't coddle my slaves."

She bit her lip—hard—and he smiled as if he knew exactly what she was thinking.

"You shouldn't be driving that team," he said. "It will hurt your hands. I don't want any wife of mine to have the calluses of a field hand."

"Then you will be disappointed," she replied. "I helped my husband in the fields." *Both* husbands, she added silently.

"You will never have to do that again," Robert said. "I never did understand why John allowed you to work like a . . . peasant."

Turning in his saddle, he beckoned to Cecil Martin, and they waited in silence as the overseer galloped across the field to join them.

"Send someone over here to drive the wagon up to the house," Robert said.

Would he send Ian? It would not be out of character for Robert to humiliate him in front of her. And the plan would be so much easier if she could tell him. . . . But Robert soon disappointed her.

"One of the slaves," he told Martin, "not the bondsman. And tell him to make it quick."

The overseer rode back to the field and spoke briefly to one of the dark-skinned workers. While the man ran toward the wagon, Fancy saw Martin's whip come down on her husband's shirtless back again. Martin was doing it, she knew, expressly for her benefit.

She looked at Robert. "If that happens again, I won't marry you."

"Yes, you will," he said flatly. "Because that is minor in comparison to what I can do."

"It doesn't matter that I despise you?"

"Not at all," he said easily. "As I said before, I'll enjoy taming you. Come, sister, it won't be so bad. You'll have servants, wealth, position. Your sister . . . will get the best of care. Your children will learn manners."

Fancy felt Fortune flinch, and she hoped Robert hadn't noticed. He thrived on weakness.

When the field hand reached them, Robert ordered, "You will drive the wagon to the house for the ladies."

The man was drenched with sweat and panting heavily. Fancy moved over on the seat, and the servant, his eyes fearful and his hands shaking, climbed up and took the reins. They were silent during the long ride up to the house. Then Robert dismounted and helped her down from the wagon. Fortune didn't give him the opportunity to touch her, jumping down quickly on her own.

"Get back to the fields," he told the driver.

The man dismounted and started down the road at a trot. Robert watched him critically as he handed the reins of his horse to the young boy Fancy had seen on her earlier visit. Then he turned back to Fancy and took her arm. "We have many things to talk about," he said, leading her toward the house. "We must set a date."

At the foot of the steps, he looked back at Fortune, who, Fancy knew, was not following them.

"Come, come, my dear," he said to her. "Don't be shy."

Fortune backed away, and he let out a sound of exasperation.

"Since your . . . *visit* to our farm the other day," Fancy said, "Fortune has been quite distraught. She's afraid of you. She can wait out here with the horses, perhaps water them."

Irritation flitted across his features. "I have slaves to do that."

"Animals calm her," Fancy said. "I can't discuss wedding plans if she becomes sick."

"She will have to get over being *sick*."

"Do you want to discuss this wedding or not?"

She issued the challenge, but he didn't pick up the gauntlet immediately.

Looking around, he asked, "Where are the children?"

She gave him a thin smile. "You forget. Noel was hurt. He couldn't make the trip. Someone is looking after him."

"He is better, is he not?"

His pitiful attempt at concern made her feel ill. Fancy didn't know why he bothered.

"Yes," she replied shortly, mounting the steps to distract him from Fortune.

"You see, I told you he wasn't badly hurt," he said smugly.

The door opened as they reached it; the butler must have been watching them through the window. She swallowed again as she noticed how the servants at Marsh's End hurried to do their master's bidding. Fear was pervasive, a living, breathing thing.

Robert escorted her into the parlor, but when he

would have handed her into the chair by the hearth, she chose to sit primly on one end of the small velvet sofa that faced the window, making sure she had a clear view of the wagon.

"Now, my dear Fancy," he said, seating himself at the other end of the sofa. "I think we should post the banns immediately. We can set the wedding in three weeks."

"What about my mourning period?"

He shrugged. "I'm simply taking care of my brother's wife. I doubt there will be any undue comment. Now, about your sister . . ."

"What about my sister?"

"I've been thinking." He paused. "There is a school in Boston that takes . . . simple girls. Since John's death I've been considering the problem, and it seems that it would be the right thing to do. And I'm sure the magistrate would agree."

Apprehension gathered like a storm inside Fancy, though she tried hard not to show it. She knew what Robert meant by "school." The place was an asylum for lunatics. And she knew why he was suggesting it. He had no intention of keeping Ian alive, but before he killed him, he needed another weapon to force her compliance. In Fortune, he had found it.

Don't panic, she told herself. Stick to the plan. He can't kill Ian if Ian isn't here. Your task is to give Fortune enough time to do what must be done.

She chewed her lip, trying to decide which tack to take. Should she act compliant? No, that would raise his suspicion. Anger and defiance, on the other hand, seemed to fascinate him.

Casting a quick glance out the window and noting that Fortune had not yet returned to the wagon, Fancy fixed him with a determined look.

"My sister will stay with me," she said firmly.

"Not unless she learns to comb her hair and dress according to my position," Robert replied.

"Will you shoot her, too, if she does not?"

"Don't be tedious, Fancy. In the first place, I didn't shoot Noel. In the second place, I told you that the boy threatened a deputy. Another deputy shot him. I had nothing to do with it."

"You had everything to do with it. If you hadn't been trespassing, trying to steal what's mine, it would never have happened."

"Ah, yes, your bondsman."

"And my farm."

"John's farm," he corrected. "And it should have been mine. Along with that stallion and the two mares."

"I *know* John didn't write a second will."

"But how will you prove it?"

He was goading her. Fancy knew it. But it suited her purpose to let him. It wasn't hard to act incensed. It was much harder not to let her anger get out of control.

She let her eyes shift briefly to the window again. Still no Fortune.

"Proof is what counts, isn't it?" Robert continued. "Sheriff Vaughn will never believe a responsible husband would leave a widow alone with a convict."

"You pay Vaughn to believe whatever you tell him," she shot back.

"You misjudge me again, Fancy," he said, his voice changing to what she supposed was meant to be a seductive tone. "I'm only concerned about your welfare." He reached across the small space that separated them to place his hand over hers. "You are my brother's widow."

"You never cared about John," she said, willing herself not to push his hand away. "You made his life miserable. He would never have turned to you."

"But he would have. He did." His smile was, as usual, unpleasant. "I know why John married you, Fancy. I know he thought you needed help. Why is it so impossible for you to believe that I might be compelled to do the same now, when you so clearly need help?"

"Perhaps because you didn't feel compelled to help *him*, when he so clearly needed it. Instead, you made certain that no one would help him. If anyone had, he might be alive today."

Fancy was surprised to see Robert go pale in the face at her biting remarks. Indeed, he actually seemed upset by the thinly veiled accusation that he had contributed to his brother's death. She wouldn't have given him credit for having anything resembling a conscience.

After a long pause, Robert spoke quietly. "John was always welcome to come here. It was his choice to turn down my offers of hospitality, which, as you say, might have saved him."

"Your 'offers' meant giving up his land," she pointed out.

"It never should have been his land," Robert retorted. "Marsh's End was not meant to be divided. I was the firstborn son, and by rights, the entire estate, including all the land and the horses, should have come to me."

"Your father didn't agree."

"My father was not in his right mind. He got soft when he became sick. Just as John was soft. You cannot build an empire by being soft."

Fancy looked at him in disbelief. "Is that why you steal and cheat and plot? Is that why you've driven families from their land? Is that why you work your people to death? Because you think you're building an *em-pire*?"

"Not *an* empire. *Our* empire," he corrected her with astonishing ease. "And it *will* be ours. I want sons, and they will be princes. You will come to understand, and appreciate what I give them."

Bile rose in her throat. He looked so earnest, as if he believed everything he was saying, as if he thought she would forgive what he had done if only he could make her understand.

It was he who did not understand, she thought, and he never would. He had no capacity to feel what others felt. Even more frightening, he truly believed that he was taking care of his brother's family—that his brother's family was *his* family, just as his brother's land was *his* land. His land, his horses. His wife.

All his property.

Fancy couldn't continue the farce any longer. She was sick. Soul sick. But another glance out the window sent a wave of relief coursing through her. Fortune was standing by the wagon. They could leave. In fact, the sooner the better.

She rose abruptly from the sofa. "I have to go. I must get back to Noel."

"What about the banns?" Robert said, rising with her. "We have to go to the church together to have them posted."

"I can't go to Chestertown while Noel is ill."

"Two days," he said. "You have two days. I will come for you Thursday morning, and we'll take my carriage to Chestertown."

Then he would discover her marriage. By then surely Reverend Winfrey would have filed the certificate.

But by then it wouldn't matter. Ian would be gone from here and out of harm's way. She could openly defy Robert then. She would fight him in the courts, and she would win.

Fancy tried to steady the trembling of her hand as Robert took it and raised it to his lips.

"I expect Ian Sutherland to be healthy by the time you come for me on Thursday," she said.

"I guarantee it," he replied. "Your wedding present."

She nodded.

"I'll send someone to drive you back. I don't want anything to happen to my bride."

"I have my gloves, and I've been driving myself for years," she said sharply. "Until we are married, I will continue to do so."

"Very well. Until we're married," he said with surprising affability.

The butler was waiting to open the door for her. Robert held on to her elbow as they descended the front steps, then helped her up onto the wagon seat.

His hand lingered on her arm as he said, "I will see you on Thursday."

"I'll be ready." *Ready to tell you that your would-be bride is already married to your missing bondsman.*

Chapter 25

Ian stooped to pick up another rock. *Don't think about the pain. Pick it up. Don't drop it.* Dropping it would mean another lash of the whip. Holding the rock, he dragged his feet toward the wagon. *One step at a time. Don't trip. Don't fall. Just put one foot in front of the other.*

He had learned at Culloden, during the vicious day of fighting and the frantic attempt to escape after the battle, that he could force his body to do the impossible, that there was always some place in his mind where he could go and endure.

Now it was thoughts of Fancy that sustained him. Her smile. Her clear brown eyes. Her gentleness and selfless generosity. The way she looked as she rode a horse, her hair streaming out behind her and her cheeks glowing. The way she felt lying beneath him, warm and soft and welcoming. It was those thoughts and more: Amy's sweet hug and Noel's bright, inquisitive gaze.

When he saw her driving up the lane in the wagon with Fortune beside her, he thought at first it was an illusion, that his pain-drugged mind had conjured up the image. But then he saw Marsh ride toward her, and he realized she was quite real, sitting right there—but so far away. Did she see him? What was she doing here? He dug deep for the strength to straighten his back and stand tall. He would not let her see him bent and cowed.

When the wagon continued up the road toward the

house, with one of his fellow workers driving it and Marsh himself riding beside it, he watched, helpless with rage, as Fancy was taken from his sight.

Hours went by, or so it seemed as he was forced to go on with the work of clearing the uncultivated field. It was the last such field, he'd heard a slave say, at Marsh's End. The hundreds of cultivated acres were on the verge of giving out, their soil exhausted by over-planting. As he worked, fantasies of escape flirted with reality. Under the scorching sun, with agony dulling his mind, it was difficult to tell the difference. Mayhap he could ride out with Fancy when she left. Mayhap he could hide in her wagon. But the irons around his ankles, biting into his flesh, soon reminded him where fantasy ended and reality began.

He could not run anywhere. He could barely walk. His ribs hurt. The burn was still agonizing. Blood oozed from the sudden vicious slices of the whip. His entire body felt as if it were pierced by nails and burned by embers; yet any time he stopped, or even slowed, the whip whistled across his bare back again.

Nay, he could not escape on his own. Not now.

But he had to survive. He had to control his anger. He had to get stronger. And then . . . then he would kill Robert Marsh.

When he saw the wagon coming back down the road, Ian glanced up to see where Martin was; then he straightened up to take a longer look. No driver this time. Only Fancy and her sister on the wagon seat. She did not stop or glance in his direction, but she appeared unharmed. Why had she visited her brother-in-law? Was she bargaining for his life? With her own? The thought was unbearable. Yet deep in his soul he knew she was capable of exactly that. Dear God, but it was bitter knowledge.

Ian lost track of time. The sun approached its zenith,

and, though the overseer allowed slaves and bondsmen alike a drink from the water barrel on the back of the wagon, no mention was made of food. Ian knew he would not last much longer. His head was spinning, the muscles in his arms and legs felt rubbery and out of control, and the pain in his side and head were beyond agony.

Don't think about it, he told himself again. The raucous sound of a bird flying overhead penetrated his awareness. Vaguely, he realized he'd been hearing the call for several minutes. And a familiar racket it was, too.

Caw. Caw. Caw.

A crow.

Impossible, he thought. It couldn't be. And yet the bloody thing wasn't going away.

Wiping sweat from his eyes with the back of his hand, Ian saw that Martin was on the far side of the field, berating some poor slave. He was safe—for a moment, anyway. He shaded his eyes and looked upward, squinting as he searched the sky.

The crow was circling directly above him. Still disbelieving, he gave the low whistle he'd heard Fancy use when she wanted Trouble to fly to her.

Instantly the bird swooped and flew past him.

Bloody hell . . .

He glanced again toward Martin. Then, satisfied that he wasn't being watched, he bent slightly, as if he were working, and whistled again. This time, when Trouble swooped, Ian held out his arm. With a flutter of wings, the crow landed.

Ian noticed the bird's thickly wrapped legs immediately. Quickly, he untied first one, then the other strip of leather, releasing two tiny pieces of parchment. These he slipped into the rope-tied waist of his trousers.

"Sorry, old girl," he whispered to the crow, "but I don't have a thing to give you. You'll have to fly back to your mistress if you want your treat. Go on. Go to Fancy." He held up his arm, and Trouble flew off, cawing loudly, heading for the woods beyond the field.

Ian itched to read the notes. He turned to see what Martin was doing. Damn, but the man had managed to ride almost all the way across the field in his direction without him noticing. To Ian's horror, the overseer had seen the crow and had a pistol in his hand, aimed at Trouble, ready to fire. . . .

Ian fell to the ground, shouting loudly with pain, an instant before the gunshot split the air. The bullet went wild, and Trouble disappeared among the trees.

Cursing, Martin looked sharply in his direction, then galloped toward him. Ian tried to get up before Martin reached him, but he wasn't able to move fast enough. The whip landed across his flesh. Then it landed again. And again.

He fell back to the ground, and this time he couldn't seem to rise. He tried, but nothing worked. Not his legs. Not his arms. He felt his back being lashed open. Felt the blood running across his lacerated flesh. Thought about oblivion. Just a few more moments now. If he lay perfectly still and didn't try to move . . .

Then he thought of the two pieces of paper in his pocket.

Ian put his hands flat against the earth and pushed. Suddenly he felt two hands hook under his arms and heave, pulling him upward. It gave him the lift he needed. He struggled to his feet and stood swaying for a moment before regaining his balance. He nodded his thanks to the man who had helped him, a dark-skinned slave who had been working silently all day a few yards away from him.

The man's eyes flickered briefly downward, toward

Ian's waist, where the parchment was hidden. Ian held his breath until the man raised his gaze again. Knowledge flickered in the dark eyes, knowledge and empathy and shared pain. Ian released his pent-up breath and gave the man another nod of gratitude.

"Git back to work, you lazy bastard," the overseer said.

Ian bent to the task once again. The sun was going down. Finally the overseer galloped back across the field to meet a man who had come looking for him from another field.

Ian took the papers from his trousers and quickly scanned them. Then read them again, this time more carefully. The letters were nearly illegible, but he was sure he hadn't misread them. His first reaction was anger that Fancy was taking such a chance. That she was out there, at this very moment, waiting for him. Didn't she realize what would happen to her if she was caught helping him escape? What would happen to her sister? To her children?

She was risking everything for him. *Everything.*

And he knew he could do no less for her. Katy might already be lost—he might already have failed her. He'd known that for a long time, even as he'd clung to the last threads of hope. But he could do something for Fancy and the children. He loved them, dammit. He'd tried so bloody hard not to, but there was no denying the fact now. He would protect them, even if the effort cost him his own life.

Ian slipped the papers into his mouth and swallowed them. A few more minutes. Mayhap an hour. He could do it. He could survive. He *would* survive.

Dusk fell, and the overseer turned the exhausted field workers toward the slave quarters, which, Ian had noticed on the walk to the field that morning, were located behind the barn where his own prison stall awaited him.

He shuffled along, his back bowed. It required little effort on his part to portray a man totally destroyed; he merely allowed the agony and exhaustion to get the better of him. He wanted Cecil Martin to discount him as a threat. He wanted the overseer to get careless.

As they approached the open area between the slave quarters and the barn, the slaves shuffled wearily toward the communal pot that hung over the central fire. Martin let them go and urged Ian onward alone, toward the barn.

"You'll get yours later," the overseer growled.

As he shuffled wearily into the barn, Ian's gaze scanned the interior. "Closest hay," the note had said. A bale of hay lay next to his prison, tossed there, he guessed, for use the following day when the horses' stalls were mucked out.

He waited until he was a few feet from the hay, then he stumbled. Falling against the bale, he shoved his hands into it, rummaging quickly. He felt iron an instant before the overseer's boot connected with his thigh. At least it wasn't his ribs, he thought dryly, thanking God for small favors.

His mind working feverishly, he groaned, rolling slowly to his back, ignoring the pain it caused the tears in his skin. He brought the pistol out of the hay in his right hand, then held it in both hands—aimed at Cecil Martin.

Ian saw the man's face redden with alarm, but the red faded when he saw Ian's expression. It became distinctly pale.

"Yer askin' fer more trouble," the overseer said.

"Am I, now?" Ian smiled. "Strange, but I believe you are the one in trouble. I would enjoy putting this ball in yer heart. You donna know how much I would enjoy it."

"You will hang."

"Mayhap, but you willna be there tae witness it. And 'twould be worth it tae put you in the ground. Now unlock these leg irons."

"I don't have the keys."

"Tha' is really too bad." Ian cocked the pistol, "because I'm a dead man anyway, and I wouldna be minding the company. At least partway."

Martin's face crumpled. "Marsh will kill me."

"Tha' possibility is several moments off, compared wi' the certainty of this verra second." He heard the burr in his voice thicken, as it always did when he was angry.

"If I give you the keys . . ."

"No if aboot it. You gi' them tae me, or I take them from your dead body."

Martin reached for the ring of keys that hung from his belt.

"Verra carefully," Ian warned.

Martin's movements were so slow that Ian finally hurried him up with a wave of the pistol. He hoped to bloody hell it was loaded.

When Martin held the keys out toward him, Ian said, "No, ye do it. Ye are good wi' locks."

As Martin reluctantly bent over Ian's ankles, Ian brought the pistol down hard on the back of his head, then caught his heavy body as he slumped. Taking a knife from Martin's belt and tucking it into his own trousers, Ian tried several keys before finding the one that unlocked his leg irons. Panting, sweating, and cursing under his breath, he used what was left of his strength to take off the man's shirt and boots and roll Martin into the prison stall where, with some satisfaction, he attached the leg irons to the overseer's ankles.

He found a length of rope and tied Martin's hands behind him, then cut off a piece of the man's trousers and stuffed it in his mouth to gag him. Being free of the leg irons gave him a moment's elation. He shook his head to clear it. Perhaps he *could* carry out the plan Fancy had laid out for him.

Hurriedly pulling on the shirt to cover his lacerated back, he picked up the overseer's hat, which had tumbled to the floor, and pulled it down low over his forehead. He took the boots, too, and making a quick survey of the horses in the stalls, he chose what looked to be the fastest and quickly saddled the animal. Keeping his body low against the horse's neck, wondering how long it would be before the stable help finished their meal and entered the barn, he rode twice up and down the wide corridor between the stalls to get a feel for the animal beneath him.

On the second turnaround, as he approached the open barn door, he heard voices coming in his direction. He couldn't wait any longer, but neither did he want to create a disturbance. With the hat drawn over his face and with Martin's shirt and boots, he hoped he would be mistaken for the man. Touching his heels to the horse's sides, he sent the animal trotting out of the barn.

No one paid any attention to him. Most of the workers were eating, their eyes turned downward.

He managed to keep his impatience under control until he reached the gate and turned out of sight of the house. Then he dug in his heels and felt the surging power of the animal under him as the horse moved into a gallop.

He was free!

Fancy paced nervously back and forth along the bank of the creek. Tim was sitting under a nearby tree, occasionally throwing stones into the sluggish, rain-hungry water. Fortune had already driven the wagon home, and she had taken Trouble with her, both of them having completed their parts of the plan perfectly.

Indeed, the crow—the weakest link in their chain—had surpassed Fancy's wildest expectations. As soon as she and Fortune met Tim at the creek, they'd taken Trouble, still in the cage John had once built for their stray pets, through the woods on foot, getting as close as they dared to the field where Ian was working. Then, with Fortune holding Trouble, Fancy had tied the notes to the crow's legs.

With the message-bearing bird, Fancy had crept slowly to a spot behind a huge oak that grew a few yards back from the edge of the field. She'd spent several minutes saying Ian's name and pointing to him. Then she'd given the command and sent Trouble on her mission.

Fancy's heart had stopped when Trouble refused to leave her. The crow had searched the ground for supper, taken short flights to various treetops, and generally ignored all of her entreaties to "find Ian." But on the fifth try, the crow had soared into the sky, circled the entire field several times, then focused in on her quarry.

Hidden on the far side of the field, Fancy had seen Trouble dive toward the ground, but then she'd lost sight of the crow. She'd had to wait, desperate with worry, for the crow to return to discover that her pet had fulfilled her mission.

The notes were gone. But was it Ian who had found them?

That question was only one of many that tormented Fancy as she waited now. As the hours passed and Ian didn't appear, her anxiety—and her doubts—deepened. Maybe he hadn't been able to find the gun Fortune had managed to slip into the hay bale while Fancy spoke with Robert in the parlor. Maybe they hadn't returned him to the barn but to some other quarters. Maybe he hadn't been able to steal a horse. Maybe he was on foot. And maybe he didn't remember this place by the creek, where they'd come the day after the fire, where he'd made love to her on the sandy Maryland soil.

Dusk was passing into night, and it was fully dark beneath the trees when Fancy saw Sir Gray, tied with the other two horses by the creek, lift his head from the tall grass, twitch his ears, and let out a soft whinny. She and Tim exchanged a look and then glanced toward the road. It ran a half mile from the creek, and was rarely used on weekdays, when most farmers were in their fields; they had seen no one since late afternoon.

But horses were never wrong. Someone was coming.

Grabbing Sir Gray's reins, Tim mounted the gelding—in preparation for flight, if necessary. Fancy waited next to the mare. She had stopped breathing, and her heart was pounding so loud she was sure Tim could hear it.

All at once a strange horse broke through the trees, a rider lying low on its back.

Ian. She would have recognized the way he looked astride a horse amid a thousand men on horseback.

She left Tim with the horses and ran to meet him. Then he was off the horse and holding her. Could it be real? She smelled his sweat and blood, but even that pungency was welcome. Her fingers traveled lightly over his back and she felt the dampness on the shirt.

She stepped back, eyeing the too large clothing.

"Courtesy of Martin," he said.

Without speaking, she unbuttoned the shirt and looked at his back. Her hands trembled as she saw the ragged lacerations.

"Dear God," she whispered, moving away, afraid of

hurting him even more than he must be hurting. "What have they done to you?"

"I've been through worse," he said.

"That is not comforting," she scolded.

But he had no patience with her concern. Taking her shoulders in his grasp, he spoke urgently. "Noel. How is he? I saw him—"

"He's fine," she assured him, then heard his breath rush out in relief. "The bullet went through his upper arm, and he lost some blood. But there's been no sign of infection. This morning he was up and about and champing at the bit to come with us."

Ian's eyes closed briefly as he murmured, "Thank God. Thank God, he's all right." Then urgency seemed to grip him once more. "We have to go," he said. "They won't be far behind." Still, he took the time to lean over and kiss her hard. "You are a little fool, you know. If anything had happened to you—"

"Robert will have no idea how you got the gun," she said quickly. "He'll believe his overseer was careless. "I'll tell him I've heard that before."

"You willna go near him," he said flatly.

"Not for a while," she agreed. "I have to go to Annapolis. Robert has forged a will that says John left everything to him—the farm, the horses, and even you. But Douglas Turner and I will appeal to the governor. Turner saw John the day he purchased your indenture. He can testify that John gave him the last will he made. I'll fight Robert—in court." She took his hand. "Tim will take you to a place where you can hide until it's safe. Once Big Tim finds Reverend Winfrey—"

"Hide!" Ian exclaimed. "You think I will hide like a bloody coward and leave you to face Marsh alone? Fancy, when he finds me gone, if he has no' already, he will be out for blood!"

"Exactly," she said. "And it will be *your* blood he wants, not mine."

Ian shook his head. "I willna do it. I willna hide while you risk your life. Wherever you are going, I will go with you."

"No." She shook her head. "You mustn't."

"The hell I *mustn't*," he growled, his burr giving way to a clear and unaccented imitation of her speech.

"But, Ian, I'm going to Chestertown to get Turner, and that is exactly where Robert will expect you to go!"

"I willna let you ride there alone at night. Not when you can be sure, at this very minute, that your brother-in-law is planning a war."

"Ian—" Desperate to keep him safe, Fancy let out a frustrated sigh. "I can take care of myself."

His rough, blistered hand touched her cheek. "Aye, lass, I know you can. But you shouldna have to." And then he kissed her again, long and thoroughly. When he lifted his head to look down at her, his breathing was as ragged as hers. "I love you, Fancy Sutherland," he said.

"Oh, Ian," she whispered, feeling hope and joy rush through her heart. "I thought I would die when I got home to find that Robert had taken you. I've been so afraid he would kill you before I could—" She broke off on a sob.

"Hush," he soothed. "I may be a little worse for wear, but I am no' dead. Thanks to you." His lips brushed her forehead. "Fancy, listen to me. I ha' lost everyone else I ever loved. I couldna bear to lose you, too."

"Nor could I bear to lose you," she murmured. "And that's why I want you to go where I know you'll be safe. Please, Ian. Please, let Tim take you where you can rest and and get well without fear of being discovered. You can't fight Robert in this condition."

He was silent for a long moment. "You are certain about Turner? You can trust him?"

"Yes," she said, nodding. "He will not betray us."

"And this governor of yours?"

She smiled at him, a sad smile. She had learned how hard it was for him to trust anyone. "There are some decent men," she said. "Some who care about justice. John told me many times that Governor Braden is that kind of man."

He sighed. "Then I willna argue further. John Marsh's word is enough for me." He sighed again. "Verra well."

Taking his words for assent, she felt relief flood through her, and she stood on tiptoe to give him a quick kiss. "Thank you."

"Where is this place?"

"Just outside of Chestertown," she replied. "It's said to be haunted, and no one goes near it." She pressed a bundle into his hands. "Here's some food."

He searched her features in the darkness. "You're a bonny brave lass."

"You must go now," she said, "or we'll all be in danger."

Her words propelled him into action. As they walked together to where Tim was standing with the horses, he kept his arm around her waist, and she felt him leaning against her—because he needed her support, she realized. She knew his strength and resilience would carry him through anything. Still, she thought, it was a good thing he had agreed to rest and let her take care of herself. Otherwise, she would have been forced to hurt his pride by telling him the truth: at the moment he was not strong enough to hurt a fly—never mind her brother-in-law.

Ian took Sir Gray's reins from Tim, and Fancy took the horse Ian had stolen from Robert's stable to the edge of the clearing and gave its rump a slap. It took off in the direction of Marsh's End, heading back to the known source of food and water.

The three of them mounted and rode together through the woods to the road. Tim continued on, to the edge of the trees on the other side of the road. But when Fancy stopped, Ian stopped beside her.

"We separate here," she said to him.

He nodded. "Be careful, lass," he said. "Remember that you carry my heart with you."

Before she could say anything else, he turned Sir Gray and took off after Tim.

Chapter 26

Robert was enjoying the warm summer evening. He ate his supper—a delicious crab soufflé—then went to his study to wait for Cecil Martin, who arrived every evening at nine sharp to deliver his daily report. He drank a brandy while he waited and went over some accounts.

Nine o'clock came and went, and Martin did not arrive. An hour went by without any sign of him.

Puzzled, Robert asked the house slaves if they'd seen the overseer, but they claimed they had not. He went outside and asked around the yard and even in the slave quarters, but he got only blank faces and empty stares.

Still not concerned, he went back to the house, drank another brandy, and worked some more on his accounts. Finally, though, as midnight approached, he grew genuinely troubled. It wasn't like Martin to miss an appointment, much less disappear altogether.

With an oath, Robert drained his glass and headed toward the barn—and the tack room, where Martin was known to hide when he wanted to get drunk. That hadn't happened in quite a while, however, and Robert hoped it wasn't happening now. While Robert enjoyed his liquor, he had little patience with employees who drank on the job. He had warned Martin several times, but the damned man knew so much about his business that Robert dared not discharge him. Still, Robert knew how to instill fear in the overseer.

But the overseer wasn't in the tack room or any of the other storage rooms in the barn. Irritated at having an otherwise perfect day ruined, Robert was about to go back to the house. He would take up the matter when Martin appeared in the morning. But before he went to bed, he'd improve his mood by checking on his new bondsman. Doubtless the Scotsman was suffering nicely after a day in the fields under Martin's whip.

Robert opened the stall gate and for a moment his heart stopped: Cecil Martin lay chained and gagged in the Scotsman's place.

Rage, immediate and intense, took over. Robert swore, loud and continually as he untied his overseer and removed the gag. Then, at Martin's panting direction, he searched through the hay scattered on the barn floor for the key to the leg irons. All the while, Martin blustered on about the damned Scotsman having a gun and tricking him. The second Martin was on his feet, Robert hit him in the jaw and knocked him down again.

A minute later they discovered that one of the horses was gone—one of his finest horses. Enraged, Robert ranted to himself. How could Martin have been so *stupid*? How could he have let that bastard Sutherland get the best of him?

In the heat of his fury Robert realized that it wasn't only Cecil Martin whom Sutherland had bested. The Scotsman had bested Robert as well.

The man must have been gone for hours. And no one, not a single slave, had seen fit to inform him. He had no doubt that they knew. Oh, yes, they knew.

Dragging Martin along behind him, Robert stomped into the slave quarters, where he roused everyone from bed for questioning. He got nothing from them but the same dull-eyed answers: "No, massa, we ain't seed nobody. Jest Mistuh Martin." The stable hands said they'd heard some noises in the stall, but they'd been told not to speak to the Scotsman, so they'd ignored the occasional thumps.

Nearly purple with rage, Robert hit one slave so hard that he thought he might have broken a finger, which only made him want to hit someone else. But what he *really* wanted to do was chain Cecil Martin back in the Scotsman's stall for punishment. If only the overseer weren't the only person on the plantation he could trust, and he needed him to summon the law to go after the Scotsman.

Robert stomped back to the house, with Cecil Martin scurrying in his wake. In his study he scrawled a note for Sheriff Vaughn. He wanted a posse. He wanted dogs. He wanted Vaughn out there tonight, chasing down his runaway. Handing Martin the note, he sent the overseer on his way. Then he loaded his pistol and his musket, and when that was done, he sat down to wait.

But the possibility that the Scotsman might actually be gone for good made him wild. Without Sutherland, Fancy would never marry him. She'd made that plain enough. He needed that damned bondsman, and he needed him now!

Jumping up from his chair, Robert paced the floor. He wanted to start the search, dammit. Only the certain knowledge that he would be wasting time kept him from bolting. He didn't know where Sutherland was, or even which direction he'd taken. He had to wait for Vaughn and the posse. And then . . . oh, yes, *then* he would find that Scottish bastard. And when he did . . .

With a shouted curse, Robert grabbed the brandy decanter off the sideboard and flung it across the room. With another curse, he shot out his arms and swept the matching glasses to the floor. The crash of smashed crystal echoed in his head.

He couldn't stand it. He had to *do* something.

Someone must know where the Scotsman had gone. Someone had to have seen which way he went. But who?

The boy. He worked in the barn. He'd taken the Scotsman food and water. And though he'd been ordered not to talk to the prisoner, Robert was quite sure the useless brat had disobeyed. Just like his brother, who'd tried to run away and died for it.

Robert would have gotten rid of the boy too, sold him off long ago, if he weren't the grandson of his coachman, Isaiah. Isaiah was the best man Robert had ever seen with horses—aside from his brother, John, of course, God rest his foolish soul—and owning Isaiah made him the envy of Kent County. Isaiah had moped when his older grandson had died under Martin's lashing, and for a while it had looked as if the old slave would try to run, too. But when Robert had threatened to sell Isaiah's younger grandson south, into the deadly rice fields, Isaiah had shaped up quick enough.

The boy. He would go after the boy while he waited for the posse. He would get the truth.

Snatching up his quirt, Robert strode to the slave quarters for the third time that night. No one was in the yard. Every slave and bondsman had gone back to bed, he guessed, though he doubted they were asleep. Not after the tongue-lashing he'd given them—and they knew they could expect worse in the morning. He imagined them cowering in their beds, afraid of what he might do.

They damn well *should* be afraid. He was not a man to cross.

It occurred to him briefly that they might have been afraid to come to him, that no one wanted to tell him that the Scotsman had escaped. But the half-formed thought was fleeting. He was their master. He had a right to treat them any way he chose. It was their God-ordained duty to serve him.

Robert went directly to Isaiah's cabin, the best and nearest of the slave quarters. Isaiah opened the door immediately, and Robert looked past him, over his shoulder.

"Where's the boy?"

"I doan know, massa. I haven't seen him."

"You lie to me, and I'll have your hide and his."

Isaiah was silent.

Robert raised his quirt and gave Isaiah's face a whack. It was the first time he'd ever hit the coachman, and he expected the usual cowering reaction.

Isaiah didn't move, and the stone-faced dignity on his bleeding face fueled Robert's anger. Yet it was clear to him that he would get nothing from the man. And if he didn't leave now, at that moment, he might vent his rage on Isaiah and end up destroying one of his most valuable possessions.

"Send the boy to me," he said shortly. "I won't hurt him."

"I'll do that, suh, when I see him."

Robert backed away, suddenly baffled. There was no fear in the man's face. If his slaves lost their fear, he would lose everything. He was alone on the plantation. Even Cecil Martin was off fetching the sheriff. It wasn't the first time he'd been alone at Marsh's End, and he had always felt quite safe. But something had happened in the past few hours. In the eyes of his slaves and bondsmen, he'd been bested by one of their own, and it seemed they had all taken a measure of courage from Sutherland's escape.

He had to get that bastard back. It was no longer just a matter of needing Sutherland to force Fancy's hand. He needed to prove that no mere bondsman could get the better of him. He needed to remind every slave and bondsman on the plantation of his or her proper place. And to do it, he realized, the Scotsman had to die. He couldn't let the man live, not even to get Fancy or the farm.

Robert felt a hundred pairs of eyes on him as he walked back to the house. He locked the front door behind him, and, as fear overrode his anger, he picked up the pistol and musket from the table in the hall and took them with him to the study. He locked that door, too.

There he waited for the posse.

Rufus knew he was dreaming. It couldn't be horses he heard. He had been drifting in and out of consciousness, and he had no idea how long he had been in the well. He only knew that his throat was swollen from lack of water and that his stomach was a ball of agony. He couldn't speak, much less yell.

For a time he thought he had finally heard the legendary crying of the ghostly children. Or was it his own internal voice, weeping for himself?

This time, though, the sound he heard was louder. The neighing of a horse. He didn't think horses became ghosts. He listened intently. Another whinny. And hoofbeats.

Was it his assailant? Had the man returned to make sure he was dead? Rufus considered whether or not he should try to make some kind of noise. He knew it was useless to try to shout; his voice was gone. His hands fumbled against the dust-dry dirt floor of the well and then along the walls. His fingers closed around a stone. He threw it with all his remaining strength, but it merely clattered against the side of the well a few yards above his head.

A male voice. Calling something.

He threw another stone, thinking what he needed

was a miracle. Surely God wouldn't put one within reach, then desert him.

Another stone. And another. The voice came closer. He listened for the rough accent of his attacker, but instead he heard something familiar. It was Big Tim Wallace. He would swear to it.

He tried to speak, but only a croak came out. A moment later he saw a man's form leaning over the side of the well, silhouetted against the starlit sky.

"Reverend Winfrey?" Tim's booming voice was now unmistakable.

Rufus pounded a rock against the side of the well. "Here," he tried to say.

"By God," Tim said. "How in hell . . . ?"

Rufus thanked God. He thanked the small spirits that had kept him company. He thanked Tim. But none of his words were audible.

"I'll get a rope and haul you out of there," Tim called down to him. "Are you bad hurt?"

Rufus tried again to talk. All that came out, though, was a whisper that never made it up the stone walls. He hit the wall with the stone, as much out of frustration as in an attempt to communicate.

His rescuer yelled down. "Tap on the wall. Two taps for yes, one for no. Are you bad hurt?"

Every bone in Rufus's body hurt from being thrown into the well, but he'd established that nothing was broken. And now, yes, he was quite all right. He would see his wife again. God had provided a miracle.

One tap.

"I'll have to find some rope. I'll be back. Do you understand?"

Two taps.

"How long have you been down there?"

Rufus banged on the wall three times.

He heard swearing above him, and he begged God

for forgiveness for the transgressor. Then he saw something falling and he threw his hands up to catch it. They closed around a leather flask and, realizing what it was, he instantly put it to his mouth and gulped greedily. Rufus knew he shouldn't drink that quickly, yet his body craved water. He slowed down, letting the water trickle into his mouth and down his dry throat. It tasted better than anything he had ever had before.

He tried his voice again. A croak came out. Nothing more. He knew Tim Wallace didn't want to leave him. But it was all right now. Everything was all right. He leaned back and thought of his wife again. Hours. Just hours now, and he would hold her.

"I'll be back directly," Big Tim reassured him, then the silhouette disappeared, and he heard the sound of fading hoofbeats.

Comforted now, Rufus sipped more of the water. He could barely believe how much remained in the flask. He eased more water into his body. He wanted to treasure every single one of God's blessed drops.

The dogs lost the scent. The horse that had disappeared with the Scotsman wandered back, leaving the dogs with no trail. A tracker, using a torch, could find no other trail.

Robert immediately posted a reward of five hundred pounds for the Scotsman and sent one man from the posse to Chestertown to commission the printing of posters. The others would curry the woods.

The Scotsman was on foot now, Robert reasoned. Unless he had help.

Robert thought of Fancy but dismissed the idea. She had been with him the entire time she was at Marsh's End. Fortune had been outside but she hadn't the wit or the nerve. Hell, she couldn't even talk.

No, Martin had been careless with his gun and was reluctant to admit it.

Robert returned to the house, exhausted and angry and more than a little worried, only to find another visitor: the man he had hired to remove the interfering minister. He had paid Samuels ahead of time and told him he never wanted to see him again. So what the hell was he doing here, cluttering up his hallway?

Samuels stood, shifting from one foot to the other and stinking of whiskey. He'd probably spent every cent he'd been paid on drink.

"I told you . . ." Robert began, but upon seeing Samuels's knowing smile, he stopped. "Follow me." Striding down the hallway, he led the man to his study.

Once the door was closed, he scrutinized the drunk more closely. Greed gleamed in the hazy eyes.

"I had somebody look at the papers I found on that preacher," Samuels said, taking a dirty piece of parchment from his pocket. "That Scotsman I heared you be looking fer. He's married to that woman who owned him. Thought you might wanna know, since yer man said you planned to wed her."

The blood drained from Robert's face. Married! Fancy was married to that convict! Why, the little bitch had led him on! He would be the laughingstock of Kent County.

Robert hadn't thought he could get any angrier than he had been when he found Sutherland gone. But as he stood there, staring at the filthy wretch grinning at him, everything became a red blur and he found himself swaying on his feet.

He tried to get ahold of himself. This . . . this lout mustn't know the depth of the wound he'd inflicted.

Feigning nonchalance, Robert forced his fists to unclench. "The man I paid you to find. He's dead?"

"Aye," Samuels replied.

Robert took the parchment and tore it up. "There was no marriage. And if I hear differently, if I hear that you said anything about it to anyone, I will kill you."

For an instant, fear flickered in Samuels's eyes, but greed won. "My memory has a price," he insisted.

Robert wanted to kill him then and there, but members of the posse were still around. One of them might have seen Samuels come inside. Later. He would kill him later. But now he would have to pay him something.

"Stay here," he ordered. In his bedroom he took some gold coins from a bureau drawer. He held them for a moment, reluctant to let them go, then went back downstairs to the office, where he thrust them into Samuels's hand. "If I see you again," he said in an icy voice, "you will wish I hadn't."

The man grabbed the money and nearly ran from the room.

Robert followed Samuels into the hallway and watched until the front door closed behind him. He stared at the door for a long while. Then he let his gaze travel slowly around the large hallway and up the wide staircase of the great house.

He had almost given Fancy this house. He had almost made a convict's woman his wife. She had lied to him, lied with a straight face. And he hadn't had a clue she was doing it.

He went outside. It was nearly dawn, and more men were milling around, ready to start a search that might net them more money than they would otherwise have seen in a lifetime. Gray light was edging along the horizon.

Robert hurried to Isaiah's cabin. He would take the buggy, and the fastest horses. He would find Fancy and beat the truth out of her. She must know where the Scotsman was. She was *married* to the carrion. The thought that she preferred a penniless condemned convict to all the wealth and prestige he could give her grated on him.

Well, she would be widowed again soon enough. And then she would have an accident, and he would become guardian of the children; he would raise them the way a Marsh should be raised. He could still have everything he wanted.

Robert told Isaiah to head for Fancy's farm.

If she wasn't there, he would take the children. That would bring her fast enough.

It was not long after midnight when Fancy woke Douglas Turner. She pounded on his door until he finally came to open it. If she hadn't been so anxious, she might have smiled at the nightshirt flapping in the light breeze and the cap perched on his thinning hair.

Fear had ridden with her through the dark evening. She kept thinking someone was following her, but whenever she looked back she saw nothing but the usual assortment of farmers and peddlers on the road.

She breathed easier, however, when she saw Douglas Turner at the door, especially when the irritation on his face changed quickly to concern. "Mrs. Marsh . . . Sutherland. What are you doing here at this time of night?"

"Robert claims there was another will," she said. "That he owns everything."

Looking harassed, Turner glanced up and down the street. "You shouldn't have come here at this time of night. People—"

"You don't understand," she interrupted. "Two days ago—three days now—Robert and Sheriff Vaughn and his deputies came to my farm when I was here with you. They seized . . . my husband, and took him to

Marsh's End. One of the deputies shot my seven-year-old son."

"Dear God!" The lawyer's gaze suddenly became alert. He opened the door wider and ushered her inside. "This is outrageous," he muttered, leading her into his office. "Your son. Is he—"

"He's all right," she said, seating herself in the now familiar chair. "Robert claims that John wrote another will, leaving him all of the property, including the indenture John purchased."

Turner shook his head. "There can be no second will. As I told you, John came here the same day he purchased the indenture. He made it very clear then that everything was to go to you."

Fancy nodded. "I know that, but I'm almost certain that Robert has paid the necessary officials to uphold his claim. In any event, he convinced the sheriff that Ian belonged to him. His plan was to use Ian as a hostage."

"A hostage?"

"Yes. Robert wants to marry me. I let him think I would agree, provided that Ian remained alive. Otherwise, he would have had Ian charged with attacking him, which would amount to a death sentence."

"Marsh doesn't know about your marriage to Sutherland, then?" Turner said.

She shook her head. "Ian would be dead now if he did." She was silent for a moment, then added, "If Robert discovers that Ian is my husband, he'd kill him before I could contest the will. And that's why I . . . helped him escape."

Turner stared at her. "You . . ." Then, shaking his head, he sighed. "Why didn't you come to me first?"

Twisting her hands together in her lap, Fancy admitted, "I was afraid to wait. If Robert had heard the slightest hint that Ian and I had wed . . . I had to get him away from there."

Deep furrows had formed in Turner's brow, but Fancy interpreted them as concern rather than censure.

"Where is your husband now?" he asked.

She didn't reply. She was unwilling to trust that information to anyone.

When she remained silent, Turner sighed. "Very well. I have a copy of the will. I'll take it to the governor in Annapolis. If nothing else, he can place custody of your Mr. Sutherland in my hands until the matter is settled. But I'll need your marriage certificate."

"I don't know if it's been filed," she said. "Reverend Winfrey hadn't yet done it when I was here before, nor had his wife seen him. One of my neighbors, Tim Wallace, is looking for him."

"Reverend Winfrey's word would help," Turner said, then added, "I have to be in court this morning, but I'll go to Annapolis this afternoon. A packet leaves every afternoon at three."

Fancy would have preferred to go that very minute, but she supposed she had no choice. And knowing that Ian was safe, she could wait a few more hours.

"It isn't entirely necessary," Turner continued, "but it could make a difference if you went with me. Would that be possible?"

She nodded. "Of course. And thank you."

He shrugged off her thanks, studying her closely. "You need some rest. Let me get dressed, and I'll take you to an inn."

"I have to go—"

"Not at this hour, you do not," he said kindly. "The Crown and Arms is just two doors down. I often send visitors there. It is a decent place, and they will look after you."

Why was it that every man she met felt she needed

looking after? John, Ian, both of the Wallaces, even
Robert. And now Douglas Turner. Did she truly appear
that helpless?

"It is late . . . or is it early now?" she said.

"Past midnight," he said. "And you need some rest
if you're going to Annapolis this afternoon. It's a very
long ride."

Fancy nodded. She had no intention of wasting time
sleeping. She had to see her children, assure herself
they were all right. And if she was going to see the
governor, she needed some clothes. If she rode all
night, then changed horses, she could be back here by
three. And Ian was safe at the old Adams place.

"I'll be back this afternoon," she said, rising.

Turner rose from his chair and followed her outside
to her horse. He helped her into the sidesaddle. "Don't
worry," he said kindly. "The governor is a fair man."

She nodded, thanked him again, and waited until
he'd closed the door, believing that she would go to the
inn two doors away. Then she headed out of town.

Despite the early hour, the only adult at John's farm
was a woman. A large, angry woman.

Robert felt the devil was at work against him. He
was being thwarted at every turn.

Alighting from the carriage, which in itself was
grand enough to intimidate most people, he'd approached the porch where the woman stood in her
night clothes, hands on her hips, guarding the door.

Her face was vaguely familiar, but he couldn't place
it. He paid little attention to the hundreds of yeomen
farmers in Kent County. They all looked alike to him,
with their worn faces and mended clothes and scores of
children.

"I'm looking for Mrs. Marsh," he said curtly. "I'm
her brother-in-law."

"I know who you are," the woman said, "and I ain't holding it agin Mrs. Marsh."

Robert took a moment to digest the surly reply. No one talked to him like that. Still, he needed something from her, so he ignored her tone and tried to gentle his.

"The children may be in danger," he said. "An armed servant escaped from my plantation. I've come to take my sister-in-law and her children to safety."

"They're safe enough where they be."

"And where is that?"

"Mrs. Marsh left me in charge. The children are safe. That's all you need to know."

"You have no right to keep them from me. I'll summon the sheriff."

"You jest do that. I heard you done it before, but ain't no one here you can harm this time."

"I think I'll just see for myself." Robert tried to push past her, but she would not be moved. His still aching muscles were no match for her bulk or her stubbornness. "Get out of my way, woman, or I'll see you destroyed."

"Like you've destroyed others?" she said. "Well, we have some money, me and mine, and you can't do a thing to us. Now be on your way. My sons will be checking on me any time."

All at once he remembered who she was. The widow Phillips. She had three brawny sons who competed in pugilist matches. They usually won.

He didn't need another beating in the immediate future, and as humiliating as it was to back down in front of a woman, Robert decided to return later, with more men.

"How long has Mrs. Marsh been gone?" he asked.

"I don't pay any attention to her comings and goings," Mrs. Phillips said. Then she marched inside the house and closed the door in his face.

Robert turned around in time to see a small smile playing on Isaiah's lips. Or at least he thought he saw a smile. It was gone so quickly he wasn't sure.

Where could Fancy have gone? Was she hiding inside?

He didn't think so. From what he knew of Fancy, she wouldn't hide from him. But where could she be?

It was seeming more and more likely that she had abetted the Scotsman in his escape. So wherever he was, she was probably with him. Where would he go?

Climbing back into the carriage, Robert spoke to Isaiah.

"Chestertown. Quickly."

It was the closest seaport. And Sutherland would be desperate to flee from a place where he was a wanted fugitive with a price on his head.

Chapter 27

Rufus waited patiently, but his heart beat rapidly when he heard hoofbeats again, and then Big Tim Wallace's loud, comforting bellow: "Reverend, I'm back."

Elation washed over Rufus as a rope dropped into the well and landed in his lap.

"Can you tie it around your waist? The horse will pull you out."

"Aye," he called, amazed that his voice was coming back. He grasped the rope and did as he was told, then tugged on it. He felt himself being lifted. He tried to use his legs against the sides of the well, but they didn't seem to work. His body bumped from one side to the other. But eventually he came to the top and Tim pulled him out, lifting him as if he weighed no more than a baby. Tim set him on his feet, but his legs wouldn't hold him, and he sank to the ground.

"How did you find me?" he asked from where he lay, looking up at Big Tim.

"I've been searching for you. Your wife said you were overdue, and I backtracked. The Bakers said you left there three days ago, so I searched the sides of the road. Then I remembered this place. It would be a perfect place to hide—" He stopped in midsentence.

Rufus knew, though, what he was about to say: "A body." He had almost been that body. Despite his best efforts, he felt himself trembling. He looked down and saw the dried blood on his clothes and he knew he must look like the most desperate of men. "God must have led you to me," he said.

Tim looked embarrassed. "It was Mrs. Sutherland who sent me to look for you. She thought her brother-in-law weren't up to no good. Looks like she was right. Care to tell me what happened?"

"First," the minister said, "do you have something to eat?"

Big Tim smiled and went to the horse standing quietly behind him, the rope still tied to its saddle. He looked in the saddlebags and took out some hard biscuits. "Here, Reverend Winfrey," he said. "Don't eat too quickly, though."

Rufus took the bread, bowed his head briefly over it, then eagerly took a bite. After finishing the two biscuits and licking every last morsel from his lips, he returned his attention to Big Tim. "So you are wondering how I came to be at the bottom of a well."

"I am," Big Tim said.

"It was three days ago, midafternoon or thereabouts, that it happened," the clergyman said. "I was returning home when a man stopped me on the road. He said he'd been waiting for me, that his mother was dying and needed religious comfort. I followed him here, but then he took out a pistol. He was going to shoot me, but God intervened. The man said he couldn't shoot a preacher, so he hit me over the head. I woke up in the well."

Tim was incredulous. "He wouldn't shoot you—but he left you to die of thirst and starvation?"

"Odd, isn't it?" Rufus said. "But I see God's hand in it. He meant for you to rescue me."

Tim didn't try to hide his skepticism. "I'm sorry, Reverend, but I fail to see God's hand in this matter. Do you know why this man would have wanted to harm you?"

The minister shook his head. "I thought at first that he wanted my horse. But then I realized, since he knew my name, that he had been waiting specifically for me and that his purpose was more nefarious than simple theft."

Big Tim Wallace was silent for a moment. "I'm afraid you're right. Four days ago Robert Marsh had someone set fire to Fancy Sutherland's tobacco and steal Ian's indenture papers. Then he claimed Ian as his property. The sheriff said Robert had a new will, giving him all of John Marsh's possessions."

"One day before I was attacked." Rufus nodded, light dawning in his eyes. "And Mr. Sutherland?"

"Marsh has him. Fancy will fight Robert, but she says if Robert knew she had married Ian, he might kill him, or . . ."

Sudden dread flooded the preacher. "Whoever attacked me took my papers, including the marriage certificate."

"Can you ride, Reverend Winfrey?" Big Tim asked urgently.

Rufus wanted nothing but to go home. He hurt. He was hungry. He wanted to see his wife. But if Robert Marsh would burn fields and forge a will, there was no telling what else he might do. He had to warn Fancy, and he needed to go to the magistrate. He nodded.

"We'll ride double. And we'll visit your wife first to let her know you are safe," Tim said. "I half worried her to death."

Rufus felt a smile spreading across his face for the first time in days.

Hidden in the shadows of a stately town house, Ian leaned against one of its walls and waited patiently outside the attorney's office for Fancy to emerge.

Bloody hell, but he felt drained. It was all he could

do to stand, but he feared that if he sat down, he might never get back up. For a moment he longed for Little Tim's company, but he had sent the boy to find his father. Tim had protested, but in the face of Ian's immovable will he'd capitulated.

Ian had never had any intention of letting Fancy out of his sight. He had wanted to argue with her at the river, but he'd seen quickly enough that they would be there all night if he tried. Best to allow her to do what she thought she must, but keep a protective eye on her. He was certainly not going to hide while she risked everything. He was through being a helpless captive.

It had not been too difficult to persuade the younger Wallace to follow Fancy rather than sneak off to some abandoned farm to wait. The boy hadn't liked the idea of Fancy gallivanting around the countryside alone, either. It had been much harder to persuade him to leave Ian in Chestertown and go in search of his missing father. Though he hated dangling the boy's father's safety in front of him, Ian didn't want Tim with him if he was captured. He already had too many lives on his conscience.

He did, however, take the boy's leather vest to pull over the bloodstains that now dotted the back of the overseer's shirt. He had also borrowed the boy's gloves to cover the brand on his hand. He had done what he could with his physical appearance. It was his physical endurance that was in question. Bloody hell, but he was spent. The door to the attorney's office opened, and he saw Fancy come out. He sank back into a recess alongside the home, holding his hand against Sir Gray's neck to calm the animal. He smiled at her determined walk as she strode to the mare. He would have gone to her aid then and there, if a tall, dignified man in a night robe hadn't helped her into the sidesaddle.

He watched her turn the horse toward her farm—

and Robert's plantation. He damn well wasn't going to allow her to do something foolish. He waited several moments, then followed, keeping to the side of the road in the shadow of the trees.

Fancy concentrated on the road ahead. And on staying awake. Earlier traffic—peddlers starting out toward outlying communities, farmers making an early trek into Chestertown to find a good location to hawk their produce—had thinned. She hadn't seen anyone in an hour, though she looked back now and then. The feeling of being watched remained with her, but she'd concluded she was jumping at shadows.

She thought about the danger Ian was in. Word would be out in Chestertown today. Robert would offer a hefty reward for his capture, and every ruffian and scalawag would be hunting for her Scotsman. Thank God he was safe.

It was well after dawn when she came up on Robert's plantation. She had no wish to see her brother-in-law, but she imagined he was in Chestertown, raising a posse, and his land lay directly between her farm and town. Just being close to home gave her renewed energy, and Lady Mist seemed to take strength from her, or perhaps she just knew she was close to fresh feed and rest. The mare's gait quickened.

As she rounded the sharp curve where the road swerved away from the river, both Fancy and the mare were startled by a fast-moving carriage coming from the other direction.

The mare shied, neighing. The carriage swerved, its team of matched chestnuts passing in a blur. The back of the carriage fishtailed, and a corner of it bumped the mare's flank.

The mare reared and stumbled, throwing Fancy from the saddle. She felt her ankle twist beneath her as she landed, but she quickly tried to rise to catch the mare's reins. It was too late. Spooked, the horse had moved out of reach.

And when she looked back toward the carriage, her heart turned cold. Descending from it was Robert Marsh, a dark look on his face.

"Mrs. *Sutherland*," he said. "I was hoping I would find you."

Ian shook himself, forcing himself to remain awake. A few more miles and she would be home safely. Mayhap he could find a place to rest then.

He had trailed far behind Fancy, catching only glimpses of her, and when he did, he dropped back out of sight. Several wagons passed him, along with one mail coach. He'd been half dozing when suddenly, from up ahead, he heard the loud, distressed whinny of a horse.

Spurring Sir Gray forward, he closed the gap between him and his wife, slowing as he drew closer to where he gauged she should be. Approaching a sharp bend in the road, he guided Sir Gray to the inside edge of the roadway, moving cautiously, determined not to run into a posse unaware.

Then he heard Fancy's angry voice. And Robert Marsh's harsh one.

Cautious no longer, he kicked the stallion into a gallop. On the other side of the bend, he saw Fancy struggling with Robert Marsh in the middle of the road. Robert's carriage sat just behind them, and Robert was trying to haul Fancy into it. She was fighting every step of the way, her hands pummeling Marsh's back.

Ian slowed the stallion as he shouted, "Put her down!"

Marsh swung around, saw him, and instantly dropped Fancy to reach for the pistol in his belt. He got his hand around it but didn't have time to draw before Ian was out of the saddle and on him.

The pistol skidded onto the road, half flung as Marsh raised his arms to ward off Ian's fists—and to strike back. Ian gasped as a fist landed square on the wound in his right side. Marsh took advantage of the moment, and Ian, stunned by pain, was powerless to stop the punch that landed in his stomach. Or the next one that, again, struck his wound.

As he doubled over, he saw Marsh go for the pistol. Ian's hand shot out, and he grabbed his opponent's foot, pulling him down. He managed to land a blow, then another. But he couldn't breathe, much less see, for pain; his side felt as if boiling oil had been poured into it. Marsh strained forward, trying to reach the pistol lying only inches away from his outstretched hand. Ian thought he saw Fancy trying to get to it first; she was still a few yards away, and she was hobbling, but if he could just hold on. . . .

Ian's hand slipped on the smooth leather of Marsh's boot. With the sudden release of tension, Marsh lurched forward, and his hand touched, but couldn't grasp, the pistol. The weapon skidded farther across the dirt, stopping about a foot in front of the horses. Seized by fury, Robert scrambled after it.

All at once Ian heard a shout.

"Ho, there."

A rider, then two others, came around the curve, their horses veering to miss the mayhem in the road. The carriage team sidled away, stamping and neighing in agitation. One of them half reared. Robert's coachman was trying to control the horses and back them up, but they became more agitated—pawing, straining at their bits, dancing forward.

In the flash of a single second, Ian saw Robert try to

rise from the center of the road, stark terror in his eyes, then he saw the coachman lose his grip on the reins.

Ian's gaze shot to Fancy. She had also started toward the pistol and now stood only inches from where Robert knelt in the dirt. With his heart in his throat, Ian rose to his feet and launched himself at Fancy. The confused and frightened horses, unable to see the people in the road and terrified at the noise and smell of blood, moved forward, their hooves coming down upon Robert Marsh before they surged ahead, just as Ian grabbed Fancy and rolled them both to the side of the road.

Ian heard a cry of agony, then the sound of wheels hitting human flesh. The carriage kept going, the horses crazed now. In the carriage's wake, Marsh's body lay crumpled like a broken doll.

"Oh, God . . ." Fancy cried.

"Donna look," he ordered, holding her head against his chest.

Ian pressed Fancy close for a moment, then loosened his hold. She too could have been lying in the road, as still as her brother-in-law. "Are you all right, lass?"

"I-I'm not hurt," she managed, but her whole body was trembling.

"Stay still," he ordered gently. Then, pushing himself to his feet, he left her as she began to sob quietly, her face buried in her hands, and moved to press his fingers against Marsh's throat.

The man was dead. And God forgive him, Ian could feel nothing but relief.

Straightening, he turned to see three riders—the same riders who had spooked the carriage team—dismounting from their horses. One walked over to squat beside Fancy and speak to her.

The Wallaces. And Reverend Winfrey. The minister

knelt next to Ian and closed Robert's eyes. His lips moved in prayer.

Marsh would need more than that, Ian thought uncharitably.

He stood and walked slowly toward the Wallaces. "Where did you find the minister?"

Big Tim answered. "Someone threw the good man into a dry well at the abandoned Adams place—the place where you were supposed to go."

"A well?"

"We figured it was done at the behest of the gentleman over there." Big Tim gave Ian a crooked smile, nodding toward the body in the road.

Tearing his gaze from what remained of Marsh, Reverend Winfrey slowly got to his feet.

Just then the carriage came back around the curve in the road, stopping several yards away. The driver, a tall black man, had clearly regained control of the team. With great dignity he descended from the carriage seat and walked over to look down at Marsh's body. He stood very still for several moments. Then he turned to look at each of them, focusing last on Fancy. "I couldn't stop the horses," he said.

"I know, Isaiah," she said softly. "I know you couldn't."

Ian wanted to thank the man, had to clench his teeth to keep from saying the words. To thank him would have been to say he thought a murder had taken place. And Ian would never know whether the man could have regained control—or whether he had purposely let go of the reins in that one crucial second.

" 'Twas not your fault," Ian told the man, who met his gaze with dark, unfathomable eyes. "We all saw what happened, did we not, Reverend Winfrey?"

The minister looked at Fancy for a moment, then nodded. "It was an accident."

"What should I do?" the driver asked.

"Go to Fancy's farm," Ian replied. "We'll take his body to Chestertown."

Reverend Winfrey shook his head. "No, Mr. Sutherland, you should not go near Chestertown. Just when we were leaving, word was getting out about a reward. A good two hundred men are out combing every field and wood for you at this very moment. The Wallaces and I will accompany Robert Marsh's body into town, and Isaiah will need to go with us. Reports will have to be made, and no doubt Mrs. Sutherland and I will have to sign statements."

Bloody hell. Forced to wait again. And the worst, Ian thought, was that Reverend Winfrey was right.

Fancy rose to stand beside Ian, turning toward the coachman.

"Isaiah," she said, taking one of his hands in hers. She saw that they were shaking.

"Don't you worry about Isaiah, missus. I'll be all right."

"I'm not sure you should return to Marsh's End at all."

He stood his ground. "Mr. Martin, he won't do anything without someone telling him to. And I'll let him know you seem the likely person to own the place now."

"I don't want Marsh's End," she said. "I don't want any part of it."

Isaiah's face fell. "Don't say that, missus. Someone else may sell us off . . ." His voice trailed off.

Ian winced slightly as Fancy slumped against his side, but he stood there, taking her weight, giving her time to fully comprehend what had happened. He felt her shudder, and he tightened his grip despite the discomfort it caused him.

Reverend Winfrey called to Isaiah, and as the coachman moved away, Ian turned Fancy in his arms and pulled her into his embrace.

" 'Tis all right," he murmured. "You are safe now. And so are the children and your sister. The war is over, lass, and you have won."

He felt her stiffen, and she pushed back to look up at him.

She met his gaze with tear-reddened eyes. "Does that mean you are going away?"

The question caught him completely off guard. He hadn't been thinking about leaving. He'd only been trying to reassure her.

Brushing the tears from her cheek with his fingertip, he said, "We can talk about that later, lass."

For an instant, panic flashed in her eyes, but then, as her gaze darted toward Marsh's body, she nodded. "You're right. This isn't the time."

Reverend Winfrey came to stand beside them. "Now that Marsh is dead, I assume there will no longer be a reward for Mr. Sutherland. All the same, I think it would be best if he stays out of sight for several days, until the word gets around."

Ian met Fancy's gaze as she tilted her head to look up at him again. "Will you go to the Adams place *now*?" she said. "They will be combing this whole area. No one, though, will go near the haunted farm."

"The man who kidnapped the minister did," he reminded her.

"And that's why no one found him," Wallace interceded.

"Will you go?" she persisted stubbornly. "I must go to the governor with Mr. Turner and have you declared free and the charge of escape dropped."

"I'll go with you," Ian insisted.

"There's no longer any danger for me. But there is for you as long as men think there's a reward for your return." She thought for a moment, then added, "And that means I would be in danger too."

His frown deepened. She was right. And by being at the farm, he might bring danger to the bairns. Since he had once lived there, it would be one of the first places searched by bounty hunters.

"I'll stay with the children," Big Tim offered. "No harm will come to them with me and Pansy Phillips there. Little Tim can show our Scotsman how to get to the Adams place, then return home to take care of the stock."

"Ian?" she pleaded.

"Aye," he said finally.

She frowned. "That's what you said the last time you agreed to go to the Adams place and wait until I came for you. And here you are."

He gave her a lopsided smile. "Now you know the worst, lass. I do lie upon occasion. But I'll stay this time, until you return."

Her brown gaze searched his for a moment before falling away. And he knew, as he helped Isaiah roll Robert's body up inside a lap rug and load it into the carriage, that she was far from satisfied with the situation. She was afraid he was about to leave her.

The Wallaces helped him collect Fancy's horses, which had wandered into the field alongside the road. Once they were gathered, Ian lifted Fancy onto the mare, then watched as she rode away with the others, the carriage following slowly behind them.

Holding Sir Gray's reins, Ian stared at the empty road long after the dust from the carriage wheels had settled.

For a moment, he forgot about Little Tim, waiting patiently to lead him to the Adams farm. He had what he wanted: freedom. Fancy would not hold him. And he no longer needed to worry about her; she and her family were out of danger, and she would have all the money and help she needed to raise her bonny fast horses and to send her children to a real school—and herself, too, if that was what she wanted.

He could leave. He could do what he had sworn to do on the awful day when Derek was hanged. He could now return to Scotland and find Katy.

But to do so, he would have to leave Fancy. And that would mean leaving his heart.

Why was it that freedom suddenly tasted so sour?

Fancy reached the Adams farm three days later at dusk. Ian lifted her down from the mare's back and crushed her to him.

In the three days since she'd been gone, he'd slept on a blanket under the trees, his body healing quickly, as always. He had snared several rabbits and cooked them, and he had drunk from, and bathed in, the clear, cold stream that ran nearby. He'd walked a great deal, feeling strength returning to his body.

Mostly he had thought. About Scotland. About Katy. About Derek waiting for him to join him. He'd thought about honor and loyalty. And he'd thought about love.

Fancy raised her face to be kissed, and he obliged her. He wanted to kiss her hard. He wanted to hold her and never let her go. He wanted to bury himself in her. But there were things to be said between them first, things to be settled.

Ending the kiss gently, he said, "Tell me what happened."

She held his gaze as she replied. "The magistrate ruled Robert's death accidental. At Douglas Turner's behest, Governor Braden recognized John's will as the true one. I inherit all of John's possessions. And you are legally free. We have a document from the governor, recognizing your purchase of the indenture. Douglas Turner is placing a notice in all the newspapers declaring the reward void." She hesitated, then added, "Noel, as Robert's only living male relative, will inherit his estate."

Ian considered the irony: Fancy was not only safe; she was wealthy. Robert Marsh, in trying to get her small plot of land, had made it possible for her to gain an empire.

He smiled. "So now you will be mistress of Marsh's End. You will be able to do so much, lass, for yourself and your family, and for so many others."

"I know," she murmured. "I just wish . . ."

"You wish what?"

Her gaze fell from his, and a moment of silence passed before she answered. "I wish that I wasn't going to be doing it without you."

Ian put a finger under her chin and tilted her face upward, to his. "Are you so certain that you will be?" he asked.

Her brown eyes, so wide and solemn, filled with tears as she looked at him.

"I donna want to leave you, lass," he said. "You are my heart and my best reason for living."

Her eyes widened. "But your sister . . ."

Ian sighed. "Aye, there is Katy, whom I also love dearly. And I donna know if she is alive. But I do know that the *chances* of her being alive are very slim. I could go to Scotland and find a grave or mayhap only hear that she was killed." He raised an eyebrow. "And for that piece of news, I too will probably be killed. And I donna want to die. Not now. I want to live with you, and help you raise Amy and Noel—and mayhap some bairns of our own."

Ian's heart raced as he watched Fancy's countenance change before his eyes, hope replacing despair, happiness replacing grief. Her hope and happiness were also his.

"I will never give up looking for her," he said. "If I have to write to every man in Scotland, I'll do so. But I also know she would not wish me to die for her."

She started to say something, but his finger stopped her. "I've been living inside a wall of grief since the day I watched Derek hang," he said, "and to atone for him having died when it should have been me, I thought I had to die, too. I convinced myself that my death would honor my brothers and my clan." He shook his head. "But in truth it would bring no honor to anyone. No one would notice the death of the last Sutherland. But mayhap I *can* bring honor to my clan with my life."

"Oh, Ian." Her breath caught on a small sob. "You already have. You have given us so much. You gave Fortune her voice, me courage, Noel the gift of reading, Amy love. Even when you were fighting so hard not to." She touched his cheek and smiled such a lovely smile that he thought his heart might burst with fullness. But she wasn't quite finished, for this time she put a finger to *his* mouth as he struggled for words. "I know that the Sutherlands must have been a proud and brave and loving clan," she added, "because you are the best man I've ever known."

"No," he demurred, humbled. "John . . ."

"I know," she said. "I loved him, and I always will. But he is gone. And I am here, with you, and I'm *in* love for the first time in my life."

He took her hand in his, rubbing his thumb over the backs of her fingers. "Will you still have me, Fancy? A penniless convict who has nothing to give you but his love?"

"Oh, yes, I'll have you," she replied. "But it isn't true you have nothing to give me." An urgent excitement crept into her tone as she continued. "Ian, I want to free the slaves at Marsh's End, but I'm afraid they won't know what to do with that freedom or how to protect themselves from people who would take advantage of them. They need to learn to read. We need a school, and we need you to run it."

He drew back, startled. "You want me to teach?"

"I want you to be my husband. But, yes, I want you to teach, too."

She was offering him the world, and he wondered whether she realized it. She was offering him an opportunity to do something important, to convert a plantation that used slave labor into one that could show people another way to do things. His mind was already leaping ahead, exploring the possibilities.

A lump grew in his throat. He loved to teach. He'd learned how much he loved it these past few weeks with Fancy and Noel and Amy and Fortune. Nothing had ever captured his heart and mind as much as seeing the blaze of understanding flare in their eyes.

"And I'll help you find your sister."

He frowned, but when he started to speak, she cut him off.

"Ian, don't you see? We have the money now to hire the very best detectives to do the searching for you. If Katy is alive and they find her, we can bring her here, to us."

And if she was dead, at least he would know. He had resigned himself to a life of not knowing, realizing it would always cause him pain. He didn't know, but he hoped, that the pain would fade in time. He *did* know that if he left Fancy—and the whole vibrant future that lay ahead of them—the pain would never fade. Not for him. And not, he thought, for her.

They were destined to be together, he had come to believe, for it no longer seemed an accident or a horrible trick of fate that John Marsh had brought him home that day to meet his wife and children, then gone to bed to die. Rather it seemed like part of a plan. A gift to him from John Marsh, who now surely lived in heaven.

And who was he to reject such a blessing from above?

Fancy placed a hand on his chest, over his heart. "Please, Ian, don't give up yet. But for the letters you wrote, we haven't even tried."

"Aye, we'll hire the detectives," he said. "And there's one thing I would ask of you in this new bargain we are making."

"Anything," she replied.

"I would ask you to marry me again. I want to say the words that make you my wife, and hear the words from you that make you your husband, as they should be said—out of love for each other." A smile curved his lips as he added, "And I want a proper wedding night, in a proper bed, with no children or animals in sight and all the time in the world to make love to you."

He could see the color rising in her cheeks, but she held his gaze steadily as she replied. "That would be very nice. But in the meantime would you settle for a blanket under the stars?"

He raised an eyebrow, his smile widening.

"I brought some things—another blanket, some clothes." She gave a little shrug. "I thought we might stay here tonight."

The idea had definite appeal, and it was becoming more appealing by the second as she continued to toy with the front of his shirt, doing little things with her fingers that both tickled and aroused him.

"The children?" he asked.

"Mrs. Phillips is there, with Fortune, taking care of

them." She gave him an unconsciously seductive look through lowered lashes. "I thought maybe some time alone . . ."

"You thought rightly." Lowering his head, he kissed her. He had never loved her more. His bonny wife who was both fanciful and practical, compassionate and determined, tender and brave.

He helped her spread the blanket she had brought. Then, in the moonlight, they undressed each other, his hands moving slowly, seductively, along each curve of her body. He leaned down and kissed her throat with barely leashed passion.

A sound came from deep inside her, and his kiss deepened as her hand entwined itself in his hair. Love in every caress, each an expression of a wondrous, magical feeling. Then his mouth moved downward, to her breasts, licking the sensitive skin, tasting one taut nipple, then the other, loving the feel and the smell of her, loving the sounds she made. Loving her . . .

Fancy could hardly bear it. Her hand went to his face, then wandered down along his neck as his lips returned to hers and pressed hungrily. Deep inside her, that now familiar sensation started to build, that liquid, quivering heat that turned her bones to water and made her want to melt into him. Her arms closed around him, and his tongue probed her lips, then slipped inside her mouth, catching her own tongue, sliding around it, the urgency growing until the air around them was hot and heavy.

Every part of her tingled with anticipation, the need inside her growing as Ian's mouth moved again, starting a journey down her body, tenderly exploring every part of her, moving finally to the triangle of hair just above her legs. Just as she thought she would explode with desire, he moved, arching his body above hers, and he trapped her mouth in a kiss so dizzying, so dazzling that it sent her into worlds she'd never known existed.

He entered her then, warmth and power flowing into her as he plunged deeper and deeper, seeking the core of her soul. She found herself straining to meet each strong thrust, her body and mind spinning in a whirl of sunbursts, climaxing in one magnificent blaze of heat.

Afterward they clung to each other, savoring the intimacy. Her hand went to his cheek, thick with dark bristles, then to his hair, which curled around her fingers.

They stayed there, their bodies still connected, their arms wrapped around each other, as love flowed between them. There was wonderment in the embrace, a beauty that she would always cherish.

She didn't know how long their wordless communication continued before he gently withdrew from her and rolled to his left, taking her with him to hold as if she were the most priceless treasure in the world.

She shifted slightly, and she heard him draw a quick breath.

"Did I hurt—"

"Nay, lass," he said. "The pleasure was far greater than any discomfort. Now lie against me and let me hold you."

And so she did throughout the warm night, sleeping occasionally, waking and feeling his body next to hers and knowing safety. And love. And belonging.

They made love again as the first gray light of dawn pierced the dark blue of night. The stars and the moon were slowly receding.

She wanted to keep them there in the sky above her. Daylight meant leaving, and she didn't want to go.

"I wish I could keep the stars here forever," she said wistfully.

He sighed, and his fingers lazily twirled a lock of her hair as he said, "One of my ancestors was said to be a starcatcher. Before going off to war, he told his betrothed he would catch her a star to show his faithfulness and affection, and she demurred, saying she preferred it to remain in the sky, where she could look at it and know he was safe. But she always thought of him as her starcatcher."

It was Fancy's turn to sigh. "That's a lovely legend."

"Aye, it is, though I always thought it a wee bit fanciful. I never understood it until I met you," he said, rolling to his side and propping himself up on an elbow to caress her face with his fingers. "But now I think that star guided them through rough and dangerous times, just as you are the star that has guided me through the darkness, Fancy. I was lost until I found you. All I knew was hate and grief and bitterness."

Her hand touched his cheek. "No," she said. "Right from the beginning, the children saw something wonderful in you. As did Lucky."

"Lucky would find something wonderful in anyone who showed him attention."

"Nay," she said with gentle mockery. "You had a gentleness, no matter how hard you tried to hide it."

His mouth took one of her fingers that explored his face and nibbled on it.

She thought about the legend in silence a moment, then mused, "Starcatcher? He must have been wonderful."

"He was said to be a fair laird and a peacemaker, which was most unusual among the Highland clans," he said, letting go of her finger, "but I think I'd rather be known as a starfinder. I did find you, and . . ."

"And Noel and Amy and Fortune . . ."

"And Trouble," he finished with a chuckle that rumbled from deep inside him.

How much she loved that rare chuckle. She intended to make it far more common.

"Oh, Ian . . . Starfinder. I like that name. I like it very much." Reaching up, she took his hand and kissed it. Caught in the gentle whimsy, they looked up at the sky. One last star was still visible. Their star.

Then suddenly Fancy thought she heard laughter. Beside her, Ian went still, and she knew he had heard something, too.

They looked around, but saw no one. Then another burst of laughter came from the direction of the ruined farmhouse. Childish laughter. A branch from a tree swayed as if a swing were attached to it.

Ian's brows knitted together as he searched the landscape. Nothing. They would have heard horses approach. They were alone.

The laughter died away, and they looked at each other.

"The breeze," she said. But there was no breeze.

She suddenly felt an odd, tingling warmth, and again she was certain Ian felt it, too. Then their eyes widened as they heard something like a sigh.

They stared at each other in the silence that followed.

"The ghosts?" he said.

"But they always cry," she replied.

He bent to give her a brief, tender kiss. "Perhaps they finally found something to smile about."

Then they heard it again. Laughter. Loud and clear, fading slowly until it was gone.

"Reverend Winfrey said a miracle happened here," Ian said thoughtfully.

She smiled, thinking that the good minister was right.

They dressed, then sat together, their fingers entwined as they watched the sun rise to shower the earth in its golden glow. It had survived the night to claim the dawn.

Epilogue

Ian was supervising the replanting of tender tobacco plants when he saw a carriage turn in at the entrance of Marsh's End. He sat up in the stirrups to get a better look, trying to identify the caller, but the carriage was unfamiliar.

He nodded to one of the workers to take over, then spurred his horse toward the house. He and Fancy and their family had been living in Robert Marsh's old home for almost two years, but the place was not their permanent residence. Neither he nor Fancy would ever be entirely comfortable in a home that had been occupied by her brother-in-law, and so they were building another house not far away. They would move into it very soon.

The original plantation house would become a school, which seemed poetic justice to Ian—that the building be used to educate those whom Marsh had persecuted.

In the meantime, lessons were being held on the ground floor of the house, while he and Fancy and the children occupied the upper floors. Ian found great satisfaction in the beginnings they'd made. He often sat in the schoolroom and listened to the teacher they'd hired, sometimes taking over a session himself. He enjoyed watching knowledge and hope light eyes that had been dulled for too long.

He had worked out a plan wherein the slaves spent one hour of every day in lessons. When they had learned to read and to write, as well as to do simple ciphers, they were given their freedom, unafraid that they would be taken advantage of. Most decided to stay on and work for wages, and they served as an inspiration to the others. Before this year's end, all would be free.

As he approached the stream that separated the south and north fields, Ian gave Gray Ghost the signal to jump. He felt the stallion gather himself, muscles bunching, then take the five-foot hedge and the stream beyond it as if it were nothing. He thanked God, as he often did, that Isaiah hadn't decided to leave the plantation when he'd passed his lessons and earned his freedom. The former slave had taken over the training of the horses. Under his guidance, Gray Ghost had won the major Chestertown race for the past two years and had been put to stud. Both Gray Ghost's and Royalty's stud fees had soared, and Sutherland horses were now highly prized.

Indeed the entire plantation was prospering. Not that their good fortune was entirely without cost. Many—most—of their neighbors were horrified at the radical methods he and Fancy had chosen to employ; specifically, they were afraid of the implications of giving slaves their freedom. Still, although they had been censured and sometimes shunned for what they were doing, the tobacco and corn production at Marsh's End far surpassed that of any other plantation, and a growing number of planters were asking questions.

Ian felt happy and fulfilled in a way he had never expected. When Fancy had given birth to Derek three months ago, he had thought nothing could make him happier.

Except one thing.

He knew now that, if he lived to be a hundred, he would never stop grieving for Katy. So far, their search for his sister had come to naught; the only thing their inquiries had accomplished was to stir his hopes. They had received one disappointing letter after another, each one a dagger in his heart. Fancy still had hopes for the Edinburgh detective Douglas Turner had employed, but Ian had almost given up.

Gray Ghost cantered into the drive at the same time the carriage drew up in front of the house. Ian saw Fancy standing on the front porch, holding their son, with Noel and Amy beside her. Before Ian could dismount, he was pleased to see Douglas Turner alight from the carriage.

The lawyer—now their good friend—turned to help someone down. A young girl. A girl with green eyes and dark hair. She was wearing a green dress and clutching a basket in her hands.

Ian's heart stopped. "Katy!" With a hoarse cry of shock and joy, he jumped from the horse's back and ran toward her.

"Ian?" she said uncertainly.

But when he held out his arms, a smile bloomed across her face, and he scooped her up, basket and all, hugging her close to him as tears clouded his eyes. "Katy," he whispered again. "Oh, God, I can't believe . . ." He squeezed his eyes closed. "I didna think I would see you again."

"Nor did I think to see you," she said. "Oh, Ian, we all thought you were lost . . . gone forever."

"Where have you been, love?"

She hesitated. It was then he noticed how thin she was, how old her eyes looked.

"I was safe. I was with Mrs. Cleary."

Ian remembered her. Mrs. Cleary, a healer, lived alone in the Highlands. Many considered her a witch and kept their distance, but Ian had always liked her.

"The English carried almost everyone off. They were looking for any remaining members of our family.

They came close once, and I heard them say they had killed all the Sutherlands but one, and they would finish the job." She shivered. "They laughed. I thought you were dead, too." Tears hovered at the corners of her eyes. "We moved from place to place until Mrs. Cleary got sick."

He felt his throat thicken. He could hardly breathe. Those dreams. She *had* been calling for help.

"How did you get here?"

"When Mrs. Cleary died, I went home. I walked. I didn't know what to do. Davey Gunn found me. He was ever so kind. He'd heard someone was looking for me. He took me to Johnny and Meggie Macrae, and I found out that you were alive! They sent me here."

"The Macraes!" He had finally written to them at Fancy's insistence, though it had cost him dearly in pride. He hated them as he hated no others because he felt betrayed by them. He had never been able to accept that they had not saved Derek.

"I have something else for you."

Douglas Turner's voice made Ian aware once more of his surroundings, and he turned to the lawyer, but he did not release his hold on his sister.

"The Macraes sent a letter with Katy," Turner continued. "She and an older lady appeared at my office this morning. They got my address from the detectives you hired. Apparently they decided to send Katy immediately rather than wait to exchange letters."

Setting Katy on the ground, keeping one hand on her shoulder, Ian took the letter Turner handed him. As he stared at it, he was vaguely aware of the lawyer taking a portmanteau from the carriage and setting it on the ground.

"Enjoy your reunion," Turner said.

Ian mumbled something vaguely in thanks, vaguely heard the carriage rattling off, back down the road.

Still numb with shock, he looked from the letter to Katy. It had been more than three years since he had seen her last, and she had grown considerably. She was tall for her age, and slender, but her green eyes held an uncertainty—the scars of war and grief, he thought—that was enough to break his heart.

"We've been trying to find you," he said. "Dear God, we've been trying for so long." He felt the dampness of tears on his cheeks, and when Fancy's hand came to rest on his shoulder, he looked at her and saw tears in her eyes as well.

Holding Katy's hand, he smiled and said, "This is Fancy, my wife and your sister-in-law. And this is Amy and Noel. I suppose you are their aunt, as well as this little one's." With a nod toward the bundle in Fancy's arms, he added, "This is Derek."

"Derek?" Her voice trembled as she said the name, and Ian knew she was thinking of their brother.

"Aye," he said. "He was the bravest of us all."

Katy looked at the baby with wonder, then took her hand from Ian's and touched the boy gently. "Can I take care of him sometimes?"

"Of course," Fancy said. "You're part of this family. And you'll soon meet Fortune, who will be married this year. Would you like to be in a wedding?"

Ian watched his sister's eyes grow wide. When she looked back at him, still uncertain, still frightened, he wondered what it had been like for her these last few years. She'd lost everyone she loved, had been hunted like an animal. He held her close.

And, as usual, his family rallied around him.

Amy, now six, looked at Katy with avid curiosity. "Are you really my aunt? Like Fortune?"

Katy looked puzzled, and Ian grinned. "We'll sort all that out later. I imagine this young lass is hungry."

Katy hesitated, then gave Fancy an anxious look. "Can I keep my ferrets?"

Ian couldn't believe she had been able to save them. He knew how difficult that must have been. His heart nearly broke for her.

"Ferrets," Noel said with sudden interest. "You brought your ferrets?"

Through the lump in his throat, Ian reassured her. "I think your ferrets will be right at home."

Katy stooped and set the basket she'd been clutching on the ground; when she took the top off it, two elongated creatures squirmed out. "This is Adam and Eve," she told Noel, whose eyes grew wide with delight.

"Just wait," he said as he touched one of the winsome animals. "I have a crow named Trouble, and a raccoon named Bandit, and a dog with three legs . . ."

"Bandit is mine," Amy insisted, "and Lucky thinks he belongs to Ian."

Undeterred, Noel continued as he led the way into the house, "and a cat named Unsatisfactory, and a . . ."

Ian caught Fancy's gaze, and she giggled. Then, sobering slightly, she glanced at his letter.

"Are you going to read it?"

His grin faded as he opened the parchment in his hand and began to read:

Ian,

We tried to save your brother, but my father could save only one of you and selfishly he chose you. He always loved you, as did I. The fact that your family chose the Jacobites and we the king didn't change that. After you were transported, I went to Brinaire, hoping to find your sister, but she was gone and I believed she was killed with the rest. But when I received a visit from a man you hired to find her, I started looking again. Thank God we found her, and with joy I send her to you. I had hoped I could buy your freedom and reunite the two of you, but I understand you have already done that. God bless.

Your brother,
Johnny

The last of the lingering bitterness drained from Ian. The Macraes had truly done far more than could be expected of them. He knew now that he had blamed them partially because he'd felt so helpless himself.

Fancy was looking at him worriedly, and he handed her the letter, watching with pride as she read it. She could read and write very well now, and she consumed books with the eagerness of a miser discovering a rich vein of gold.

"You will thank him?" she said.

"Aye," he said. "And more. The Macraes have always admired good horseflesh. Perhaps we can send them one of Royalty's colts."

"I think that's a fine gift for sending me a new daughter," she replied softly, taking his hand.

"And new critters," he reminded her.

"As long as there's no elephant," she said.

He leaned over and kissed her. His star. Bright and strong and steady. And now his heaven was filled. There was no longer a hole where a star should be.

Hand in hand, they followed the children inside.

Don't miss national bestseller Patricia Potter's next starry romance coming soon from Bantam Books

Star Rider

In a young country torn apart by the aftereffects of a brutal war for independence, Annette Carey is forced to watch her father brutalized at the hands of the patriots. She pledges her life to avenge him.

After being kidnapped at an early age by the British army, John Patrick Sutherland vows retribution, constantly reminded of his anger by the physical and emotional scars he bears. Known only as Star Rider, he is an unrelenting enemy of the British Empire and all that it represents. Even as Annette and John Patrick risk their lives to indulge their passion, both know that they must eventually give each other up, determined never to betray their cause. But neither are prepared to fight what lies deep within their hearts.

"Shana Abé writes with intense, unforgettable emotion." —Jane Feather

Look for these richly romantic novels by

SHANA ABÉ

A Rose in Winter

Lady Solange, wed nine years to a wicked lord, escapes her waking nightmare, and must rely upon the lover that she scorned years ago to convey her to safety.

____57787-5 $5.50/$7.50 Canada

The Promise of Rain

A woman flees the court of King Henry for a deserted isle, where a handsome enforcer ignites her deepest desires.

____57788-3 $5.99/$7.99 Canada